Witch Fall

A WITCH SONG Companion Novel

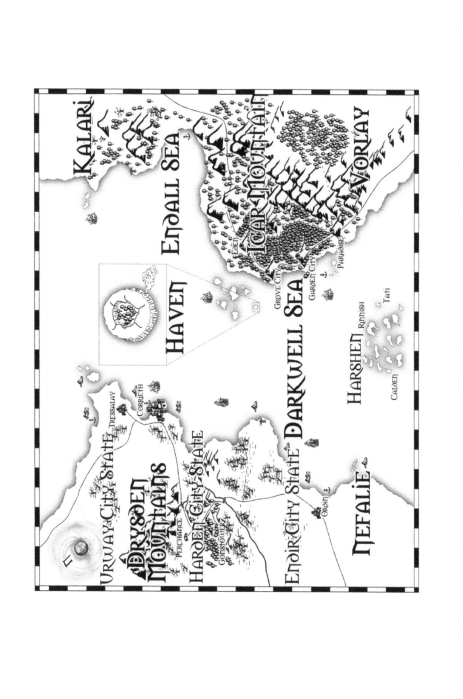

Witch Fall

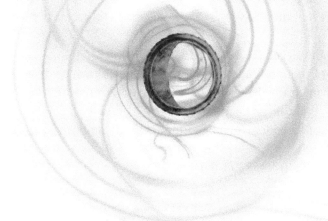

A Witch Song Companion Novel

by Amber Argyle

Starling Publishing

Editing by Linda Prince
Text design by Kathy Beutler
Map by Robert Defendi
Cover art by Laura Sava

ISBN-13: 978-0-9857394-6-1
ISBN-10: 0985739460

Also available as an eBook.

Library of Congress Control Number: 2014930923

Printed in the United States of America
10 9 8 7 6 5 4 3 2 1

Visit Amber Argyle at her author Web site:
http://www.amberargyle.com

Dedication

To Corbin, Connor, and Lily,
for teaching me what love is

CHAPTER 1

Lilette left the island like she came into it, amid a wave of suffering and death. ~*Jolin*

Lilette pointed her hands above her head and leapt off the cliff. Eyes closed, she reveled in the feel of falling. She sliced through the cool water at the base of the waterfall, kicking until she reached the rocky bottom.

There, she paused. Everything looked different down here. The water caught the sharp sunlight, bending it into slanting shafts of turquoise. The figures of the other girls on the bank were wavering and insubstantial—as if they were mere reflections instead of flesh and blood. It was like looking at the outside world through a mirror. But which side was real, and which was the reflection?

Lilette wished she didn't have to go back, that she could stretch this moment beneath the cool water into forever. But her lungs began to ache for air.

I will escape my fate, she promised herself. It had taken her nearly two weeks to gather enough sleeping herbs to drug Bian's family. Tonight, two days before her wedding, she would slip the herbs into the evening meal. After everyone was sound asleep, she'd gather her supplies and slip away.

Lilette's toes pushed off the rocks. She swam upward and broke the surface to take a gasping breath.

Pan stood at the rim of the cliffs, her arms folded over her chest. "Come on, Li. The others want to head back soon."

Her words had a hard, biting edge that made Lilette inwardly cringe. She gazed downstream and felt a sudden urge to just swim away and slip into the jungle, evading Bian and his sons while gathering enough supplies to survive the week-long journey at sea. After that, she would have to steal a boat, and then it was merely a matter of navigating by starlight.

Simple, really.

"You think he sent us here alone?" Pan said as if guessing Lilette's thoughts.

Of course not, Lilette mused bitterly. After her last escape attempt, he'd had her guarded day and night.

"I'll call for them if I need to," Pan went on, her voice flat.

Lilette hadn't just lost Salfe that night. She'd lost her only other friend too, for Pan had made it clear she would never forgive Lilette for causing her brother's banishment.

"Come on," Pan said. "I need to practice fixing your hair."

Lilette let the weight of her body pull her under again and swam to the edge of the pool. She pulled herself out of the water, her bare legs flashing pale as her hands and feet found the crevices to haul her up the cliffs.

At the top, Pan was waiting for her. "This is how things are for a woman, Li. With Fa dead, the village lord decides who you marry. If you'd just accept it, you could be happy."

Lilette winced at the mention of Fa's name. The sun hadn't even set on the day of her surrogate father's death before the village lord had announced she would be marrying him. "If you really believe I could be happy with Bian, you don't know me at all."

"He never shouts at my mother or my aunties," Pan replied as if speaking to a small child. "And he plays with his daughters almost as much as his sons."

Lilette knew better. She'd been born into a world where women ruled because they were the ones with magic. But that was oceans and a lifetime away from the Harshen islands.

She pushed the rising fury deep into her belly. In the darkness following her parents' deaths, Pan had sat beside her, bringing her pink iridescent shells and combing her hair. Over the years, as Lilette longed to go home to her older sister, Pan had coaxed her out of the hut and down to this very pool.

Lilette thought she had locked her heart safely away. But if that was true, why did Pan's coldness and Salfe's banishment hurt so much?

The water had turned Pan's normally frizzy dark hair into gorgeous curls. Lilette hesitated, then reached out and tugged one, a sad smile on her lips as the curl sprang back up. "We'll never get to come swimming anymore."

Pan batted her hand away. "Not everything changes just because you're a wife."

"Everything changes." Lilette gazed into the jeweled tones of the water, hoping to see a different future reflecting back at her.

Pan seemed to soften. "Is it so very bad, marrying my father?"

Lilette's hands curled into fists. She wasn't going to marry Bian. By the Creators, she was escaping tonight. She would make it back to her homeland and the sister who was waiting for her. Afraid her eyes might betray her, she avoided Pan's gaze and took a deep breath. She'd have a better chance at freedom if Pan dropped her guard. "Maybe you're right. Maybe it's not so bad."

Lilette pulled on the tunic and loose trousers Bian had given her. She allowed a very small part of herself to enjoy the finery. The tunic hung to the middle of her calves, with a side slit that reached to her upper thigh. She tied the pleated silk sash around her waist and pinned a jade brooch to the front of it. Unlike her homespun cotton clothes, which had knots and bumps from her hand spindle, this was silk, so soft it was like wearing tensile oil. Both robe and tunic were a rich blue. Lilette hadn't worn color since she'd washed up on the island eight years ago. She and Fa had never been able to afford dyed cotton—let alone silk.

She'd forgotten what it felt like to wear something that didn't rub sores under her arms. She ran her hands down the length of her stomach, remembering the closets of fine clothes she'd once had. As usual, she forced away the memories of her previous life, surprised that any of them still surfaced.

She slipped on her new, finely tooled sandals. Pan's sigh held an undercurrent of envy. "He was so generous with your bride price."

No one seemed to care that Bian was old enough to be Lilette's father, that he already had three wives and dozens of children. All that mattered was that he'd showered her with fabulous clothes, brooches, and winking rings—all of which only made his wives hate her. The fact that Lilette didn't want the gifts or the attention only seemed to make them hate her more.

Pan looked Lilette up and down. She reached out, stopping just shy of touching the fine silk before withdrawing her hand. "Sit down."

Lilette sat gingerly on a large rock Pan had draped with palm leaves to protect her clothing. She studied the other girls, Pan's younger sisters. All seven of them were chatting happily as they plaited flowers in each other's hair. They all looked very much alike with their darker skin, curling black hair, and laughing, almond-shaped eyes—very different from Lilette's golden skin, pale hair, and brilliant turquoise eyes.

Pan's quick fingers worked rich-smelling oils into Lilette's hair before tugging a little more roughly than necessary at the knots with the comb. "You're hair is so thin," Pan complained as she bound Lilette's hair into complicated rolls and poufs. She placed three white orchids, the symbol of fertility, behind her ear. Lilette brushed her fingertips along the petals, resisting the urge to rip the flowers from her hair.

Pan's next younger sister knelt behind Pan and watched them shyly. "Sing for us, Auntie," she said.

Lilette held back a wince at being called Auntie. She studied the cluster of girls who would be her stepdaughters if she failed to escape tonight. She imagined Bian's dark eyes watching her, possessing her, and she shuddered.

Lilette took a deep breath and sang one of Fa's songs.

Down to the depths of the stream you must pour
Heartache and loneliness, hurt, and what's more,
Missed opportunities passing you by.
Mistakes and aches, let them fly
Into the stream of forgetting.

The world around Lilette stilled, waiting for something more, but she hadn't sung the words in the Creators' language—the language of power. She'd buried her knowledge of that language so deep she could only remember one song, and that one only recently.

As last note drifted away, the elements slowly went back to sleep. In the quiet that followed, Lilette fingered the phoenix carved into the decorative comb Salfe had given her. It was the only thing of value she truly owned. The only thing she'd take with her when she escaped.

Pan tugged the comb from her fingers and slipped it into Lilette's hair. "Not quite straight," she murmured and shifted it. The comb suddenly jerked out, taking some of Lilette's hair with it. She yelped and whirled to look at Pan. At the look on her friend's face, the words she might have said froze in her throat. She followed Pan's gaze to see a man watching them from the shadows—probably Quo, one of Pan's many brothers.

But instead of running away in shame for having been caught watching the women swimming, he slowly rose to his feet. Lilette took a breath to threaten to tell Bian, but the man stepped into the light. Lilette didn't recognize him, which was impossible. She knew everyone on their small island.

"Hello, Lilette."

Her mouth came open in a noiseless gasp. He'd spoken in her native tongue—Kalarian. And used her full name. No one had called her that in eight years.

She rose to her feet and took in his dark hair bound in a queue, the fine features and full mouth. But it was the poised way he stood, the leather-and bronze-studded armor he wore that gave him away. She realized with a start that she did know this man.

Chen had come to kill her, just as his father had killed her parents. The fear that had long slumbered in Lilette roared to life, and the air seemed thin and wavering. "It can't be."

"Who are you?" Pan's voice came out breathy.

Where were Bian's sons? Lilette was suddenly frightened for them. They would be worse than useless against Chen.

"Quo? Zu? Ji?" Pan called. When they didn't answer, her face paled and she cleared her throat. "What do you want?"

"He's come to murder me," Lilette answered.

Chen's brow furrowed as he turned to her. "Murder you? No. You will become my concubine."

Lilette narrowed her gaze. "I don't believe you."

Pan puffed out her chest in a show of bravado. "You can't have her. She's already taken."

Lilette rested her hand on Pan's shoulder in warning.

"Yes," Chen agreed. "Long ago." He motioned with one hand. Dozens of men eased from the shadows of the jungle, the sharp sunlight of midday revealing their leather armor reinforced with bronze studs. Each man carried two long swords at his waist or across his back. Some also carried halberds, the wicked blades resembling half moons. The heavily armed men blocked the way back to the village.

Lilette and the others made to dive into the pool, but soldiers appeared at the base of the cliff. They were surrounded.

"Quo! Ji! Zu!" Pan cried for her brothers, this time her voice full of fear instead of supplication.

"Are you looking for them?" At a gesture from Chen, the soldiers brought forth three boys who were almost men. Each was bound and gagged, eyes wide with fright. Quo's cheek was swollen and his face bloodied.

Chen eyed Lilette up and down. "This isn't going to be nearly as arduous as I thought."

She knew firsthand this man's ruthlessness. If she didn't do something soon, everyone would die. "Let them go."

He cocked an eyebrow. "Are you giving me an order?"

She swallowed. "If what you say is true—if you really mean to make me your concubine—I'll come quietly."

Chen looked pointedly at the men surrounding the females. "You'll come either way."

Lilette's hand snaked out and grabbed Pan's knife from its sheath. She held the blade to her throat, hoping against hope he'd spoken the truth before and didn't mean to kill her.

Some of the cockiness fled Chen's face. "You won't use that."

Lilette pressed down and the tip bit into her skin. Her flesh parted, the metal sliding inside her. Blood dripped down her neck, soaking her beautiful robes.

"Chen!" said one of his soldiers, a man with a scar that stretched from one mangled ear all the way across his cheek before biting into his nose.

Chen stretched his hand toward Lilette, palm forward, and spoke to his men. "Let them go. I have no need for them."

Pan's eyes seemed enormous in her pale face. "Li—"

"They're going to take me anyway," Lilette whispered. "Just go! Don't look back."

Pan took in the soldiers with their swords and spears. In her fist, she still gripped Lilette's decorative jade comb. Hands shaking, Pan stepped forward and gently slid the comb into place. Her lips beside Lilette's ear, she whispered, "I'll send my father and the other men after you."

"No!" Lilette hissed. But Pan was already herding her sisters toward a gap the soldiers had created, their dispassionate gazes watching the girls pass.

"The boys too." Lilette's voice cracked.

Chen's gaze darkened, and Lilette knew she would pay dearly for their freedom. After a moment he nodded. Bian's sons stumbled after their sisters.

Only when they were all on the other side of the soldiers did Pan look back.

"Don't," Lilette mouthed.

Pan pushed her sisters forward. "Run!"

A sick horror rose in Lilette's middle as she realized she would probably never see Pan again. She considered using the blade. It might be a kinder fate than what awaited her. But soldiers were already swarming her, and the knife was ripped from her grip by the scarred soldier.

Chen came to stand before her. When he made no move to kill her, she went weak with relief. "Why?" she choked out.

His dark eyes bored into hers. "Because our daughters will have your power."

Metallic taste of fear filled Lilette's mouth. When she'd prayed to the Sun Dragon to free her from marrying Bian, she should have been more specific.

"Why not sing?" Chen asked. "You were rumored to have been strong enough."

She realized he'd been expecting it—testing her, even. She refused to meet his gaze. But the thought hadn't even occurred to her. She scoured her mind for the words of the Creators' language—the language of power. But she only remembered one song, and it was worthless against these men.

His brows rose. "You've forgotten, haven't you?"

She glared at him, hating the tears of frustration in her eyes.

Chen turned and began marching away. "Form up."

The soldiers tightened into formation around her, but none moved to touch her. They started marching, forcing Lilette to move with them. She continued to wrack her brain for one more song, any song, but she'd shoved her memories down too deep for too long.

The dense canopy blocked out the sun, leaving little light for the growth of underbrush. So when the plants around Lilette started to thicken and the men had to hack at them with their swords, she knew they were close to the edge of the jungle. And at the end of the jungle was the sea.

The hard ground became loose and sandy before they stepped out of the jungle into the oppressive light and heat. A zhou was anchored off shore. It was easily five times larger than the largest fishing boats in the village, with three wide sails and dozens of men on deck.

Lilette knew what fate awaited her once she was onboard. She tried to dart between two soldiers. One caught her, his grip firm as he pushed her into the middle of the group. She whirled and tried again. Another soldier easily caught her and forced her back toward the center.

Emboldened by their carefulness with her, Lilette shot toward the scarred soldier and kicked him with all her strength. She'd hoped he would falter, but he absorbed the impact, and the blow seemed to hurt her far more than it had him. He grasped her about her waist, holding her firmly. She beat against his chest.

The formation halted. While Chen watched, two soldiers caught her wrists and bound them with soft cords. The flowers in her hair had come loose. They swung against her check, their sweet smell nearly making her gag.

Chen carefully tucked them back into place behind her ear. "If you're not careful," he said dispassionately, "you're going to hurt yourself."

He backed away from her and resumed his place up front. "We can't afford any delays," he said almost apologetically. "Fight any more and we'll bind your feet and carry you. Understand?" The wound at her neck had broken back open, spilling blood down her neck and chest and making her tunic cling to her. She nodded dizzily, and Chen gave her a small smile. "Good girl."

He turned toward the scarred soldier. "Get her in the boat."

The man took her elbow and dragged her down the beach to a small rowboat that had been towed onto shore. He easily hefted her inside. She looked into his eyes and was surprised to see a hint of compassion. "Please." *Don't do this to me. Let me go.*

His gaze darkened and he turned away. Something whistled through the air and landed with a thud near his feet.

Lilette nearly cried out with joy to see a fishing spear quivering in the ground. She knew the spear had been a warning—the men of her village could easily impale a fish from twenty breadths.

"Phalanx formation!" Chen ordered.

Soldiers who had been climbing inside the boat leapt back out and loped forward, their spears held before them. Men from her village stepped slowly out of the jungle. Bian was among them, as was Quo, his eye now swollen completely shut. The men held fishing spears, long knives strapped to their waists.

The two groups appraised each other. Lilette's villagers outnumbered these men, but even she knew that fisherman against trained soldiers didn't make for good odds.

Bian took a step forward. His hair was shot through with gray, his skin weathered by the sea, but he still carried himself like a younger man. "Who are you, and why have you taken my wife?"

Chen reached into his armor and pulled out a drawstring purse, which he tossed at Bian's feet. "To compensate you for her bride price."

Slowly, Bian bent and lifted the bulging purse. He opened it and his eyes widened. One of the elders said something and Bian passed the purse over.

Another villager called out, "You cannot buy another man's wife."

Chen tipped his head to the side. "She's not a wife until the marriage is consummated. Until then, the contract may be bought out by another."

How could Chen possibly know so much about her betrothal?

Bian studied the soldiers surrounding Lilette. "By law, you cannot take her if I do not agree to the exchange."

Chen lifted his swords. "If you wish to die, come and try to take her then."

The scarred soldier stepped closer to Chen and said softly, "You slaughter an entire village and there will be consequences, Chen."

"Remember your place, little brother," Chen said. "These peasants are no threat to us."

Brother? Lilette's gaze shot back to the scarred man, searching for the boy she'd once known. To her utter shock, she found him there, in the eyes that had once been gentle and full of life. Now they were just empty.

"Han?" she said softly.

He flinched, as if his name on her lips was utterly repulsive. What could have happened to him to turn him into this? He'd sat beside her for hours, patiently teaching her how to speak Harshen so she wouldn't be so lonely.

Lilette closed her eyes. She knew who these men were. "Let them take me, Bian. If you don't, you'll all be killed."

Chen took a deep breath and called loudly, "Listen to her, fisherman, for the path you tread is narrow as a blade."

Bian watched her, regret plain on his face. "You underestimate us, Lilette. I have waited too long to let you go now."

Chen made a sound low in his throat. "Believe me when I say I have waited longer. I am not here to barter, fisherman. Take the gold and your lives and be gone."

When Bian hesitated, Han's voice pierced the quiet. "A widow has no husband."

Bian stared at Lilette, and she saw he would not give her up. He threw the purse at Chen's feet. She gaped at the glittering gold pieces lying in the sand. "No, Bian!" she cried. "They are elite!"

Her words evoked a deadly stillness, for even in her isolated village, the elite were renowned as the highest trained soldiers of the empire. It was they who guarded the royal family.

One by one, the villagers dropped to their knees, their foreheads pressing into the sand three times as they kowtowed.

"You had only to name yourself heir, and she would have been yours." Bian's voice shook. Finally, he understood the danger.

Chen cut a glance at his brother. "Now we have no choice. She told them who we are."

All the fear and tension drained out of Lilette, replaced by a bone-numbing horror. Had her revelation sentenced her villagers to death? "No!" she screamed. She lunged for Chen, determined to stop him somehow.

Han caught her about the middle, his arms locked tightly around her no matter how much she strained. "Chen, it's murder," he said.

"If you cannot stomach it, get her onto the ship," Chen growled as he drew his swords. He turned his back on Han to address the elite. "Make sure none of them escape. If we fail, we risk a war."

With that, he stalked toward the villagers, most of whom grabbed their discarded weapons and stood their ground, but a few kept themselves prostrate.

"Chen, leave them alone!" Lilette cried.

Han tossed her into the boat. She tried to bolt back out, but he blocked her way. "You can't stop it. You'll only make it worse for them."

Listening to her villagers' death cries, she felt the fight drain out of her. "Please," she wailed as the elite cut through the villagers.

Muscles straining, Han pushed the boat into the water and pulled himself in. Lilette automatically leaned to the other side to keep the craft from capsizing. Belatedly, she realized she should have overturned it.

Chen had reached Bian. He easily sidestepped Bian's spear thrust and pivoted, his sword biting into flesh. Bian's eyes widened in surprise. He wavered on his feet. Chen pulled back and struck tip-first into Bian's heart. He fell to the beach, lifeless.

Lilette thought of her would-be husband's wives. All those children—Pan foremost among them—and her heart cried out in anguish.

Quo screamed in outrage and threw his spear. Chen twisted and the spear glanced harmlessly off his reinforced armor. Then he lunged forward, and even from this distance, Lilette could see the fear in Quo's face, fear as he turned to flee. Chen ran him down and shoved the sword in his back.

Han took Lilette's face firmly between the thumb and fingers of his massive hand. She looked into his empty, dark eyes. "Lie in the bottom of the boat and cover your ears," he told her.

Perhaps it was cowardly. Perhaps it was weak. But Lilette did as she was told, pressing her fists into her ears to block out the sound of her villagers dying.

CHAPTER 2

Lilette hated orchids. I never thought to ask her why. ~Jolin

Below decks, the ship had been quartered off with silk curtains. The hull was peaked in the center and curved toward the floating deck. Lilette had curled into the farthest corner of the stern, the orchids dangling limply beside her head. Her arms were wound tightly around her legs as she tried to forget the images of Bian's murder. The blood. The horrific sounds of the massacre. All because she'd called out that the men were elite.

She could hear the soldiers coming aboard, their boots clomping on the deck above her. She was alone except for Han, but she knew it would only be a matter of time before Chen came to check on his prize.

In Harshen, there were dozens of island fiefdoms of differing sizes, each with its own name and lord. But all of the fiefdoms paid obeisance to the emperor. Chen would take Lilette to the capital island, Harshen, to the imperial city of Rinnish. And once she was there, Chen would never let her return to her fellow witches, her sister. Never let Lilette become what she was always meant to be. The future she had dreamed about and fought for her entire life shattered like stones scattered across the mirrored surface of a pool.

The ship creaked as the sails caught wind. The intervals between the waves grew shorter, indicating the craft was picking up speed. Lilette had finally left Calden Island, but she hadn't escaped.

Chen would be coming down soon. The thought of what he would do to her sent her rocking back and forth to keep from falling apart.

Han crouched before her, watching her, studying her. Finally, she took a deep breath and forced herself to meet his gaze. His eyes flicked to the dampness on her cheeks. "Sometimes a fall is required to change our path." He took hold of both her arms and pulled her to her feet. "You have been set on this path, Lilette. There is no going back, so you might as well stand and be strong. Do what must be done."

Until tonight it had been so long since anyone had called her Lilette. Most Harshens couldn't pronounce the name. It belonged to another life, another person. "Everything has been taken from me . . . again," she said softly.

"You rebuilt a life once. You are strong enough to do it again."

A life built around finding a way home. That hadn't changed. She would escape this. She would find her way to her sister. And she would make Chen pay. She glared at Han. "You don't know anything about me, not anymore."

The corners of his mouth twitched as if he was fighting a smile. "Fight the battles you can win. Retreat from the ones you cannot."

"And if I cannot retreat?"

He tugged the flowers from her hair and tossed them aside. "Then you surrender with dignity." His gaze held hers, and for the briefest moment the emptiness receded, and his eyes were filled with such depth and clarity that her trembling began to still from the inside out.

"What happened to you?" Lilette managed around what felt like a rock lodged in her throat. She and Han had played in the gardens for hours, feeding the exotic animals in the enclosure and hiding from their mothers in the incense-filled walls of the shrine.

Just like that, the emptiness returned to his eyes. "Remember what I said." Han stepped back from her moments before the curtain was swept aside.

Chen moved to a cabinet and withdrew a bottle and an ornate ivory cup. He filled the cup to the brim and drained it in one swallow.

Han took a step toward his brother and gestured toward Calden. "This was badly done."

Chen poured another, downed it, and poured another. "Couldn't be helped," he replied, then wiped his lips with the back of his arm. His skin and hair shone with drops of water, as if he'd washed himself. Cup in hand, he stepped closer and examined Lilette.

She channeled all her fury into her gaze, hoping he could read her unspoken promise to kill him.

He chuckled dryly. "I see you remember me."

As if she could forget the son of the man who had killed her parents! Even as a child of twelve, he'd been ruthless. And now he'd finally come for her, leaving a host of death in his wake. "You're a murderer."

His jaw tightened. "I am Heir Chen, chosen son of Emperor Nis, speaker for the Sun Dragon." His gaze held a warning. "And if I'm a murderer, it's the Sun Dragon's will that I be so."

She uncurled herself from the floor and drew herself to her full height, which was nearly the same as his. "And I am Lilette, daughter of Lellan. A keeper of the realms and the gods."

He didn't respond, instead crossing his arms and swirling the liquid in his cup. "There were no survivors found in the wreckage of the ship you burned, and yet here you are. Alive when all else are dead." He took another drink. "And then you revealed who we are to your villagers, forcing me to kill them. So you tell me, Lilette, who has more blood on their hands?"

She lunged for him, but Han held her back. She brought her knee up and almost caught Han between his legs, but he twisted, narrowly avoiding the blow. His arms were like iron bands.

She stopped struggling. "How did you find me?"

The picture of ease, Chen watched her. "How did you survive when no one else did?"

Guilt coursed through her. She'd only remained hidden this long because everyone else had burned or drowned. But if Chen could refuse to answer her questions, she could refuse to answer his. "The emperor only has to ask, and he could take any woman he wants," Lilette said. "You didn't need to kill them."

"I'm afraid the situation called for more secrecy than that."

"Why?" she asked angrily.

Chen's dark gaze met her blue one. "What do you think the witches would do if they knew I'd taken one of their own?"

Despite his washing, there was still blood in the crease beside his nose. "What do you want of me?" Lilette finally asked.

Stepping closer, he lifted her jaw with a crooked finger, examining her. "Many things. But in this case, exactly what I paid for. You will be one of my concubines."

Bile rose in her throat. "Never!"

Anger flashed across his face and he leaned forward, so close she could smell the alcohol on his breath. "Some resistance is to be expected—after all, I took you by force. But my patience only extends so far. "

If being Bian's captive had taught her anything, it was that escape would only be possible if she lulled her captors into complacency. She backed away, and Han let her go.

"So you really don't mean to kill me?"

The harsh expression on Chen's face eased. "You needn't be afraid. I take good care of the things that are mine." She backed into the hull as he stalked toward her. She knew he would kiss her. It took all of her determination to hold as still as possible as his lips lightly brushed hers.

He broke away and the backs of his fingers caressed her hair. "Pale as starlight, with eyes the color of the brightest sea."

"Brother, this may not be the time to woo her," Han said dryly. "She has just lost everything of her old self."

Chen frowned. "Ah, yes. My coward of a brother calls for caution."

Han's expression was unreadable. Chen glanced around the small space, no doubt noting the bamboo hammock and a few silk pillows. He turned back to study Lilette, indecision playing across his face. Finally, he nodded. "With your song to propel us, we shall reach the bay by morning."

"But I . . . I told you," she stammered, "I've forgotten all the songs."

Chen held up a finger. "But you've remembered one—the very one I need."

She gaped at him. "How could you know that?" On the day Fa lay dying, she'd remembered the song to call the wind. She'd used that song to propel their boat to shore to find the physicker. It hadn't been enough to save Fa.

Lilette didn't resist as they took her to the upper deck. Her gaze was drawn to her island in the distance, but she quickly looked away.

Chen handed her a copy of the song—he'd obviously come prepared. But she knew this one. It was the only one she remembered.

It was almost a relief to sing herself away, to separate herself from the pain and horror of the last hour. When the ship cut through the waves as fast as the sails could bear, they took her back below decks.

Chen watched her—he'd been watching her for hours. Lilette wasn't sure how much longer she could resist the urge to try to kill him, regardless of the outcome.

Finally, he backed away from her, his eyes never leaving her. "Truly, you are the most blessed of women."

And then he was finally gone. Han lingered a moment, staring at the ground, before following his brother out.

Blessed? She'd just been forced from her home, her villagers killed for trying to keep her. Her parents had been murdered, and her sister was gone. How could Chen call her blessed when she'd never see any of them ever again?

Her parents had died trying to escape this fate. Lilette leaned back against the stern, then slid down to rest her head on her drawn knees.

**

The next morning, she woke knowing she wasn't alone, that someone was watching her. With a gasp, she jerked upright in the hammock to find Chen leaning over her. An amber pendant dangled from his throat. It was set in gold, an emerald-eyed sun dragon curving around it.

Lilette was certain he hadn't been wearing it yesterday. Slowly, she forced herself to relax, to appear compliant.

"You are very beautiful. Your skin—it's as golden as white wine and as soft as silk." He seemed to be waiting for some kind of response. But all she could think of was that he'd finally washed the last of the blood off the side of his nose. How many men had he killed in addition to Bian?

"The proper response to a compliment is 'Thank you, Heir, or Heir Chen.' Either honorific is fine." Chen straightened, and the pendant settled in the hollow of his throat. "You must adjust faster. It won't be so hard when you come to the compound and have servants to attend you and beautiful things to wear."

Lilette blinked at him.

He took a step back. "Stand up."

The only battle worth winning is the one for my freedom, she reminded herself. On a ship full of elite and surrounded by ocean, she could not win. Moving stiffly, she did as she was told. Chen reached out and helped her down. She had to force herself not to recoil from his touch.

He gestured to a package resting on the cabinet. "We've sighted Harshen. By midday, we'll have docked in the harbor. I have brought you something suitable for your station. A maid will attend you shortly." He waited again. When she still said nothing, he took a deep breath as if calling upon his patience. "Again, a thank you would be appropriate."

She bit down on the words she wanted to say, crushing them between her teeth. "Thank you, Heir." Her voice came out raspy and low.

Chen shook his head. "You must learn manners before I can ever take you to the palace. Learn them fast." He waited again, an eyebrow raised.

Lilette reined in her temper by imagining her boning knife sticking out of his chest. "I will, Heir."

He nodded, seeming somewhat mollified. He pulled back the curtain just enough to reveal a kneeling middle-aged woman who wore a blank expression. "Prepare her to enter the palatial compound," Chen ordered. "She's not ready for the niceties, so keep it simple."

"Yes, Heir Chen." The woman kowtowed, touching her forehead to the floor three times.

Chen swept away, not bothering to wait for the woman to finish.

CHAPTER 3

Somewhere along the way, Lilette learned only to fight the battles she could win. ~Jolin

The servant rose to her feet, her eyes downcast. Without a word, she began helping Lilette out of her bloodstained robes.

"What time of day is it?" Lilette asked.

"Midday." The servant clucked disapprovingly at the jade comb in Lilette's hair, tossing it to the floor.

"That's mine," she protested.

"Cheap jade," the woman responded. "Not fit for the heir's concubine." As the woman turned to retrieve the bathwater that had been set outside the curtain, Lilette snatched the comb. One of the wings had chipped. Her mouth in a tight line, she unpinned her brooch.

She concealed both in the blanket on the hammock. She didn't care so much for the brooch, but perhaps she could sell it when she escaped. As for the comb, it was the last thing Salfe had given her. She would not lose it.

The woman moved like she would help Lilette wash herself. Lilette held out a forestalling hand. "I will do it myself."

The woman nodded, but watched critically as Lilette washed the dried blood from her chest. "You only kowtow to the emperor and his heir. The imperial lords and his other sons are your equals, so you simply bow in respect, a bow they will return. All others kowtow to you."

Lilette planned to escape before then. "How will I know the emperor?"

The woman snorted. "Emperor Nis wears the pendant, same as his son."

Lilette nodded. "And how will I distinguish between those who bow to me and those who kowtow?" she asked, nervousness making her fingers clumsy.

The woman nodded as if pleased that Lilette had asked a sensible question. "Only the members of the royal family can wear the image of the five-clawed dragon—the Sun Dragon. You wear a four-clawed dragon. Anyone below you must kowtow."

The woman directed Lilette to lean over the basin of water for her hair to be washed. After the woman finished washing it, she wrung it out and let it hang down Lilette's back while combing through it. When she was finished, the woman started making elegant rolls and fans.

Pan had combed Lilette's hair only yesterday. She had to be alive. The alternative was too heart-wrenching.

After sliding a jewel-encrusted comb into Lilette's hair, the maid pulled out new robes of red and gold. These garments put her previous clothing to shame. They were covered in hand-dyed panels depicting golden dragons, lotus flowers, and orchid-covered hills. Lilette hated them immediately.

A white powder was brushed on her face, and her eyes lined with kohl. Her lips were stained red, her cheeks pink. Then the woman stepped back and studied her handiwork. She nodded. "It will do."

While she opened the curtain and spoke with someone on the other side, Lilette took her comb and brooch and slid them into the pocket of her robes.

Lilette waited, her insides squirming. A moment later, the curtain was swept aside for Chen. He'd traded his soldier's clothing for red robes just as glorious as her own, the key difference being the swords belted at his waist—weapons she wished desperately for. The serving woman immediately dropped to the ground and began to kowtow.

Lilette hesitated. It grated her to demonstrate obeisance to the man who'd taken everything from her—twice. But if Chen thought her complacent, he wouldn't watch her as closely.

Forcing her knees to bend, she touched her forehead to the floor three times. When she had finished, she sat on her heels, waiting.

He stared at her. "Truly, you were meant to be mine."

"Thank you, Heir." It took everything she had to keep her face expressionless. *Patience,* she reminded herself. *Keep him complacent until you have a chance to escape.*

Chen turned away, clearly expecting her to follow him. She forced herself to do as he expected, four steps behind as was proper. He led her up the ladder to the ship's deck. And then she caught sight of Harshen's capital city, Rinnish.

Memories boiled up inside Lilette, completely engulfing her with the scent of burning. The choking smoke that had filled her lungs until she couldn't breathe. Her mother's fingers digging into her arm. Shouts and swords and blood. Running, running— always running.

Then, the city had been a burning ember against the raging night sky. Lightning had cast everything in bone-white relief, giving it the appearance of a graveyard of blood and stone. Now the city thrived with color and life. Buildings with wide porches and turned-up roofs had been rebuilt, more beautiful and grand than before.

Rinnish had grown around the circular bay, the wealthiest section on a round isthmus. On a gentle mountain at the very heart of that grandeur, the palatial compound lorded over the city. From this angle, all Lilette could see were the imposing ramparts built of yellow bricks and capped with a walkway and towers. She didn't need to see the palace to know there was a wide porch on every level, that the walls were painted in red and gold, that the copper roof had developed a turquoise patina.

She'd lived there during the weeks of her parents' ambassadorship. She knew the compound, knew the garden behind it nearly by heart. Just as she knew all the grandeur and beauty only served to hide the rot buried deep within.

She started from her contemplation of the city when Chen swore violently. He and Han were speaking with a man she'd never seen before.

Chen shot her an unreadable glance. Unease stirred within her. The other man bowed to Chen before leaving the ship at a trot. Chen worked his jaw before gesturing to Han. Lilette eased closer to hear what they said.

"Take her to Father's harem. Keep it quiet."

Han's brow wrinkled. "Are you sure that's a good idea?"

Chen's gaze flicked to her. "Father regularly adds to his harem. No one will suspect anything. Still, keep her out of sight." He gave a sharp command for the elite and they marched off the ship.

Lilette worked hard to keep her elation from showing. With Chen and the elite gone, she'd only have to escape Han. "Who are you hiding me from?"

Han motioned to her robe. "Take it off."

Han's eyes didn't miss her palming her brooch and comb, but he didn't say anything as she shrugged out of the robe. She sighed in relief as she shed the extra layers of clothing. It was the beginning of the hot season and the robe had been stifling. She was left standing in nothing but her sleeveless tunic, which was just as beautiful. It had panels of an island surrounded by stormy seas. No dragons.

Han handed the robe to the woman who'd helped her dress— Lilette hadn't even noticed her waiting beside the hatch, her eyes downcast. "The plan has changed. Give me the plain one."

Lilette groaned as another robe was brought out, this one with a hood. As the woman wrapped it around her, Lilette studied Han. He had none of the refined beauty of his brother. His features were stronger, his body all muscle, his scar pale against his dark golden skin.

"Are you done staring?" he asked coldly as he pulled the hood over her pale hair.

She slipped the comb and brooch into the pocket of her new robes. "I don't understand what's going on."

Han shifted to watch Chen disappear into the city. "Count yourself lucky." He glanced around warily. "Stay close to me."

He took her arm and walked beside her. Both actions were considered highly inappropriate—she was not his to touch, and a woman should always walk four steps behind a man.

Han guided her down the gangplank and onto the dock. They bypassed the causeway, stepped into the mud, and made their way past derelict buildings. The pungent smell coming from them was a mixture of something sour and something dead. Used to the fresh-ocean-and-jungle smell of her home, Lilette covered her nose with her sleeve and took shallow breaths.

Men emerged from the shadowy doorways, their gazes fixed on her. She instinctively shrunk back. "We're not safe here," she hissed at Han.

"We're safer here than most places in the city," he said without shifting his gaze from the men.

As if feeling his eyes on them, the men looked at Han. As one they paused before slinking back the way they'd come. Lilette glanced at Han and understood why. Those men reeked of danger and shadows, but Han wore death like men wore armor.

Deciding now was not the time to escape, she moved a little closer to him. They passed a building that was clearly supposed to look glamorous, but instead looked like flashy refuse. A few scantily clad women called out lewd suggestions to Han. Lilette gaped at their audacity, which made the women cackle merrily. She faced forward and tried to ignore their leering insults. "How much longer?"

Han led her around a corner and paused to look back. "Any spies would have a hard time fitting in here."

"Spies?" She didn't think her situation could get any worse. Apparently she was wrong.

They finally left the derelict buildings behind. Gradually, they began to pass tightly clustered houses, most with simple beaten-dirt walls and thatched roofs.

Eventually those homes gave way to small, wooden houses with turned-up corners and battered-silk screen windows. The streets here were paved in yellow bricks so old the corners had been worn off, the centers of the bricks bulging a little under her slippered feet.

The numbers of people steadily grew. Lilette and Han passed many carts—some pulled by a horse or ox, some by people. Finally, they turned up the market street. Merchants were thick, their booths filled with everything from food to jewelry beneath glass cases.

Most of the hawkers wore knee-length tunics with loose trousers. Their shorter hair was held back with a simple cord. Their wives or daughters wore slightly longer tunics and loose trousers as they worked the booths, wrapping the items and taking care of the customers.

Girls ran around with their hair unbound, while all the adult women had theirs tied back in simple braids or buns. As Lilette and Han moved through the street, the merchants and people grew thicker, the booths filled with more elaborate goods. Hawkers called to her, their voices blending together and breaking apart like a flock of songbirds in flight.

Lilette brushed her forefinger on the sharp edge of her chipped comb. If there was ever a perfect time to escape, it would be now, in the chaos and press of people. Without her dragon robes, she appeared to be one of the wealthier women, and hopefully that meant no one would question her.

They passed a woman reclining in a rickshaw, her hair in an elaborate style that could only be accomplished by the skilled hands of servants.

People jostled and bumped them from every side. Han still held Lilette's arm, so she threw herself forward as if she'd tripped. Han held on, but he was slightly off balance. Cocking her knee, she kicked back at him. He twisted to avoid the blow.

With a swift jerk of her arm, she was free. She scrambled under the rickshaw and ran, dodging between people and carts. She looked back, a lock of hair sweeping across her face.

Han was a mere few steps behind her. His hand shot out. She twisted and dove beneath a cart, then came out the other side. Crouched below the masses of people, Lilette slipped under a table covered in blankets.

The merchant backed away from her, her mouth open to protest. Lilette held out her jade brooch, her thumb running regretfully across the lotus carving. The woman's mouth snapped shut and her fingers snatched up the brooch, which immediately disappeared within the folds of her robe. She looked up, scanning the crowd. "He isn't far. Be silent." The woman resumed calling out to the crowds.

Lilette's heart pounded in her chest. She held perfectly still as sweat rolled down her temples.

After a moment, the woman motioned toward the alley behind them. "Go."

Pulling her hood low over her face, Lilette stepped into the shadows between two buildings built so close together their roofs overlapped. She forced herself not to look back, not to run. She reached the street on the other side and peered out.

She didn't know where she was or where to go. All she knew was she had to put as much distance between herself and Han as possible. She kept walking, her head down to hide her obviously foreign features, one hand holding the hood low.

She crossed this street and came out another one, but she hadn't taken three steps before the ground beneath her feet began to rumble. One hand out for balance, she froze at the sight of a creature as tall and wide as a house coming toward her. She gaped at the hopelessly wrinkled animal covered in black silk and gold tassels. Its nose reached to the ground, and its ears fanned out beside its head. Its sheer size caused sweat to break out across Lilette's body.

A boy sat at the animal's neck. Behind him, a ridiculously elaborate palanquin-like pavilion rested on its back. Inside the palanquin was a veiled woman. And surrounding both woman and creature were elite, two soldiers deep.

Remembering herself with a start, Lilette darted into the nearest alley. Just as she crossed the mouth, someone grabbed her. Han. He shoved her behind a tall cart, then pressed his body flush against hers. It was unthinkable. A small cry of protest rose from her throat, but he only covered her mouth with his hand.

"Did she see you?"

Lilette took a breath that was full of the smell of leather and steel and murmured unintelligibly beneath his fingers. He let up enough for her to speak.

"Who? What?"

"The woman in the howdah, did she see you?" Han asked.

So that's what the palanquin was called.

In the small space between cart and wall, Lilette watched the creature lumber past in an oddly swaying gait. She let out all her breath. "I don't know."

He cursed, soft and low. "Why did you run?"

She went limp and boneless, feeling like all hope had been bled out of her. "How could I not?"

Han's gaze went hard. "Do you think my life so valuable that my father wouldn't kill me for losing you?"

Her eyes heavy with tears she refused to let fall, she met his gaze. "You don't care if Chen forces me to be one of his concubines. Why should I care if the emperor kills you?"

Han worked his jaw before pulling a knife from an ankle sheath. She braced herself, but he only cut the bottom of his silk tunic and proceeded to bind her wrists. Her hands immediately went numb. She refused to let the discomfort show.

He made no apology, nor did he loosen the bands. "Don't try that again." He took hold of her arm, stepped to the end of the alley, and peered out.

Lilette eased forward and watched the creature's hind parts and a branch of a tail grow smaller. "What was that?"

Han's expression was grim. "An elephant."

She wet her lips. "Is it dangerous?"

"A bull elephant is. That one is female. They're fairly passive."

"Then why are you afraid of it?"

Han eyed her, his expression unreadable. "It's not the elephant that's the problem—it's the woman riding it. And it's not me who should be afraid."

"I never stopped being afraid," she whispered.

He let out a frustrated growl. "Being one of his concubines is an honor. He is your heir."

"He is my shackles." Lilette considered running again.

Han's grip tightened on her. "Don't. When you can't win, you retreat."

She looked into his eyes that were so dark they were almost black. "I have no retreat."

"Then you take your surrender like a man."

Lilette gave him a level stare. "But I'm a woman." *And we only let you think we've surrendered before we gut you,* she added silently.

He grunted. "I'll bind your feet and carry you over my shoulder if I have to." With his hand locked around her arm, Han tugged her forward. "Come on." He looked around as if gathering his bearings before starting down another alley. She had to trot to keep up with him.

The road slanted upward. They left the crowded, noisy streets below and passed numerous walled compounds with winged entrances and imposing gates, behind which she caught glimpses of grand houses and gardens. The tantalizing scent of food and growing things wafted toward her.

She was strong and healthy from hours spent working with Fa on their fishing boat, but she was still breathing hard when the enormous gates of the palace came into view. Instead of heading for them, Han pulled her into a noodle house. He gave a familiar nod to the owner and started up the stairs. At the top, they crossed the room to a veranda covered with tables and chairs. Jade columns supported the roof. Han wove among the scattering of people eating a late midday meal. A few shot Lilette curious glances—she was obviously not of their race and her hands were bound, but none moved to interfere. Not when her captor was an elite, and she was just another worthless woman.

Along one side, they came to an enclosure with wines along one wall, ceramic pots of herbs along another, and a large brazier filled with teapots—it was some kind of drink station. The servant at the brazier nodded to Han as if they knew each other.

Han produced his knife and cut the bindings around Lilette's wrists. "Don't let her past you," he said to the man, who raised an eyebrow before his gaze settled on her.

Han stepped onto the railing, gripped the edge of the roof, and hauled himself up. She leaned over the railing and gaped up at him. He extended his hand. "I need to see what's going on past the gates, and I'm not letting you out of my sight."

She glanced back at the server for help. He only moved to block the exit, his arms over his chest. Not seeing another option, she hoisted herself up to stand on the rail. Han gripped her wrist and pulled her up beside him. One hand on the slanting clay tiles, he climbed to the roof ridge. "Watch yourself."

Trying to ignore the two-story drop, Lilette crawled after him on hands and feet, the grit from the roof tiles sticking to her damp palms. Han crouched behind the roof ridge, which was carved to resemble a scroll, and peered at whatever lay beyond. After hesitating a moment, she eased up beside him. The ramparts loomed before her, a whole two stories taller than the building she sat upon. The gates faced south, toward the ocean. As she watched, they opened to admit the elephant and the elite, giving her a partial view of what lay beyond.

The palace stood in the center of an enormous courtyard, a pair of sun dragons flanking the wide front steps. Lilette's gaze strayed to the green peeking out behind the palace—the gardens. She and Han had played there for many hours as children.

Behind the palace in the west corner was a smaller compound that jutted against the ramparts. Two shorter walls half the height of the ramparts enclosed the space.

The harem.

Pointedly turning her eyes away, Lilette watched as the veiled woman on the elephant raised a long, slender arm to greet the crowd, her ring flashing with green stones. The gates swung shut.

Lilette's vision swam and she realized she'd been holding her breath. She sucked in a lungful of air.

Han's gaze made one more sweep of the courtyard before he backed away from the roof ridge, only rising when they were completely obscured.

She followed him. "What were you looking for in the courtyard? Who is the woman on the elephant?"

He paused. "A very big problem."

"Which one, the woman or the ele—" Lilette didn't have a chance to finish. A tile cracked beneath her foot and slid out from under her. She plunged hard and fast for the edge. She twisted so she was belly down, her fingernails clawing at the tiles, but she couldn't gain purchase. She was going to fall.

Suddenly, Han's iron grip was around her wrist, and this time she gripped him back. His feet scraped as he slid down beside her. She was too busy trying to convince her body she was no longer falling to realize he hadn't let go of her wrist. She opened her eyes to find him lying beside her, staring at her with something like sadness in his gaze. Abruptly, he released her and scrambled to the edge of the roof.

Scooting down on her bottom, she asked again, "Bad for whom?" By his set jaw, it was obvious he wasn't going to tell her any more—Fa had often worn that same expression.

She peered down two stories to the street below and wet her lips. "How do we get down?"

Han crouched low, his hands on the roof line, and then swung down. His momentum carried him forward and he landed in a crouch on the veranda before turning back to her. "Drop down and I'll pull you in."

Her heart pounding, Lilette sat on the edge, her legs dangling. She hesitated.

Han leaned forward and looked up at her. "Don't think about it. Sometimes you just have to move. I won't let you fall."

Taking a deep breath and holding it, she rolled onto her stomach and slowly pushed her legs back into open air. Leaning out over the banister, Han grabbed her ankles. As she lowered herself, his hands slid up to her knee, then her thighs. When she was hanging by her hands, he grabbed her waist and pulled her forward. She slid down his chest before he settled her gently on the floor. Slowly, he reached over and placed her hood back over her hair.

His friend, the servant, was grinning. Heat rose in her face.

Han stepped back as if her touch had burned him. He cleared his throat and said gruffly, "I didn't want you to fall."

Wordlessly, she nodded.

Helping himself to a rag, he ripped it in half and tied her hands again. He shot a glare at the servant before hauling her back the way they'd come.

CHAPTER 4

Harshen and its people took so much from Lilette, but she could never bring herself to hate them. They gave as much as they took. ~Jolin

Lilette's body felt impossibly heavy as the palace's massive gates loomed before them. Six elite wearing imperial-soldier uniforms watched them approach. They held wicked-looking half-moon spears before them. Lilette's stomach seemed to shrink within her.

Han paid the guards no mind. At the last second, the palace gates opened and the elite parted to let Lilette and him pass.

They crossed the rectangular courtyard heading to the harem. "Keep your head down," Han said under his breath. "You don't know the danger you're in."

For whatever reason, she believed him. She stole glances at the palace. Each of the four stories was surrounded by a wide veranda complete with a turned-up corner roof. Potted plants grew thick and green everywhere. As they came closer, Lilette made out the intricate carvings on the beams, doors, and window frames. She remembered them suddenly—five-clawed dragons, some on land and some in the sea.

Before the palace was a staircase of perfectly symmetrical lines. In front of the steps, a group of elite guarded a large gathering of men and women. The men wore black armor, the women long, flowing garments in varying shades of green.

Han must have noticed her staring. "You must never so much as touch one of the steps. To do so is to be immediately killed." Sweat started under Lilette's arms. "Because I'm a woman?" Han shook his head. "Only people who've been granted permission by the emperor may touch his home. You have been given no such privilege."

Actually, she had been, as a child. The privilege had apparently been revoked.

Just as Lilette drew even with the gathering, the doors swung open. A woman in a strange, billowing tunic trotted down the steps. The sight of her blond hair, blue eyes, and fair skin sent a shock through Lilette. She couldn't take her eyes off the woman. Han picked up their pace, but Lilette resisted his efforts to hurry her, and he seemed unwilling to make a scene by dragging her.

Chen appeared behind the woman, his arm outstretched as if to stop her, and Lilette wondered briefly if this strangely dressed woman was his wife.

"As an ambassador, you are a guest of the imperial house and of Harshen. You will obey our laws," Chen's voice rang out.

Not his wife then. Or at least Lilette hoped not.

The woman whirled to face him. "You better remember who holds the power in this world, little heir, because it isn't you."

Lilette's jaw dropped. It had been years since she'd heard a woman—besides herself—challenge a man like that. But that wasn't what stopped her. Deep inside, her memories were stirring. She knew this woman.

Chen reared back as if he'd been slapped. His hands clenched into tight fists. The elite shifted to grasp their swords, and Lilette had a better view of the people they had surrounded. Over thirty women and at least twice that in soldiers. The women gripped hands, but not out of fear. Instead, their faces shone with power and confidence. Elite soldiers began converging from around the compound. The tension in the air felt like an ember about to burst into flames.

Lilette planted her feet to keep from taking that last step into obscurity. And then she realized what she should have seen all along. The women were witches—ambassadors from Kalari.

She gasped, the sound cutting through the tension. The woman on the steps glanced in her direction. Lilette stared at her from beneath the hood, and their gazes locked. Lilette's mouth fell open. It was like looking at her reflection in a pool of clear water.

The woman was her sister.

Han must have seen Lilette's realization, for even as a scream for help built in her throat, he clapped his hand over her mouth and yanked her out of sight. She kicked and drove her elbows into him, desperately hoping Sash would somehow recognize her. But Lilette had been a child of eight when she'd gone missing, while Sash had been sixteen, nearly a woman.

Han dragged Lilette behind the palace. She didn't stop fighting until he dumped her in front of the harem's lower wall and small gate just inside the gardens. She collapsed, desperately trying to swallow the sobs that tore through her body. Sash had been more like a second mother than a sister. Always taking her to play, bringing her treats. As Lilette had grown older, Sash had accompanied her musical performances with her strings and her voice.

Han stood between Lilette and the sister she'd been longing for since childhood. "My whole life I've been trying to get back to her. And she's here—my sister is here! Just let me go!"

Refusing to look at her, Han focused on the two guards who stood on either side of the gate. They made no move to let Lilette and him pass like the other guards had. Instead, one took a mallet and struck a glancing blow to a gong before settling back to statue-like stillness.

A dozen heartbeats later, the door opened and a strange person walked out. Lilette wasn't sure if it was a man or woman, as the person wore a man's robes but had a woman's face. Lilette was even more confused when the person bowed to Han and said in a woman's voice, "How may I serve you, elite general?"

"Madame Lilette is to be taken to the secluded compound." Lilette staggered to her feet and backed away from Han and the guards. "Please." It was only one word, but there was a tone of fear and dread behind it.

Han kept his gaze trained on her, his face unreadable. "I am sorry."

He had been her friend once—her only friend in a foreign land. They had scaled every tree in the gardens behind the palace, searching for fruit. She could still taste the sweetness of oranges on her tongue, feel the dew-soaked grass on her bare feet as they ran in the shadows of the trees. And now he'd betrayed her.

The guards slid forward, flanking her. She studied the wall—twice the height of a man—before focusing all her loathing at Han. "May your flesh rot on your bones."

His attention shifted to the man-woman. "Watch her. She'll try to run." And with that, Han simply turned and walked away.

Lilette watched him go, hate tearing her apart from the inside out. She wished she could sing. Wished she could remember the words to bring down the palace and all its walls.

Her enemies outnumbered her and were bigger and faster. If she made a run for it, she'd be caught and restrained further. She must wait for the right time. It would come. It had to.

She faced the person waiting for her as her mind pieced together faded rumors and overheard bits of conversation from her childhood. He—for it *was* a he—was a eunuch, and eunuchs were the servants and guards of the harem. He was very plump, from his rolling stomach to his bulbous nose and round face. But beneath all that fat was a hardness she recognized. This man had risen to his position by decisively defeating all who challenged him.

"I am Minor Chief Wang. I oversee the emperor's harem." He spoke as easily as if bound women were brought to him every day. Maybe they were.

From inside his robes, he pulled out a small flask and handed it to Lilette. "If you will take a swallow of this."

She eyed the flask warily. "What's in it?"

"A harmless tincture."

She didn't believe him. He was watching her too closely. "And if I refuse?"

"There are other, less pleasant ways to ensure your cooperation."

The guards stepped closer. Lilette wanted to fight, but she was tired of being manhandled. And she wouldn't win. *Patience,* she reminded herself. *The opportunity will come.*

Her expression hard, she took a mouthful of the liquid, then held her wrist to her lips and spit as much of it into her sleeve as she dared.

"Half a mouthful is nearly as effective as a full dose," he told her. He took the flask and twisted it closed. Then he cut the rag that bound her wrists. "If you will come with me."

It was not a question. After rubbing the circulation back into her hands, Lilette slipped her hand inside her pocket and brushed her thumb along the sharp edge of the phoenix. She studied the ramparts, soldiers pacing across the top, and considered making a run for it. But where would she go?

"Running will earn you twenty lashings with a bamboo rod," Chief Wang said matter-of-factly.

When Lilette didn't move to follow, he cocked his head to the side. "The outer gates are shut. There are hundreds of elite throughout the compound—and that's if you can outrun the ones before you, which hasn't happened yet. But you're welcome to try. Usually once is all it takes before a concubine settles down and accepts her new life."

The guards at the gate inched closer. When still she didn't move, Chief Wang gave a long-suffering sigh, took a hold of her bruised arm, and tugged her past the guards.

On the other side of the door, Lilette glanced around. Beautiful trees were heavy with fruit, and fragrant flowers bloomed everywhere. Off to the right, a fountain trickled water into a circular lake filled with swans. A monkey called down to her from a tree.

The plants were so rich and full, it reminded Lilette of the jungle of her home. Her eyes welled with tears she refused to let fall. "This is the harem?"

Chief Wang continued walking, his gait hunched over and pained. "Yes. The emperor's wives, concubines, and younger children all reside here." Wang glanced at her, his gaze taking her in from top to bottom. "You have been granted the most secluded of our residences."

"And what of the heir and his concubines?" she asked.

He raised a thin eyebrow. "The heir lives in the palace with his wife. He has no concubines."

So Chen had made an exception for her. She peered between the trees and saw several small homes. Everything was balanced and flowing. But the serenity was broken by the daunting ramparts, guards prowling along its walkway. It was still a prison, albeit a beautiful one.

Lilette heard murmurs and music before a handful of women came into view beside the lake. In their colorful tunics, they were all beautiful and bright as a summer morning. There were also many eunuchs. All wore black robes, their heads shaved bare under their flat, conical hats with little tassels in the center. They turned to watch her curiously as she passed.

After a while, the houses began to thin until Lilette didn't see anyone else. Swinging from branch to branch, the monkey continued to follow her. Chief Wang steered her down a side path to a secluded house. Unlike the others, this one had a wall half the height of the harem wall. The monkey perched on the top and called to them.

"Compounds within compounds," she murmured.

Wang ushered her past the gate, beyond which was a sprawling garden and large house. "You may not leave this compound without the emperor's permission."

So she would be alone here. Good. That would make it easier to escape. "What about the older ones?"

Wang shot her a quizzical look.

"The older children," Lilette clarified as they stepped onto the porch of the house. "You said the younger ones live here. Where do the older ones live?"

"At twelve, all children are taken to the mountain palace." Wang slid the screen door open and strode inside the house. "The boys are trained as soldiers or monks. The girls are trained in the wifely arts."

Lilette placed her hand protectively on her belly as resolve hardened within her. *I will find a way out,* she promised herself before following Wang inside.

Before her was a long room. In the center was a short table surrounded by delicately embroidered cushions. A small, cold brazier stood off to the side. Screens partitioned both ends of the house, which smelled of lemon oil.

"Your personal servant is still being chosen. Until then—" Chief Wang uncovered a tray filled with tea, fresh fruit, and spring rolls stuffed with fresh vegetables. "I had this brought a few moments ago. Your servant will arrive to groom you before the heir comes sometime tomorrow."

"Not tonight?" Lilette held her relief at bay until Wang confirmed it.

"He wanted to give you time to adjust."

She hid her shudder by studying the intricate, four-clawed dragons carved into the beams along the walls and spine of the house. She ran her fingers lightly over one of the sharp claws, wondering how many hours the carver had spent chiseling away at the beam.

"I must warn you, if you pass the compound's gates, you will be beaten. If you ever leave the harem walls, you will be killed."

After staring her down, Wang left. "And don't feed the monkeys!" he called back. She didn't move until he crossed the garden and shut the gate behind him. Already, Lilette's senses were dulled by whatever he had drugged her with.

She searched the home, looking for anything useful for her escape—knives or rope, or jewels she could sell. Nothing in the main room. She slid open one of the side screens to reveal a bare room—two sleeping mats lying side by side. Her mouth suddenly dry, she quickly shut the screen.

It was becoming harder to focus. She shook her head to clear it and crossed the room to the other silk screen. Behind it were shelves with pottery and baskets and another sleeping mat, obviously for her servant. She rifled through the baskets, but they were empty of all but a trace of rice or leaves. No knives.

Not even a bit of twine. So she'd have nothing but her wits and her body. It would have to be enough.

Back in the main room, Lilette knelt before the tray of food. She shoved all but the rice and one of the rolls inside a tea towel she'd found in the second room, then tied off the towel and stuffed it into her robe. Starting toward the door, she nibbled on the tangy roll she'd saved, but at the thought of the two sleeping mats side by side, her throat grew so tight she could barely swallow.

She strode outside. The monkey called at her. Remembering Wang's parting comment, she tossed the roll to the base of the tree. The monkey snatched it and raced back up. Just as she reached for the gate, the full effect of the drug slammed into her.

She reeled back, wavering on her feet. Her legs went limp and she collapsed in a heap. Before she knew what was happening, everything went dark.

CHAPTER 5

Lilette once told me she didn't trust beauty—hers or anyone else's. That it was a great illusion. ~Jolin

L ilette woke to a clinking sound. She found herself on the cushions beside the short table. Someone had moved her. Fighting the exhaustion still dulling her senses, she pushed herself up on her elbows and saw a kneeling woman placing a teapot on the brazier. She wore an ankle-length tunic and trousers of fine black silk. Her hair was piled on her head and held in place by chopsticks.

Lilette glanced out the open screen. The light had gone soft—it was evening. She'd slept nearly half the day. She moaned in frustration.

The woman poured some food into a copper pan. It sizzled and immediately sent the dark, sweet smell of brown sauce into the air. But what should have smelled delicious only made Lilette's stomach turn. She rolled her knees under her, the towel stuffed with food sticking damply to her side. "Who are you?"

"My name is Sima. I have been assigned as madame's servant. I will live with you and see to all your needs. Today, I am to prepare food and begin preparations for madame before the heir comes tonight."

Lilette's head jerked up. "I thought he was coming tomorrow."

Sima pursed her lips. "Is he? Good. That will give us more time."

It would be much harder to escape with this woman watching her. "I don't need a servant. Please just go."

"I'm afraid that isn't possible." Sima cleared her throat. "Tell me, why did the heir choose you?"

Lilette looked past the doorway, to the ramparts. The sun was just beginning to move behind them. Her time was running out. She staggered to her feet and took a few faltering steps toward the door.

Sima was beside her in an instant. "It wears off slowly. Sit, rest. It will pass by tomorrow."

"I don't have time to rest," Lilette ground out. She'd made it to the door and then stopped.

A man waited outside. At the sight of her, he started forward. Sima held out a forestalling hand. "She just wanted some fresh air. She's coming back now."

Though her whole body ached to fight, Lilette allowed Sima to pull her back inside and settle her on the cushions.

"You didn't choose to be here?" Sima sounded surprised.

"No," Lilette whispered, her heart pounding with desperation. "I did not choose it."

Sima's brow drew together. After a moment, she sighed. "No one ever leaves. Even those who have help."

Lilette clenched her fists at her sides. There had to be a way. If not now—she braced herself as the fear slammed into her—then soon. "Will I ever be allowed to leave this compound?" It would be much easier to escape if she were already beyond these walls.

Sima stirred the vegetables. "Sometimes, if the hot season is especially bad and the needs of the empire are not too demanding, we go to the summer palace in the mountains at the center of the island. It is beautiful and remote enough that we are allowed to travel beyond the palace walls." There was an undeniable hint of longing in the woman's voice. "Even then, most concubines never leave the compound. A select few have spent time in the palace itself, if the emperor wishes it."

Lilette knew Chen would never risk taking her from the safety of these walls. Escaping would take time and careful planning, neither of which she had. She closed her eyes and imagined herself home, sitting on the shore, the sun bleeding red as it sank into the sea's vast waters. The images calmed her.

Sima set the food before Lilette, who refused to look at it. The woman sat on her heels, her hands resting on her legs. "Will you not eat, madame?"

Lilette moved the food farther away so she wouldn't have to smell it. "I am not well."

"Did you eat all the food I left for you earlier? The tray was empty."

Lilette sighed. She couldn't tell the woman about the food stuffed in her robes. "It was delicious, thank you."

Sima sniffed. "If I am to teach you court manners, I must know more about you. Might I ask you questions, madame?"

Lilette wiped the sweat from her face. "I suppose."

Sima closed the brazier vents to snuff out the fire. "You speak as a Harshen, though clearly you are not. Where are you from?"

Lilette took a deep breath, determined not to let her emotions surface. "From one of the smaller islands." She didn't tell her about being born a Kalari—it was not a story she told. Ever.

"What was it called?"

Lilette's head was beginning to hurt. She rubbed her temples. "Calden."

Sima cocked her head to the side. "You do not look like a Harshen."

Lilette's stomach rolled inside her. Groaning, she pressed her hand to her middle.

"Madame? If I am to instruct you, I must know where to begin."

Lilette's mouth watered uncontrollably. She held her fingers over her lips and tried to concentrate on keeping the vomit down. "I came to Calden Island when I was very young. A man named Fa took me in and raised me as his daughter. He died a few weeks ago."

She tried and failed to push the memory of his death from her mind. So much blood that it had stained the surface of the sea. She could taste it as she had dove down to kill the eel that had bitten through an artery in Fa's arm.

Sima watched her carefully. "Why did the heir choose you as his concubine?"

Lilette didn't understand what these questions had to do with her learning the proper etiquette. "Doesn't matter."

For the first time, Sima met Lilette's gaze. "Have you performed all your duties as a concubine yet?"

Lilette swallowed her outrage and tried to rise to her feet, but she was suddenly dizzy. She stumbled and threw her hands out to catch herself, but there was nothing to hold onto. She tripped on the cushions and crashed into the brazier, burning her hands and spilling hot coals across the floor.

She blinked to steady her vision, but everything was fuzzy and disjointed. "I am not well."

Sima knelt next to her but made no move to help, no move to smother the coals smoking on the beautiful wood floor. "Answer my question."

Sima's hands were right in front of Lilette's face. She stared at the ring on the woman's finger. A curving dragon, its scales bright gold, its face impossibly detailed with emerald chips for eyes. But what stunned her most was the dragon's claws—five of them. Only the royal family could wear a dragon with five claws.

Sima bent down and clenched Lilette's jaw in her impossibly smooth hands. "He's risked a war for you. I want to know why."

This close, Lilette could smell the woman's pear-blossom perfume. Servants wouldn't wear something as lavish as perfume. And the eunuchs served the harem. A different sort of fear reared up inside Lilette. "Who are you?" But she didn't wait for her answer. "The woman on the elephant." Chen's wife.

Han had warned Lilette to be afraid. Her stomach cramped. "What have you done to me?"

Sima's hold tightened, bruising Lilette's jaw. "I will give you the antidote if you tell me why."

"But . . ." Lilette sputtered before clamping her mouth shut. She'd only had one bite of the spring roll. Surely that wasn't enough to kill her, yet her body told her otherwise. Lilette's heart raced, pumping the poison faster through her veins. She did not want to die.

"Because I am a witch. His father tried to take my mother when I was a child. I was meant for Chen."

The woman's expression turned to disgust. "Did he think to sire his own private choir of witches? It would never work. The witches always find their own." Sima laughed suddenly. "Well then, his destruction will be easy to orchestrate. I won't even have to kill him. The witches will do it for me."

Lilette's head ached. "The antidote."

Sima's gaze narrowed. "One more thing. What was your mother's name?"

Lilette wiped the sweat from her brow with the back of her wrist. "Lellan. Her name was Lellan."

Sima scrutinized her for a long moment. She gave a small nod of satisfaction before releasing her and gathering the food and tea. Lilette's hand shot out, trying to grab her arm, but there were two arms now, and she'd reached for the wrong one. The woman easily batted her away and started toward the silk screen.

"Wait! The antidote!"

The woman chuckled dryly as she tossed the food and the remainder of the tea into the soil. "There isn't one. Never was." She stepped out of sight.

"Should we wait until it is finished?" came a man's deep voice. Definitely not a eunuch.

"It's too risky. Besides, it only takes one bite, and the whole plate was empty. No one could survive that," Sima answered tartly.

One bite was still one bite too many. Lilette stopped fighting her nausea and vomited onto the fine silk cushions. She reached into her robes and tossed the towel of mangled food onto the floor. She had to get out of the house, get help. She struggled to her feet, using the wall to shore herself up until she peeked out the door.

Sima and the man were gone. It was nearly dark. Lilette put her hands out for balance and started forward, but promptly tumbled down the steps. She lay gasping, her heart flopping in her chest like a dying fish. She pressed the heel of her hand against her ribs to keep it from beating out of her chest.

She rolled to her side and came face to face with the monkey she'd thrown the spring roll to. It was lying under a shrub, dead. Looking past the carcass, Lilette fixed her gaze on the gate. She had to reach it. Years of balancing on Fa's fishing boat were the only reason she made it to her feet and kept her balance all the way to the gate.

Lilette's hands were numb and tingling, her shaking limbs impossibly heavy, but she managed to grab the latch and pull it open. She lurched through the gate. Everything tipped and swayed around her. Leaning on the wall, she threw up bile. She pressed the back of her cold wrist to her mouth and followed the wall back the way she'd come.

Her heart finally started to slow down. For a moment, she felt better. Her vision cleared and she was able to move without clutching onto something for support. Her pace picked up measurably. It didn't last long enough, though. Everything was surrounded by a halo, like each object was backed by its very own sun. She swayed and stumbled like someone deep in her cups. She bumped into something, reeled back, and looked up, up, up.

Through her muddy thoughts, she recognized the ramparts. She'd gone the wrong way. Filling her lungs, she screamed for help. Silence answered her. With tears in her eyes, she faced the way she'd come. She could feel her body shutting down. See death teasing her along the outer curve of her vision. Already it was too late.

But Lilette had never given up before, and sheer habit kept her moving when nothing else would have. She turned and lurched back the way she'd come. But death grew more bold, more ominous. She tried to bat the darkness away with her hands, but it only laughed as it came swarming in.

She fell to the ground, her whole body convulsing. Death leaned over her, and its breath puffed against her face. It smelled of orchids.

CHAPTER 6

With complete power comes pride. Pride breeds corruption.
Corruption begets vulnerability, which pride refuses to see.
And so begins the vicious cycle of destruction. ~Jolin

L ilette wasn't sure how long she'd been lying on the ground
before death's arms reached beneath her and picked her
up. She struggled against it, willing her body to fight the poison
coursing through her.

"Be still," said a deep voice.

She immediately relaxed. Not death, but a man. Had he
fought death off? She rested her aching head against his broad
chest. "Hurts."

"What happened to you?"

Rain began tapping against her skin. "Woman. Poison."

"Hold on, little dragon." He took off at a run. Later, she would
remember little of it. Mostly just sensations. The muscles of his
arms relaxing and contracting with each of his running steps.
The steady beat of his heart, so different from the occasional
thump of hers. The scent of his damp leather armor.

The way he held her and his smell tugged at the fraying edges
of her memory, but she didn't try to weave the threads together.
She didn't care enough to try.

He paused twice—the last time to slide open a door. A woman
gasped. "What are you doing here? You can't be here!"

He grunted, the sound vibrating against Lilette's forehead.
"Apparently I can."

She struggled to open her eyes as he set her on a sleeping mat. "It's her, isn't it? Lilette?" said the woman.

"She's been poisoned," he replied.

After a moment's hesitation, delicate hands pressed against her chest. "She's cold. Her heart is weak."

Lilette finally managed to blink her eyes open and stared up at one of the most beautiful faces she'd ever seen, pale green eyes a shocking contrast to her dark features. The woman's eyes were round, her face longer. She was definitely not Harshen.

She pried open Lilette's mouth and sniffed. "She's vomited." She came eye level with Lilette. "Were you pricked or did you consume it?"

Lilette's body didn't seem to be connected to the rest of her. "The spring rolls."

The woman nodded. "What did it taste like?"

Everything was so blurry. She squinted, but it didn't help. "Like . . . spring rolls."

The woman disappeared and the man leaned over her. It was Han, his scarred face twisted with concern

This didn't surprise her. Some part of her had recognized him when he picked her up. And somehow she didn't want to kill him.

From close by, a bell rang. Lilette glanced out the window. It was full dark now. The woman came bustling back into the room. She positioned Lilette's head on her knees and held a cup to her lips. "Drink it."

Lilette didn't have much of a choice as the liquid was poured into her mouth. She immediately gagged. She recognized the taste from a lifetime of clearing out old fire pits. A sludge of ashes mixed with water.

"Keep it down," the woman warned. "It will absorb the poison."

Lilette swallowed to keep her gorge from rising, but as soon as the mixture hit her stomach, she immediately threw it up.

"You want to live, you'll keep it down."

The cup was tipped back again. It was gritty and horrible, with chunks of charcoal sticking in her throat. Lilette swallowed, and with everything she had left she fought the urge to vomit.

The woman just kept pouring more down her throat. "I've summoned my eunuch. You better slip out of here before anyone sees you," she said to Han.

He scoffed. "I think I can handle your tailless dog."

The woman's eyes hardened. "He won't keep your secrets, and they'll kill you if they find out you set foot in the harem." Her face softened and she reached out and touched the jagged scar that stretched from his cheek to his mangled ear. "My son, I'm so sorry."

He pulled away from her. "I don't want your pity."

Tears welled in her eyes. "Go. Before it's too late."

He cast one last glance at Lilette, his gaze unreadable, then turned and strode out.

The woman held the cup to Lilette's lips once more. Tears dripped from her face onto Lilette's cheeks as if they were her own. Lilette was certain the tears were not for her.

The woman stroked her head. "My name is Ko. Yours is Lilette?"

Her bowels cramped and she curled into a ball. "Yes." She moaned in pain. "Han is your son?"

Grief crossed Ko's face. "Yes."

"Chen too?" Lilette gasped.

Ko shook her head. "No. His mother died a year ago." That made Chen and Han half-brothers.

The eunuch arrived. He was younger than the first Lilette had met, his face practically boyish. "Alert Chief Wang that Madame Lilette has been poisoned. Quickly."

The boy ran.

More eunuchs came. Ko ordered them to bring in more braziers, water, and stones to make steam. "We'll sweat the poison from her. Seal up the windows."

One of the eunuchs pressed his hands together and bowed to Ko. "Honored madame, you should go. We will care for the girl."

Lilette squeezed the woman's hand, silently begging her to stay. She wasn't sure when she'd started holding it.

Ko squeezed back. "I will stay with her." It wasn't long before the stuffy heat of the hot season had grown unbearable. Sweat coursed down Lilette's skin while the eunuchs fanned her. She silently willed her heart to keep beating.

Ko kept pouring water into Lilette's mouth. Sometimes she threw it up, sometimes she kept it down. Chen arrived with Wang and the court physician, another eunuch with straggly gray hair circling his mostly bald head, his long mustache resting on his protruding belly.

The whole room of eunuchs rolled smoothly into their kowtows. Ko bent low but didn't move from her position as a cushion for Lilette's head.

Chen took one look at Lilette and kicked over a brazier. "Who did this?"

Eunuchs scrambled on all fours to scrape the coals and ash back into the brazier before it burned the house down.

When no one answered him, Chen knelt beside Lilette. His hands hovered above her body before coming to rest gently on her shoulders. "Who did this to you?"

She blinked blearily at him, the halos around everyone making her squint. "A woman." Her voice was barely a whisper.

He rested a hand on her clammy forehead. "What did she look like?"

Lilette shut her eyes. "Her face was longer." She had to rest. "Her eyes close set." Another break until the dizziness passed. "She wore a five-clawed dragon ring with . . . with emeralds for eyes." She lay back, exhausted from the effort of speaking.

Chen reeled back on his heels, his face flashing with disbelief that quickly melted to fury. He glared at the physician, who was already mixing powders into boiling water. "She dies, you die. Understand?"

The man bowed, clearly terrified.

Chen shot a final look at Lilette before storming out. Eunuchs followed him, closing the screen and sealing it to keep the steam from escaping.

Ko watched the physician dump in more powders, her brow creased. "What is that?" Han's mother asked.

The physician stirred the concoction briskly. "Honored madame, it is poison to counter poison. Ashes from poisonous frogs, centipedes, and snakes. I also mix it with ground shells to trap her soul inside her body."

Ko stared at him. "You're giving her more poison?"

He tipped Lilette's face up and helped her drink it. She choked and gagged. "This is just the first of her treatments. We must cleanse her body of toxin. Strip off her raiment."

Eunuchs slipped her out of her tunic and proceeded to treat Lilette in ways she hoped to never experience again. When it was all finished, she was too exhausted to keep her eyes open and in too much pain to sleep. She listened to Ko humming as eunuchs fanned her.

Eventually, there was a flurry of dry air. A cool silk sheet was pulled over Lilette's body.

"How is she?" It was Chen's voice.

The physician answered. "I have done all I can for her."

"And?" Chen's voice held an undeniable warning.

The physician didn't answer. Lilette knew what his silence meant, but she was too weak to fear death.

"Lilette." She stirred a little. Her limbs were so heavy. "Lilette. Open your eyes."

She blinked them open to find it was morning again. Chen stood above her. His hand was locked around the back of a woman's neck. "Is this who poisoned you?"

It was his wife, Sima—or whatever her real name was. Only now her robes were the finest Lilette had ever seen. Her hair was pulled back in elaborate twists, with jeweled combs and orchids sparkling across the top.

Lilette nodded once. Chen's eyes flashed.

His wife couldn't seem to catch her breath. "I didn't even know she existed!"

"With the amount of spies you have all over the palace, Laosh, I think not." He threw her to the ground. As if from far away, Lilette watched as the woman scrambled to her feet. Chen advanced on her while the eunuchs remained prostrate.

Laosh reached the wall. There was nowhere else for her to go. Chen slowly drew his sword. "And she is not the first."

His wife glared up at him. "You swore when you married me that you would take no other! You promised my father."

He lifted his sword above his head. "Part of our arrangement was that you provide me with sons. Your barrenness voids our contract."

Her eyes flashed a warning. "Kill me and my father will raise his armies against you. He'll destroy your city, your people. Everything!"

"Even your father cannot save you from the law, Laosh."

She screamed until the sword came down, silencing her. Lilette had just watched Chen kill his wife. She waited for the horror to come. The disgust. But it didn't. Instead, all she felt was a numb detachment, like nothing she saw was real.

Chen stepped back, a look of revulsion crossing his face. "Eunuchs, clean this mess up. Send her body back to her father. He can go to the trouble of burying her."

He strode toward Lilette, blood dripping from his sword. "She is dying?"

Silence was the reply.

He cuffed the physician. "Answer me!"

The man lay blinking where he'd fallen on the floor. "Yes, Heir. She is dying."

Chen turned and left without a backward glance.

CHAPTER 7

Lilette saw something that night, something that haunted her the rest of her days. ~Jolin

Lilette's heartbeats grew farther and farther apart until she again floated in the uneasy space between life and death. As if from a distance, she sensed movement and unease. Finally, an explosion jolted her into consciousness. Even through the blankets darkening the room, she could see flashes of lightning. Wind blasted against the house.

Chen stood in the doorway, sword in hand, water dripping from his clothing. Before him was a woman, this one very different from the last. She was gaunt and looked about Lilette's age. Her wet, chin-length hair, the color of ashes mixed with dirt, was parted exactly down the middle and tucked behind her ears. Her strange, floor-length tunic had a fitted bodice and billowed out below the hips.

She was one of the witches. Lilette tried to make her mouth work, to say something—anything—but she couldn't move past the wall of pain and weakness.

"I am told you are the best healer, so heal her," Chen said to the woman.

"I've already told you, I'm not a healer, I'm a potioner," she replied in almost perfect Harshen. "But it's true, I am the best— and an argument could be made that the best potioners are also the best healers." A look of curiosity swept over her face as she took in Lilette. "What happened to her?"

Chen clenched his teeth. "She's been poisoned, which is why I need a potioner."

The woman's eyes narrowed. "With what?"

He handed her a familiar-looking tea towel. "We found this in her house."

She opened the towel, and her eyebrows came up as she surveyed it. She picked a few of the limp greens out of the spring rolls and held them up to the light.

She nibbled the end of one before spitting it onto the floor. She wiped her tongue on her rain-dampened sleeve. "A simple yet very effective variation of morte. It's rather rare, only available from the black-market witches, and without the antidote, always fatal."

She smacked her tongue on the roof of her mouth as if to clear out the aftertaste. "Have you questioned the poisoner? It would be helpful to know how much was consumed."

Chen's eyes flicked to the corner. The eunuchs had scrubbed the floor, but the blood had stained it a dark brown.

The woman followed his gaze and gasped. She turned to face Chen. "What happened here?"

He refused to look back at the stain. "The poisoner admitted to the crime and was punished."

"So you just killed him?" the woman whispered.

Chen didn't bother to correct her. "I am the heir. My word is justice."

She clamped her mouth shut. "I want no part of this."

She made to move past him, but he blocked her. "You would really let her die because of something I did?"

She glanced over her shoulder at Lilette as if she'd forgotten she was there. "I can at least provide the antidote." She squared herself in front of the rotund physicker. "What have you given her?"

The man laced his fingers and set them on his stomach. "We are sweating her—"

The woman shook her head as if disgusted. "Clearly. The heat is going to kill me, and I'm perfectly healthy. What else?"

He frowned and glanced at Chen. The heir simply waved for him to continue. "The ashes of poisonous creatures to battle the poison inside her, and ground shells to trap her soul within her body," the physicker said.

The woman blinked at him before turning to Chen. "Is he trying to kill her?"

The physicker sputtered a reply, but the woman ignored him. "Fine. I'll help her," she said to Chen. "But I want him out."

The heir gestured to the physicker, who looked relieved as he left the room.

Kneeling beside Lilette, the woman brushed her hair off her damp forehead. "I'm Jolin." She squinted at Lilette's skin, as if she was seeing something puzzling there. From her pocket she pulled a contraption made from round bits of colored glass connected by thin wires. She set it on her nose and stared at Lilette.

Jolin pulled a rose-colored glass over her eyes and gasped. "It's you." She whirled to Chen. "This is the woman we've been looking for—the one our listeners sensed."

Lilette almost wept for joy. Finally! She wanted to ask about her sister, but the pain was a wall she could not cross.

"She is my concubine," Chen said steadily. "You cannot take her."

Jolin frowned. "All keepers must come to Haven for testing."

"Not this one."

"Creators' mercy—"

"Don't invoke your gods on Harshen soil," Chen warned.

"They're your gods too," Jolin murmured so softly Lilette was sure no one else heard. *Smart girl.*

Jolin's stormy eyes turned back to Chen. "All right, I'll save her. We'll discuss the rest later."

He tipped his head, his lips pursed. "We will discuss nothing."

She muttered something unintelligible, and a sense of purpose seemed to settle over her. Never taking his eyes from Jolin, Chen backed out of the room.

She pointedly ignored his retreating figure. "Open the windows and let this unbearable heat out."

Ko shook her head. "We must sweat out the poison."

Jolin started pulling seeds from a belt at her waist. "This heat is killing her faster than the poison. Open the windows and one of you" —she seemed to be struggling to find an appropriate word for the eunuchs— "*men* bathe her with water and fan her until she cools off."

A breeze tickled the tiny hairs on Lilette's body as some of the oppressive heat escaped. As cool water slid across her skin, she sighed in relief.

"I'll be back," Jolin said before she headed outside. When she returned a few minutes later, she held a handful of dark green leaves. "Out!" she commanded the eunuchs. "Can't think with all these crows flapping about," she muttered.

As they shuffled outside, Jolin ground the leaves in a mortar. Then she added cold water, each twist of the pestle seeming to instill her with a stronger sense of purpose. Moments later, she tipped the mixture into Lilette's mouth.

It tasted fresh, green, and a little bitter. Lilette swallowed it reflexively, her body somehow recognizing it as something desperately needed. Suddenly, the cramps in her stomach eased. With some of the pain and unbearable heat diminished, a few of her muscles unclenched and she relaxed. She closed her eyes as her heart began to slow even more.

"Good. The antidote is already working." Jolin leaned down so close that Lilette could feel her. "You will have to fight if you want to live."

With some of her pain abated, Lilette found she could speak again. "I've never stopped fighting."

Someone pressed an ear against her chest and said, "We came to look for you, you know. We felt your song, though we figured you were farther southeast. You're one of us—one of the keepers. You sing and the world obeys."

Exhaustion wore at Lilette, and the woman's words became muddled in her head. Lilette wished she'd leave her be. She was so tired.

"I need you to stay awake, witchling," Jolin said. "We didn't come this far only for you to die now."

"You're too late," Lilette managed. She could hear Jolin working over her mortar.

The woman gave a short laugh. "If you were in anyone else's hands, you would be lost. Luckily, you're in mine, and I'm the best."

Despite her words, Jolin sounded truly worried. She began singing in the Creators' language—the language of power. Lilette had long ago forgotten the words, but the sound and rhythm were as familiar as her own heartbeat.

Lilette felt someone pushing her up from behind. It was Ko. The pool of sweat in the hollow of Lilette's throat now ran between her breasts. Someone poured something into her mouth.

"These herbs will speed up your heart," Jolin explained. "Don't die before they begin to work."

She and Ko laid Lilette on her back again, and she felt herself shutting down. It was getting harder to breathe. Moments later, Lilette's heart beat once and paused.

"No," Jolin exclaimed. "Just give the herbs a moment to work. Just give them a moment."

Lilette came back from the edge of something darker than sleep to answer. "I'm sorry." Everything started to blur. She willed her heart to beat again, and it did—once. Then the room grew brighter, light suffusing everything around her until it flashed a blinding white.

The last sound she heard was Ko's sobs. And then the strangest thing happened. Through the brilliance, a long, thin shape appeared. After a moment, the shape took the form of a woman and suddenly Lilette knew her. "Mother?"

Lellan reached out and cupped her cheeks. "Daughter, I haven't much time. You must listen."

Beyond Lellan was the most achingly beautiful music. It filled Lilette's body with a longing, a pain deeper than anything she'd ever imagined. "I'm dying."

Her mother's smile fell. "Not like this. The work needs a martyr."

Lilette tipped her head to the side. "What do you mean?"

"We aren't supposed to watch, and we certainly aren't to interfere, but I cannot abide this. Terrible things have been set in motion. It will destroy the whole world."

Lilette pried her attention away from the bewitching music to focus on her mother. "I don't understand."

Lellan pressed the pads of her fingers to Lilette's forehead. Immediately, Lilette was inundated with scenes of chaos and destruction—whole cities burning, armies colliding with the force of a breaking wave, tornadoes and monsoons ripping life off the face of the earth. Last, Harshen sank into the ocean—the palace itself the final thing to disappear beneath the churning waters.

Reeling, Lilette let out a cry of horror. She told herself those terrible things hadn't happened—that they could *never* happen.

Lellan closed her eyes. "Save those you can."

Lilette took a shuddering breath.

"I have laid the groundwork for you," her mother went on. "Everything you need has been prepared. Find Grove City."

"But Chen . . . I'm trapped in his harem."

Lellan's eyes flashed. "Chen is right about one thing—you are a weapon, but not one he can wield. Prove that his weapon can turn on him."

Lilette's breath came short. She was slipping away, something pulling her toward the light and music. And she suddenly didn't care about saving the world. She yearned for the music—only the music.

"There isn't time. If I don't stop this now, you will die." Lellan gripped both her arms. "You are my daughter—a warrior of the world, not a plaything for princes. Will you do what is necessary?"

It took everything Lilette had to turn away from the music and light. "Yes."

Her mother nodded. "Live." The word came out as a song, and Lilette's flesh responded to the command. She sank back into her body. Lellan knelt beside her and pressed her lips against her daughter's forehead. "Light guide thee."

Her mother stepped into the brilliance, which faded before disappearing altogether. The music grew farther and farther away. Tears welled in Lilette's eyes, and an ache filled her body that had nothing to do with her illness.

Ko was slumped over weeping, her head in her hands. Lilette took a gasping breath. Her heart pounded, filling her with a burst of blood. She sucked air into her starving lungs.

Jolin jerked upright and pressed her ear against Lilette's chest to listen to her heart.

"A drink," Lilette mumbled.

A smile spread across Ko's face.

Jolin slapped her thigh. "I knew I could do it!"

"Please," Lilette begged, her throat so dry the words came out like two stones rubbing together.

Ko called to the eunuchs just outside the room. They scrambled to work, practically tripping over themselves to serve her. She sat back on her heels. "How is this possible? She was dead. You said so yourself."

Jolin tucked her hair behind her ears. "It was the potion I gave her. It speeds up the heart."

As Lilette stared into the space where her mother had disappeared, a longing filled her chest. Already, she desperately missed the music.

CHAPTER 8

*I brought a woman back from the dead. Sometimes my prowess
astounds even me. ~Jolin*

"You knew our company came here looking for her," said
a feminine voice.

After several seconds of silence, a man replied, "Yes."

"Yet you led us to believe you didn't know where she was,"
the woman said.

Lilette roused herself from sleep to listen to the conversation.
She didn't know if she'd slept for hours or days, only that it was
light out.

Chen's arms were folded across his chest. "If I'd told you
where she was, you would have tried to take her."

Jolin stood before the heir, fists on hips. "All witches must
come to Haven for learning. It's the law."

Chen glared at her, his thumb tapping the hilt of his sword.
"Not Harshen law."

"I know what you're trying to do," Jolin growled. "I promise
you, it will not end well."

"You know nothing."

Lilette didn't miss the bitterness in his tone. She worked some
moisture into her mouth and whispered, "Take me with you."

Jolin glanced at her, triumph flaring in her eyes. "I knew it! I
knew she couldn't want to stay here."

Lilette allowed herself a moment of satisfaction, but it quickly ended when Chen motioned to two eunuchs behind him. "Bring me her seed belt."

"What? What are you doing?" Jolin backed up, kicking at one of the eunuchs as he lunged for her. The eunuchs stripped the belt from her and backed away.

Lilette started to sit up, determined to help Jolin, but Ko held her down. "Stay still," the older woman whispered. "Anything you say or do will only make it worse."

Chen took the belt, running his fingers over some of the compartments. "Make sure neither of them leaves the house."

Jolin's chest rose and fell as she breathed hard. "You can't keep me here!"

Chen shot her a withering look. "I'm afraid I no longer have a choice. If the witches know Lilette is here they will retaliate, and my entire empire will be in danger. I cannot allow that."

Lilette wanted to strangle him.

Jolin tried to march after him, but the eunuchs blocked her way. "Then why bring me here in the first place?"

Chen turned back, considering her. "She was too weak to speak. It never occurred to me that you could tell what she was merely by looking at her. And she was dying." His voice caught on the last, as if he really cared.

"She's white! You had to know I'd figure it out."

Chen chuckled. "It's not like she's the only white concubine in the harem. My father has diverse taste in women."

"Without knowledge," Jolin ground out, "she's as useless to you as a falcon with clipped wings."

After a moment, Chen said, "I see the truth in this. That is why *you* will teach her."

"I will do no such thing!" Jolin barked. "I'll not teach your concubine how to fight us."

He took a step toward her. "You will teach her. I'll make sure of that."

"You're afraid—that's where all this anger is coming from. Is it because I'm a keeper? Or are you just afraid of anything more powerful than you?"

Chen clenched his fist. "If you had seen the things I have seen, knew the things I know, you would be afraid too."

Jolin glanced at his fist. "Touch me and you'll regret it."

"Your song isn't strong enough to do any real damage." Her hand flashed out as she slapped him. "It's not just my song that can hurt you!" The eunuchs lunged forward and restrained her.

Chen pressed his fingertips against his reddened cheek. "The law for striking the heir is death. As reward for saving Lilette, I'll spare your life. But you will have a lashing to teach you better manners. After all, I can't have another concubine with so little respect for her heir."

Jolin gaped at him. "You wouldn't dare." He tipped his head to the side and gave her a crooked smile before she said, "My keepers would never allow it!"

He shrugged. "You caught whatever plague my concubine had. It causes boils all over the face. Very disfiguring to the body."

Jolin struggled against the eunuchs holding her. "You have no idea the viper's nest you're poking."

"Don't I?" Chen laughed, but there was no humor in it. "Five lashes," he said to the eunuchs, and then he turned and left without a backward glance.

The eunuchs began dragging Jolin away. "Please—" Lilette said as she reached toward them.

Ko rested a hand on her shoulder. "They don't have a choice."

Jolin kicked and squirmed. "You will pay for this. I swear it! The witches will bring down a curse on your heads."

"Don't fight them," Lilette said weakly. "Save it for when it will do some good." But Jolin was screaming and fighting so hard, Lilette doubted she heard.

When they were out of earshot, Ko whispered, "Jolin should be grateful it's only a lashing."

"He can't force her to be his concubine. It's not right," Lilette said.

"He can do whatever he wants."

Lilette knew that better than anyone. "Will the witches believe him?"

Ko's gaze was fixed on the floor. "I don't know."

A eunuch brought Lilette another bowl of rich broth. Though Ko had to help her sit up, she was able to grip the bowl and sip it herself. It was such a relief when her body welcomed the food instead of promptly rejecting it.

"How long have I been asleep?" she asked.

Ko refilled her cup of tea. "Almost a whole day."

Lilette passed a hand over her face in frustration. A whole day wasted. "Did Jolin say anything about my sister?" She set the empty bowl down. "I saw her with the other witches."

Ko shook her head. "I'm sorry."

Lilette finished a few cups of the tea the eunuchs had made according to Jolin's instructions. Then Ko dismissed all of the eunuchs.

Despite her worry for Jolin and her distress for her sister and the others, Lilette fell asleep. She woke in the late afternoon, feeling as if she was no longer hand in hand with death.

A eunuch who'd been kneeling in the corner kowtowed and backed from the room. Ko came in moments later with more broth, this time with noodles. Lilette pushed herself into a sitting position for the first time in two days. Such a small thing, but it felt like a victory. Though she trembled, she was able to slurp the food on her own. Ko left for a time while the eunuchs bathed Lilette. Then she slept again.

When she opened her eyes next, it was cooler and the light was soft—it was morning. That made it three days since Laosh had poisoned her. Five days since Lilette had left Calden. A pang of homesickness shot through her.

A breeze flowed through the open windows. Another eunuch brought Lilette some plain rice, fruit, and tea. Then Ko knelt beside the sleeping mat and dismissed all the eunuchs.

Lilette slipped a piece of mango into her mouth. Sweet and tart, with a metallic aftertaste. "How's Jolin?"

Ko sighed. "She's been fighting, so they gave her the sleeping tincture. She hasn't woken yet."

Lilette steeled herself. She would have to be patient, but patience had never come easily to her.

"You need to be very careful how you address the heir. Only the emperor is more powerful," Ko said bitterly.

Lilette stared into the distance and hoped her song made her stronger than Chen. Her fingers felt big and clumsy as she gripped the chopsticks.

Ko watched her. "Do you remember me finding you wandering the compound, lost and disoriented? My helping you here?" There was a tension about Ko, a tightness to her face, and she looked exhausted.

Lilette swallowed her mouthful. "Han brought me here."

Not meeting her gaze, Ko stirred the rice. "You were very sick. You must have imagined that."

"Why are you so afraid that I'll remember?"

Ko bowed her head. "They kill any whole man who enters the harem, besides the emperor or the heir—and even he must be escorted by the chief eunuch. No man may lay eyes upon the imperial concubines if the emperor does not wish it—even if that man is my son." Ko finally looked up, pleading plain on her face. "Please."

Lilette could not deny her. Not after everything she'd done. "Your secret—his secret—will become my secret."

Ko let out a deep breath. "After you and your family escaped, they took him from me and locked down the harem so even the children could not leave. The night he brought you here was the first I've seen him in eight years." There were tears in her voice, though her face remained a tight mask. "I barely recognized him—my own son."

"Chief Wang told me they took the children at twelve," Lilette said. Han had only been ten when she left, while Chen had been days from twelve.

"They wouldn't tell me why they took him early," Ko said softly.

Lilette's determination to escape hardened within her. She would not bear children only to give them up and never see them again.

Gazing out the window, she studied the guards patrolling the ramparts. How had Han gotten inside? How had he found her? "Is there a way out?"

Ko stared at the mat she knelt on. "We are the best-guarded treasure in the whole empire. To leave the compound without permission is to die."

If Han had managed it, so could Lilette. She wasn't afraid of death. Not anymore. In fact, a part of her longed for it. Though not eating for the last few days had caused her stomach to shrink, she forced herself to finish her food.

Ko gathered up the dishes and left just before Jolin came stiffly inside and slid the screen shut. Her eyes were bleary, her hair limp. There were tight lines of pain on her face.

With a groan, she eased down and pressed her ear to Lilette's chest. "It's stronger." Leaning back on her haunches, she pursed her lips. "I could have sworn it stopped beating. I'm not usually wrong—about anything." She seemed to be trying to convince herself.

Afraid her face would reveal the truth about what really happened the night she had died, Lilette looked away.

"Are you truly Lilette?" Jolin finally asked. Lilette nodded.

"I remember you. Before you disappeared," Jolin went on. "I went to see you sing once—I had never heard anything like it. You were bound to become the next Head of Light, as I am to be the next Head of Plants. After your ship sank, you became a legend. The only body never found."

Lilette winced. She suddenly remembered singing for crowds—thousands of them. "Head of what?"

Jolin didn't seem to notice Lilette's distress. "The Head of Light is always chosen because she has the strongest song. I should be Head of Plants, a position chosen for proficiency with potions. But Garen is fighting me."

Lilette didn't understand half of that. Jolin tipped her head to the side and asked, "What happened to you?"

"I survived."

"Here?"

Lilette glanced in the direction of her island. "No. They only found me a few days ago."

Jolin sucked on her teeth in thought. "They couldn't have followed the same trail we did."

Lilette shot her a quizzical look. "Trail?"

"Witches, called listeners, are always on the lookout for stray witch song. When they hear it, they send a ship to find them and bring them back. In this case, they heard a very strong song and sent our company to find you."

So that's how the Witches had known to come looking for her. If Fa hadn't forbidden her from singing, they would have found her years ago, and she could have gone home. But then she would have never known the man who raised her—his quiet kindness and iron determination. "So how did Chen find me?"

Jolin's fingers gently prodded her back, and she grimaced. "Keepers have listeners. Emperors have spies."

Lilette mulled that over silently, wondering who from her island had betrayed her. "I'm sorry he beat you."

Jolin's jaw clenched. "The chances of Chen's success in this endeavor are diminutive. As soon as the listeners realize we're here, they'll come for us. And then the Keepers will force him from his throne and behead him."

Lilette blinked at her. "You're certain."

"Oh, yes." Jolin huffed. "And I'll make sure they throw in a good lashing before they do." Her eyes glinted with dark delight.

Lilette stared off into nothing. "And naked. They should make him face the crowd naked."

Jolin nodded. "Brilliant."

They were silent, reveling in their own dark fantasies. At almost the same time, their eyes met and they burst into laughter.

"Come on," Jolin said. "You have to move if you want to get your strength back."

With Jolin's help, Lilette rose to stand for the first time in nearly three days. She felt shaky and weak, but the pain was gone. "My sister?"

Jolin threaded her arm through Lilette's and helped her walk slowly around the room. "She insisted on heading the search. She was under the delusion that the listeners had found you. Obviously it wasn't such a delusion after all."

An ache flared in Lilette's chest. Sash had stayed behind to finish her schooling as a witchling, while Lilette and their parents had come to Harshen. "What did she believe happened to us?" But what Lilette really wanted to ask was why her sister hadn't come looking for her.

"That your ship caught fire and everyone died," Jolin answered.

"And no one questioned it?"

Jolin looked away. "They had your mother's body."

Lilette took a few more steps, already winded. "And why did you come?"

"For the plants," Jolin replied. "We have so little contact with Harshen. Their plants are unique to the islands. I couldn't turn down a chance to study them." She took a deep breath. "They sent over thirty of us—a bit excessive, but Harshen has a reputation for treating women poorly. We wanted over three full-strength circles.

"We stopped here to request permission from the emperor to search Harshen for you. Not surprisingly, he wasn't cooperating. Then Heir Chen came to our quarters and offered a trade—heal his concubine and he'd grant our request." Jolin chuckled dryly. "No wonder he was so eager to agree. He wanted us out of the city and away from you."

"What were those glass planes you wore over your eyes?"

Jolin pulled them out of her pocket and handed them to Lilette.

"Spectacles. I invented them. They show me the true size of an aura, which directly correlates to how strong a witch is. Most witches have gold or orange auras. Yours is almost white. And you are very, very strong."

Lilette put the spectacles on and stared at her hand. "I don't see anything."

"Not everyone can." Jolin appraised her. "You're doing surprisingly well for a woman who basically died two days ago."

Lilette didn't feel well. She felt battered and weak, but she was still moving, albeit slowly.

Jolin helped her sit down and glanced at the closed screen. She leaned in closer. "And what of Ko? Do you trust her?"

Ko had stayed by Lilette's side for days, holding her hand and tending to her. Somehow a bond had formed in that time, but treason was bigger than a newfound friendship. "Only so far."

"Until we know for certain, we should be careful what we say around her," Jolin said.

Lying back, Lilette nodded. Then a rare smile overtook her face. "Are you really going to teach me?"

"I can't. Whether you are willing or not, your song will be used against Haven. I can't be responsible for that."

Something sharp twisted inside Lilette. "Please. It's all there—the creators' language and the voice lessons—it's just locked inside me. If I can just remember a little of it, the whole will come flooding out." It had to.

Jolin closed her eyes. "He will turn you into a weapon."

Lilette's mother had called her a warrior. And Jolin could teach her to become one. Lilette was surprised how much she longed for that. "He can't wield me if we escape."

Jolin studied her. "And you will come to Grove City for learning?"

Lilette let out all her breath in a rush. "Yes."

Jolin was silent a moment, her face hard. She glanced at the closed screen. "Very well." The words seemed to cost her a great deal. "You're woefully ignorant, so I'm just going to stick to what might be useful. Singing as a choir, we can control nature—the seasons, the storms."

"I remember that," Lilette breathed as the warm memory surfaced. Her mother singing in a circle with the other witches, strange colors dancing around them as the world shifted in response.

"Individually," Jolin went on, "a witch's song controls plants— singing a seed to a full grown tree you can then manipulate. The stronger the witch, the faster and better the response."

Another, much darker memory assaulted Lilette. Singing with her mother in a dim corridor as men bore down on them with spears. Her song had woken a beast that had crashed down on the men with lightning and wind.

She'd only been child at the time—incapable of understanding that the elements were simply responding to her call, that killing men who threatened her family was justified.

Jolin must have seen the anguish on Lilette's face. "I'm sorry."

Lilette wiped the tears from her cheeks. It had been a very long time since she'd cried. "No, I need this—need to remember. It isn't right to forget people who loved me so much."

Jolin took a deep breath and winced as if in pain. "Let me hear you sing."

"I can only remember one song, and I understand little of the creators' language."

"Just sing anything," Jolin said.

Lilette sang a fisherman's song. Jolin listened, her face screwed up in concentration. As the last note eased to silence, she took a deep breath. "Your voice is very beautiful," she admitted reluctantly. "And the more beautiful your song, the stronger."

Jolin began teaching Lilette the Creators' language, the language of power. The words molded themselves to her tongue before cutting through the air like a bird in flight. The elements came alive around Lilette.

Jolin made her perfect each song before they moved onto the next. The more Lilette sang, the more the memories locked in her mind pressed against the barrier holding them back. By nightfall, her head ached and she was so tired she could barely keep her eyes open.

After dinner, she and Jolin slept in the same room. Lilette's dreams were full of swimming with her father, mother, and sister playing in the sand on shore.

Her dreams were interrupted when Ko shoved aside the screen, a lit lamp in her hand. Lilette sat up, holding up her hand to shield her from the brightness. A glance out the window revealed that it was sometime in the darkest hours.

"Vorlay's armada has been sighted," Ko said breathlessly. "Their king has come to make Harshen pay for killing his daughter."

CHAPTER 9

I saved her life. She never thanked me. ~Jolin

Jolin shot to her feet. "What?"

"Chen's wife, Laosh, was the one who poisoned Lilette. She was a Vorlayan princess, and Chen killed her," Ko explained. "There are over a hundred ships, all of them flying Vorlay's colors."

Struggling to make her weak body work properly, Lilette pushed herself to her feet. "That's impossible. Laosh has only been dead four days! How could they have received word so soon? And Vorlay is over three weeks away with good winds."

"Laosh had more spies than the emperor, and she was fond of her pigeons." Ko turned back to face the main room, which the eunuchs were entering. "Light the lamps. Then wait at the gate and do not leave until the emperor sends word."

"But madame, the harem will be the last to receive word," said Ko's eunuch, his head bowed.

"I said go." Ko looked pointedly between Lilette and her personal eunuch.

"Go with him," she said to the eunuch. "Hurry."

The two men exchanged glances and donned their outer robes. Before they left the house, each lit his lamp, a bowl of oil with a bobbing cork and wick in the center.

Lilette began to dress as quickly as her slow fingers would allow. Jolin helped her finish, and they shuffled into the main room. In the dim lamplight, Lilette glanced around. The house was much like the first one—a long rectangle with rooms on both ends of a main living area. The eunuchs slept in the room where food was stored. There was the room Lilette and Jolin had just left, and a fourth room that shared a wall with it. Ko came out of the room and set a lamp in the window.

"They'll be gone for a while." She knelt before the brazier and lit it with the cork from another lamp. "Sit down, both of you," she said. "You're making me nervous."

Lilette hesitated before moving to obey. "What do we do now?" Jolin asked.

Ko disappeared into the kitchen and came out with bowls of rice and vegetables. "The only thing any woman can ever do—wait." She motioned to the bowls. "And while we wait, we can make breakfast."

As Lilette helped Ko cook, she realized the room where she and Jolin had been sleeping was Han's. He'd changed so much since he was a boy. His gentle smile used to come easily as he followed Lilette everywhere. What had turned him into such a hard man?

After eating, the three women cleaned up the dishes in silence. Light gradually touched the sky. Soon, the light overshadowed the lamps. When Ko blew them out, the cork plugs bobbed in the oil. Just as Lilette was about to demand they go find out what they could themselves, the outer door slid silently open and a eunuch she'd never seen before slipped inside.

Most of the eunuchs were a little plump, their bodies strangely hairless, but this one was on the thin side. There was something harder about him—not just his body, but the way he carried himself. Nothing like the soft hands and manners of most of the eunuchs. He looked different from the other Harshens as well. It was something in the shape of his eyes and the length of his face. With a start, Lilette realized he was the same race as Ko. The eunuch's gaze took in Lilette and Jolin, and his expression closed off.

Ko pushed herself to her feet. "Lang, what's going on?"

His gaze flicked warily to Lilette and Jolin. "You trust them?" he asked in disbelief. "They're witches."

Ko took a deep breath. "They're not like the others."

He grunted. "I very much doubt that."

"What—" Jolin began.

"Is Vorlay's armada really out there?" Ko interrupted.

Lang's lips pressed into a thin line. "Yes, they're surrounding the island now. The emperor has sent out his ships, raised the harbor chain, called up all his troops, and armed the citizens."

"Will it be enough?" Lilette asked.

His frank gaze met hers. "No. Vorlay is a beast compared to us. Chen was a fool for killing their princess."

Lilette slapped her leg in frustration. "Then why did he do it?"

"Because the same poison was used to kill his mother about a year ago."

Lilette's mouth fell open. "Then Laosh . . ."

"Killed at least four people," Lang finished. "Most of them were murdered as part of her political maneuverings."

After several seconds of silence, Ko said, "You're underestimating Emperor Nis."

"Nis has relied too long on our distance from other nations to keep us safe." Lang's voice was tight with anger. "Harshen has a third less ships—few of them war ships. The city doesn't have ramparts to speak of. The defensive line will be spread out and ineffective. The palace compound is well fortified, so it will endure for a little while after the city proper falls. But walls cannot stand forever, not against battering rams and arrows and soldiers with hooks and rope. Fighting back will buy us some time, nothing more."

Lang made a sound low in his throat, his gaze settling on Lilette. "It would have been much better for Harshen had you just died when Laosh poisoned you."

Guilt and anger twisted Lilette's insides. None of it was her fault, but she had been the catalyst. "Laosh chose her own path."

Lang huffed. "And the heir chose ours."

Lilette shook her head, still not really believing it. "They couldn't have come this far so quickly. It's not possible."

The eunuch studied her coolly. "Isn't it?"

Lilette rubbed her temples and pictured the charts she'd seen in Bian's home. "This time of year, the winds are wrong. Tacking into the wind, it would have taken them weeks to travel from Vorlay to Harshen."

Lang crossed his arms. "It is said they had help."

"What are you implying?" Jolin demanded.

He met her gaze head on. "That the witches in Kalari are helping them."

Lilette froze as understanding washed over her.

"Don't be ridiculous," Jolin exclaimed. "We don't involve ourselves in wars between nations."

Lang's brows came up. "Do you have another explanation for how they made a three week journey in three days?"

Lilette bit her lip. He was right. It was the only explanation that made sense.

"No," Jolin admitted.

"See what you see instead of what you're told to see," Lang said.

"What is that supposed to mean?" Jolin spat.

Lilette rested her hand on her friend's arm. The only people capable of moving the armada that quickly were the witches. She knew it and so did the others—Jolin just wasn't ready to accept it yet. "What of the witches in the palace?" Lilette asked Lang.

"They were supposed to leave this morning, but Vorlay's arrival put a stop to that."

Jolin's face drained of color. "They believed Chen's ridiculous story?"

"None of them carefully inspected the body before they burned it," replied Lang. "I suspect the boils put them off."

Lilette gasped. "But the listeners would have heard us sing."

"They wouldn't have been able to differentiate us from Sash and the others." Jolin gripped Lilette's hand. "I must escape. You must come with me."

Incredulous that Jolin would say as much in front of this eunuch, Lilette elbowed her. "You too, Ko," Jolin added quickly.

Lilette rolled her eyes. That wasn't what she'd meant, but she couldn't say it in front of Lang.

"I can't," Ko murmured. Her face had gone gray, her eyes pinched shut as if to block out some terrible sight.

Lang raised a hand toward her before dropping it back to his side. "Ko . . ."

She met his gaze, tears lining the rims of her eyes. "I can't. My son is here."

"Is he not already lost to you?" Lang said so softly Lilette could barely hear him. Ko turned away. He opened his mouth, then closed it again. "If the witches truly are helping Vorlay, we stand no chance. I'll get you off the island if I can, and hide you if I cannot." He reached forward and brushed the backs of his fingers down her cheek.

Ko took his hand briefly in hers. "And if you fail? You know what the emperor will do to us."

Lilette gaped at them.

"Ko, please," Lang implored. "I have the resources this time. I swear I'll keep you safe."

"I can't," she whispered.

He reached into the folds of his robe and handed her a dagger. "Then take this."

Ko blinked at the wicked gleam of the blade. "Lang . . ."

"Take it." He curled her fingers around the hilt and turned his attention to Lilette and Jolin. "Many of the elite guards have been reassigned as leaders of the militia. You stand a chance at escaping tonight. Climb the harem wall and hide. When morning comes, join one of the groups leaving the compound."

Fear curled around Lilette's belly, leaving her cold and shaking.

Lang studied her, his eyes glittering. "I will bring you some eunuch's clothes. You'll be less conspicuous that way. They'll be hidden in the tree outside your room. May the Sun Dragon see you safely to your journey's end." He sent Ko a longing look. Then he turned and was gone.

"Safe journey," Ko seemed to whisper to herself after he had gone, tears still brimming in her eyes. She glanced down at the dagger in her grasp and retreated to her room.

Jolin leaned over and whispered, "She's in love with a eunuch?"

"Shh." Lilette glanced back at the doorway. "He's still a man, isn't he?"

"Strictly speaking."

Ko stepped back into the room, and Lilette could only hope she hadn't heard Jolin. Ko knelt down and wiped her face. "He has loved me faithfully and at great risk to himself for nearly two decades. You could only hope to find such love someday."

Jolin flushed bright red. "I apologize for what I said."

The sudden silence was uncomfortable. Ko sat back on her heels. "You need to understand what happens if you're caught," she said softly. "Before the palace steps, with the emperor and the heir watching, they will behead you. Your body will be given to the peasants, who will display you in pieces before selling the remains for curses."

Lilette shuddered. "How many times has this happened?"

Ko turned away, refusing to meet Lilette's gaze. "Once in my lifetime. No one has tried it since."

From the pain in Ko's voice, Lilette knew that whoever had died had been close to her. "Who was it?"

"My sister." Ko sniffed. "We were twins—the daughters of King Mu'Fa of Jinji. Our father valued a trade agreement with Harshen more than my sister's marriage to a merchant's son. Lang followed us here. He managed to sneak into the harem. He and my sister tried to talk me into escaping with them, but I was already pregnant."

Tears rolled freely down Ko's face. "Carrying a child wouldn't have stopped the emperor from killing me. I couldn't risk it."

Lilette rested her hand on Ko's shoulder. "He caught them, didn't he?"

Ko nodded. "Emperor Nis could have killed Lang too. Instead, he made him watch. When my sister was . . ." —a sob caught in Ko's throat— "Lang begged for death. Instead, the emperor made him a eunuch and locked him in the harem."

She took a deep breath and wiped her cheeks. "At first, Lang simply looked after me because he blamed himself for my sister's death." Ko shrugged. "How could I not fall in love with him? That kind of honor and determination . . ." She gave a watery smile. "And I made sure to teach my son that same honor."

Lilette thought of Han's small acts of kindness and selflessness. He may look like his father, but he'd learned his goodness from his mother.

Jolin suddenly jumped to her feet. "Someone's coming!"

Lilette could hear singing, so far away she couldn't make out the words. There was something dark and sinister about it—it was almost more of a chant. Something wrenched inside her, a feeling of terror like a silent scream.

"My keepers are fighting," Jolin cried. She started toward the outer door, but it opened before she was halfway there. A handful of eunuchs were on the other side, the chief eunuch among them.

Had the eunuchs overheard their talk of escape? Were they coming to take them to their execution? Lilette pushed herself to her feet—to do what, she didn't know.

Two of the larger eunuchs came in, quarterstaffs in hand. Ko cried out and backed to the other side of the room. The eunuchs advanced on Jolin. "You will come with us, keeper."

Backing away, she snatched a heavy pot and held it like a club. "Why? What's going on?"

The eunuch's quarterstaffs shot out. One connected with Jolin's side, and the other smacked her hand. With a gasp of pain, she doubled over as the pot went flying.

"Stop this!" Ko cried.

The eunuchs seized Jolin and dragged her toward the door. Lilette started after them. "Leave her alone!" One of them stepped in front of her. She bounced off his chest and fell hard. Curse her weak body!

"Remember what you promised, Lilette," Jolin pled. "It's more imperative now. Find a way!"

Lilette pushed herself up and moved to follow Jolin, but one of the eunuchs grasped her. She fought and struggled against him, but she was as weak as a child. "Jolin!"

The chief eunuch shot her a look of disgust. "See that she stays here." The eunuch dragged Lilette deeper into the room. Trembling and gasping for breath, she tried to dig her heels in, but only succeeded in losing her slippers.

Ko came to stand beside her. "I will deal with her. Release her."

"When she's calm," the eunuch responded.

Ko shot Lilette a pleading look. "Fight the battles you can win. Retreat from the ones you cannot."

Now Lilette knew where Han had learned the phrase. Knowing the older woman was right, she complied. The eunuch held her a moment more before letting go. Arms crossed over his chest, he stepped back and blocked the doorway.

With shaking hands, Lilette pulled her hair away from her face. A bit of color on the floor caught her eye. She reached down to pick up Jolin's spectacles—she must have lost them in the scuffle. They were bent, but the glass was still intact. Lilette slipped them into her robe.

Ko motioned for Lilette to follow her into Han's room and shut the screen behind them. Lilette slumped down on the sleeping mat. "Han learned that phrase from you?" she whispered.

"Yes." Ko must have seen the worry lining her brow, for she added, "Jolin will be all right. They've no reason to hurt her."

How could she be so calm when Lilette felt she might burst apart at any moment? She could still hear the chanting, feel the occasional quake as the elements tore through her. "What's happening?"

Ko's careful fingers paused. "I warned you that the emperor was cunning."

Lilette pushed herself up. "What do you mean?"

"Perhaps he saw what Lang did—that he could not win this war. And so he took the strength he needed."

Lilette's eyes went wide. "By using the witches as a weapon."

Wasn't this what her mother had shown her—the world filled

with blood and death and chaos—all orchestrated by witch song? Not the least of which was Harshen sinking into the sea.

If Lilette didn't find a way to save her sister and the others, that's exactly what would happen.

CHAPTER 10

*It has taken me decades to admit that Chen and the emperor
saved our lives that night. It has taken me longer still to admit
that our deaths would have been a relief to the keepers. ~Jolin*

Lilette waited all that day, until full dark, long after the
eunuchs had gone to sleep behind their screens. Ko passed
her a wooden jar of kohl and the knife Lang had given her. "You
sure you still want to go through with this?"

"I have to," Lilette said.

"Why? You barely know Jolin. And you haven't seen your
sister in nearly a decade."

"You would do the same for your sister. I know you would."
There was more at stake than Lilette's sister, though. Her mother
had warned her that if she didn't free them, the whole world
would descend into chaos.

"Use the kohl to darken your hair, and be careful." Ko left,
silently shutting the screen door behind her.

Lilette pulled her hair into a tight bun on the top of her head.
Then she smeared kohl on the hair at her temples and the nape
of her neck—areas that would not be covered by a eunuch's hat.

Shoving her jade comb into her pocket, she hurried to the
window. She pushed aside the silk screen. The tops of the outer
walls were lit with hundreds of torches, their light blotting out
the stars and illuminating the elite prowling behind the parapet.

Lilette pulled herself onto the sill and climbed out. She found
the eunuch's clothes right where Lang said they'd be. She took

off her fine robes and hid them before pulling the cotton robes over her smallclothes. She donned the round hat and tucked the knife in the sash of her robe, then slipped into the moonless night.

When she reached the small lake, what she saw in the water made her halt in disbelief. She dragged her eyes from the shimmering reflection to the sky itself. A column of light and soft colors rose into the night. In the center, a woman floated higher than even the palace. Her hair twisted up like a flame as she slowly spun.

The whole scene was the most beautiful, terrible thing Lilette had ever seen. More of her memories broke free. Memories of lights and songs and women twirling toward the sky. But those memories were incomplete, as full of holes as a sea sponge.

At the sound of voices, Lilette froze. The chief eunuch. She ducked behind a pleasure boat moments before he appeared through a cluster of trees. He was speaking with another eunuch, a paper lantern in his hand.

"They have already sunk half the ships! The soldiers are fighting the Vorlayans in the city, but without reinforcements, they are falling back."

Lilette was tempted to follow, to learn more if she could, but she could actually hear the witches' words now—beautiful words twisted for a dark purpose.

She broke into a faltering run. Her tunic was drenched in sweat by the time she reached the harem wall. It sounded as if the witches were just on the other side. Keeping to the shadows, she searched the flat expanse. It was more than twice her height and too smooth to climb. The trees were cut back and therefore of no use in scaling the wall.

Well, I am a witch, aren't I? she thought. It was time to use that to her advantage. She found a sturdy tree. Her gaze traveled up the latticework of branches. If she was well and had her full strength, it would have been an easy climb. After hiking her tunic up above her knees, she grasped a branch. It seemed to take hours, and she had to rest more and more often, but finally she'd gone as high as she dared. The barrier softly lit up the night and cast green and purple light on the airborne woman's face. It was Sash. Lilette wanted to call out to her sister. It was unbearable to have her so close and yet completely unreachable.

Lilette looked up at the ramparts, glad for the branches that obscured her from the sentinels' eyes. It probably wouldn't have mattered anyway. All their gazes were trained beyond the city or the witches. She still couldn't see below the harem wall, but that was about to change. Fixing in her mind one of the songs Jolin had taught her, Lilette sang softly for the tree to grow. Soon the sweat of fear ran down her body.

The tree grew a little higher, opening Lilette's view to what lay just beyond the harem wall. About a dozen witches were arm in arm inside the barrier. She scanned their faces for Jolin but didn't see her.

As if they were one mind, the witches stopped chanting and Sash took over. She chanted with the strength of them all, but with one voice, calling for the waves to swamp the ships. The elements writhed in pain, the rhythms screeching against one another. Even as Sash was gently lowered, wind gusted with enough force to level a city.

"Another song. This one directed toward the northeast," a voice ordered. The emperor stood atop the walkway, looking like an older version of Han. Lilette shuddered.

"They're already retreating! Let them go!" Sash demanded, now nearly at eye level with the emperor.

"I must ensure they can't come against us again," he said.

"I won't do it!" Sash cried as she sank below him.

Lilette couldn't understand why Sash and her witches didn't just blast the emperor with lightning—level the whole city with a violent storm.

The emperor turned his full attention to Sash. "Your witches brought our enemy to my city, and then you pretend innocence! I will do what I must to protect my people."

Lilette's breathing came hard. This was wrong, horribly wrong. Why wasn't her sister fighting back? Then the emperor made a gesture.

Sash whipped around. Lilette followed her gaze to the other side of the barrier. Obscured by the strange lights, dozens of men and women knelt in rows, their hands tied behind their backs. An elite stood above each of them.

Lilette's hand flew to her mouth to silence her gasp of horror. Half of the witches had been forced to sing, while the other half and all their guardians were held at sword point.

She had a sudden flash of memory—guardians holding a shield wall, fighting and dying to maintain the passage. Griz had held her to his chest and run. Lilette had never forgotten those guardians. Her father had been one. Their duty was to protect the witches, guarding their backs as their songs began to take effect.

Fury rose in Lilette. Something sacred and good and right had been violated—twisted into something evil.

Sash gasped. "You're asking us to murder thousands of men!"

"Don't pretend this isn't something the witches haven't done for centuries," the emperor replied.

She glared at him, pain naked on her face.

"I won't let Vorlay slaughter my people," he went on. "You witches think you can meddle in the affairs of men but never suffer the repercussions. Well, you came here as spies. That makes you prisoners of war!"

"I keep telling you, we're not spies! And those songs couldn't have come from Grove City. It's not our way!"

"You told me yourself—the listeners hunt down anyone who sings outside of your city. If someone is singing, you know about it."

Sash was crying now, and Lilette scrambled for a solution—some way she could help. But what could she do beside getting herself caught?

"We must have missed something," Sash said as her feet touched down on the ground in the center of the circle. "I don't know how, but I promise, I will find out."

The emperor motioned again. In unison, the elite drew their swords from their baldrics and held them poised over the witches' heads. A whimper of fear and horror clawed its way up Lilette's throat. She pressed both her hands to her mouth to keep quiet.

The emperor paused before saying, "Make your choice, Sash. Either you capsize those ships, or we kill your witches and guardians."

Lilette's sister tipped her head to the side as if listening to something. Without any direction from her, the witches began singing as one. Sash shot up into the night sky, her strange dress swirling around her legs. But she did not look up, did not move until it was her turn to sing.

When she did, her song was punctuated with sobs. And this time as Lilette listened, something began to happen. She was remembering.

CHAPTER 11

We showed the world we were weapons. From that moment on, everything changed. ~Jolin

Memories long lost churned inside Lilette. Her mother singing with her as a very young child. Their songs gliding through the air like a fish through water. The world responding to words that molded themselves naturally to Lilette's tongue. Her father dancing with her amid flowers that glowed with a strange light. Her sister playing a musical instrument for Lilette as she sang for a crowd of thousands.

She also remembered her mother and father arguing, their words cutting and hot. Her mother had been offered a place as a Harshen ambassador. Her father wanted to go. Wanted Lilette away from the pressure and demands that came with a child destined to be the next Head of Light. Her mother didn't think Harshen was safe. In the end, her father had won.

And there was more. Lilette remembered the Creators' language. The songs. The harmonies. All of it came rushing back. And she knew that she was powerful. One of the most powerful witches alive.

From overheard bits of conversation, Lilette learned that Vorlay's entire armada had been sunk, down to the last ship. Any Vorlayan soldiers in the city were cut off from any means of support or retreat. It wouldn't be long before any pockets of resistance would be overpowered. The invasion was over.

With their dark purpose fulfilled, the witches released each other. Cracks spread across the barrier until it exploded in a shower of dying light. The elite rushed in and bound and gagged the witches. Lilette watched, appalled. She knew the women's power—she held a piece of it inside herself—it was unthinkable that something so strong should be so easily subjugated.

Someone shouted. A woman was struggling against the men holding her—men dressed in the black robes of the eunuchs. "You will pay for this evil you've forced us to commit," she shouted up at the emperor with his impassive face. "The deaths you've stained our hands with!"

One of the eunuchs brought his staff up and swung it down on the woman's head. She collapsed, hitting the brick courtyard so hard that she skidded forward before coming to rest in a heap. As she lay there unmoving, the torchlight caught her face.

"Jolin!" Lilette cried. Clapping a hand over her mouth, she immediately pressed herself flat against the smooth bark, hoping no one had noticed a voice coming from the harem. After a moment, she dared peek around the tree. Elite soldiers were hauling Jolin away, their torches illuminating her head hanging limply from her neck. Blood matted her hair.

The rest of the witches and guardians were herded farther into the gardens until Lilette could no longer see them through the trees. Her breathing came fast and hard. She glanced up and noticed Chen watching the spectacle, his face emotionless.

Hate built inside her chest. He'd taken everything from her— her family, friends, future. Her mother was right. Lilette was a weapon; all these women were. And if she could just find a way to free them, her power would be multiplied a hundredfold.

She waited for hours, until the generals and soldiers had gone, until the garden was dark and quiet. She sang softly for the tree to grow even more. It stretched up and out, until branches cast comforting shadows over the harem wall's sloping roof, which was about as wide as she was.

Not trusting her reflexes, Lilette lay down and scooted along the length. She dropped down on the wall and pressed herself flat against the rough tiles. For a long time she watched the dark garden, noting the placement of torches and the guard towers spaced along the ramparts. A soft glow of torchlight illuminated the tops of the trees about a hundred paces from where she lay concealed. That must be where they were keeping the witches.

She fingered the knife she'd stuffed in her robe. She'd seen how powerful they were, how strong. All she had to do was cut a few of their gags free. The witches could call down a storm that would bring the city to its knees, just as Lilette and her mother had done long ago. Then they would steal a boat by the docks and escape.

Eventually a pair of guards marched by, their half-moon halberds catching the starlight. They didn't carry torches, so the shadows would conceal them and make them harder to avoid.

Once they passed, Lilette slid over the side. She hung by her fingertips before she dropped, then pressed her body against the wall. She paused, her heart in her throat, and when no one sounded a cry of alarm, she entwined her fingers inside her wide sleeves and hurried through the garden.

She came to a clearing with a fountain surrounded by flagstones. She remembered this place. Remembered playing for hours with Han in the fountain. Now it held bound and gagged witches. The guardians were nowhere in sight.

A pavilion had been set up above the witches, with a glowing torch on every pole. Elite surrounded the witches in groups of ten, with the whole surrounded by more elite. Desperate to know if Jolin was alright, Lilette tried to pick out her friend among the witches, but they were all huddled together in a tangle of bodies.

Not daring to come closer, Lilette kept to the shadows along the perimeter, counting guards. Two guards per witch. She hadn't counted on that. She'd figured the witches would be bound and watched by just a handful of guards. Nothing like this. Clearly, Chen and the emperor knew just how dangerous the witches were.

If Lilette were to free them, she needed a way to draw away the guards. The beautiful palace, lit up with distant torchlight, caught her eye. A smile stole over her face. Now if she could just manage to avoid being caught.

Eight long years had passed since she'd been in the garden, but she hadn't forgotten the shrine. She moved in its general direction and stumbled upon the guardians. The emperor obviously didn't see them as nearly the same threat as the witches. They were kept inside a metal-barred enclosure that had once held exotic animals. Fewer than a dozen elite stood guard at the gate.

Lilette counted the guardians as best she could—over sixty. It would be much easier to free them and let them fight their way past the elite guarding the witches. She skirted the enclosure, and it wasn't long before she caught the sweet smell of incense. She followed the smoke to the wide pillars and slipped inside. Names of all the emperors for the last thousand years were carved into the five walls, sticks of burning incense before all of them.

The stones were cool beneath her slippered feet as she approached the dais, upon which was a statue of the five-clawed dragon curled around the sun. Hundreds of sticks of incense in various states of burning lay before him—prayers for a Harshen victory. All those sticks of incense were lit by holding them to one of dozens of cork lamps floating in glass jars of oil.

Wetting her lips, Lilette took one of the lamps, careful not to spill the hot oil. She couldn't hide anymore, not with a lamp lighting her up to the night. So she walked straight toward the palace as if she belonged.

Taking a deep breath, she left the safety of the shadows and stepped onto the porch. The door wasn't guarded—the only way into the gardens was through the palace, so there wasn't really a point.

Knowing the exact tapestries she would light on fire, she reached for the handle.

"Stop," someone said in a commanding tone.

Her first instinct was to run. But she forced herself to stay still. She was winded after only walking. There was no way she could outrun two elite guards.

They came toward her, their half-moon spears lowered. She kept her eyes trained on the floor, hiding her pale coloring in the shadows.

"Who are you? What is your business?"

"I'm Chang," she said, her mind working quickly. "My madame lost her comb in the garden and sent me to fetch it." She held out the comb Salfe had given her as proof.

One of the men lowered his spear long enough to take it from her. She had to resist the impulse to snatch it back. The other guard squinted at her in the dim light. "You're not one of the palace eunuchs."

Oh, no. "I'm new."

The first guard tucked her comb into his pocket. "Easy enough to find out. We'll take him to the master eunuch." He clamped a hand on Lilette's shoulder while the other guard opened the palace door.

Nausea hit her hard. This would not end well.

The guard steered her forward, and she entered the palace for the first time in eight years. The smell hit her—incense and scented oils. Carved reliefs of phoenixes and dragons covered the walls. Tall columns of green marble were spaced throughout the room. It was dark, but Lilette knew the walls were painted red—the color of passion and life. Motifs in tones of jade and gold adorned the high ceiling.

The main room was broad and open, filled with low tables surrounded by cushions. The guards directed Lilette toward the back of the palace, in the direction of the small, screened rooms where the palace eunuchs slept.

Her mind scrambled for a way out, something that didn't end with various parts of her body being sold for curses. She was vaguely aware of the front doors swinging open. An elite wearing full battle armor strode in. Was he here for her too?

Gripping the lamp hard, she lurched forward, deliberately spilling oil on the nearest wall. But the sudden motion caused the lamp to go out, so the wall didn't catch fire. Dread filled her whole body, making her limbs heavy. One of the elite swung the shaft of his spear, hitting her across the shin. Lilette dropped to the ground as pain shot up her leg.

"What are you doing?" he barked. "You'll set the whole palace afire, you fool!"

"Get up," the other growled, his gaze flashing to the elite who'd come in after them.

Lilette gasped for breath. She didn't think her leg was broken, just terribly bruised. She started to push herself up, but she was shaking so badly her body wouldn't respond.

"Come on," the second guard said through clenched teeth. "You eunuchs are all so soft. Not even men at all, are you?" He jabbed the butt of his spear into her side. "Get up!"

Lilette cried out in pain. Her vision went black before coming back in streaks of gray. Pain shot through her side with every breath. "Please, just give me a moment."

"I have better things to do than act as nursemaid to some gelded weakling. Get up!" The guard raised the butt of his spear above his head.

CHAPTER 12

A true test of any civilization is how they treat their women.
~Jolin

L ilette braced herself for the pain, but it didn't come.
"I said, what's the meaning of this?" The armored elite was standing above her, his hand wrapped around the spear shaft to prevent the guard from striking her again.

Both guards took a few steps back. "We found him in the compound after dark. Said he was sent to find his madame's lost comb, General." He held it out as proof.

In her peripheral vision, Lilette watched the general stare at the comb. He squatted in front of her. Knowing he was her only hope, she tipped her face into the light.

For a single beat of Lilette's heart, disbelief crossed Han's face before his expression shifted back to impassable. He tapped her comb against his leg as he stood. "This is only one of them. Where's the other?"

Her mouth came open and she gave a slight shake of her head. "Other?"

He rubbed his forehead as if her mere presence exhausted him. "I know his madame, one of the emperor's favorites." Han tugged off his helmet and ran a hand through his sweaty hair. "She's not going to be happy."

The soldiers shifted. "Sorry, General. We didn't know."

Han's voice went low and dangerous. "Did I ask for your excuses?"

"No, General," they said in unison.

There was blood on his armor and on his neck. He'd been fighting Vorlayans. "How about we forget any of this happened? My guards won't report you leaving the palace at night. You don't report their . . . manhandling."

The elite nodded eagerly. Her hand clenching the cramp in her side, Lilette nodded.

"Do you remember where you found the first comb?" Han went on. "Chances are the mate is somewhere close by."

What was he going to do with her? Was he really helping her? Relief threatened to overwhelm her, but she held the emotion at bay. Fear was the only thing preventing her from collapsing. She kept her eyes averted. "Yes, General."

"Well, let's go find it then. There'll be no living with the madame if she doesn't have her combs." Han tipped his head back the way the guards had come. "Get to your rounds." The soldiers left as if death itself chased them. Knowing Han, it probably did.

He reached down and pulled her to her feet. "This is a deadly place to be. We need to move." His voice was dark and angry.

She leaned limply against him, all her weight on her uninjured leg. "Where are you taking me?"

"Back to the harem."

She tried to pull away from him but was shaking so badly she could barely stand. "No. I have to free my sister."

He shook his head. "You can barely walk. You're going back into the harem whether you like it or not."

Lilette glared at him, but inside she knew he was right. She would just have to wait for another chance at escape. She let out a humorless chuckle. "So I surrender. Again."

Han took hold of her elbow. "No soldier would be seen carrying a eunuch." His voice was gentle. "Lean on me. We'll make it look like I'm dragging you." Her leg cramped in protest, but she hobbled forward despite the pain.

Han grunted. "Were you actually trying to burn the palace down?"

"I had to do something." After slowly descending the palace stairs, they entered the comforting shadows of the garden. He guided her toward the harem wall. With each dozen or so steps, the trembling in her limbs faded.

"Why are you helping me?" Lilette asked. "Why not just turn me in to your father?"

Han glanced at her sideways. "I have no desire to see your head anywhere but at the top of your shoulders."

She winced at the thought. "And before? How did you find me the night I was poisoned?"

He nodded toward the top of the ramparts, where a tower lorded over the harem. "I was up there. I saw you wandering below, obviously sick or injured. I saw you fall."

Her brows drew together. "But you're not a guard. There's no reason for you to be atop the ramparts—especially so soon after returning home." Then the realization hit her. "You . . . you were looking for me?"

He didn't deny it. Lilette looked into his eyes, like chips of onyx in the starlight. "They would have killed you, had they found you."

"Yes."

She could walk by herself now. She put a little distance between them. "I don't understand. Why would you risk it?"

Han studied her. His scar was on the other side of his face. From this aspect, with the starlight to soften his harsh features, he looked almost handsome. "It's been a long night, Lilette. I have watched many, many men—none of them soldiers—die. I don't have any more to give."

By now, they had reached the wall. He looked down the length of it. "How did you intend to get back over?"

"I didn't."

His gaze lit on her and he shoved his helmet back on his head. "Wait here while I get some rope."

Her hand shot out, capturing his arm. "We don't need it."

He paused and looked back at her.

Closing her eyes, she concentrated on the ground inside the harem. When she found what she wanted, she sang softly. A vine snaked into sight and crawled down the wall.

When she looked up, Han was staring at her, something akin to anger in his eyes. "I thought you'd forgotten the language."

"I remembered."

He looked around, then slipped out of cover and gave the vine a hard tug. "This should hold." He quickly tied the end to a tree.

She glared at the wall. This was going to hurt. But before she could move to climb it, Han stepped in front of her, his strong hands encompassing her waist. "Wrap your arms around my neck, and your legs around my waist."

Her arms tucked around her ribs, she automatically stepped back. "What?"

He looked up one side of the wall and down the other. They were exposed here. "Hurry." Han meant to carry her over the wall. "I can do it," she said.

He raised an eyebrow. "This climb would take more strength than you had before you were injured."

"No. Ko would never forgive me if something happened to you."

He made a low sound in his throat. "I'm not keen on the idea either, but do you see another option?"

Lilette slowly shook her head.

"Then come on."

She pursed her lips. Wrapping her arms and legs around his body sounded far too intimate.

His expression hardened. "Am I really so repulsive to you?"

"You don't repulse me." Gripping his shoulders, she tried to hop up with one foot.

Han rolled his eyes and lifted her. She wrapped her legs and arms around him. Beneath the armor, his body was all muscle, hard everywhere she was soft. She had the sudden urge to explore his chest with her fingertips. She pushed away the thought, glad it was dark enough he couldn't see the blush spreading across her face.

He gripped her legs behind the knees and lifted her higher onto his stomach. "Lock your feet and wrists and hold on." He grabbed the vine and started climbing.

She couldn't believe he was strong enough to heft both of their weight. She glanced over his shoulder to the ground far below. A feeling of helplessness washed over her. Her well-being was completely in his hands. If he slipped—if her vine couldn't take both their weight—she would fall.

Closing her eyes, Lilette pressed her forehead into his shoulder and concentrated on the steady tensing and relaxing of his muscles, the narrowness of his waist, his chest expanding with each breath.

Han heaved them onto the wall's roof. She scrambled to the other side of the peak and leaned against it, her breath coming fast. "We should—"

He clapped a hand over her mouth. Startled, she began to pull away, but he drew her into his arms. Heat crept up her body. "Han . . ."

"Shh," he whispered in her ear. "I can hear them." He released her enough to peer over the raised roof.

And then she heard them too. "The vine." She reached for it, intending to tug it out of sight.

He pulled her back into his arms. "Movement and sound draw attention. The vine stays."

She heard the steady rhythm of the guards advancing toward them. She could feel Han's heart pounding through her clothes. Eventually, the steps grew softer as they marched away. Lilette let out the air in her lungs.

Han looked down. "You're not going to make that by yourself."

She huffed. "Down is easier than up."

He sighed and gripped the vine. "Come on. It'll be faster this way. I'll cut it down after I'm safely back on my side."

She opened her mouth to argue, but he wrapped her in his arms and swung over the side. She had to grab him and hold on to keep from falling. Her heart pounding with fear, she pressed her face against his chest and concentrated on breathing.

"You can let go now."

Startled, she opened her eyes to discover they'd reached the ground. "I almost fell," she whispered. She dropped out of his arms, gasping when her injured leg took her weight. She hopped, one leg cocked.

Han's arm shot out, steadying her. "I told you before, I wouldn't let you fall." He pulled her out of sight behind the tree and pressed the palm of his other hand into her sore side. She hissed a breath through her teeth.

"I don't feel any knots. That's a good sign." He gently lifted her tunic. A bruise had spread from her hipbone to just above her waist. He shook his head in sympathy. "It should heal. My mother has a salve."

She was suddenly aware of how near he was, both his hands on her, their faces a mere hand span apart. She tried to pull away, but he held her firm. "I've watched so many die tonight—I won't see you be one of them. What are you doing, sneaking out of the harem? And going into the palace? I thought you were smarter than that."

When Lilette didn't answer, he took a small step closer—so close she could feel the warmth from his body. "You're to be the next empress—the most powerful woman in the empire. You'll want for nothing. Why risk death to get away from that?"

The next empress? "What?"

Han's face darkened, but he didn't respond.

She pinched her eyes shut to block out the images of being a wife to Chen. Could she trust Han? Despite everything, she'd seen glimpses of his former kindness. He had saved her life twice, risking his own. If Lilette was going to get out, she needed help. She wouldn't find anyone better. "If I asked, would you help me escape?"

He studied her, his eyes glinting in the starlight. "We are enemies, you and I."

Hopelessness washed over Lilette. Without his help tonight, she would have been caught and probably killed. If he refused, her chances of succeeding were almost nonexistent.

"You should go." The hardness in her voice could cut a stone. "Thank you for returning me to my prison. Again."

She turned to leave, but Han caught her hand. "Do you remember the first night you fled Rinnish?"

"How could I forget?"

He gently tugged off her hat. She froze as he unwound her bun and ran his fingers through her hair. She wasn't sure why she allowed him to touch her, but it felt so good. "You were my best friend," she finally admitted.

"Do you remember someone coming in the middle of the night to warn your parents to flee?"

Lilette whipped around to face him, her hair flaring across her shoulder. "All I remember was waking to my mother forcing me out of my bed."

He looked sad, and vulnerable. It was so unlike the man she'd come to know that she blinked in surprise. "You? You warned us?"

His scar twitched. "I overheard my father talking to the elite. They were to come for you just before dawn. He wanted to marry you off to Chen."

She touched Han's scar. "Is that why you have this?" He tried to pull away from her, but Lilette stepped closer. He dropped his head and murmured, "My father was furious."

She ran her fingers across the uneven skin. The movement was so slight she wasn't sure, but she thought Han leaned into her touch.

"I wanted you to know that we may be enemies, but I am also your friend," he whispered. "I have always been your friend."

She wasn't sure what made her do it, but she leaned forward and pressed her lips to his. His mouth opened in surprise, but then he took hold of her face and kissed her. His lips were soft and gentle, but she felt a slight tremor somewhere deep inside him, as if he was holding back.

He pulled away and rested his forehead against hers. "Lilette . . ."

The way he said her name with such longing—had he learned to build armor around his heart too?

Every part of her ached for more. He rolled a lock of her hair between his fingers. "I never knew it came in the color of winter sunlight."

"I've never seen winter." Lilette's voice came out breathy and soft.

"The light is thinner, the colors washed away."

She pressed her lips together to keep herself in check. "Han . . ." This—whatever this was—didn't fit in with her plans of escape, or Chen's plan to marry her.

Han let her hair slip from his fingers before he stepped back. He tipped his chin toward his mother's house. "You need to get back. Can you make it?"

She felt hollow without him next to her, and now words had abandoned her. She nodded. With a rush, he launched himself at the wall, his footing and handholds sure.

Lilette whipped around at the sound of voices in the distance. They were too far away for her to understand their words, but they were definitely calling for someone. And of course that someone was probably her.

"Lilette," Han whispered. She turned back to him. He'd reached the top of the wall and paused, his face in shadow. "Don't try to escape again."

Without answering, she slipped into the shadows.

CHAPTER 13

Han terrified me. He was violence personified in muscle and scowls. But Lilette seemed drawn to terrifying things. ~Jolin

Voices called Lilette's name. Cold waves of fear pulsed through her. She was dressed in a eunuch's clothes, with kohl in her hair, and bruises on her body. No explanation she could give would satisfy Chen. She looked around, hoping to find something, anything, to help her. And then she saw the lake. Creators' mercy, this was a foolish idea—most of her ideas usually were. But she didn't have anything else.

She stripped out of her eunuch's robes, shoved them inside one of the boats at the dock, and waded into the lake until it reached her waist. The water was cool, but the bottom was muddy. Keeping her mouth and eyes firmly shut, she scrubbed the kohl from her hair, rinsing at least a dozen times.

Soaking wet with less-than-savory water, she crossed her arms over her nearly translucent smallclothes. Forcing herself not to limp, she moved toward the voices.

It wasn't long before she caught glimpses of torchlight flickering through the trees. One of them yelped in surprise when she burst into sight. "Are you looking for me?" she asked innocently.

He looked her up and down, his brows drawn in confusion. "Yes, honored madame. The heir has come to see you, but you were not there." He whistled for the others. They escorted her back to Ko's house.

Ko was pacing in front, her hands wringing together. She froze when they came into view, her expression giving away nothing, and Lilette wondered if her friend had betrayed her.

The chief eunuch huffed into sight, his strange, hunched-over gait exaggerated by his wide steps. "Where have you been?"

She gestured to her dripping clothes. "Swimming."

His eyes narrowed. "Do you know what you have done?"

"I'm sorry."

"Sorry?" he sputtered. He opened his mouth to say more, but Chen stormed into view. The chief eunuch clenched his jaw, his throat working around the words that seemed to choke him.

Chen still wore his battle armor, though with its condition he clearly hadn't been in the midst of the fighting. His gaze pierced Lilette to the core. He took in her barely clothed state, and she had to resist the urge to cover herself with her hands. "You were not to leave Ko's home," he reminded her.

She bent into her three kowtows, then blinked up at him.

"I came to share our decisive victory with you, but you were gone. Where did you go?" Though his words were soft, the tension beneath them frightened her more than shouts would have.

She rose to sit on her heels. "It was so unbearably hot. I went for a swim."

Chen frowned. "In the lake?"

"I used to go swimming at night all the time." A blatant lie. She'd always been too tired to bother. "I miss the water." At least that was true. She let her eyes fill with tears—genuine ones.

He motioned to the eunuchs. "All of you go." He jabbed a finger at Lilette's personal eunuch and Chief Wang. "You two wait for me inside with the other concubine."

Everyone filed quickly away. Chen took Lilette's arm to pull her outside the house and out of earshot. He pinned her against a tree. Pain lanced through her injured side. She forced herself not to react, not to cry out.

"You were trying to escape."

"No," she gasped, her head swimming with pain. "I was—"

"Lilette, there are things even I can't protect you from. If you're caught, do you know what my father will do to you?"

"The same thing you did to Laosh?"

Chen released her as if she'd burned him. "I spared her a public execution—and the torture that comes with it."

Lilette reeled her anger in. *Trust,* she reminded herself. *If he trusts me, opportunities to escape will come.* "I'm sorry."

He blew out through clenched teeth.

"I promise I wasn't trying to escape. I just went swimming."

He studied her, his dark eyes glinting. "Are you willing to prove it?" He stepped toward her, his gaze trained on her lips.

Lilette forced herself to tip toward him and press her mouth against his. His mouth was wet and cold. All she could see was soldiers lined up behind the keepers, hear the dark, pounding chant. See Chen watch impassively as Jolin was bludgeoned. As the kiss went on, Lilette couldn't stop the bone-deep tremors that started inside her.

Finally, he pulled back. As if daring her to stop him, he touched her through her thin smallclothes. "The lords from the other islands are due to arrive before midday for the war council, and a feast is already scheduled. The perfect opportunity to prove yourself."

"But the kiss—"

"It helped." His grin was wolfish. "But you still have a long way to go."

"Prove myself how?"

He tipped her chin up. "By becoming my wife."

She'd played right into his hands. "No." The word slipped out before she could stop it.

"Think of all the good you could do as empress."

She searched his eyes. "Why are you doing this?"

His expression closed off and he stepped back. "Because it's the best thing for my country. And believe it or not, it's the best thing for you."

Lilette clenched her hands into fists at her sides. Still, if she lived in the palace, all she'd have to do was slip into the gardens to free the witches. "Is no even an option?"

"Of course," Chen said. "I'm not a monster."

She took a fortifying breath. "Very well."

"What?"

She shifted her weight off her aching leg. "I said yes."

He nodded to himself, a smile gracing his perfect lips. "You'll see, Lilette. This is the best thing for everyone. And I will be good to you. I swear it." He motioned for her to follow him. "The eunuchs must be awakened. They'll have to work all night."

"Wang," he called as they approached the house.

The chief eunuch opened the door and gave a bow.

"For failing to keep an eye on the princess, her eunuch shall have five lashes," Chen declared. "You will have seven. Lose her again and it will be both your heads."

"Yes, Heir," the chief eunuch said.

"Now that's taken care of, we have a wedding to plan. Wake all the eunuchs." Chen cradled Lilette's cheek and kissed her again. He pulled back, his breath on her lips. "Until then, my sweet wife."

It took everything she had not to wipe her mouth with the back of her hand. She gave him what she hoped would pass for a shy smile.

Chen rubbed his thumbs along her collarbones before motioning the chief eunuch to walk with him. "She's far too thin. Is she eating enough?"

Wang bowed. "I will personally see to her diet, Heir." Over his shoulder, he shot Lilette a look of such hatred that she winced. Her personal eunuch trailed after them, his steps quick.

Lilette entered the house, then sidestepped Ko's eunuch and pushed into Ko's room. She slid the screen closed, scrubbed her lips with her sleeve, and spit onto the floor. Breathing hard, she ground out, "Did you tell them I had gone?"

Ko shook her head. "The heir came to visit you." Her mouth tightened. "He would have bedded you."

Lilette pressed her hand against her mouth, her heart racing. If she didn't escape by tomorrow night . . . but she would be in the palace then. She'd only need to slip into the garden. Faking submission these past few days would surely pay off. It had to.

"Why did you come back?" Ko asked quietly.

Lilette winced. "I was caught."

Ko's eyebrows flew up.

"Han intercepted the guards. He let me go."

"It's a good thing, or all three of us would be dead."

Lilette let that soak in, realizing how close they'd all come to being caught. She lifted her smallclothes, revealing purple-black bruises that the shadows and her thin film of clothing had hidden. "Han said you had a salve?"

Ko rooted around in a chest while Lilette examined her shin. To her surprise, it hadn't bruised, but she could feel a wide knot under her fingers.

Ko smeared the salve onto Lilette's abdomen before wrapping it with an old sash. She handed her a jar of paste. "Take a fingerful of this. It will help with the pain."

Lilette took the jar, but hesitated to consume any.

"I think," Ko said after a moment, "it is very dangerous to be your friend."

A cavern seemed to open up inside Lilette. Over the course of her life, she'd lost everyone she'd ever grown close to. Why would Ko be any different?

"Lang and I have risked our lives for you. My son has risked his life—too many times. Promise me you'll keep him out of this."

The cavern yawned and stretched. A blush crept up Lilette's cheeks. Did Ko know something had happened between Han and her? Though it sent a stab of pain through Lilette's belly, she forced herself to say the words. "I swear."

She put a fingerful of the paste in her mouth and pulled a face as the bitterness fanned across her tongue.

CHAPTER 14

*Chen was an evil man with a thirst for blood and no hint of
compassion. He was beyond redemption. ~Jolin*

Lilette awoke when her eunuch opened the screen. There
were more eunuchs behind him, dozens of them—so
many they filled Ko's home.

As she pushed herself up to a sitting position, Lilette winced
at the twinge in her leg. Judging by the light, it had to be
midmorning.

Her eunuch came inside, a tray of food in his hands. He eased
to his knees and kowtowed. Moving as one, the rest followed.
Lilette caught sight of Ko kneeling as well. Lilette frowned.
From this day on, she would be a princess. There were only three
people in the empire to whom she would kowtow.

Her eunuch rose and set the tray before her. She could smell
breakfast—sausage, tea, and fried rice flour—and felt sick with
hunger. She took a bite of fried sausage roll and closed her eyes
in pleasure. She studied her servant's hollow eyes and drawn
face. "Have you tended to your wounds?" she asked softly.

He stiffened. "I have been bandaged, Princess."

She flinched at the honorific, and her side protested the
sudden movement. She wondered at the aspirations of eunuchs.
Did they desire to bask in the leftovers of their madames' glory?
Her eunuch certainly seemed thrilled with the idea of moving to
the palace with Lilette. "Have you taken anything for the hurt?"

He continued working. "Softening the hurt would also soften the punishment. It is not allowed."

She tipped her head to the side. "I am the princess. I allow it."

The eunuch was still for a moment. "Your wishes are mine, Princess."

He left, presumably to do as she had requested. One of the few things she would miss when she escaped this place was his cooking. She wished she could take him with her. But he was accountable to the chief eunuch, and therefore the heir, so she couldn't trust him.

Ko came in a moment later. "You dishonor him." Lilette opened her mouth to protest. "As he bears the hurt, his honor is returned to him. You treat him as a weakling."

Lilette made to go after him, but Ko's hand on her arm halted her. "If you retract your order, you lose face."

Lilette swallowed a groan. She had more important things to worry about than her eunuch's feelings. Ko left without another word.

Knowing what lay ahead of her, Lilette forced herself to eat. As soon as she finished, the eunuchs removed the tray and proceeded to undress and bathe her. They were gentle with her bruises, though none commented on them. She was not allowed to help. Every time she tried, a look of shame came over the eunuch's faces.

They rubbed rare oils into her skin, dusted her face with rice powder, lined her eyes and brows with kohl, and painted her lips lobster-shell red. She was draped in yards of red and gold silk—all of it painstakingly hand-dyed. They combed her hair into elaborate rolls and fans.

After they had finished, Lilette stared down at herself. She wore combs in her hair and brooches on her clothing—all of them priceless heirlooms. Her silk robe alone was worth more than Fa would have seen in a lifetime. And she had to admit that a part of her reveled in the beauty surrounding her.

The crowd of eunuchs left the room. As if he'd been waiting for them to finish, Chen stepped inside with six more eunuchs, four bearing elaborately carved trunks with ivory and jade inlays. The other two carried smaller chests.

At a signal from Chen, the eunuchs opened the trunks and bowed out of the room. Inside the larger trunks were silk robes in every hue. The smaller two chests held silk-lined trays, each filled with priceless jewels in a rainbow of bright colors. Unable to help herself, Lilette ran her fingertips across the glittering stones. There were ruby brooches, diamond and pearl hair combs, mother-of-pearl and sapphire bracelets, and a cabochon ruby set at the end of a dagger of solid gold. Under the cover of her billowing sleeve, Lilette grabbed the dagger and slipped it inside the folds of her sash.

"These have been in my family for generations." Chen came up behind her and reached around her body to pick up a ruby brooch that dangled from a chain. He attached it under her sash. She held her breath, hoping he wouldn't feel the dagger there.

She let out a breath when he moved back, observing the brooch as it dangled above her knee. "I remember my grandmother wearing this one—it was her favorite." He smiled as if at a fond memory, and Lilette struggled to imagine him as an innocent child curled into his grandmother's lap. "When you come into the palace, you shall do so in grand style."

"The palace," she echoed, her thoughts sticky and slow in her head.

He bent down and kissed her softly. "There will be a great feast in our honor, and you will move into my apartments."

Creators' mercy, she had to find a way free before tonight. Chen reached behind his neck and undid the clasp that held his amber pendant. He tied it around her neck, the metal still warm from his body. The gold dragon flared against the red of her wedding robes.

One side of his mouth pulled up. "Yours isn't finished yet. But you should wear the royal pendant on the day you join us." He fingered the stone. "This one has been a part of Harshen for generations."

Lilette wanted to rip it off and throw it against the opposite wall. Her eyes slipped closed as she took a deep breath. "That's very kind of you." And it was. He was making it hard to hate him. But she was a very determined person.

He kissed her again before motioning to the eunuchs waiting at the door. They surrounded her on all sides, reminding her that she was a prisoner here. Lilette paused at Ko's threshold, searching for the familiar warmth on her face, but there was only fear and dread.

Her heart wrenching in her chest, Lilette turned away and walked down the stone-lined path, her shin and side aching dully. The emperor's concubines came out to kowtow, then sat on their heels and watch the procession, some of them whispering behind their painted silk fans.

Lilette kept her head erect, her eyes straight ahead. As she approached the harem's gates, they swung open. What lay beyond made her stutter to a stop.

The elephant was surrounded by elite soldiers in their finery. Even more overwhelming was the presence of the empress, one of Chen's many stepmothers. Chen went before her, bowing. She bowed back.

Memory overwhelmed Lilette. She was on her island again, the day Chen had come for her. She was surrounded by soldiers, unable to choose for herself as her villagers had died.

Her breaths came faster as she realized how much the two days resembled each other. She had fought back, her villagers had fought back. And they had lost. She had to find a way for this day to be different.

One of the eunuchs at her side bent low. "Princess?"

Remembering herself with a start, Lilette approached the empress. The eunuchs slid to the side, bending seamlessly in their kowtows.

A half second late, Lilette joined them. When she was finished, the empress motioned for her to rise. "I am Empress Yuwen. You will bring honor to our family."

Lilette bowed again, but her throat dried up and she couldn't speak.

The empress motioned for Lilette to join her. "I have already seen to your apartments and ordered the finest silk for you to choose from. We will review your wardrobe tomorrow." She continued on with the dishes to be served at the feast, but Lilette had stopped listening.

She stepped up next to the elephant, which had been painted with gold patterns. Black silk draped it from front to back, tassels hanging from every point. Tentatively, Lilette reached out and laid a palm on the creature's side. It was rough and warm, with a thin bristling of hair. The animal turned to look at her, long lashes covering intelligent eyes set in a mottled pink-and-brown face.

She felt a sudden kinship with the elephant. So strong, so powerful, and yet draped in finery and forced to submit to the will of those much smaller and less worthy than herself.

Chen slapped the elephant's shoulder and cried, "Lift leg!" over and over until she complied. He pulled back his robes, stepped onto the elephant's raised leg, and swung up. Three steps later, he was settled in the howdah.

A eunuch gestured to a palanquin. "If the princess will stand here."

She stepped onto it and gripped the bars on either side. Smooth as the wind through her fingers, eunuchs gripped the poles and lifted her above their heads.

She was now level with the sedan chair. Chen pushed aside the curtains and held out his hand. Though it grated her, she took it and stepped onto the elephant's back. She could feel the animal's warmth radiating through the thin trappings. In awe, she sat on the silk-lined wooden chair.

Chen's wife had ridden this same elephant on Lilette's first day in the city. And before that day had ended, she was dead. If that pattern followed through, Lilette would be dead by Chen's hand tonight. She cringed.

The boy sitting on the elephant's neck kicked the backs of its ears and ordered, "Go! Go!" The elephant lumbered forward, its wide gait making Lilette sway from side to side and sending the tassels swinging. A thrill raced through her. Before her loomed the palace gates. Standing in front of them was a contingent of elite six rows wide and thirty deep.

The gates swung open moments before Chen and Lilette reached them. The elite surrounded them. Calling out commands, the boy directed the elephant into the city, his foot kicking the elephant's ear when he wanted the creature to turn.

People lined the streets and cheered, throwing orchids and lotus blossoms onto their path. The flowers' delicate fragrance filled Lilette with a sense of foreboding.

The elephant picked up a cluster of white flowers with her incredibly long nose and tucked them in her mouth. The boy scolded the animal.

"No," Lilette called out loudly enough to be heard over the crowd. "Let her eat them."

He looked back at her in shock before he turned to Chen, who nodded his permission.

"What is her name?" Lilette asked.

"Jia Li," the boy said before turning away. The elephant continued munching happily as they made a circuit around the streets.

Chen took Lilette's hand. She had to force herself not to pull away. Even with the shade of the roof above her, she was stiflingly hot under the layers of clothing. Sweat trickled down her face, and she worried that the rice powder was running.

Finally, they turned back toward the palace. For a fleeting moment, Lilette wanted to slip from the elephant's back and run. She closed her eyes and listened to the cadence of the marching soldiers around her, the cheers of the people. She had nowhere to go.

They finally reached the compound, where the gates stood open. A long red carpet, surrounded by the elite, led straight to the palace steps. Around the elite, hundreds of commoners filled the courtyard to overflowing. There were no cheers or cries of approval. Instead, each and every person, down to the smallest child, slipped into a kowtow. Such a sign of respect made Lilette uneasy. She'd done nothing to earn it. Not yet.

The palace compound was huge, but Jia Li's massive strides ate up the distance. Lilette rubbed her feet on the elephant's back, silently thanking the animal for carrying her. Jia Li flapped her ears as if she understood, and Lilette was tempted to smile.

"I'll give her to you if you like," Chen said. "You can take her out whenever you wish, as long as the elite go with you."

Lilette refused to meet his gaze. "Was Jia Li *her* elephant?"

When Chen didn't answer, she turned to face him. "Was she? Was she Sima's elephant?"

His face paled. "Is that what she told you her name was?"

Suddenly uneasy, Lilette smoothed her robes. She'd forgotten that wasn't the former princess's name.

Chen's gaze was far away. "'Sima' is Vorlayan for 'the betrayed.'"

CHAPTER 15

I have come to wonder if we abuse the elements as we did that elephant. ~Jolin

Lilette fixed her gaze on the serpentine dragon statues flanking the palace steps. Her gaze traveled up the red-lined steps, to the pinnacle, where the emperor stood in front of the open palace doors. What struck her most was how ordinary he was, with his wide stomach and his expression of disapproval. He assessed her with a shrewd, calculating gaze.

She suppressed a shudder as Jia Li came to a stop at the base of the palace steps. The boy gave the elephant a bunch of bananas.

Chen called out for Jia Li to lift her leg. He held a loop attached to a harness around the elephant's neck and chest, swung onto her leg, and dismounted.

The platform was brought out again. Taking a deep breath that sent a jolt of pain through her side, Lilette gripped the rails and stepped onto the surface. The eunuchs lowered her smoothly to the ground.

Masses of people surrounded her, all of them pressing their foreheads to the ground—all except the elite, who stood still as stone. She made her way slowly through them, hesitating at the palace steps—after all, Han had said she would be killed for merely touching them.

"You may enter my home," the emperor said. With robes lifted, Lilette stepped between ranks of officials to stand before them. "For your dowry, you offer my son children with the power of the keepers' songs," the emperor continued. "In return, we offer a bride price of titles, land, silks, and jewels. I have found the bargain worthy."

He nodded to his wife. She motioned to two eunuchs, who stepped forward, bearing a headdress between them. The monstrous thing, easily as big as Lilette's head, was a half orb embedded with stones the color of shallow water.

"It has nine dragons and nine phoenixes. The number signifies your exalted status," Empress Yuwen explained. The dragons were actually golden sculptures that seemed to be climbing among the flat bodies of the phoenixes. "The four bobins" — the empress motioned to the couplings of wings that fanned out from the side of the crown— "signify you as wife of the crown prince." The empress's crown had six bobins.

Pearl strands dangled from the sides of the headdress, geometric patterns of gold giving them shape. The eunuchs placed it on Lilette's head. It was terribly heavy, and the pearls clicked in her ears and brushed her shoulders when she moved. She could already feel a headache beginning in her forehead.

"It is done," the emperor proclaimed. "All arise."

And just like that, Lilette was married. The rustle of thousands of people moving to their feet was deafening. She could feel their gazes on her, though with her back to them, they would see nothing more than her fabulous robes and the boulder of a headdress.

The emperor raised both his hands to the air. "Let us now celebrate with a feast!"

As if they'd waited for the signal, eunuchs immediately moved through the crowds, handing out oranges from baskets tucked under their arms.

Chen stepped down and offered his arm. Keeping her face impassive, Lilette took it. This close, the details of the palace were amazing. Nearly translucent panels lined the entire front, all standing open to let in the occasional breeze. An interlocking, woven pattern ran below all the windows, the weave meant to keep out demons from below. The double doors featured carvings of serpentine dragons, which Lilette was studying when eunuchs opened the doors.

Inside, the main room took up nearly the entire floor. Officials and scholars in their best silks slipped into their kowtows beside low tables surrounded by cushions. Lilette tried to catch sight of Han, but she couldn't find him.

The emperor and his wife went to the center table, which was raised above the others. Lilette followed them in a daze. Her bruises hurt, and she was so thirsty and hot. The headdress had made her head go numb. She maneuvered her way through kowtowing crowds of people, their faces a blur.

She took her place at the table. Eunuchs brought the first course. Lilette downed the wine and asked for water. They refilled her cup three times before she felt satisfied. She knew she should eat, since she would need all her strength for what was coming, but anything she put in her mouth stuck in her throat.

The men at the table spoke, their voices rising and falling without meaning. Lilette was glad women were discouraged from speaking in the palace, and glad her silence was marked as a sign of humility instead of terror.

Just as the meal started winding down, unease settled over Lilette. In less than a heartbeat, nature went from smooth and flowing to writhing in pain. In a daze, she rose to her feet. The room went silent.

"Lilette?" Chen said.

"Something is wrong." She'd felt this before—this sense that something was deeply amiss, when the witches' songs had attacked the Vorlayan armada. And long before that, when she and her mother had called down lightning.

Lilette's eyes widened as she understood. "They're singing against us." And then she remembered her mother showing her scenes of death and destruction that had ended with the island sinking below the waves. "Grove City is attacking!"

Chen was on his feet now, his arms on her shoulders, trying to convince her to sit down.

"You have to let them go! Let them go or the witches will destroy you!" Lilette shouted at the emperor.

His gaze flashed to the back of the palace. The screen there had been slid aside, providing a perfect view of the gardens where the witches were held. "See they are all secure!" the emperor commanded. Elite standing guard shouldered their halberds and started running.

"No!" Lilette said. "It's coming from Grove City." No sooner had the words left her lips than the palace bucked beneath her, sending her flying. Her ridiculous headdress toppled off and cracked nearly in two.

The world roared in protest—a sound full of breaking and crushing. The palace shook as if it would come down around them. Lilette tried to crawl away, but the ground shook her to the floor. She curled into a ball, hoping the entire structure didn't crumble on top of her.

Somehow, Chen managed to reach her. He wrapped his arms protectively around her, and she was so terrified she turned to him and buried her head in his chest. The shaking seemed to go on forever, but when it finally ended, she peered out. She barely recognized the room. Tables had been upended, food had spilled, carved reliefs had cracked, and sculptures had toppled.

"You have to let them go, Chen," Lilette murmured against him. "They'll destroy us all if you don't."

"Shh," he said comfortingly before pulling her to her feet. Frenzied eunuchs rushed about the room, tending to everyone.

"You knew that was coming?" the emperor demanded of her.

Lilette braced herself. "I knew something was coming. I did not know what."

Suddenly Han was there, his gaze on her in Chen's arms. "There's always a second one. Get everyone out!"

Everyone rushed outside. Lilette gasped in a breath full of dust and fear before the second wave hit. Chen wrapped his arms around her and held her tight, making her bruised side ache anew. This one didn't knock her down, nor did it last as long. When it had finished, Lilette was surprised the palace still stood.

"It is an ill omen," the empress said, her gaze fixed on Lilette.

The emperor's face was red. "Have our witches fight back! Level Grove City!"

Lilette shook her head. "For a song that powerful to travel such a distance, hundreds of witches must have been singing." Even she knew that. "You have just over thirty."

The emperor's face went even redder, and his gaze focused on her bare head. "That headdress has been in my family for generations. Where is it? What have you done?"

Lilette crossed her arms over her chest. If he had to blame someone, apparently it had to be the witch closest to him.

Chen moved between her and his father. Han edged up from behind. "We must see to the city, Emperor. There will be injured. Collapsed buildings. Fires."

The emperor began roaring commands, ordering elite into the city and calling for the imperial soldiers to be mobilized.

Lilette watched soldiers running from the palace. With them gone, it would be much easier to escape. She put her hand in her pocket and rubbed her thumb along the chipped edge of the phoenix wing. She just had to slip away.

But she hadn't taken two steps before Chen found her. He looked around. "Where are the blasted eunuchs when you need them?" He pushed her toward his brother. "See that she's taken safely to my rooms and keep her there!"

Han grunted. "Where are you going?"

Chen had already started running. "To prepare the witches for a counter song if we're attacked again!"

Han motioned for Lilette to walk in front of him. "This is only the beginning," she said once they were out of earshot. He clenched his jaw as they stepped back into the chaos inside. "They will not relent," she continued. "And you don't have enough of us to fight them. If you let us go, we can negotiate on your behalf."

They passed a pair of gold-plated lions guarding the symmetric staircase. "I saw this happen," she insisted. Han showed no sign that he was listening. "The witches will sink the whole island."

He spoke through clenched teeth. "You're saying you're some kind of seer?"

They'd started up to the second level. "I was shown it, by one of the Creators."

Han stiffened. "You saw the Sun Dragon?"

If Lilette's mother couldn't be called a Sun Dragon, who could? "Yes. And I saw Rinnish sink below the waves, witches and all."

Han briefly closed his eyes. "Kalari won't destroy the city, not with their witches still inside."

Lilette's shoulders fell. "They will have to in order to prevent this kind of thing from happening again."

Han paused before an intricately carved door. He pushed it open to reveal a room with an actual bed littered with silk cushions. Beautifully carved tables had tipped over, spilling the glittering contents of jewelry chests across the floor.

She hurried to the opposite door and stepped onto the porch. Parts of the city were burning, smoke rising into the midday sky. Other parts had collapsed into rubble. People would be buried there, their homes becoming their graves. Lilette pressed her hand to her mouth.

This was just the beginning. "I have to free my sister and the others. It's what I was saved for."

Han rounded on her. "Save them? They're guarded by over seventy elite. The guardians are in the enclosure where the lions used to be kept. And only the emperor has the key."

She swallowed against the tightness in her throat. "Han, you have to let me go."

"So you can die?" He gripped the banister, his knuckles turning white. "Do you know what you're asking me? When you're caught, my father will have you killed. Neither Chen nor I will be able to stop him." Han stared at her fabulous robes. "My brother will never forgive me. He trusts me. And he's your husband." Han's voice broke on the last part. "Then my own father would kill me."

He wasn't going to let her go. "Death is not something to fear, Han." She reached into the folds of her sash and gripped her knife. She tipped forward as if to kiss him. He took hold of her arms to push her away. "I'm sorry," she breathed, then swung her arm out in an arc and slammed the butt of the dagger into his temple.

He collapsed in a heap on the floor. Lilette stared at the blood-red stone in the hilt. She should kill him. He would be coming for her when he woke. But she couldn't bring herself to do it.

Chapter 16

That tremor was a warning from the keepers. We all knew
it. And all of us secretly wondered how expendable we were.
~Jolin

Lilette unstrapped Han's armor and stripped off his
clothing, trying hard not to look at the scars that cut
across his body like the lines of a map. She tore off her elaborate
robes and dropped them on the floor. Standing in nothing but
her smallclothes, she wrenched the combs and flowers from her
hair. She found a basin of water and scrubbed her face and neck
clean of powders.

Next, she snatched a silk purse, stuffed it with jewels, and
tied it to her waist, then pulled on Han's tunic and trousers. She
twisted her hair up off her neck and tugged on his leather-and-
bronze-plated helmet. It promptly fell over her eyes. She stuffed
it with squares of washing linen. The helmet's flaps covered her
neck and ears, and there was an optional faceguard. She strapped
it on, tightening it with the leather straps. It was stuffy, but now
only her eyes showed. Too bad they were blue.

Luckily, Han was only a little taller than she, so although they
were baggy, the clothing and armor fit her fairly well. His large
boots would be the biggest problem.

Creators' mercy, she was terrified. She opened the screen and
peeked outside. She cast one final glance at Han's motionless
body before fastening her eyes to the floor and retracing her

steps through the wide corridors, the swords at her back clanging together with each of her steps.

She trotted down two flights of stairs to the main room. Eunuchs and elite bustled about. No one made a move to stop her as she rounded one of the golden lions and headed straight for the gardens. She was halfway there when Chen strode through the garden doors, Wang at his side. She ducked her head, sick with fear. The nearby elite paused to bow as Chen passed, so Lilette did the same.

"Keep an eye on her. I don't trust her," Chen said as he drew even with her. "And tell my brother to meet me at the stables. We're needed in the city."

Chen pulled his helmet onto his head and didn't look back as Wang trotted up the stairs, his belly bouncing. The moment Wang arrived at the rooms, he'd find Han unconscious and Lilette missing. It would be over before it had even begun.

It took everything she had to wait to burst into a run until she reached the shadows of the garden. She raced toward where they kept the Guardians, her heart pounding frantically and weakness assaulting her. But she couldn't slow down. Couldn't stop.

She'd nearly made it when the alarm rose up from the palace. It was too far away for Lilette to make out the words, but the meaning was clear. Wang had discovered her missing.

Knowing there was no time for subtlety, she didn't slow down when she reached the enclosure where the guardians were kept. She simply ran to the gates. Unfortunately, her breath was coming so hard she couldn't talk.

Hunched over, she braced herself against her thighs, as much because she was about to fall over as because it would hide her face. She waved toward the main gates. "Earthquake, distraction," she said to the elite guard. "Vorlayans in the compound."

Her distress must have convinced them, because all but two of the elite ran off. Two she could handle.

She followed the ones who were leaving. As soon as she was hidden from view, she found the tallest tree in sight and climbed until she could see the guardians and the two remaining elite.

There wasn't time to hesitate. Chen would guess where she'd gone. Elite would be coming.

Unstrapping one side of the useless faceguard, Lilette sang between gasping breaths. Of course the two remaining guards heard her, and of course they came running. But that's why she'd climbed the tree, to buy herself time.

She considered singing a song to bind them, but she didn't dare take the time for it. Instead, she sang for the plants to wrap around the bars holding the guardians prisoner.

The two elite found her quicker than she'd hoped, and immediately started climbing the tree. Arms trembling with exhaustion, Lilette climbed higher, still maintaining her song.

On the fifth repetition, she'd gone high enough that the tree had started to tip with her weight. She made the mistake of looking down, and her head went light.

A branch broke beneath one of the elite's feet. He scrambled for purchase, barely managing to hang on. When he regained his footing, he and the other guard didn't try to climb any higher. Instead, they hacked at the tree with their swords.

Cries of outrage came from the guardians. They yanked harder on the bars. Hundreds of vines had curled around the bars, squeezing and tightening until the empty spaces bulged. One of the slightest guardians—he looked no older than a boy, with a shock of copper hair—squirmed through the bars and darted toward Lilette.

An elite below her gave a shout when Copper Hair appeared at the base. Quick as a monkey, he clambered up. A grim-faced elite dropped down to deal with him. The other hacked harder at the tree.

With a crack, the trunk suddenly dropped beneath Lilette. She screamed as it fell forward. It jerked to a stop, and the momentum swung her around until she was dangling by her fingertips just a few lengths from the elite.

A gurgling shout sounded below her. Lilette looked down in time to see one of the elite plummet from the tree. He hit the ground and didn't move again. Copper Hair barely paused to tuck his sword away before he was climbing again.

Lilette met the remaining elite's gaze and saw murder bright in his eyes. He must have known he was going to die, but he was going to kill her first. He stepped onto one of the branches and eased toward her, his sword outstretched.

"Hurry!" she called to Copper Hair.

The elite steadied himself and swung his sword. Lilette had no choice but to let go. She screamed as she fell, crashing through branches, her arms desperately flailing.

A hand shot out, grabbing hold of her trousers and nearly pulling them off her. She squealed and glanced up to see Copper Hair looking down at her, his expression strained as he held on. Half a moment later, another guardian grabbed the back of Lilette's breastplate and pulled her onto the branch with him. Copper Hair nodded at them both before scrambling after the remaining elite.

The tree was crawling with guardians now. They helped her to the base. She promptly collapsed and lay panting. Her side throbbed, and stars swam in and out of focus before her.

A man, his dark hair streaked with gray, hovered over her, wearing a stunned expression. He had dark features like a Harshen, but his eyes were different—more rounded—and his skin had a reddish-brown tone. "You're not Sash?" he said in Kalarian.

"No. I'm her sister, Lilette." She struggled to sit up while pulling her trousers back on. At any other time, she would have been mortified, but she was too relieved to be out of the tree to care.

He reached down and pulled her to her feet. "How—"

"No time. They already know I'm missing." She handed him Han's swords—they were useless in her own hands.

"I'm Second Leader Geth." He took them, keeping one for himself and handing the other to a mountain of a man with kind eyes. Two other guardians stripped the swords from the dead elite.

Geth nodded to two of the guardians who dropped out of the tree—Copper Hair and another small man, each of whom had a sword now. That left six swords to share among what appeared to be over fifty guardians. "The rest of you grab sticks or rocks," Geth ordered. "Let's go."

He motioned for Lilette to come with him. "Soon as we're in position, I want you up a tree again, singing." She blanched at the thought of climbing another tree. "Bind up as many of the elite as you can. I'll leave Galon to guard you."

Geth and the guardians spread out as Copper Hair—Galon— came in beside her. When they were close to where the witches were being kept, Lilette spotted a fairly tall, sturdy-looking tree. Touching Galon's arm, she motioned toward it. He nodded wordlessly and secreted himself in the foliage at its base.

She climbed, her hands stinging with scratches from the previous tree. She concentrated on gripping one branch at a time, and never once did she look down. She came high enough to see the witches and the elite who guarded them. It appeared Chen hadn't pulled any of them to clean up the streets. With about two elite per witch, their numbers were fairly even with the guardians.

Taking a deep breath, she fixed the song in her heart. As soon as it passed her lips, the guardians charged. The elite saw them coming and positioned themselves between the charge and the witches.

It was a terrible thing, watching unarmed guardians charge men armed with two blades. But they did it, fiercely slamming into the enemy and knocking them back.

Lilette's song faltered when the witches rammed the elite from behind. The witches were bound and gagged, completely defenseless. But the elite didn't turn and slay them. Instead, they beat them back with hilts, and then turned to face the guardians again.

The guardians were brilliant to watch. Even with her ignorance of sword fighting, Lilette could see their skill. They ducked blades, kicking out with feet and hands. They twisted into the elite's guard and came back with one of their swords.

And they died. Even with the guardians' skills and determination, elite reinforcements would arrive any second, and then it would be over.

They didn't just need to win, they needed to win quickly. Lilette steadied herself. She had to sing perfectly. She had to save them. She put everything she had into it, her voice chiming over the fray.

Vines shot out of the ground, wrapping around the elite's feet and tripping them, slowing them down. Another voice joined hers. A guardian had managed to free one of the witches. As she sang, she started yanking gags out of other witches' mouths.

Within moments, half a dozen witches were singing, their voices blending with Lilette's. In turn they moved to other witches, freeing their mouths.

Growing impossibly fast, plants shot from cracks between the bricks. They stretched, catching at the elite's feet and binding them. Guardians promptly finished them off, taking their swords—two swords to arm two men. It was over.

Lilette scrambled down the tree. Not trusting her trembling body, she took great care. When she reached the bottom, she braced herself against the tree to keep from falling over.

The witches had switched their song and might need her help. She looked around expectantly for Galon, but he was nowhere to be seen. "Galon?" She took half a dozen steps before freezing. He lay still on the ground, his hair a shock of color against his pale face. She dropped beside him and held her hand in front of his mouth. His breath touched her fingertips.

A sound made her turn. Two dozen elite stepped into view— Chen and Han among them. Lilette's faceguard was down. Her gaze flitted across Han—fully clothed and armored—to Chen, who wore the same dead expression as when he'd killed Laosh.

Lilette bolted, but she hadn't made it five strides before Chen grabbed her hair. She clawed at his grip, tears welling in her eyes from the pain. He forced her to her knees. She twisted just enough to see him raise his sword, his face conflicted.

A hand shot out and gripped Chen's sword arm. Han came into view, and he wore death as armor again. "What did you expect her to do?" he hissed. "You took her by force, married her by force."

"She has betrayed our people!" Chen shouted.

"Our people! Not hers!"

Chen tried to jerk free. "This is a kindness. You know what Father will do to her."

Han shook his head. "I can't let you kill her."

Chen released Lilette. She pitched forward, landing hard. She gathered herself and looked back to find Han sprawled on the ground. Chen's hand fisted. "She was raised among us!" he said.

Han shot to his feet. "Because we killed her family."

Chen's expression changed to something unreadable. "No. The witches did that."

A lie.

Han held out a placating hand. "Just let her go."

Chen tightened his grip on his sword. "That's why Father chose me as the heir instead of you. Because I do what must be done."

He turned toward Lilette and raised his sword. She cowered as it came down, but it was blocked with a clang of steel. Han had drawn his own weapon. He threw his brother's sword back.

In a flash, Chen's expression changed from disbelief to betrayal. "You sure you want to do this, little brother?"

Drawing his second sword, Han took a fighting position between Lilette and Chen, one blade high, the other low. "I can't let you kill her."

He and Han moved forward at the same time, their blades quick. The fight looked more like a dance than a brawl, deadly and impossibly fast. But even untrained in swordsmanship as she was, Lilette could tell Chen was quicker—or perhaps just more determined to kill his brother.

Before she could shout a warning, an elite came at Han from behind and kicked his legs out from under him. He landed hard but automatically brought one sword up to block a blow to his head. Lilette let out a strangled cry that immediately transformed into a song.

Dirt and rocks exploded around Han as roots the size of her wrist shot out and snatched at arms and legs, pinning elite where they stood. *Why didn't the plants react like that before?* There wasn't time to ponder it. The elite were already fighting their way free of the vines. Lilette pushed to her feet just as a shout rang out behind her.

"Guardians to me!"

Lilette turned to see dozens of guardians running toward them. Geth charged toward Han, sword raised.

"Not him!" She launched herself between them, her gaze locked on Geth, daring him to harm Han.

He seemed to understand, for he redirected his charge. "Get back with the others!" He and the guardians slammed into Chen and the other elite.

Lilette started off, but turned back when Han didn't follow her. "You have to come with me now."

Blood trickled from the corner of his mouth, and his expression was dazed. Her focus shifted to a blur of motion. An elite had sneaked up behind Han.

"Behind you!" Before the words had fully left Lilette's mouth, Han spun, his blades blocking a thrust and a swing. This time, there was no hesitation as he twisted the tangle of swords in a circle, his body twisting with them. His elbow came up fast, landing square in the elite's nose.

As the man reeled back, Han ran toward Lilette. She fell in beside him, knowing he would be a target now just as much as she was. She led him to where Galon lay unconscious. Han didn't even have to ask. He threw the smaller man over his shoulder and took off after her.

CHAPTER 17

"The monster of my story was as beautiful and calm as a sunrise." ~Lilette, quoted in Jolin's biography

L ilette headed toward the clearing, and only then did she notice the singing. She slowed to listen to the unfamiliar song of growing and tearing. Her eyes widened when she realized what the witches were doing. Guardians had replaced the elite in the protective circle around the witches. Those in front of Lilette slid into a fighting stance as she came closer.

Thankfully, Han knew better than to reciprocate the action. "He's with me," Lilette said quickly.

The guardian directly in front of her narrowed his gaze. "And who are you?"

"Lilette!" Jolin cried. She darted between guardians and enveloped her in an embrace that made her side throb with pain. Lilette hugged her friend back, not caring how much it hurt.

Jolin turned to the guards. "This is Lilette, Sash's sister. She's the reason we escaped." Her gaze took in Han, and her smile faltered.

"He helped me escape," Lilette explained. Immediately the guardians stood down, and Han left Galon in their care.

Jolin motioned for Lilette to follow her past the perimeter. "Come on, there's someone you need to meet."

Trotting to keep up with Jolin, Lilette didn't let Han out of her sight. Jolin led them to the center of the singing witches and paused in front of a woman with white-blond hair that matched Lilette's.

"Sash!" Jolin said. "I found Lilette."

Sash whirled around and her gaze locked with Lilette's. It was like a lodestone between them, so strong they both moved to each other's arms, both of them crying.

Sash pulled back first, and Lilette couldn't help but notice the blood on her hands. "There's so much between us that needs to be said." Sash took a deep breath as if steeling herself. "When we're safe."

"But what are you doing?" Lilette pointed to the ramparts.

"Making our escape." Sash backed away. "Sing with us. We need all the help we can get."

Listening hard to the song, Lilette began to sing. Sash nodded encouragingly. Suddenly, Lilette realized she'd abandoned Han to go to her sister. She panicked—someone might hurt him simply because he was Harshen.

To her relief he stood nearby watching her sing, his gaze unreadable. She approached him as she would a wounded animal, her movements slow and even. She took hold of his hand. He winced but didn't let go.

The crowd parted for Geth as he strode toward them. He nodded to Sash. "They're rallying at the palace, gathering elite back from the city to come against us in force. The gates are already closed against our escape."

"I expected as much." Sash pursed her lips and studied the green half-circle eating away chunks of the north ramparts. Crushed bits of brick rained down. "We're almost there."

Geth jerked his thumb over his shoulder at Han. "What about him. Isn't he Chen's brother?"

Lilette stepped between Han and Geth. "He saved my life— helped me when no one else would."

Sash looked at Lilette and then Han. "Leave him be. For now." She glanced around. "Where's Leader Gyn?"

The guardian shook his head.

Sash frowned. "Very well. You are first leader now, Geth."

The man gave a curt nod. "They're coming!" someone shouted.

The witches turned as one. Taller than most of them, Lilette could see over heads and past shoulders. Elite soldiers rushed at them from the east. A few of the front runners reached the guardians, who shifted their defenses to block them.

"Stick to the ramparts," Sash ordered. "Let the guardians take care of it."

Han's hand went for his sword, but he hesitated. Lilette wondered how many of them were his friends—men under his command.

"Will you fight?" Geth asked.

Han swallowed hard. "I'll defend myself, Lilette, but I won't kill them. I can't."

"Stay by her then—protect her," Geth said as he ran toward the fight.

"We need the safety of the barrier," one of the witches called out.

Sash studied the advance. "Form up! Wait for my mark."

Another witch grabbed Sash's arm. "We can't wait! It has to go up now!"

She shoved her toward the circling witches. "Do as I say."

Lilette glanced around, wondering what to do. Jolin pushed her into the circle with the others. "Sing—we need you!"

Following the others' lead, Lilette straightened to her full height and sang with all her strength. After a moment of faltering, her voice moved seamlessly with theirs.

The elite broke through the guardians, and the fighting grew intense. More guardians around the perimeter ran to help.

At the sound of rushing, Lilette whirled around. A dozen elite were charging toward her. With a groan full of pain, Han pushed past her and slid to his knees under a wild swing, his swords snapping up and into an elite's body. Han rolled to the side and rose in a crouch, his blades flicking out, hitting the unarmored throat of one of the elite. He gurgled as he fell.

Han was no longer simply defending. He was killing his men. For her. An ember seemed to ignite in Lilette's chest, and her song changed. She wasn't even sure of the words she used. But the men cried out in pain and dropped their smoking swords before retreating.

Han turned toward her, someone else's blood running down his face. Around them, the witches sang again once, twice, three times. But for Lilette there was only Han, the pain she knew was there, buried under his stony exterior.

She didn't say she was sorry. The words would have seemed hollow. Instead, she simply turned sideways, making space for him to come back into the circle. After glancing behind him once more, he did.

A crack split the air. Through the plants, a fracture had appeared in the ramparts. More vines curled around rectangles of bricks, crushing them into rubble that tumbled down in little piles. Yellow dust billowed into Lilette's face and coated her lungs, making her cough.

Sash marched in a circle in front of them. "Switch to pushing back the elite." Her voice rose to a shout. "Guardians, on my mark!"

The witches' songs shifted to stopping the elite. A wall of green rose up between elite and guardian, pushing the elite back.

"Guardians," Sash called. "Inside the barrier!"

As soon as the last guardian was inside, the witches gripped hands and their song switched from pushing the elite back to forming the barrier. Without songs to hinder them, the elite surged forward.

"Now!" Sash cried.

Seconds before the charging elite would have hit them, there was a sound like a clap of thunder. The percussion pulsed around them, blasting a hole through the weakened section and knocking the elite to the ground.

The witch holding Lilette's hand suddenly screamed. Lilette's eyes widened in horror at the sword sticking out of the woman's middle. Her eyes glazed over and she slowly toppled forward, revealing an elite behind her.

Lilette tensed to run, but the man was already dead. He slowly collapsed in two halves—the barrier had split him neatly in two.

A sob hitched in her throat, and the barrier flickered as if it would go out. The witch next to her stepped over the bodies and gripped her hand.

Lilette became aware of a voice in her head. *Lilette! Lilette, look at me!* With a start, she realized it was Sash. *You must focus.*

"How is this possible?" Lilette murmured, but Sash had already turned from her and issued a silent command that reverberated inside Lilette's head.

A song took shape in Lilette's mind. Somehow, she knew it because everyone else did—as if their minds were linked.

"That's exactly what it is," Jolin said beside her. "Now stop thinking so loud. It's making it hard to concentrate."

The witches sang. Belatedly, Lilette joined them. The air thickened before her sister shot into the sky.

"Retreat!" one of the Harshens cried. "Find shelter."

As elite scrambled for cover, Sash climbed above the ramparts. With a change of song, the witches' voices stirred up a vicious wind. Elite armed with bows toppled from the ramparts, their screams ending with a sudden silence.

Their next song twisted the wind down on the garden. It ripped trees from the ground, flinging them like sticks. Sash surveyed the damage, her mouth tight with something like indecision.

We have to bring down the city, said one of the witches in Lilette's head. Others echoed her sentiment.

Sash held out her hand. *I don't know how, but Grove City has already done that. I won't kill more innocent people than we already have.*

The witches stopped singing. The barrier cracked and shattered into shimmering flecks that drifted like burning bits of light. Moments later, Sash touched down.

"Guardians, clear the way and cover the rear!" Geth called as he surged over the rubble toward the breach in the ramparts. Guardians moved to the front and back of the witches.

"Stay together and move!" Han followed them, one sword drawn as he watched for any elite coming up behind them.

Side by side with Jolin, Lilette scrambled over the rubble and through the shredded garden. After only a few minutes of running, her legs trembled and she gasped for breath. She was falling behind. "Just go without me," she panted.

Growling in frustration, Han threw her over his shoulder. With his powerful strides, he quickly caught up with the others. Once they passed beneath the breach, he set Lilette down with her back against the ramparts. Sweat running down her face, she gasped for breath, relieved to have something solid between her and the elite.

"We need a barrier tree to block this up," Sash called to those around her. "Surely someone managed to hide a seed?"

A woman stepped forward, swept aside a jumble of bricks, and shoved a seed into the earth. The witches around her began singing.

Oh barrier tree, I sing to thee,
Take up thy boughs and cover me.

In front of them, a green shoot burst out of the ground. Within moments, it was taller than the witch, with branches and leaves curling toward the blood-red sun.

Lilette watched as the tree's boughs covered the sky. Within a few minutes it had gone from a seed to a tree as ancient as the rocks around the waterfall back home.

Their song turned dark and sinister.

Let no one pass.

Lilette gaped as the tree moved. Not shifting with the wind, but reaching to snatch an elite by the waist and hurl him back the way he'd come. The tree reached down for more elite, who hacked at it with their swords as they screamed in terror.

"Geth," Han called, "you have trouble."

Lilette followed his pointing finger. The palace compound was built on a rise. Below them, weaving through the webbed streets of the city, were pockets of imperial soldiers—all marching toward them from the northwest.

Leader Geth glanced about, as if searching for some kind of escape. "We can't cut through that." He pointed along the ramparts. "The only other way is to the east."

Lilette groaned as Han pulled her to her feet. At least she'd caught her breath enough to keep up with the others as they dashed parallel to the ramparts. After only a few dozen steps, she ran into the back of the witch in front of her. The whole group had slammed to a halt.

Wiping sweat from her temples, she stood on her tiptoes and found the way blocked by another group of elite. Smoke billowed around Lilette. The tree was on fire. Though it continued to grab soldiers and throw them back, its branches were breaking off, and burning leaves twirled on the air currents.

Through the smoke and fire, Chen appeared at the apex of his elite. The witches were trapped.

CHAPTER 18

The poisoning left Lilette breathless and weak whenever she exerted herself. I could never bring myself to tell her it was a malady she would live with the rest of her life. ~Jolin

The witches packed together under the late-afternoon sky, guardians surrounding them.

"Keepers, there need be no more death. Surrender!" Chen said.

Lilette promptly ducked behind another witch. Her hand found the phoenix comb, and she squeezed it for reassurance.

Sash met Chen's gaze. "Give me a moment to confer with my advisors."

"One minute. No more."

"Keeper Sash, your orders?" Geth asked.

She met Lilette's gaze, tears glazing her eyes. "We don't have our seeds, our potions." It was almost like an apology.

"You can't surrender," Lilette said softly. "He'll make you all concubines, and probably kill all the guardians." And her.

"You don't understand." Sash took a deep breath. "Our songs won't be strong enough to fight them without a circle."

"But we can't hold a circle forever," Jolin said. "Three days at most."

Sash smiled sadly. "I know."

Horror washed through Lilette. "No! You can't!"

"This was my expedition. My responsibility." Sash took a deep breath. "Lilette, I'm going to need you to take my place as point."

Lilette shook her head. "I don't know how."

"Doesn't matter. What matters is that you'll get them out."

"But I just found you," Lilette whispered. Sash drew her in for a hug.

"Keepers!" Chen barked. "What is your answer?"

Sash squeezed Lilette tight. "When you arrive in Grove City, Merlay will find you. Trust her and no other."

Sash pulled back and spoke just loudly enough to be heard by the thirty or so witches around them. "I need volunteers to stay behind and create a circle."

"I don't understand what's happening," Han whispered.

Jolin blew out a breath. "Those in the circle will stay and fight, while the rest of us try to escape. And I can't be one of the ones to stay."

"Why?" Lilette asked quietly.

Jolin shook her head. "It'll be a small circle—they need the strongest singers to make it work."

Lilette gasped. "She chose me as point so I couldn't stay behind." Her sister was just as brilliant a tactician as Chen.

Gray head bent, one woman stepped forward. As she moved, she took the hand of another. The two locked gazes, a lifetime of memories passing between them. Both moved forward at the same moment.

Lilette turned at a flurry of movement off to the side. A girl wrapped her arms around one of the older women. "No, Grandma, don't," she begged.

The older woman hugged her fiercely. "Just don't—" She shuddered and took a calming breath. "Just don't waste it." Another keeper pulled the young girl away.

Sash was crying hard now. "It's not enough."

"Keepers, what is your answer?" Chen asked again, his patience obviously gone.

"There aren't enough." Sash wiped her cheeks. "You older women—those of you who are injured—you won't be able to run. This way if you die, you'll be dying for something." Four of the younger keepers joined them.

Sash gave a shaky smile. "Does anyone have any water? We'll be able to last longer with it." A few water skins were passed forward.

"Thank you, your sacrifice—" Sash began.

"They're forming a circle! Charge!" Chen cried.

"Form up!" Sash ordered. "We'll clear the courtyard and guard your backs. Creators' mercy, I hope you make it."

The women curled into a circle, eight women strong. "Get down," Sash said.

All the witches and guardians around the circle dropped, Lilette and Han half a beat behind. The other witches joined hands, their song shooting forth just as the elite surged forward.

The barrier again rose into the sky. A shock wave rippled out from the witches, whipping the flames from the dying tree and flinging the brittle, burning branches into the nearby elite.

The witches sang three times, their songs dark and deadly. Then Sash rose into the night sky and sang with the combined power of many.

"What is she doing?" Lilette asked.

Jolin covered her head with her hands. "Fighting."

The ground beneath Lilette shook as if the whole world was being rent asunder. Han pulled her into his arms, his body hunched protectively over her—just as his brother had done earlier.

In the city, more buildings collapsed. Lilette knew innocent people were dying, and a piece of her seemed to wither and die with them.

A jagged wall of earth rose between the palace and the city, cutting the army off. The witches in the circle started a new song, their faces determined. The sky turned dark. Black clouds boiled above them, lightning flashing along the bottom. Rain pelted them. Within a matter of seconds, dozens of lightning strikes flashed down inside the compound.

Lilette thought of all those women and children in the harem, and her blood turned to ice. "Lang got her out," she said to herself. "He got her out!"

Han held her tighter. After what felt like forever, the strikes stopped. Opening her eyes, Lilette braced herself on her arms. Shouts rose up from behind them. She shifted, bits of earth scraping under body. The elite were coming at them from along the outside of the ramparts. Within moments, they would be surrounded.

"Go!" Sash cried. "Before it's too late!"

Han lunged to his feet and took up position behind them. It was time to run again. Water dripping from her face, Lilette surged back through the crumbled brick ramparts with the rest of the keepers.

The unmistakable smell of burning flesh assaulted her senses as she entered the compound. Rain pounded her hunched shoulders, and she started forward into the ruined garden.

All around her were the still forms of the dead. Steam or smoke, perhaps both, rose from their bodies. A small cry of pain rose involuntarily from deep inside her, and she found herself looking for Chen's body.

Han wrapped his arm around her shoulders and turned her face away. "Don't look."

She leaned into him, focusing only on his chest as they stumbled through the pathway of the dead. She had the distinct impression her body would soon falter. She was so far beyond the limits of her strength, but there was no choice but to go forward.

Behind them, lightning struck down the imperial soldiers in the city—the circle was attacking the army now.

The harem wall bordered the garden's west side. Lilette's gaze was drawn to it, but there didn't seem to be smoke coming from inside. "They didn't attack it." Relief coursed through her. Even if Lang didn't get Ko out, she might be all right.

When they bolted straight through the palace, eunuchs scattered in fear. The guardians flung open the palace doors and motioned for them to hurry. "Across the courtyard to the gates. Quickly now!"

But Lilette staggered to a stop. Before the gates, the ragged remnants of the palace elite had gathered. Geth pushed his way to the front of the group. He tipped his head toward Lilette and spoke low. "We haven't time or numbers for a rear guard. Watch your backs." Then he waved his sword above his head and sprinted forward. "Guardians, to me!"

Lilette stepped closer to Jolin. "What do I do?"

"Sing," Jolin said simply.

Lilette hesitated. "Keepers, follow my lead."

Marching forward, she started singing. Jolin and the other witches took up the song. Immediately, plants started snatching at the elite's feet, tripping them.

When they were halfway between the palace and the gates, Han stiffened beside her. He took half a step to the side and then ran to kneel beside a still form.

The guardians clashed with the elite, the sound making Lilette flinch, though she couldn't take her gaze from Han. "Jolin, keep them singing." She trotted up beside him and forced herself to look.

No one could mistake the stunning robes, even damp with rain and partially charred. Lilette bent down and picked up the elaborate crown at her feet. It was burned on one side. Han slowly turned over the emperor—his father. He was dead.

Han hung his head, his hands fisted at his sides. Lilette started to reach for him but hesitated. After all, she'd caused this.

From behind her, she heard a cry of pain and whirled to see Chen standing on the palace steps. The witches gave startled cries and darted away from him, but he ignored them. He sprinted forward and skidded to a halt on his knees beside the emperor.

He pressed his hand on his father's still chest. His gaze swept across Lilette to land on Han. "How you could do this?" Chen's voice broke. He gestured to the utter destruction of the compound, his voice rising with every word. "You let the witches free? Helped them kill elite—your own men—and our family? Stole my wife? Why?"

Han did not flinch. "It's wrong. Invading Vorlay will destroy us."

Lilette's eyes widened. Chen was planning an invasion, and no doubt planning to use her sister and the others to do it.

"Our islands lack so many natural resources," he explained. "Is it wrong of us to want to better the lives of our people?"

Han's mouth tightened. "Using the keepers as our weapon will spark a war we will not win. The entire empire will be destroyed because of your folly. Our people will be the ones to pay the price."

"You've known all this for days and done nothing," Chen replied.

Han spoke through his teeth. "You would have killed Lilette."

Rising to his feet, Chen pulled his swords from their sheaths. "I bested you once, Brother. I can do it again."

Lilette opened her mouth to stop Chen. Jumping up, Han cut her a look that instantly severed her song. "Do not interfere. Not this time," he said.

Her mouth clamped shut. She wanted to protest, but she remembered what Ko had said about regaining honor. Han had to do this alone if he was to ever live with himself.

Amid the sounds of the guardians and keepers battling the elite, the brothers circled each other. "When I win," Chen said, "I will take back what's mine."

Han's jaw hardened. "Just to kill her?"

Chen's gaze flicked to Lilette. "You take her to Grove City, she's as good as dead anyway."

"Liar!" she cried.

Han made a choking sound. "Lilette, go. I can't fight him while I'm worried about him coming after you. Join the others."

Knowing he was right, she backed away. The brothers lunged at each other, their swords cutting through the air with a hiss before clashing in a ringing of steel.

Wiping rain from her face, Lilette took in the elite battling the guardians and the witches singing with all their might. They were outnumbered, and the guardians were clearly exhausted. They might manage to fight their way through, but so many would die seeing it done. There had to be another way.

Lilette caught sight of the stables, which were two stories high. An idea forming in her mind, she ran toward them and threw open the doors. The dozen or so grooms jumped. Their eyes swept over her and they bowed. Lilette realized with the weak light, all they could see was her armor—Han's armor.

After tying up her faceguard, she stepped out of the rain, her gaze traveling down the rows and rows of horses in their stalls—all of them saddled and armored. A grim smile touched her mouth as she dropped her voice an octave. "See that all the horses are ready. Now." She strode straight down the center of the stables without looking to one side or the other and stepped through a short gate into a two-stories-high room. She startled at movement far, far above her.

She craned her head back to find herself not a half dozen steps away from the elephant. Though the howdah was gone, Jia Li was still outfitted in rich trappings covered in tassels that swayed as she studied Lilette with intelligent eyes. Her enormous trunk prodded Lilette's arms, as if searching for something.

A slow smile spread across Lilette's face. "Oh, yes. We can use this."

Keeping her movements smooth, Lilette undid the pin that held the bar across the entrance and opened it wide. Pretending she knew what she was doing, she repeatedly slapped the elephant's shoulder and said, "Lift leg!" To her utter delight, the elephant sort of crouched down and raised her leg.

Fear and a burst of excitement rushed through Lilette. She stepped onto the crook of the elephant's leg and scrambled up. And promptly slipped off onto the beast's rear. The elephant looked at her with something close to amusement in her eyes.

Brushing off her backside, Lilette tried again. She hiked her foot up and stepped on the elephant's leg. Her other foot went in the loop hanging from a sort of harness around Jia Li's neck. Lilette still wasn't at the top. Grabbing the loop, she pulled herself belly first over the elephant's neck and swung her leg around.

The elephant straightened up, a motion that felt like a tree swaying. And Lilette was once again much higher than she liked. But at least it was warm and dry beneath her damp legs.. Scooting forward, she blew out all her breath and nudged the back of Jia Li's ears. "Go." The elephant started forward, and in two steps, they were out of the stable. Lilette kicked behind the elephant's left ear to turn it left—only the animal turned right. "Gah!" She tried again, kicking the opposite ear. Jia Li turned left. In five strides, Lilette could see the entire battle.

She scanned the keepers. "Jolin!"

Her friend broke away and gaped up at Lilette. Jolin's face was slack with wonder—she'd probably never seen an elephant before.

Lilette pointed back to the stables. "Get the witches on the horses. There are a few stable hands, but they shouldn't be much trouble. I'm going to break down the gates."

"What—" Jolin cried, but Lilette was already nudging the back of the elephant's ears and heading straight for Han. The two brothers were still fighting, their blades carving paths through the rain. Han moved like a shadow, his strikes swift and smooth, but Lilette had the distinct impression he was holding back.

"Han!" she called. "It's time to go."

Chen's head turned at the sound of her voice, leaving himself open and vulnerable for half a second. Sword gripped in his fist, Han punched his brother in the temple. Chen crumpled to the ground. The rain tapped against his leather armor as if to wake him.

Han looked up at Lilette, his face filled with darkness. She reared back and Jia Li came to a stop. The murder slowly dissipated from Han's eyes, replaced with hopelessness. "If you stay here, you'll die," Lilette said. When he still made no move, her voice went soft. "I need you."

He looked down at his brother. "I should kill him."

"Can you live with yourself if you do?"

Han slid his swords home. "Not like this."

She slapped the elephant's shoulder. "Lift leg!" She reached out to Han. After snatching a bow and quiver from a dead man, he scrambled up behind her.

Lilette turned to see keepers coming out of the barn astride the horses, the women's dresses tucked up around their thighs. Each woman held the lead ropes of additional horses.

"Leader Geth!" Jolin yelled.

Geth glanced back at her before calling out the order to fall back. His men began retreating toward the horses as the witches' song held the elite back.

Lilette gripped Jia Li's harness, her fingers turning white. Han nocked an arrow. "They won't touch you," he promised her. She hoped he was right. The mounted witches pulled back on the reins, slowing their mounts so the guardians could take the extra horses. They spurred forward and took up flanking positions around the elephant.

"Follow me!" Lilette turned Jia Li toward the gates and nudged her ears until she was half trotting, half loping. Elite leapt out of the elephant's way as they cut toward the gate.

Behind her, the bow twanged as Han loosed arrow after arrow at elite who tried to stop them. "Cursed thing is wet. Range and accuracy are off," he muttered behind her.

Clearly realizing they had to stop the elephant, the elite sheathed their swords and scrambled for bows. Lilette ducked low to make herself a smaller target. One man swung at Jia Li, cutting her across the chest. The elephant trumpeted in fear and dodged away from any elite who came too close. Arrows rained down on them, but the witches sang from atop the horses. A wind shot out, turning the arrows.

Finally, they reached the gates. Without hesitation, Jia Li lowered her head and charged it. Han swore and pushed Lilette flat against the elephant's head, covering her body with his own. There was an enormous crack. Splinters and wood went flying.

Lilette felt a sharp sting as something imbedded in her arm. Han grunted in pain. Then they were through. Guardians and witches burst into the open in front of the palace. They crashed down the city streets, lightning and thunder at their backs.

CHAPTER 19

Elephants are useful for many things—most especially for clearing things out of the way. ~Jolin

Dozens of lightning bolts struck behind the palace compound. Sash and the others were still alive and fighting. Before them, a scattering of imperial soldiers converged.

Han tossed the bow and the empty quiver. "I'm out."

Lilette patted her sheath—she still had the jeweled dagger. "Which way?"

"There." Han pointed from behind her. "Take merchant's row."

Lilette turned the elephant down the street and looked back. The witches still followed her. Surrounding them, the guardians had their swords out.

Shouting came from the one of the side streets. Imperial soldiers ran toward them. Knowing they couldn't afford to be trapped, Lilette nudged Jia Li to go faster. People and animals moved out of the elephant's way. Anything that didn't was simply run over. More than one merchant cart was knocked down, its wares trampled in the streets.

"Not much farther now," Han said.

There were more shouts, and Lilette turned to check on the keepers. Still coming. Feeling some of her tension ease, she faced forward. "Oh, no."

"What?"

Wordlessly she pointed to the blockade of carts. Han leaned around her and promptly cursed. With no side streets, there was nowhere to turn.

"Can she go any faster?" Han asked.

Lilette shook her head.

"Hang on!" He gripped her middle so tight her side pulsed with pain. He pressed her flat beneath him just as Jia Li hit the blockade. She blasted through carts and broken furniture that had been piled higher than a man, but quickly lost momentum. Lilette kept kicking. Jia Li trumpeted, her ears flapping at the sides of her head.

With a yell, imperial soldiers charged them from above. Han leapt to his feet, his swords whirling above her. Clutching her dagger, Lilette hugged Jia Li's neck. "Come on, girl. Come on!"

From the ground, the soldiers cut at Jia Li's legs.

"No!" Lilette sobbed. "Leave her alone!" Trumpeting, Jia Li reared up, shaking loose the soldiers and Han with them.

"Han!" Lilette reached for him, but he was already gone.

Jia Li dropped back to all fours and began picking up broken bits of furniture with her trunk, flinging it at the soldiers swarming them. "Good girl!" Lilette rubbed her rough skin. Guardians quickly joined the fray, protecting Jia Li as she cleared a path for them.

Finally, they were free. Witches booted their horses forward, guardians swinging up behind them. Lilette looked around for Han.

"Lilette!" he called. "Go on! Don't stop!" He grabbed a loose horse and jumped on its back.

She could see the docks. They were going to make it! She kicked Jia Li back to full speed. A group of soldiers darted in front of them and disappeared in a narrow space between buildings.

Before Lilette could make sense of it, they shouted. "Now!" A rope as thick as her leg snapped up. Jia Li skidded, trying to avoid it, but she couldn't stop. She trumpeted as she hit the rope. Lilette went flying, skidding across the paving stones before coming to a stop.

Quickly she assessed her injuries—nothing seemed to be broken. She braced herself on her arms and looked back. From atop their horses, guardians were fighting more soldiers. Jia Li lay where she'd fallen, her enormous body seeming so much smaller now. Oblivious to the chaos around her, Lilette stumbled toward the elephant and knelt beside her head. Jia Li was covered in cuts, blood pooling around her. How could something so magnificent and strong fall?

Lilette reached out and rested her hand on Jia Li's face. The animal looked at her and touched Lilette's stomach with her trunk. With a start, she remembered the boy giving her a bunch of bananas. The elephant wanted a treat.

"I'm so sorry, girl. I don't have anything."

Jia Li kept searching until her trunk flopped on the ground and her eyes went unfocused. A strangled cry left Lilette's lips.

A sudden hand gripped her shoulder and pulled her to her feet. Han lifted her onto a horse's back. "Come on! We're not dying. Not today." He swung up behind her. His arms came around her, and he urged the horse forward. Lilette turned back to watch Jia Li's body and the pursuing soldiers grow smaller.

"Lilette! Answer her!" Han shouted practically in her ear.

She swiveled around to find Jolin riding directly beside them. "Which one?" Jolin asked.

Shaking herself, Lilette followed her gesture. There were hundreds of ships docked in the wharves or simply tied to some free spot on a pier.

Lilette's mind grabbed onto something familiar to keep the grief at bay. She scanned the ships and found a suitable-sized zhou with a sea-going, curved hull and tumblehome topsides. It appeared to have some sort of hold and sat low in the water, meaning it was loaded, hopefully with food. The craft's sails were stretched between horizontal battens, making them look like the membranes between a bat's wings. It would be fast, hold all of them, and handle all but the roughest seas.

"That one," she said, pointing.

The horse balked at stepping on the pier. Abandoning the animal, Han pulled Lilette from the saddle and shoved her in front of him. "Run!"

But Lilette's body refused to obey, and her legs buckled. She struggled to push herself up until Han tossed her roughly over his shoulder and sprinted down the pier. The guardians brought up the rear, ready to fight off any soldiers who came after them.

Han hustled up the gangplank and deposited her next to the gunwales. A cluster of sailors took one look at the armed guardians and dove off the side.

"Does anyone know how to operate this ship?" Geth called out.

Silently cursing her illness, Lilette searched the crowd, hoping someone else would step forward. After all, she'd never run anything larger than Fa's fishing vessel, which only had one sail. But there was no one. She took a deep breath. "I can." She hoped. "But I don't know the way."

"I can navigate us by the stars," Jolin spoke up. "And witches never run into bad weather."

Lilette pushed to her feet. Her body trembled and her coordination was off, but she could move. "See if you can find some charts." Jolin left and Lilette glanced up at the sails. "Untie them. Two guardians at the bow—watch for snags in the harbor." Lilette moved to the stern and studied the enormous rudder. "Three guardians to man this."

"Uh, miss, you better hurry." She turned to find Galon behind her.

"You're alive!" She started to smile, but he pointed toward a group of soldiers coming down the pier. "Pull in the gangplank!" Lilette ordered. "Untie the ropes! Witches, sing us a wind!"

Guardians hurried to untie the ship while the witches sang a wind to fill the sails. Others sang for the kelp to shoot out of the water and snatch at the soldier's legs.

A handful of soldiers ran onto the ship just before the ship moved out of range. The guardians met them, dispatching them within moments.

A low-toned gong cut through the chaos. Lilette froze and turned toward the city, wondering what the sound meant.

"We have to get out of the harbor before they raise the ship breaker!" Han shouted.

Lilette whirled to face him. "The what?"

"A chain across the harbor mouth."

"Creators' mercy," someone said.

"Sing!" Lilette cried. "Our lives depend on it!"

A dozen witches formed a circle, the injured in the center. Their songs called forth a wind that whipped across the sails, filling them to capacity within seconds. The ship strained forward.

Lilette pushed through the press of bodies towards the bow. Han motioned to the circle. "Shouldn't you join them?"

She didn't pause. "If we stray from the channel, all the singing in the world won't stop us from running aground." She shouted commands to the guardians manning the rudder. They guided the ship into the deepest channel in the harbor. Lilette's eyes scanned for sandbanks or snags.

Stretched across the harbor in front of them, she could see water buffalo being strapped to an enormous wheel. They strained against their yokes, turning the wheel. A rusty chain as tall as Lilette scraped out of the water.

Knowing the center of the chain would be the lowest point, she aimed the ship for it. Helpless to do more, she watched with the guardians as the chain slowly clanked out of the water, one link at a time.

The wind whipped them from behind, flinging Lilette's hair in her face and stinging her eyes. One more clink and she could make out the entire long line of rusty chain. She glanced at the sails. She wasn't sure they could take more wind without tearing, but if they didn't make it past that chain, it wouldn't matter.

She started singing with the others, her voice blending with theirs. The ship seemed to move a touch faster. Then the chain passed out of sight under them. Lilette held her breath.

The ship shuddered, and a high-pitched screeching filled the air. Crouched down, Lilette waited for the crunch of the wooden hull. The ship tipped up as the chain lifted the stern out of the water. But their momentum carried them forward. When they slammed down, Lilette lost her balance and pitched into Han.

Something splintered, and Lilette gripped his armor and held her breath, waiting for the ship to come apart beneath them.

But they were still moving forward. She searched for signs the ship was taking on water—slowing down or sitting deeper. Nothing. She released her breath and let go of Han. "See if the hold is taking on water. Be thorough—if there's a small leak now, it will be an enormous one by tomorrow."

Lilette scanned for any sign of a reef they probably wouldn't be able to avoid anyway. She didn't see any darker shapes, or the break of waves on rocks. She set up a watch at the stern for pursuit and at the bow for snags.

Geth trotted toward her. "The rudder caught on the chain. It's ruined."

That must have been the splintering sound. Cursing, Lilette hustled to the stern as fast as her exhausted body would allow. Sure enough, the rudder had shattered at the narrowest point."

"Pull it up and see if you can't rig something to get us by until we can reach Grove City."

"And how do we steer in the meantime?" Geth asked.

She pursed her lips. "Right now, steering isn't as important as getting out of sight. If the ship is damaged, we won't outrun anyone."

"But with the keepers singing—" Geth began.

"Their singing won't stop us from sinking or sitting so low in the water we can't move," Lilette interrupted. "We can steer the ship with the wind, at least a little."

She felt Han's solid presence beside her. "I didn't find any holes."

They were going to make it. Lilette couldn't stop herself from glancing back at the city of Rinnish as dusk stole over the island. Through the blur of rain, smoke rose toward the sky. Lightning lit up the clouds. The palace still lorded over the city, looking pristine among the destruction.

Lilette let out a breath. "This isn't the first time I've fled this city while it burned."

Han made a sound deep in his throat. "I remember."

All these years of trying to get back to her sister, and they'd had less than an hour together. Sash had taken Lilette's place, and Lilette had abandoned her. "I'll come back for you, just as you came back for me." The wind caught her promise and carried it away. Lilette wished her sister could hear it.

Knowing the image had burned a brand in her memory, she turned away. They'd made it, but how many had fallen behind?

Guardians were hauling the injured below decks while the witches continued singing. Jolin wove through the mass of guardians and witches toward them. "I found some charts to plot our course by," she said, then turned and headed back.

Lilette motioned for Geth and followed Jolin to the hatch. They waited as Han went down first. "How long will it take to reach Grove City?" Lilette asked.

Jolin looked toward the circle of witches, her eyes narrowed with concentration. "If we keep a steady rotation of singers, five days."

Lilette went down next. Her trembling legs barely held her weight, and she went slowly so she wouldn't fall. The hold was one long room full of barrels, crates, and swaying hammocks. Someone had already lit the lamps. A couple dozen injured had already been laid out. Witches went among them, doing the best they could.

Lilette turned in a slow circle as Geth and Jolin dropped down. "Any food?" Lilette asked.

Han found a crowbar, then pried open a crate and reached inside. He pulled out handfuls of what looked like twisted ropes of fine, shining hair. "Looks like they'd just loaded their cargo—raw silk."

Lilette found one with bits of fruit peeking out. "Over here." There were barrels of water too. "How many of us made it out?"

Jolin peered hungrily between the gaps of the crate. "Twenty witches. Thirty-two guardians."

Lilette hesitated as Geth pried another crate open—this one held rice. "How many were lost?"

Jolin's face fell. "Too many."

They moved among the crates, trying to estimate if they had enough food for over forty people. "If we're careful, we should make it," Geth finally surmised.

Motioning for them to follow her, Jolin strode through the injured to the stern, where there was a screened-off partition—probably where the captain slept. She gathered a rolled-up map and a small chest. "I have some calculations to make when the stars come out in about an hour. I'll be topsides if you need me."

"Geth—" she tipped her head toward the drafting table "—bring that, if you will." But she paused at the doorway and nodded toward a group of guardians who were pulling apart some planking. "What are they doing?"

Lilette grunted. "Making a new rudder."

"Oh. Well, then. I suppose as long as they don't take any important pieces." She departed, Geth lugging the table behind her.

That left Lilette alone with Han. He eased himself onto the floor and carefully removed his shin guard and boot. The material beneath was dark and unnaturally heavy. He pulled up his pant leg, exposing a nasty gash in his calf.

Lilette took a step toward him. "When did that happen?"

"Chen gave it to me."

She knelt before Han, inspecting the wound without touching it. "Can you move it?"

One side of his mouth crooked up. "I've been running on it for half the night."

She shot him a glare. "Didn't that hurt?"

He shook his head. "That always comes later."

"I'm going for help," she said, pushing herself up.

Han reached up and gripped her arm. "Just bring supplies."

Her eyebrows shot up. "I'm not sure I'm the best—"

"Have you met our physicker? I can handle myself."

That made sense, and it wasn't like Lilette hadn't dealt with wounds before. She stepped back into the hold, weaving her way among the injured. She asked about supplies. Someone had found an apothecary kit. She managed to procure a needle, pig-intestine thread, and a bucket of cold seawater.

Kneeling before Han, Lilette rolled his trouser leg over his knee, cringing at the feel of cold, sticky blood beneath her fingers. "You're lucky. It's with the grain of the muscle instead of against it. You'll still have use of your leg. As long as rot doesn't set in."

She felt him watching her. "Have you done this often?" he asked.

She shrugged. "Fa and I could never afford the physicker." She met Han's searching gaze. "This is going to hurt. Do you need someone to hold you down?"

"No."

She poured seawater onto his wound, washing away clots of blood. Through the seeping was an unnaturally dark strip. She picked out a piece of his trousers and separated the cut with the pads of her fingers, washing and cleaning it out as she went.

Han winced and tensed up beneath her, but he never made a sound. When she'd finished, she glanced up to find him watching her, his face soft.

A blush wound up her neck as she washed the blood from her hands with more seawater. Careful not to look at him again, she called for someone to help her press the sides of his flesh together while she stitched.

When she finally finished, she wrapped the wound with strips of boiled cotton, then mopped up the blood and water, wringing the filth into a bucket. She wiped imaginary blood of her hands and studied Han as he lay on the floor with his eyes closed. His scar was on this side. A lock of hair had fallen across his face, and she had to resist the sudden urge to smooth it back. She looked quickly away and began unstrapping her stolen armor and setting it in a neat pile.

Last, she felt the weight of Chen's pendant. She began to remove it, but Han reached toward the pendant before his hand fell back to his side. "That's the token of the imperial house."

"It was his."

Han's gaze met hers. "Wear it. Promise me."

She hesitated. "Why?"

"Just promise me."

She wanted to say no, but he'd already lost so much. She could give him this. She let the pendant fall back against her chest. "All right." She settled down beside him. "What will you do? You don't have to be a soldier anymore."

He took a deep breath. "I don't know how to be anything else."

"Will you come with us?"

Han opened his eyes to study her, and his gaze felt like the lick of flames against her skin. "You might need me yet."

Lilette wrung her hands as something warm and soft built in her middle. "I . . ." Her words grew thick and heavy in her throat. "Thank you. For what you did."

"Lilette . . ." He hesitated. "What did you mean when you said you were saved for this—just before you knocked me out?"

She cast him a sheepish glance. "My mother came to me when I lay dying. She said I had to save as many as I could. I knew that if I didn't free the witches, they would destroy Harshen, and somehow that would put into motion events that would destroy the world."

He blinked at her. "So now that you freed the witches, Harshen is safe?"

She let out a long breath. "Yes."

Han was silent a moment. "I never forgot you."

The delicious warmth in Lilette's middle spread outward.

He closed his eyes again. "You climbed into the cherry tree. I could barely see you through the blossoms."

"My first day in the garden behind the palace." Sometimes she forgot that all her memories of Rinnish were not tainted by ashes and burning.

She had climbed down and Han had shown her the fountain. They'd sat on the edge, their feet dangling in the water, while the flashing goldfish nibbled on their toes, and pink petals stuck to her wet legs. "You were teaching me to speak Harshen."

"You were lonely with no one to talk to."

She studied him, trying to make his face match the face of the kind little boy. "Why did you warn my parents?"

"You were my friend," he said simply.

She lay beside him, feeling the gentle swaying of the boat. Once her muscles relaxed, she could no longer move. "Thank you," she whispered. "Thank you for saving me. Again."

CHAPTER 20

That day I realized something was different about Lilette. Her song wasn't just strong, her witch sense wasn't just accurate. Something else was happening. ~Jolin

A hand on Lilette's shoulder shook her awake. Jolin crouched beside her. Han was nowhere to be seen. Lilette pushed the hair out of her face and sat up. Inside the hold, the heat of midday had made her tunic and trousers stick to her body. Her whole being ached, her heart worst of all, for her sister was gone.

Jolin gave her an orange and a cup of water. Eyes closed, Lilette held the fruit against her lips. She heard the tearing and smelled the orange rind as Jolin peeled her own breakfast. Lilette started into hers.

"We'll begin where we left off," Jolin said. "You're a fast learner."

Lilette took a bite of tangy sweetness. "I don't need lessons in the Creators' language—I remember it."

"When did that happen?"

Memories assaulted Lilette again. Her sister twirling in the air, tears streaming down her face as Chen and the emperor forced her to kill. Lilette frowned. "I don't want to talk about it."

Thankfully, Jolin let it go. She taught Lilette witch songs until it grew unbearably hot below decks. By then, Lilette's headache was better, so they went topsides. She held her hair up to let the breeze reach her neck while she looked for Han, but he was nowhere to be seen.

For lunch, they ate rice cooked on bolted-down braziers, and chewed on salt fish. There were mangoes, so sweet Lilette groaned with pleasure at her first bite. She sucked every last morsel off the pit before throwing it overboard.

By midafternoon, her head throbbed again and her thoughts were fuzzy. She held her hands over her ears. "Stop! My head can't fit anymore."

Jolin smiled to herself and Lilette realized that had been her goal—to fill Lilette's thoughts with something besides heartache over leaving her sister. She and Jolin took a nap curled under the shade of one of the masts.

When Lilette woke, the sun wasn't quite so hot, and a woman stood over them. She was a bit older than most of the keepers on board, and pale as a snail's belly.

Jolin quickly sat up. "Lilette, this is Nassa."

The woman sat down beside Lilette without so much as a glance at Jolin. "The famed Lilette. Your song was rumored to be strong enough to guarantee your place as Head of Light one day."

Lilette remembered singing for strangers—thousands of them. As a child of seven, she longed to play with her sister, dig in the garden behind their tree, or go swimming with her father. But there were always lessons and performances.

Shaking herself out of her memories, Lilette noticed the tension between her friend and Nassa. "Jolin?" she said hesitantly.

Geth moved toward them. "It's time," he said to Jolin.

She stood and brushed off her dress. "Geth agreed to let me stop at one of the smallest islands to gather the seeds I lost in Rinnish. I'll see you later."

Lilette watched her climb onto a small boat, a dozen guardians going with her. "Such a keen mind," Nassa said. "Such a shame it is wasted."

Lilette's gaze narrowed. "Jolin's mind hasn't been wasted."

Nassa tsked. "Well, not completely. She's brilliant with potions, but she cannot sing for her concoctions or even her garden. She has to have a keeper on hand to help her. That's why she'll never be Head of Plants, no matter how many breakthroughs she has."

Lilette watched as the boat was lowered. "I thought Plants was chosen because of proficiency with potions."

"Certainly, but a Head must be a full keeper, and Jolin will never move beyond an apprentice."

Before Lilette could respond, Nassa went on. "Let's test your song then." She held out a small seed between her forefinger and thumb.

Lilette hesitated before reaching out her hand. Nassa dropped the seed into her palm. She opened a little bag, spilled black soil across Lilette's palm, and drizzled it with a bit of water.

The water seeped through the soil, pooling in her palm. Something within her seemed to wake, stirring to the sounds of the wind and water. She sang softly.

> Take in light,
> Take in air.
> Spread thy roots,
> Thy leaves grow fair.

A shoot of green poked through the soil. Roots spread across Lilette's palm, soaking up the water. Two leaves appeared, and a flower grew between them.

Nassa gaped at the plant. "You only sang once!"

Enthralled with the power coursing through her, Lilette didn't immediately register the shock in Nassa's voice. But at the wary look on the older woman's face, the thrill seeped away like water through rocks.

"Sing it into seed. We'll need the pesnit if someone develops a fever."

Lilette sang again and the pretty flower aged, the leaves going a darker, older green before turning brown around the edges. She sang again and the flower curled up like a dead spider. A shriveled petal drifted down to the dirt on her palm.

Nassa caught the falling seeds in her hand and let out a breath. "Well, that's a more normal reaction. It usually takes three songs to achieve results—it's why we have guardians. We are powerful, but we're not fast. We balance each other." She held open a small leather bag. "Put the soil back. We can reuse it."

Lilette scraped the soil into the bag and brushed her hands together to dust off the remnants. Nassa tightened the drawstrings. "Well then, I'd estimate you between a level six and seven—very strong, and you'll certainly be a solid seven by the time we finish your voice lessons."

They practiced singing for hours, long after Jolin had returned and disappeared below decks, until Lilette could no longer hit the high notes and her throat felt tight and dry. After announcing that the lesson was over, Nassa studied Lilette with a calculating gleam in her eyes. "We'll have to start you as a witchling, but you'll advance quickly to an apprentice. Practice your scales every morning. I'll join you after the midday meal and we'll work some more on your pitch, power, and delivery." She didn't give Lilette time to ask questions. She simply stood, brushed off the back of her dress, and walked away.

Lilette's skin was beginning to burn in the relentless sun. She reluctantly moved down to the stuffy hold, where she spotted Jolin separating hundreds of seeds into squares of cloth spread out in front of her. She looked miserable. She didn't glance up as Lilette dropped down beside her and wrapped her arms around her knees. Lilette wiped the sweat on her forehead with the back of her arm and asked, "Is it this hot in Grove City?"

Jolin dropped a few more seeds into a piece of cloth. "Keepers control the weather, so it's pretty much perfect. It rains every night, with a gentle breeze and pleasant sunshine every day."

"It sounds wonderful."

When Jolin didn't respond, Lilette took a deep breath and ventured, "I'm sorry about what Nassa said."

"She's a leech. She knows you could easily become one of the most powerful women on Haven, and she'll use you to further her own plans."

Lilette watched Jolin painstakingly sort a few seeds the size of a grain of sand. "I don't like her."

"Neither do I, but she's the best at what she does." Jolin's voice held more than a touch of bitterness.

"She's wrong. You're not a waste."

"I know," Jolin said softly. "But it . . ."

"Hurts that others see you that way," Lilette finished.

Jolin turned away. "It isn't fair," she said so quietly Lilette could barely hear her over the sounds of the waves against the hull. "I should be Head of Plants—I deserve it. But without the song, I'm nothing."

Lilette took her time answering. "If the witches cannot recognize you for the brilliant woman you are—if they're blinded by power—then they are fools."

Jolin wiped at her eyes. "It doesn't help when a woman as beautiful as you has a voice like that, while mine is as plain as my face." She blanched as if she couldn't believe she'd been so blunt.

"I'm not perfect, and neither are you," Lilette replied, barely containing her sudden anger. "Let's just leave it at that."

Jolin grunted. "Beauty and power go hand in hand. Just be glad you're on the powerful end of things."

Lilette chuckled darkly. "Because being beautiful has made my life better?" She ran her hands through her hair and lifted it off her sweating neck. "People use me—nothing more."

Jolin gathered the corners of the squares of cloth and tied them up with a strip of twine. "Better than to be ignored and pitied."

Lilette leapt to her feet and strode toward the ladder.

"Lilette . . ." Jolin began.

She whirled around. "You think I don't know what it's like for people to never see past your face, to see what's inside? I know, Jolin, probably better than you do."

Lilette stormed back topsides, not even realizing what she was looking for until she found him. Han stood at the bow, leaning forward with his weight on his elbows. She moved beside him, mimicking his position. He eyed her sideways before looking back out at the water.

The ship was pulling away from the island. Some of Lilette's tension drained away, replaced by sadness. Han's entire demeanor had changed, as if the sight of his homeland fading away had bled the hope right out of him.

They were leaving Harshen, leaving Sash. The circle could only hold for another day and a half at most. "Now what?" Lilette said. "Will Chen . . . will he hurt my sister and the others?"

Han pressed his lips into a tight line. "They're the only protection he has against the witches. There's no going back."

"No," Lilette said.

A shudder rolled through Han, and he looked out to sea again. "The emperor was not a good man, but he was my father, and my actions resulted in his death." His voice remained steady, but anguish simmered beneath his words. "And my brother . . ."

To save her life, Han had lost everything. Lilette took a deep breath. "No, you did not betray anyone. Sometimes love and honor conflict, and you chose honor. You were loyal to your country . . . and to me." She couldn't fathom why. She'd been nothing but trouble for him.

His gaze finally met hers, and she saw the boy he'd once been—the boy who'd had kindness beaten out of him. But it was still there—still at the core of him.

"We should be enemies," he finally said. "But we never have been."

She leaned in and rested her temple on the point of his shoulder, as she had when they were children. "No. Never."

CHAPTER 21

Some are broken by grief. Others refined. The difference is a small but oft-made choice. ~Jolin

By their third day at sea, Lilette found herself at the bow, watching for the land Jolin said would come into sight at any time.

Han walked over to stand beside her. "Geth said you wanted to see me?"

Eyes watering, she held her hand out to block some of the light. "Shh, just watch."

The sun finally slipped below the horizon, backlighting a thin, dark streak. "There." She pointed. "That's Kalari." The homeland of the witches.

He squinted into the light. "Are you sure?"

Lilette smiled up at him. "I'm sure." She looked back at the horizon, but the brief flash of land was gone. "Now we follow the coast for three days, and then we'll reach Grove City." Her voice shook as she added, "The circle is broken by now."

His gaze fell. "I know."

She braced herself to ask her real question. "You're sure he won't kill her?"

Han looked at Lilette, his gaze steady. "I'm sure."

"What will he do to them?"

"Bind them up, better than he did before."

"Will he hurt her?"

"Not unless he has to."

Lilette felt the wind caressing her face. "Will he force them to sing again?"

"To protect Harshen? Absolutely. I'm hoping that with Father dead Chen will hold off the invasion." Han hesitated. "There's talk among the guardians."

Her eyes scanned the endless horizon. "About?"

He shifted so he was a little closer. Lilette was very aware of his arm touching hers, the warmth building between her skin and his. "They say you're stronger than any other witch they've ever heard."

"What does that have to do with us?"

He went on as if she hadn't spoken. "There's even talk that you'll be a discipline head someday—I'm guessing that's like the witches' emperor."

"There are four discipline heads who rule over the four elements—earth, plants, water, and light—and all the followers for each element." Nassa had explained all this to Lilette earlier.

He studied her, a sadness weighing down his face. "They're already vying over who will be your guardian."

Lilette turned away. "Nassa says I won't have a guardian until I've passed all the courses. I'll start out as a witchling with a bunch of little girls."

Han traced the grain of the wood. "You won't stay a witchling for long." He turned to face her, his expression open and tender. She saw past the scar, past the scowl he wore to protect himself. He was beautiful—just like Jolin was. But neither of them could see it.

"The point is," he went on, "you're a little intimidating."

"I don't mean to be."

"You are who you are."

Lilette looked at him sidelong. "You could be my guardian."

"Why me?"

Her cheeks grew warm. "I'm not, well—you're very good with those swords. And you're kind. You helped me when no one else would have, and I . . ." Her words trailed into nothing.

"You can do better than me, little dragon," Han said softly.

Tears suddenly welled in her eyes. He'd made some kind of decision. She could see it in his eyes. "What are you going to do?"

He hesitated a moment. "Somebody has to fight for Harshen, Lilette."

"Fight how?"

"I have to negotiate a peace—one that involves the return of your witches and the safety and prosperity of my people."

"I will help you."

"What about becoming a witch?"

"I can do both. Besides, I promised you I would look after Harshen. I mean to keep that promise."

"Lilette—"

She whirled on him so fast her head ached. "Don't. They are my people too." Her words surprised even her. Harshen and its people had not always been good to her. But then she thought of Fa, Salfe, and Pan. Ko and Lang, and of course Han, and she could not find hatred in her heart.

His jaw tightened and he gave a quick nod.

"What's the plan?" Lilette asked.

"We plead Harshen's case. Talk to whomever we have to."

"Figure it out as we go. I like it." Sounded just like her kind of plan.

Han chuckled. "We can't exactly plan a battle without knowing the battlefield."

"Right. I agree." She tried to sound more confident than she felt. "What about . . . what about . . . ." She paused. "I know you have feelings for me."

He looked away and braced himself against the gunwales. "Lilette . . . it seems like whenever we're together, others get hurt."

Something dark formed inside her. "Don't."

"I don't think—"

"No. I won't let you say goodbye." She glared at Han, daring him to look at her. When he finally did, she leaned forward and pressed a kiss to his lips. He blinked at her, clearly stunned.

A thrill raced through her. "Think about that, Han. See if you don't change your mind."

She turned and walked across the deck, feeling more than one pair of eyes following her as she climbed into the hold. After sitting in her hammock, she drew her knees up to her chest.

Jolin came to stand before her. She cleared her throat uncomfortably. "I wanted to say I'm sorry. I'm an idiot."

Lilette huffed. "Yes, you are."

"Scoot over."

Lilette wiggled to one side. "It's hard in these things."

Jolin climbed in. "Where have you been?"

"Just plotting to save the world."

"With whom?"

Lilette refused to meet her gaze. "No one."

"Oh, I've seen no one before. Does no one wear a sword and a scowl?"

Lilette shrugged. "I might have kissed him."

Jolin gaped at her. "Isn't he your brother-in-law?"

A wicked grin crept onto Lilette's face. "Well, if they can have more than one wife, why can't I have more than one husband?"

"Lilette!" Jolin sounded appalled.

"Technically, I'm already on my second husband."

"Your second?"

Lilette giggled. "What's another one?"

Jolin's eyes were the size of sand dollars. "So . . . Han?"

Lilette clamped her hand over her mouth to keep her mad laughter inside. "Yes."

"Well, I can't see it. But then I love sardines. Who am I to judge?"

Lilette's nose wrinkled. "Sardines are disgusting."

"I know! But they're deliciously disgusting."

Lilette dissolved into another fit of giggling.

Jolin's gaze went faraway and dreamy. "I've only ever kissed one man—he was the one who introduced me to sardines. I think that's why I liked him."

Lilette burst out laughing. "Because he tasted like sardines?"

Jolin smacked her, but she was smiling. "No. Because he made me try something new. He's the reason I went on this trip. He said that in order to get conclusive results, I needed a larger sampling."

"You shouldn't listen to his advice ever again." Lilette laughed so hard she snorted. Jolin finally gave in, and soon both were laughing so hard Lilette's side felt like it might split open. But she needed this. Because if she didn't laugh, she really might go mad with grief.

For the next three days, she didn't have time to dwell on her sadness about Sash. Jolin and Nassa stuffed her head full of songs, singing lessons, and plant lessons. Lilette practiced singing until her throat hurt and her voice sounded scratchy and rough.

Every once in a while, something seemed to tighten within her, catching the song and pooling it inside. At those times, her voice grew sweeter, stronger. She caught other witches watching her, their faces filled with awe or jealousy or both.

On their sixth day at sea, Lilette was singing in the hold with Nassa. She didn't know her voice could reach so high, that she could hold a note for so long.

Nassa nodded encouragingly, a hungry look in her eyes. "Yes, very good. But you still need to work on pulling from deep in your belly—that's where your power comes from. That's how you project your voice." Nassa settled herself deeper in her hammock. "Now try again."

Lilette filled her lungs and sat up straight, her shoulders thrown back and her mind sharp. She started singing. The sounds she made were nonsense—they weren't important. It was the interplay of the notes, the rise and fall of the cadence, the power she gave up or withheld. The world perked up around her, the elements slowed like a marketful of people stopping a million different tasks at the same time to turn toward her.

"Good." Nassa fanned her own sunburned skin. "You can feel the elements, can't you? You can feel them waiting for your commands."

Lilette didn't answer. She couldn't. She was too enraptured by the power dancing from her mouth. All she had to do was change the nonsense into the Creators' language and the elements would respond—they were eager for it. As eager as she was.

Sweat ran down her back, soaking into the already-damp material at her waist. Though the day was tripping toward evening, the midday heat had baked into the hold, filling her nostrils with the smell of resin and sour sweat.

An idea formed in Lilette's mind. Her mouth formed the words, releasing them like dancers leaping from her tongue. Nassa's expression changed to worry, but Lilette ignored her. The wind teased down through the hatch, wrapping around her body and wicking away her sweat. The other people in the hold sighed in relief. Lilette smiled and concentrated on the joy of connecting with the elements.

"You did it again."

Lilette shook herself out of her reverie to find Nassa bolt upright, watching her. "You controlled the elements with a single song, and with such precision."

The rapture fled Lilette. "I'm sorry."

Nassa stared at her. "I think, Lilette, that you may be the most powerful witch ever born."

Lilette didn't try to protest. How could she when she could still feel the buzz of power inside her? Thankfully, a flurry of activity above decks distracted Nassa.

Han poked his head down below the hold, his eyes finding Lilette's. "They've spotted the bay."

She untangled herself from her hammock and tried to straighten the wrinkles out of her cotton tunic and trousers. She'd been wearing them constantly for six days and finally decided they were beyond helping. She debated slipping the armor back on, but it was so hot, and it wasn't as if she was going into a battle.

Foot tapping, Lilette waited her turn to climb the ladder. Luckily, she was taller than most of the women, so she could see the mountains—more like very large hills—that dotted the land.

One of these mountains was surrounded by circular, gray stone ramparts, with towers evenly spaced along it.

Instead of a city inside, there were trees—huge trees. Her mind kept trying to compensate for their size by insisting the ship was closer to shore than it was, which threw off her sense of distance and made her head hurt.

They turned into the bay. Hundreds of boats were docked in the wharves, but they were so tiny. Then Lilette saw the first person on shore and suddenly everything clicked into place. The trees were mountains unto themselves.

She craned her head back and still couldn't see the tops. The branches reached so high into the sky they mingled with the clouds. Light reflected off mirrors hanging from the tree trunks. But then a woman leaned out of a tree to call to someone below.

Those weren't mirrors. They were windows. And the trees weren't just trees. They were houses. Around some of the windows, balconies had grown of twisted branches. Some of those balconies were connected by elegant bridges, which people crossed, going from one tree to another. How had Lilette forgotten this?

Rubbing at a cramp in her neck, she watched keepers and guardians go in and out of the trees like ants—only through doors, which wasn't like ants at all. "I have to sit down," she said to no one in particular. She plunked down on the deck and rested her forehead on her knees.

Someone laughed at her. Lilette tipped her head back to find Jolin looking down at her. "Wait until you see Haven. Bethel isn't finished yet, but those cliffs take your breath away."

"Bethel?"

Jolin's gaze hardened. "She's the most famous keeper alive."

"Are we going to Haven now?" Lilette wasn't sure she could handle any more shocks today.

Jolin shook her head. "No. You'll need to report to the Heads. They live on the highest peak in Grove City." She pointed to a tree that towered above the rest, so high Lilette could see the top even from where she sat surrounded by people.

Lilette stared at the sky, which was slowly being blotted out by trees. "Grove City—the city is an actual grove."

"Don't you remember?"

Lilette shook her head. What else had she forgotten? "How is it the wind doesn't blow them down?"

Jolin gave her an exasperated look.

"Because the witches control the wind," Lilette said with sudden realization.

To her right, people shifted. She looked through dozens of pairs of legs and saw one in particular moving toward her. She recognized those shin guards. Looking up at Han's face, all she could think was that she'd kissed him. And she wanted to do it again.

He crouched beside her. "Are you all right?"

"Han, they live in the trees."

He smiled a little crookedly. "Well, they are witches. Come on. Geth wants your help docking the ship." Han helped her up and placed his hand on the small of her back. The pleasure of his touch spread through her.

"Creators help us." Jolin threw her hands in the air.

Once at the bow, Lilette called out orders for the sails and makeshift rudder. By now, the guardians were proficient at working both, so they didn't need much guidance. The zhou pulled into the docks and was tied off.

Geth called out to a man who came to meet their ship and explained who they were. The man looked the vessel over with a keen eye and said, "Leader Gyn? Keeper Sash?"

Geth shook his head. "Lost. I'm Leader Geth. This is Lilette. She was made Point in Harshen."

The man looked them over, his gaze lingering curiously on Lilette. "The Heads are waiting for your report. I'll let them know you're coming. The rest of you report back to your disciplines."

Report to the most powerful women in the world? Lilette tried to keep her panic from showing.

Geth studied her before he turned to Jolin. "You best come along and help Lilette become acclimated."

Lilette cast him a grateful look. With a smile, he ushered them from the ship. Just beyond the docks, she got a true sense of the size of the ramparts surrounding Grove City. Compared to the trees that towered above it, it was rather small, until one considered that it was easily the height of fifty men. Just gazing at the top made Lilette dizzy. She looked closer and couldn't see seams or bricks. Her jaw dropped. It was all one long, seamless piece of stone.

"How is this possible?" she asked.

"We are well protected," Jolin said with a touch of pride.

They approached the main gates—a statue of a witch and a guardian, standing as sentinels on either side. Their crossed weapons—a green, growing staff and a sword—formed the gate's arch and made it look like the entire wall was part of the barrier. The group passed beneath the shadows of the archway. It took Lilette easily thirty steps to reach the other side.

When she stepped into the open air, she couldn't stop staring at the trees. The tops of the doors and windows were peaked. Some were at ground level, nestled between the buttressed roots. Others sat at the top of long stairs made of the trees' roots.

It was obviously a city, but not one laid out on a grid. It should have been messy, but there was an overarching pattern in the placement of the trees, which were far enough apart for the sun to pass between them, and the curve of the path like the bends of a river. Lilette wondered how long it would take her just to walk around one tree.

Once her shock at the size of the trees started to wear off, she realized the city didn't smell like any she'd ever visited. Instead of the sickening smell of human waste mixed with smoke and food, Grove City smelled of flowers, a rich kind of resin, and the mineral tang of the ocean.

People hustled in and out of the trees, a sense of agitation in the way they moved. "Apparently, word has spread about what happened in Harshen," Jolin said.

The trees' buttress roots jutted up against the paths. Inside some of these natural alcoves, merchants had set up shops—

some complete with canvas awnings. The stalls featured hand-dyed silk, copper cutlery, leather goods, shoes, food, and many other items.

"Pretty necklace for a pretty lady!" a merchant with a curling mustache called as they approached. From the tree house behind him, a witch began singing to pots arranged before her. The plants started growing, but so did all the other plants within the sound of her voice. Around the vendor, vines edged over his table of wares, shifting the jewelry.

A dangling earring caught on the beginnings of a leaf. The plant grew upward, taking the earring with it. The merchant snatched the earring just before it grew out of his reach. A fern edged around his clothes, feeler vines climbing up his mustache. He took out a pair of shears, and with a loud harrumph, he tugged the vine free and cut the plants back at the roots. In the process, he accidentally cut off part of his mustache. All around him, merchants were hacking plants down, but almost as quickly, the plants grew back.

Finally, the witch stopped singing. The frantic cutting slowed before merchants began straightening their wares and discarding cut bits of leaves from the tables.

"Does this happen often?" Lilette asked Jolin.

"A hazard of living with this many witches in one place."

Once they began climbing the hill in earnest, Lilette found it difficult to keep up. Han studied her with obvious concern and asked her if she was all right.

She pressed the palm of her hand over her heart. "Perfect," she gasped.

He stepped closer. "I can carry you."

She shot him a glare. From in front of them, Jolin mumbled something under her breath about sardines and scowls.

"We're not in a hurry," Geth said to their guide.

Lilette hated that they had to slow down for her, but there was nothing she could do about it.

As they neared the top of the hill, the trees looked older—even ancient. The group crossed beneath a wicked-looking hedge covered in curved, cruel thorns the size of Lilette's thumb. Tiny yellow flowers with red centers bloomed throughout, giving off a sweet, light fragrance.

Beyond them, along the perimeter, two rows of trees stretched as far as Lilette could see. She immediately recognized them—barrier trees. She stared up at them nervously as she and the others came within reach, but the trees didn't move except to shift with the breeze.

At this elevation, Lilette could look back at the ramparts, and it suddenly occurred to her that it appeared much like a brazier filled with wood. "What about fire?" she asked.

Jolin waved her hand dismissively. "Fires have happened before. The witches simply call in a storm to dampen any flames. If anyone were ever foolish enough to attack us, we could grow thorns beneath their army's feet so fast they would never even reach the ramparts."

Lilette took a deep breath to calm the panic in her heart. "So the only way to fight the witches is with more witches. What's to stop someone like the emperor from trying again—and this time succeeding?"

"We were placed here at the beginning of the world to keep and protect," Jolin said. "What Emperor Nis did was an anomaly."

The words did nothing to calm the foreboding in Lilette's heart. "What happens when other countries realize how close the emperor came to succeeding? How easily the keepers can be subdued and forced to destroy an entire nation?"

Jolin shook her head. "It won't happen. Stop worrying."

"What if you're wrong?" Lilette asked softly.

"Then the world will fall."

CHAPTER 22

Lilette had the kind of beauty that men went to war over.
Sometimes I hated her for it. ~Jolin

L ilette and her group were ushered into a raised pavilion. Climbing vines clung to the trellis and made a roof of leaves. Enormous potted plants were everywhere. Some held trees loaded with ripe fruit. Other pots overflowed with flowers that perfumed the air with their heady fragrance. Some pots held different kinds of herbs lined up in neat rows. In the background was singing. Not the dark, sharp-edged songs that turned Lilette's stomach, but the gentle, growing songs that made the very air throb with life.

Keepers and guardians milled about, but they stopped what they were doing as Lilette and the rest of her group walked in. *How ragged we must look,* she thought. There had been no privacy aboard the ship, but she'd managed to wash her tunic and trousers and to scrub herself with a rag dampened with seawater. Without a comb, she'd simply run her fingers through her hair and braided it in the traditional fashion of the women of her village.

They approached the center of the enormous pavilion. Sitting on marble chairs on a dais were four women surrounded by people—it was clearly some kind of meeting. The man who'd fetched Lilette and the others from the ship approached a desk off to the side and spoke to half a dozen women in simple gray dresses with matching veils covering their hair.

Jolin leaned close and whispered to Lilette, "Each Head represents one of the elements. The redhead, Garen, is Head of Plants. The older woman, Brine, is Head of Water. Tawny is the dark one with the cropped hair—she's Head of Earth. And the young one is Merlay, Head of Light."

Merlay. She was the one Sash had said to trust. Lilette would have to speak with her when the council ended.

The women looked nothing like each other—old and young, light and dark—but despite their differences in appearance, they all wore the same mantle of authority. Lilette counted a dozen guardians stationed around the pavilion, their gazes wary.

One of the veiled women rose and went to whisper in Brine's ear. The older woman clapped her hands. "Everyone out."

"Who are the women with the veils?" Lilette quietly asked Jolin.

"They're wastrels—servants of the keepers."

The term was vaguely familiar, and the associations Lilette had were not positive.

Brine inclined her frothy gray head. "We'll keep this short, as we are all very busy with the situation in Harshen. I recognize you, Guardian, though I don't recall your name."

Geth half bowed. "I am Geth, second to Leader Gyn."

"I'm assuming Gyn is dead?" Brine asked, then scrawled something on a parchment a wastrel held for her.

"I believe so," Geth responded.

Brine waved the wastrel off. "Most unfortunate. He was a good guardian." She removed some of her own parchment and took out a quill. "We already know much of what has passed in Harshen. We simply need you to fill in the gaps." Geth nodded. "How many of you returned?" Brine asked.

Geth swallowed. "Of the thirty-six witches to depart, only nineteen have returned. Of the sixty-eight guardians, only twenty-two."

Remembering how so many of them had died, Lilette winced.

Brine marked it down in her notes. "I'll assign someone to debrief the survivors shortly."

Fury flashed through Lilette at Brine's matter-of-fact attitude. She was suddenly there again, soaked to the skin as lightning flashed. Her last glimpse of her sister's face. The elephant's heart-rending cry. Lilette squeezed her eyes shut and tamped the memories back.

"And Point Sash?" Brine went on.

Lilette had to bite her tongue to keep from screaming. Geth cut a glance at her. "She and the others stayed behind to create a circle so we could escape."

Merlay covered her mouth with her hand.

"The ones left behind—I assume they're dead?" Brine didn't even look up from her notes.

"Chen has a temper," Han spoke up. "But he needs those witches. There's a good chance they're still alive."

"And who are you?"

"Han, second son of the Golden Dragon."

Brine's eyebrows rose. "That makes you a prince."

"Yes. A prince and a representative for Harshen. I have come to negotiate our peaceful surrender."

Lilette gaped at Han as if she'd never seen him before. The emperor had over five hundred children, and only one of them was named heir. Han didn't have the authority to negotiate anything.

The Heads seemed equally shocked. "Your father authorized this?" Brine asked.

"He's dead," Han said in a voice like steel.

Brine's gaze narrowed. "So you're the new emperor?"

Han's face went red, making his scar stand out. "No. My brother Chen is emperor now."

Merlay watched him through lowered lids. "You said our witches might be alive. You don't know?"

"Not for certain."

Brine pointed her quill at him. "You have no authority to act for Harshen. Why are you wasting my time?"

Lilette stepped forward. "He can help you."

Brine shot her a look full of impatience. "And who are you?"

"I'm the empress." Creators' mercy, she really was. She hadn't realized it until now.

"It cannot be," Merlay said, her face pale.

Tawny gaped at Lilette. "But you're white!"

"You're not," she replied.

A slow smile spread across Tawny's face. "I see we're both observant."

Brine rolled her eyes and looked at Lilette again. "Are you authorized to act in Harshen's behalf?"

"I don't need to be," she answered. Han stiffened beside her, but if he could exaggerate, so could she.

Brine sighed. "I'm fast losing my patience."

"You must depose Chen," Lilette said, "and put Han in his place."

"And how are we to do that?" Brine asked brusquely. "We do not have a standing army."

"You don't need one. Cut off Harshen's rains until they release our witches and dispose of Chen."

Brine studied her. "What is your name, Empress, and how do you know so much of us?"

"She's a witch." Merlay's face was drawn. The other three Heads stared at Lilette.

"My name is Lilette. I was shipwrecked in Harshen as a child."

Tawny and Garen exchanged hushed whispers, while Merlay looked as if she might be sick.

Good. They'd heard of her. Hopefully that would help.

"So it's true," Garen breathed. "Harshen really did sink our ship and . . . kill your parents."

Lilette fought the memory, but it welled up from deep within her, drowning her with images she wished she could banish forever. "Elite boarded our ship. My mother and I barricaded ourselves in the captain's cabin. I was very young—only eight. We set the ship afire to hide our escape." Her mother was crying. Her father was dead. The ship was burning too fast, flames licking her mother's feet. The smoke was so thick Lilette couldn't breathe.

"My mother shoved me in a pickle barrel." Then she'd kissed Lilette, her lips damp with tears or sweat or both. Stuffed so tight into a pickle barrel she could barely move, her eyes stinging with a mixture of smoke and vinegar vapors. "There was an explosion." Careening through the air before slamming into the water.

"My mother didn't make it." The imperial soldiers had found her body, had pulled her into their boat. But they hadn't found Lilette. The next day, she'd managed to escape the barrel, though she'd nearly drowned in the process. She'd sung herself a current and spent two days at sea before Fa had found her and taken her in. Years later, that kindness had been repaid with death and destruction.

The silence in the room finally pulled Lilette out of her memories. Witches and guardians had gathered around her as she'd spoken.

Brine waved them away. "The meeting is cancelled. We'll resume again tomorrow." But no one made a move to leave.

"So it was you our listeners heard." Garen had a different accent from the rest—it sounded warm and rolling. She turned to the other Heads. "But why didn't they find her earlier?"

"Back to the matter at hand," Brine said. "Deposing Chen and letting his brother take his place does little to satisfy justice."

"What about mercy?" Lilette asked.

Brine's steel-gray eyes flashed. "And what mercy did Chen and his murderer of a father show the seventeen witches and thirty-eight guardians who are now dead or imprisoned by Harshen hands—let alone your parents and the guardians killed years ago?"

Lilette stared at her. "How did you expect Harshen to react when you brought Vorlay's ships to their door? They were only protecting themselves!" Why was she standing up for Harshen?

Brine shot to her feet. "We did no such thing!"

Lilette eyed her. "You did. I know it, and every one of the witches with me knows it." She looked pointedly at Jolin.

Her friend cleared her throat. "It's true."

Brine turned to the others. "Did any of you do this?"

The other three Heads vehemently denied it.

"Tawny, have your listeners felt someone singing illicitly?" Brine asked.

"Of course not!"

Brine's gaze slowly swung back to Lilette, but the Head of Water gestured to one of the wastrels. "Interview the returning witches—all of them. Now. I want reports delivered in batches of ten."

The woman hastily wrote something before darting away. Brine steepled her fingers and stared at Lilette.

"Brine—" Merlay began.

"Silence," she said, her tone brokering no argument. "In times of war, I lead. If Lilette and Jolin are telling the truth, some other force is at play, perhaps skewing our perceptions. I will hold private council with the guardians." Brine rose to her feet.

Han took a step toward her. "If your witches are still alive—if we can get them back—will you negotiate peace?"

Brine's cool gaze settled on him. "I'm afraid it's not that simple, Prince. Your father's actions have made us look vulnerable. In order to prevent things like this from happening in the future, we must have a decisive show of strength now."

Lilette gestured toward Harshen. "But—"

Brine held up her hand. "Nothing matters until we find out if our witches are still alive. We sent our spies days ago. We should hear back from them soon. If Chen uses our witches to sing, our listeners will pick up on it immediately." She lowered her hand. "And if he uses them to sing against Grove City or any other nation, I'll bring every last witch I have down on him until there's nothing left." She pivoted and marched away.

"What shall we do with the empress and the prince?" Garen called after her.

"Neither of them leaves the inner city," Brine replied over her shoulder. "Other than that, treat them as guests." Guardians and wastrels converged on Brine as she kept walking.

Merlay stepped down from the dais and stood before Lilette, her gaze searching. She seemed barely able to keep her emotions in check. "You're exhausted. Come with me."

The crowd swarmed the remaining two Heads. Conversations started up while wastrels bustled about taking notes and carrying messages. Merlay cut through the crowd.

"Wait." Lilette hurried to catch up with her. "What about my sister and the others?"

"Try not to worry," Merlay replied, not looking back. "Everything that can be done will be."

Lilette shot Han an exasperated look. "What exactly can be done?"

"Brine will meet with Leader Farth. They'll garner reports from the spies and form a plan."

"But—"

Merlay turned. "At a minimum, our keepers' safe release and Chen stepping down as emperor will be terms of their unconditional surrender. Trust me."

"You have to let me help," Lilette said. "I promised I would go back for her."

Merlay's steady gaze met hers. "And what would you do? Will you storm the ramparts? Demand Chen release her? Bring an army down on the city?"

Lilette opened her mouth but no words came out.

Merlay's expression softened. "The truth is, there's nothing you can do. Nothing but wait. Let us handle it." She offered a small smile and strode away.

Lilette didn't follow her. Jolin was trying to speak with Lilette, but the words circled like sharks—all sharp teeth and terrible speed. Lilette remembered the last time she'd seen Sash. The circle could have held for three, maybe four days. By now, everyone inside was at Chen's mercy. Lilette knew that mercy all too well.

Han took her elbow to guide her through the press of people. She leaned gratefully into him, closing her eyes to the overwhelming sights and sounds. "I lost my sister before I ever knew her," she said.

"You don't know that," Han replied. "They should be safe for as long as he needs them."

Lilette felt sunshine on her face. They must be out of the pavilion now. "And if you're wrong?"

The sounds of the crowd were fading. Lilette blinked up at the canopy, a dark lace of leaves against the indigo sky.

"You haven't lost everything," Han finally said.

CHAPTER 23

The first night Han saw Lilette, he betrayed his brother for her.
If that is not proof of love at first sight, I don't know what is.
~Jolin

The fading light cast shadows across Merlay's face as she paused in front of the strange tree, steam drifting between the walls of woven sapling trunks. She looked pointedly at Han and gestured to a nearly identical tree set a little farther back. "That's the men's bathing tree."

"You'll be all right?" he asked Lilette.

Not meeting his gaze, she nodded.

He leaned into her, his breath brushing against her skin. "Take your time. I'll be waiting." Lilette watched him walk away.

Merlay folded her arms across her chest. "Jolin, if you will excuse us."

Jolin shot an apologetic glance at Lilette before disappearing inside.

Merlay studied her. "You look like Sash. The same nose and eyes, but your jaw is finer, and her hair was wavy."

Tears sprang to Lilette's eyes. "What was she like?"

"She was smart. A good singer. And she hated fruit."

"Fruit? Who hates fruit?"

Merlay gave a little chuckle. "I know. She was odd, but she was also my friend." She was silent for a time. "I remember Lellan—you remember the ones who die." She took a deep breath. "If only Sash had known—if any of us had known you were alive, we would have come for you."

Lilette blinked back tears.

"There has been no trace of you for eight years. We all thought you dead."

"I washed up on an island and was cared for by a man who raised me as his own."

"But—" Merlay seemed to gather herself "—our listeners should have picked up on you."

"I never sang."

Merlay's eyebrows shot up. "Never?"

"Not until a few weeks ago."

"Why not?"

"The man who took me in—he made me promise."

Merlay's gaze sharpened. "Why?"

"Because our village lord wouldn't have left me alone if he'd known." Lilette didn't want to talk about Bian or her first betrothal. "Harshen told you our ship sank, but . . . why did you believe them?"

Merlay let out a long breath. "Even witches can die in fires, Lilette. We had no proof of foul play."

A wastrel approached, scroll in hand. "Head Merlay, the others request your presence."

Merlay sighed. "Very well." The wastrel bowed and stepped back.

"How long will we be stuck here?" Lilette asked.

"For you, probably not long. Han is another story." Merlay pointed down the hill. "Brine will have already sent a wastrel to alert the inner city guards that he is not to pass. Please send the word along. None of you want to be at the receiving end of Brine's temper, trust me."

Lilette pursed her lips and said nothing.

"I have more questions, but I'm afraid things are rather chaotic right now. I'll send a wastrel to bring you to me sometime in the morning." With that, Merlay started back to the pavilion.

Lilette stepped through the arched doorway. Inside was a pool of turquoise water. Steam dewed against her skin, making her feel the grit of her journey more keenly.

Jolin was already in the water, her dress neatly folded on a long shelf. "No wonder you forgot," she said softly. "I would have wanted to forget too."

Lilette didn't want to talk about it. She stripped off her clothes and dropped them on the floor with the pendant and her comb on top. "Merlay seems a little young to be in such a powerful position."

Jolin looked away. "She became a Head of Light at twenty."

"Really?"

"Heads of Light are always young. The Creators choose them by gifting a keeper with the strongest song of any woman alive. Heads of Plants are usually older—it takes years to gain that kind of proficiency with potions. The Head of Earth is the one with the strongest witch sense—usually a listener. And Head of Water is chosen because of her brilliant military tactics—she's usually the oldest of them all."

"What about what's best for the elements and the people? Who represents them?"

Jolin looked at Lilette as if she was daft. Deciding to let it go, Lilette stepped into the water. It was so hot she had to ease into it, but once she adjusted, her muscles relaxed. The dirt caked into her pores finally came free. She found a cache of soaps and scrubbed herself three times before she felt completely clean. A serving woman came in and took Lilette's and Jolin's salt-crusted clothes, leaving the pendant and comb on the shelf. Jolin explained that the clothes were being taken to be washed.

Lilette floated in the water, her hair curling around her head like the steam from a cup. Her palms grew as wrinkled as the surface of the ocean, her skin as pale as a fish's underbelly. As darkness fell, a woman dressed in gray came and lit lamps along the walls.

Floating in the water reminded Lilette of home. She missed the ocean, her fishing vessel beneath her, a pod of dolphins leaping in pace with her bow, the gritty feel of salt on her cheeks. She missed Fa's steady, quiet presence, and falling asleep to the sound of rushing waves.

Through the water, she heard someone speaking. Tucking her legs under her, she sat up. A woman stood at the edge of the pool, towels in hand. "I'm to show you to your tree, keepers."

Lilette stood, water sluicing down her skin. Jolin still floated, half asleep. "Jolin." When she didn't respond, Lilette splashed her. "Jolin!"

Jolin sputtered as she stood up, rubbing water from her eyes. She glared at Lilette before noticing the wastrel. "Time to go already?"

They climbed out of the water. The woman handed them green dresses in a plush material with embossed filigree patterns. Lilette scowled at the dress, but they hadn't returned her tunic and trousers so she had no choice but to put the dress on. Next she donned the stockings and lace-up boots.

Wet hair clinging to her face, she stared at the pendant and considered leaving it there. But she remembered what Han had told her—how this pendant had been in his family for generations. It was part of Harshen's history. It was part of Lilette's home.

She froze. She'd never thought of Harshen as home, but it had shaped her. It was part of her. She picked the pendant up, staring into its amber depths before slipping it on and tucking it inside her dress.

Jolin stood in an alcove, parting her jaw-length hair exactly down the middle. Lilette moved in beside her and wiped the condensation from the mirror, her palm squeaking against the glass. She stared at herself, blurred and distorted by the imperfections in the mirror and the water running down it in streaks. Her eyes were bloodshot, and her face was pink and peeling from sunburn. Her eyes held a hunted, hard look. She didn't recognize the girl staring back, and that frightened her more than anything.

Keeping her eyes averted from the mirror, she randomly chose a bottle of oil and rubbed several drops of it into her tresses. The oil smelled of something fresh and light—like bottled sunshine. She laboriously untangled her hair from the ends up before twisting it in a bun at the top of her head. Last, she slide her comb into place.

She felt a small measure of relief. "When will we have our things back?" Lilette directed her question at the wastrel. The armor and clothes were Han's, after all.

"Sometime tomorrow," the woman replied.

Lilette and Jolin followed her out of the tree. Han silently moved to Lilette's side as if he'd been waiting for her. He was still dressed in his leather armor, like he expected trouble even here.

"Didn't they take your things to launder?" Lilette gestured to his armor.

"I always care for my own equipment." There was a hint of mistrust in his tone, and Lilette wondered if she shouldn't have let them take his other set of clothing.

They started downhill, following the woman through the twisting paths of the inner city. Lilette moved closer to Han. His arm brushed hers, and she had to resist the urge to lean into the steel-and-leather smell of him.

As they started up a rise, the hem of her skirt tangled around her feet. His hand shot out, grabbing her arm to keep her from falling. She steadied herself against the side of his leather breastplate. "Why do you wear these things?" she asked.

"You have to hold up the hem a little, especially when you're climbing." Jolin demonstrated, her own skirt lifted in her hands.

Lilette copied her, and the hem no longer tripped up her feet, but her hand was full of skirts. It seemed a ridiculous waste of energy.

They passed another group of women wearing the wastrel's drab dress. All of them nodded to the wastrel and eyed Lilette curiously. Jolin dropped back to walk beside them. "You shouldn't stare, Lilette. Wastrels of the inner city all wear the uniform and hair veil. Witchlings and apprentices wear dark green. Keepers wear what they want."

Lilette forced her gaze away as the cluster of women continued past them. Then she looked down at her own dress. "If they can wear what they want, why dresses?"

Jolin hefted her dark green skirt to climb the steps to a door, where the wastrel was already waiting for them. "That you will have to ask of someone smarter than I."

The wastrel motioned for them to enter. As soon as they were all inside, she shut the door behind them and said, "The nearest food pavilion is a short walk down this trail. Meals are available morning, midday, and eve, with fruit and bread on hand at all times. There is a room upstairs with beds. I took the liberty of bringing a light meal for you."

Lilette marveled at the simplicity and beauty of the room. Everything was made of pale wood that blended seamlessly from floor to ceiling, and ceiling to floor. In the center stood a magnificent spiral staircase, shoots of pale wood anchoring it to the walls above their heads. Off to the side was a small cooking stove bolted to a brick platform. The tabletop sat much higher off the floor than a Harshen's low table.

She had a sudden memory of herself as a child, eating a bowl of soup, her legs swinging through the open air as she sat at a similar table. Her father had chided her to tuck her hair behind her ears so the ends wouldn't hang in the broth. Overcome with the remembrance, Lilette stared blankly at the platter of fruit, cheese, and bread.

Han brushed his fingers along the back of her hand. "Are you all right?"

She let out a slow breath and turned to him. "I've forgotten so much, and it's coming back to me now."

His expression softened. "I hope they're good memories?"

Lilette shrugged. "Sometimes."

Suddenly the door burst open behind them. Han whipped around, his hand on his sword.

A woman with brown hair threaded with gray stood in the doorway. Her gaze locked on Jolin. "You're late."

Jolin's mouth tightened. "We were delayed."

"So I heard." The woman's gaze flicked to Han's hand on his sword. Then her gaze settled on Lilette. "You should not have come back."

Lilette took a step back. "What?"

The woman stepped into the room. Behind her came two others—a balding guardian, his gaze sweeping the area as he maneuvered ahead of her, and a sour-faced wastrel.

The first woman's gaze locked on the wastrel from the bathhouse. "Who are you?"

"W–what?" the girl stammered

"Never mind," the woman said. "Get out. Your services are no longer needed. Doranna" —she motioned to the wastrel behind her— "take care of the tray."

"Don't," Jolin said, her face ashen.

Doranna gathered up the food tray and dumped it out the front door.

The first wastrel finally found her voice. "I was assigned here. You can't just—"

"Well, I just unassigned you," the woman interrupted, sitting down on one of the chairs.

"And who are you to—"

"My name is Bethel," the woman replied as she brushed some crumbs off the table. The wastrel's mouth made a popping sound as it shut. Without another word, she hurried out of the room.

"Bethel?" Lilette looked between her and Jolin. "The famous Bethel?"

Jolin sank into a chair, her eyes hidden under her hand. Lilette looked to Han for an explanation, but he hadn't taken his eyes off the guardian. "Jolin, who is this?" Lilette tried. "What's going on?"

Bethel motioned to the staircase. "Check the bedroom and then fetch us some more food." Doranna started up the stairs.

Lilette sat down. It felt awkward, being this high from the floor, and she wished for soft cushions to sink into. A thousand questions flooded her mind. She blurted the first one to make it to her mouth. "I was going to eat that."

Bethel snorted. "You don't know better. You" —she shot Jolin a stern look, even though Lilette's friend was still hiding behind her hand— "you know better."

Jolin finally lowered her hand. "Not everyone is trying to poison us, Mother."

"It only takes one," Bethel replied.

Lilette's astonished gaze settled on Jolin. "She's your mother?"

Jolin groaned.

Bethel's eyes met Lilette's. The only soft thing about her was her hair, woven into a loose braid over her shoulder. But her steel-gray eyes did resemble Jolin's. "Never eat anything without knowing where it came from."

"You think we're in danger?" asked Lilette.

"I know you are." Without turning, Bethel spoke to her guardian. "Is he proficient?"

Lilette took in the glaring contest going on between Han and the guardian, who seemed to be making up for his baldness with a thick coating of black facial hair. "Shall we find out?" His voice held a challenge.

Sensing the violence about to break out, Lilette half rose to her feet. Bethel kicked her injured shin. "Stay put."

Sucking air through her teeth, Lilette sat hard and grasped the still-swollen lump from where the elite had hit her.

Han and the guardian moved, their swords snaking from their scabbards. As they sparred, the sound of clashing swords rang in Lilette's ears. She gritted her teeth, wanting to stop the fighting, though she didn't think either man was really out to hurt the other. This was about proving something.

The men broke apart as suddenly as they had begun. "Well, Harberd?" Bethel said.

The guardian grinned. "He can handle himself."

Bethel grunted in approval and leaned back in her chair, her hands laced over her stomach. "No—I don't know who exactly you're in danger from. All I know is that someone in the inner city is flinging curses around—curses she's managing to keep hidden from all but the most powerful of witches."

Jolin laughed nervously. "If someone were singing curses, the whole city would know."

Bethel didn't take her gaze from Lilette. "Curious isn't it, that the most powerful witches have either been sent away or have ended up dead?"

"They send the strong witches on assignment," Jolin replied, "and accidents happen."

"How many?" Lilette rubbed her shin. "How many have died?"

Bethel's mouth tightened into a thin line. "Three so far. One found dead in her bed, one from an infection, one simply disappeared."

Jolin sighed. "Three women, Mother. Only three."

"And how many level sevens do you think there are in Grove City?" Bethel asked softly.

"Ten, maybe fifteen."

"There are three left," Bethel said. "Two of them are in this room."

Bethel was a level seven? Lilette's eyes widened. The silence that followed took on a life of its own, growing like shadows after sunset.

Han sat down on one of the chairs, a light sheen of sweat on his brow. "Why? Why take the strongest?"

Doranna slipped down the stairs, moving very lightly for a woman in her middle years. "It's safe," she reported. When Bethel nodded, the wastrel moved past Harberd and disappeared outside.

"Because the curses are so well masked," Bethel said. "Only the strongest can sense it."

"It's impossible to hide witch song, Mother."

Bethel shot her a look. "As impossible as using the earth in potions?"

Jolin didn't respond. Lilette's eyes widened as she turned to face her friend. "Is that what you're trying to do? What all your experiments are about?"

"It can be done," Jolin said through clenched teeth. "I know it can. Think of it—a whole new world of ingredients that we know nothing about. Minerals such as salt, sulfur, antimony . . . the list is endless."

Lilette bit her lip. "Even if it can, are you sure it's a good idea? After all, look at the damage the witches can inflict with just a song."

In answer, Jolin shoved herself back from the table and began pacing. Doranna returned with another platter of food, which she set on the table. Though Lilette's mouth watered and her stomach tightened within her, she could not bring herself to eat.

Han nudged her. "Lilette?"

She raised haunted eyes. "I've been poisoned before." She met Bethel's gaze. "I thought I would finally be safe here."

Bethel piled the food onto a plate and set it before her. "You will both come to Haven with me. There you will be safe."

Jolin paused in her pacing. "I'm staying."

Bethel took a delicate bite out of a slice of white, creamy-looking cheese. "You will come or I'll cut off your funding for your research. And there go your dreams of becoming the Head of Plants."

Jolin went so still she could have been carved of stone before she stormed up the stairs. Lilette forced herself to eat. At least it was food she was familiar with—sliced mangoes, oranges, and star fruit—all served with cheese and crackers.

There was a bottle of white wine that they shared, the fruitiness a nice contrast to the tangy cheese. When everyone had their fill, Doranna covered the remaining food with a cloth and set it aside.

Bethel rose to her feet. "All the women upstairs. You men are down."

"I'll take the first watch," Han said as he stood.

The other guardian moved to join him. "We sleep in front of the doors.

Bethel yawned and moved up the stairs without looking back.

Doranna moved to Lilette's side. "I–I knew your parents. I'm sorry."

All Lilette could do was nod.

CHAPTER 24

I don't know why all young women think their mothers fools.
~Jolin

Lilette's head felt like a boulder perched precariously on her shoulders. She pressed her fingertips to her throbbing temples. Her mouth tasted particularly foul. She rolled to her knees and pushed herself up. Her body felt thick and ridged. She barely remembered to hold up the hem of her dress as she plodded down the curving staircase.

Downstairs was already in an uproar. Broad men were hauling out straw-lined crates while Jolin hovered above them, shoving fistfuls of straw between the books. "Make sure they are packed in oiled canvas. Water is poison for books. Absolute poison." The men bore Jolin's fussing with expressions of forced patience.

Han saw Lilette first. "You look rested."

Jolin looked up at her and grunted. "He's being kind. You look like you've been trampled by an elephant."

Han shot Jolin a warning look. Lilette reached up to touch her hair. Half of it had come loose, so she shook it out and let it tumble in a messy, still-damp heap around her shoulders. Her dress was crumpled from sleeping in it. "Remind me never to drink wine again." She sighed and rubbed her eyes with the front of her wrists. "What's going on?"

Jolin was already back to fussing over her books. "Mother made an agreement with the Heads. I am allowed to take some of the inner-city library books with me in exchange for going back with her. She's already gone ahead to Haven. We're to follow as quickly as we can."

Lilette stood frozen on the stairway. All of her life, she'd dreamed of nothing but going to Haven, her days filled with singing and the knowledge she'd craved since childhood. And always with her sister beside her. Now Sash was the captive and Lilette the student.

Her gaze strayed to Han. She'd never imagined leaving him would hurt this much. He reached toward her, grasped her hand, and pulled her out the front door. They ended up behind the tree, in her sister's private garden filled with leaves and the green smell of growing things.

He looked at Lilette, his eyes as dark and depthless as the deepest part of the ocean. His gaze shifted to her mouth and she could have sworn she felt the pressure of his gaze on her lips. She moved forward a fraction, until there was nothing between them but sunlight. Then there was nothing at all. His lips were on hers, not claiming, not possessing, simply wanting. Needing. She'd never known how full of need he was, how dark and empty the spaces in his soul must be. He drank her in like she was light and hope and he'd been a starving man all his life.

For Lilette, it was as if his touch let her shine. Like she'd been shattered into a thousand specks of light and he brought her together—made her whole.

With a shudder that shook him to the core, Han pulled away from her. He rested his forehead against hers, his breath ragged. "Lilette."

She closed her eyes as he said her name like he was cupping a bird in his hands and was about to set it free. She inhaled the breath that had carried her name. "Han."

"No matter how hard I try, you're all I can see," he murmured.

She held her hands together to keep them from trembling and betraying her. "Where does that leave us?" She pulled back slightly to look at him.

"I don't know." Han closed his eyes. "You're leaving for Haven. I'm going to stay here as an ambassador for Harshen."

She nodded. "I'm glad." She trusted no one else with this.

Han hesitated, and then kissed her briefly. "Be well, little dragon." He turned and started walking away.

Lilette watched him, waiting for him to move out of sight before she allowed her legs to go soft, let herself sink into the loam. She didn't cry. She just waited for the aching to fade enough that she could get to her feet and keep moving.

***

Lilette stood at the bow, letting the cool sea wind wash over her. As the sun changed the color of the water from indigo to cerulean, jagged black cliffs rose in the distance. She was astounded by the sheer size of them, rising so high they seemed to cut into the sky. The ship headed toward a crescent moon carved into the side of the cliffs.

Behind her was a flurry of motion. Bare from the waist up, sailors took down the sails, slowing the ship to a crawl. Lilette looked for some kind of channel, some passage to get them inside the cliffs. There was nothing.

The captain ordered his men to drop the anchor. A splash was followed by the slither of ropes. The anchor dragged along the bottom of the sea before finally catching and slowing the ship to a halt. Lilette could feel the vessel straining against the pull of the water.

Jolin tightened her hands around the strap of the satchel containing all the seeds she'd gathered from Harshen. Her face was set as if she was facing down a raging storm.

"Are you all right?" Lilette asked.

Jolin slowly turned to face her. "Let's just get this over with."

The sailors had already loaded Jolin's crates of books into the smaller boat, but she insisted on checking each one, double checking the ties around the oiled canvas. "You're sure you double bagged them? Some of these books are nearly three hundred years old."

Galon grinned at her, and Lilette had to tear her gaze away from the freckles that covered his chest. He'd been assigned as their guardian to Haven. His nose was a little large, his knuckles knobby, but there was something so ineffably happy about him that Lilette couldn't help but like him.

"Yes, Keeper. I could toss them over the side now and they'd be nary the worse for wear."

Jolin straightened as if she'd been slapped. "You'll do no such thing!"

He chuckled. "'Course not. The point is I could."

Jolin pressed both her fists to her hips, obviously preparing to deliver a tongue lashing.

Lilette rested a hand on her arm. "Jolin, he's teasing you."

"Oh. Well, as long as he keeps his hands off my books."

"I don't think that's where he wants to put his hands," Lilette murmured.

Galon's grin widened. He gripped Jolin's waist and hefted her easily into the boat. She squealed in surprise. He hauled himself up beside her and held out a hand to help Lilette in.

She took it even though she didn't need it. "I never thanked you, for saving me back in Harshen."

"You saved us back, so I guess we're even." He winked at her.

He reached across Jolin to grab a misplaced oar. She stiffened as his bare chest pressed against her arm, and Lilette resisted the urge to laugh. Before sitting down, she stumbled on some kind of wedge riveted into the base of the boat. She turned to look behind her, squinting through the brightness of the light reflecting off the water. "How are we getting past those walls?"

A grin stole across Jolin's face. "You'll see." Lilette did not like that wicked gleam in her eyes.

Sailors finished loading the supplies into the boat and tied them down, the cords of muscle in their arms straining. The captain himself verified the stability of each crate. *Why do they need to be tied down so tight?* Lilette thought uneasily.

Three more sailors swung into the boat—none of them wearing shirts. Jolin tensed up as another bare-chested sailor took the seat next to her. Another stood in front of Lilette. "That's my job, Witchling." He pointed to the oar in Lilette's hand.

She huffed indignantly. "I can do it."

"'Course you can. But it isn't your job—it's mine. You've a different part to play."

With a huff, Lilette handed over the oar and scooted to the center of the bench. The four sailors picked up the oars. The boat was lowered by a series of pulleys, the sailors lined up to release the rope one handhold at a time.

The boat settled heavily into the water. The sailors dug in with the oars, their movements a perfectly matched dance. More boats filled with supplies were lowered into the water after them.

Lilette watched as Jolin's gaze traveled down Galon's wiry frame, her bottom lip between her teeth. He turned in time to catch her appraisal, and a slow grin spread across his face. Jolin's face flamed nearly as red as his hair. Lilette laughed out loud. Jolin glared a death curse at her. As soon as Galon turned away, she mouthed something that looked like "I'm going to kill you." Lilette laughed harder.

The sailors stopped rowing and concentrated on keeping the boat from drifting.

"Now you have to stand and sing," Jolin said, a smug look on her face.

Lilette's grin faded. "Why?"

Jolin rooted around in her pocket and pulled out a piece of a sheet of music. "It'll be good practice. Besides, you're a better singer than I."

Lilette took the music and quickly scanned it. She filled her lungs and her voice rang out.

Oh, sister sea plants, I ask of thee,
Take me to the place none but witches see.

The words echoed off the cliffs, adding an eerie chorus. As she began her third repetition, she caught sight of something white glimmering beneath the waves. Still singing, Lilette leaned forward for a closer look. But the image was suddenly blotted out by a thick rope of green. As the last note trailed off her tongue, ropes of seaweed shot up from below and began weaving around the boat.

A strong hand pulled her down. "This is your first time?" Galon asked. Mute, she nodded. He swore and shoved her hand into a leather loop on the seat beside her. She hadn't paid it any mind before. "Hold on to this."

She grabbed it, too confused and frightened to argue. He grabbed her leg and jammed her toes into a wedge of leather that had been bolted onto the deck. The one she'd stumbled over before. He winked at her. "Hold on. This is the fun part."

She finally found her voice to ask him what he meant when the last of the kelp wrapped them in near darkness and the boat suddenly upended. Half a moment too late, Lilette tensed, her toes digging into the wedge. A sailor grabbed her shoulder to steady her. Suddenly it was almost silent. The kelp bulged inward until it pressed against her face, water trickling past the leaves. Her ears suddenly hurt so bad she couldn't think past the pain.

"Try to blow your nose, but pinch it closed," Galon told Lilette. She didn't understand but she tried it anyway. Her ears popped and the pain was gone for half a moment before returning.

"Keep doing it," he said encouragingly. Jolin gripped her satchel and muttered something about stupid ideas.

"Are we going to die?" Lilette whispered.

"Not today," Galon responded far too brightly.

Suddenly, they were rising—much, much faster than they'd descended. The boat burst above the surface, and the kelp slithered away.

Lilette lay against the bench, her dress damp with seawater. Wherever they were was dimly lit and smelled of damp rocks and smoke. Above her was an arched ceiling, black with soot.

Galon sat up, a wide grin on his face. He and the other sailors started rowing. Lilette stayed where she was.

Jolin checked the seeds in her satchel before settling back with a sigh of relief. She laughed at the look on Lilette's face. "I'm a bad friend."

"Yes, you are."

"You can let go of the loops now."

Lilette forced her aching fingers to relax. She rubbed the feeling back into them and yanked her foot free of the wedge. "Why didn't you tell me?"

Jolin smirked. "Because it wouldn't have been nearly as much fun."

Lilette took a deep breath to remind herself she wasn't drowning and forced herself to look around. They were in a cave, but not a ragged hole in the side of a mountain. This was elegant and circular, with an arched, blackened ceiling held up by thick columns. Torches sputtered in brackets on the walls, sooty triangles behind them. Water exploded behind the boat as another one surfaced.

The sailors rowed the boat neatly into a dock, where wastrels waited to tie it off. Watching them, Lilette thought of Doranna and the others like her. Treating women like servants simply because they couldn't sing—it wasn't right.

Three sailors started unloading the boat. Galon offered the women a hand up. Jolin blushed again and let him help her out, then rushed to check on her books. Lilette wasn't so eager to disembark. She missed the sea. Blowing out her lips, she took Galon's hand.

He settled her on the dock and stepped closer. "You're students?"

Slightly perplexed, she nodded.

He made a grumbling sound. "Well, then, goodbye." He swung a crate onto his shoulder and marched off.

"What was that about?" Lilette wondered aloud.

"Is that a rhetorical question, or would you like an answer?"

Lilette jumped and turned to find Jolin behind her, thumbing through a book in her hands. "What?"

Jolin raised a single eyebrow. "Was it a rhetorical question, or would you like an answer?"

"Um, I'd like an answer. I think?"

"Students on Haven are forbidden contact with men. Had you not been a student, he probably would have asked to court you."

"Court me?"

As Jolin turned to watch Galon head toward the cave mouth with a crate on his shoulder, a disappointed look crossed her face. "The ritual by which men and women fall in love—or not," she said wistfully. "He would have taken you to dinner, perhaps. Or to some kind of jovial activity. After a sufficient amount of wooing, he would have asked you to marry him."

"He asked about us, not just me," Lilette replied. "And you were the one he was smiling at."

Jolin grasped her hands behind her back. "I am sure you are mistaken. I know what I am, and I know what I am not. Attractive to men is certainly not one of my many valuable qualities." She wouldn't look Lilette in the eyes.

Jolin snapped her fingers at the sailors. "Follow me." She marched toward the head of the cave, her head held high and her back straight.

Knowing it was all for show, Lilette snatched her small bag and hurried after Jolin. The bag contained only Lilette's spare dress and her purse of jewels—she'd given the armor and clothes back to Han.

They left the dim cave and emerged, blinking, into the light. What struck Lilette first was how like Grove City everything was. There was the same riot of green—from the pale shoots of new grass to nearly the black of the plants tucked into the shadows. Heavy with water, the air carried the smells of growing things. Plants grew on top of plants, over plants, and crawled up trees. Moss grew on the muddy ground, but a path of gravel had been laid out. It wound through the vegetation, between trees that were short and stout compared to the ones in Grove City. There were no arched bridges between balconies. Still, windows winked from between curves of bark, and peaked doors were set between buttressed roots.

"They're a different species," Jolin answered Lilette's unasked question. "I helped develop them." Lilette gaped at her friend in amazement. Jolin raised her hands palm up. "What?"

"I thought you were a potioner!"

"I have an intimate knowledge of the composition of nearly every plant ever known. It's not that hard to go from using a plant for a potion, to changing the properties between plants."

They'd reached a tree. Jolin produced a key and unlocked the door. Inside was a table and stove. Every other square of space was covered in bottles and pots and clay jars. All filled to overflowing but meticulously labeled. "You live here?" Lilette asked.

Men followed them inside and deposited the crates of books beside a wide shelf before shuffling back out. Jolin was already depositing the little sacks of seeds from her satchel into clay jars with cork lids. "Obviously."

Doranna appeared at the door. She waited for the last of the men to leave before shutting the door after them.

"Where's my mother?" Jolin asked her.

Doranna took the jars, dipped a brush in ink, and began labeling them. "Last I saw her, she was headed to the southwest side of the island." Her gaze shifted to Lilette. "You should avoid going anywhere near the cliffs. Rock fall can happen anytime here."

"When was the last one?" Jolin asked.

Doranna shrugged. "It's been weeks."

"That bad?"

"We're managing."

Lilette looked between the two. "What's bad?"

"Sometimes she's a bit . . . volatile," Jolin answered.

Lilette shifted her bag to her other hand. "Who?"

Jolin met her gaze. "My mother." She moved to start stacking the books on the shelves.

"Ah, I understand," Lilette said, though she really didn't.

Doranna was still working on the jars. "Lilette, I have been asked to apprise you of the rules. You may not leave Haven without the headmistress's permission. You must be in your rooms before full dark. Open flames are allowed only on bolted-down candlesticks, which must be blown out when you leave the room—except, obviously, for the one you carry to light another."

Jolin had nearly finished with the books.

Doranna turned the bottles so all the labels faced out. "Haven is a near perfect circle, so all paths eventually lead to the center of the island. Just about everything important is around the circle—the headmistress's tree, the food pavilion, the library.

"The bathing pools are by the cliffs opposite the entrance. Because there are no men allowed to live on the island, the pools are open to the air."

She stepped up beside Jolin and began meticulously alphabetizing each title. "Meals are served thrice in the pavilion. If you miss one, there are usually baskets of fruit, bread, and cheese, which you may take at any time as long as it is not wasted."

"You're to check in as soon as you're settled." She gestured to a woven basket by the door. "Leave your laundry in the basket and I'll see it's washed and returned the evening next. Your tree will be cleaned in the mornings."

Lilette poked around the chaos of potions, seeds, herbs, and baskets of rocks. "How do you find anything in this mess?" She held up a vial of topaz-colored liquid.

"Mess?" Jolin snatched the potion from her hand. "I know exactly where everything is, so mind you don't touch anything." She set the bottle down carefully.

"What's that one?"

"I call it ioa." Jolin's voice was filled with sadness. "It can change a person into a fish."

Lilette's eyes widened. "Why would you ever want to be a fish?"

"That's what the Heads said. A couple vials were stolen, though, by a witch who wanted to become a Head of Plants. The results were . . . less than favorable. After that, they moved me onto the island—it's more secure. I also began leaving out a key ingredient to each of my potions."

"Less than favorable how?"

Jolin took a deep breath. "A few dozen people are stuck as some kind of half-person, half-fish. Their skin turned a mottled green, their skelature changed, webbing grew between their fingers, and their teeth became pointed."

Even though she knew she hadn't spilled the potion on her hands, Lilette wiped them on her dress.

"The Heads won't let me try it on anyone else, and the witch was banished," Jolin continued. "The fish people have taken to living on an island farther south. They call themselves mettlemots. Apparently, they're quite the fishermen." She chuckled at her own joke.

At the look on Lilette's face, she quickly sobered. "I'm convinced the potion is sound. It's the method of transfer that's off. My theory is that it needs to be applied to the body's meridian line for the reversal of effects. But I can't test any of this."

Lilette's mouth was suddenly dry.

Jolin lifted her brows. "So, mind you don't touch anything." She opened a door to another room. "Come on, Doranna."

"Is that how you talk to me, girl?" Doranna continued unpacking the books and setting them on the shelves.

"I apologize." Jolin sighed. "Would you please render your assistance?"

Casting a regretful glance toward the rest of the unpacked books, Doranna stepped up beside Lilette and turned the ioa potion so its label faced out. "And?"

"Thank you so much for your invaluable service," Jolin ground out.

"I'll teach that one some manners if it's the last thing I do," Doranna said with a smirk to Lilette.

Lilette had a view of pots and plants before the door shut behind them. She studied the organized chaos surrounding her and started toward the only other door in the room. Behind it was a single bed—she hoped that was remedied before nightfall. If not, she'd be sleeping on the floor, and she'd come to like beds.

The walls were covered in shelves of books. Lilette took out her spare dress and hung it on an extra peg, then tucked her bag of jewels behind a book called *Intraspecific Hybridization,* by Jolin Lyon. Her eyes wide, Lilette tugged the book off the shelf. She walked to the back door and opened it to ask Jolin about the book. What Lilette had thought was a room was actually a garden encased by glass—a garden with hundreds of potted plants. Jolin and Doranna were planting the seeds from Harshen into large clay pots.

"You wrote this?" Lilette held out the book.

Her hands buried in soil, Jolin glanced up. "A few years ago. We keepers have long known that by crossing two plants that each have a desirable characteristic, we could create one plant with both."

"So you wrote it when you were what, twelve?" Lilette flipped through more pages.

"Thirteen, I think. I couldn't find a book that documented all our findings, so I wrote one."

"How many others have you written?"

Jolin thought for a moment. "Fifteen or so. It's hard to keep track anymore."

"You're really rather brilliant, aren't you?" Lilette said, more to herself than anyone else.

"Obviously," Jolin said.

"Why didn't you tell me all this?"

Jolin's hands stilled and she looked up. And Lilette suddenly understood. All her life, people had treated her differently because of her beauty, and now her voice. They'd done the same to Jolin because of her brilliance. Quite simply, people were intimidated by them, or resented them, or were drawn to them for all the wrong reasons. Lilette realized she and Jolin had a great deal in common. "Thank you for letting me stay with you," she said quietly.

Jolin looked relieved. "Only because I need someone to sing for my potions."

The corners of Lilette's mouth quirked. "Mmm."

"It's true. Now put that book back and make use of that ridiculously pretty voice to help us grow these."

Lilette returned the book and stepped into the garden, the smells of moist soil and green amplified by the glass. Reminded of the jungles around Calden, she felt a pang of sadness.

Jolin and Doranna had laid out dozens of pots, which Jolin had already planted with seeds. Doranna opened a jar of black paint and dipped in a brush. She added water before bending down to paint on a label in perfect letters.

"She has her first class," Doranna chided.

Jolin waved the woman's concern away. "This will be far more educational than sitting through a plant identification course."

Lilette sang, and soon dozens of seeds had sprouted and grown into mature plants. Around them, the already-existing plants stretched and broadened and rustled. Lilette marveled at the power of her voice.

"This one."

Lilette whirled to find Bethel standing behind them, a seed the size of a small pebble in her palm. "This is the one you've been searching for."

Jolin didn't meet her mother's gaze. "How can you tell?"

Bethel set the seed on a table. It wobbled a little before going still. "I didn't know what I was looking for until I found it."

Bethel turned and left without saying goodbye. Jolin didn't bother acknowledging her mother's departure. She just picked up the seed and held it to the light.

Chapter 25

Everything was connected, bonds forming and events occurring exactly when they were needed. Only after was I able to see it clearly. ~Jolin

As soon as Bethel was gone, Jolin slammed her trowel down and braced her arms against the table, her eyes pinched shut.

Doranna lifted her hand as if to comfort her, then seemed to think better of it. "She was worried when you were gone. She kept coming by your tree and staring at the door. She's just not very good at showing that she loves you."

Jolin let out a brittle laugh. "Love? The only thing she loves is the earth." She began rearranging the pots.

"Jolin . . ." Lilette began.

Jolin wiped her dirty hands on her dress. "Now you understand why I have such poorly developed social niceties." She waved in the direction her mother had gone. "Look what I had for an example."

"Jolin," Doranna said with a hint of warning.

Lilette had seen the way people looked at Bethel. "I don't understand."

Jolin went still for a beat. "Mother has always been paranoid— she's convinced Grove City is on the brink of collapsing. It's why she built the ramparts around it. It's why she built Haven out of an island of cliffs in the middle of the sea."

"Your mother—she made them?" Lilette breathed. "Then . . . why isn't she the Head of Earth? Surely no one is stronger."

"She turned them down." Jolin's shoulders sagged with the weight she must have carried with her every day of her life, living under the shadow of her mother's accomplishments. "It was offered to her even though she's rabid mad, while I create one wonder after another, and it's never enough." She wiped her face, smearing soil across her forehead. "And now you know why I don't mention it."

No wonder Jolin didn't think writing a book at thirteen was much of an accomplishment. "I'm sorry," Lilette said.

"Fetch the notes, will you?" Jolin asked Doranna. "We'll start crossbreeding the plants immediately." After Doranna had left the glass garden, Jolin fixed moist eyes on Lilette. "I'm not my mother. I never will be."

Lilette tilted her head to one side. "Why would you want to be?"

Jolin grunted, but her bearing seemed lighter. "Help us crossbreed some of these plants, and then you better report for classes."

Lilette stepped up beside her. "What exactly are you doing?"

Jolin watered the seeds her mother had pointed out. "The only reason I went to Harshen was to gather new seeds. There are entire volumes of recorded data on plants mixed with other plants to create potions, but almost nothing on plants mixed with the components of metal and stone."

Lilette raised an eyebrow. "What good does it do to mix potions with rocks?"

"That's just it!" Jolin waved her hand in the air, the quill swishing through the air. "No one knows. Imagine if you could make an unbreakable sword. Mix certain compounds to create an explosion. What if we could wake up the rocks, so they responded to us like the plants did? We could build entire cities!"

Lilette blinked. "You have dirt on your forehead."

Jolin didn't bother rubbing it away. "The point is, we don't know the possibilities. Anything could happen. It's so exhilarating!"

Lilette sang until she was hoarse. Doranna carefully categorized the new plants, and then she and Jolin began documenting each plant's characteristics.

"I won't need you again until I have my findings," Jolin told Lilette. "You may as well head to class."

Unease fluttered in her belly. "I don't know where to go."

Doranna rolled her head and rubbed at her neck. "I'll take her and bring back some lunch."

Jolin made a sound that could have been construed as agreement.

"Don't mix those pots up before I have a chance to label them," Doranna said, then started off without waiting to see if Lilette followed. "The island is quartered into four sections, each one dedicated to one of the elements—earth, water, plants, and light."

Lilette's studied her surroundings. "Why are there so many open pavilions? Don't you worry about the rain?"

Doranna gave her an odd look. "Haven't you noticed?"

Lilette slowed as she remembered that it only rained at night. "Do the keepers control everything?"

"Everything." Doranna's voice was laced with bitterness.

They stopped at a large pavilion covered in fragrant vines. Beneath it were long benches and tables. The smell of fish stew filled the air.

"Have some lunch," Doranna said. "Then stop at that tree." She pointed to one not far from where they sat. "They'll give you your schedule."

Lilette took a bowl of the stew, which looked like a congealed mess, along with some bread and fruit. She ate quickly. At the tree she received a schedule, and a wastrel who was assigned to take her on a tour. Lilette marveled at the variety of books in the library, and the clear, blue waters of the bathing spring, which was fed by an underground heated pool and a cold waterfall that tumbled off the cliff.

"Where does the water come from?" Lilette asked as she craned her neck to see the top of the cliffs.

The wastrel smiled. "Bethel made it—the water comes from inside the cliffs somehow."

Sash had bathed in that pool, walked these paths, studied in these pavilions. Lilette had longed to come to Haven her entire life. But she would give it all up again to make her sister safe.

She was shown where her classes were—trees or pavilions filled to the brim with girls, all younger than Lilette. Her schedule included Potions, Earth Studies, Singing, and even a class on politics. Lilette balked at that one. "Why do I need to learn the finer points of politics?"

"Class schedules are catered to a witch's potential," the wastrel answered.

"What about what I want?"

"Apprentices have more choices."

Lilette made a mental note to progress through her classes as quickly as possible.

The girl deposited Lilette at her last class, which, of course, was full of young girls. She was given a book and a slate board for her notes. Feeling a little humiliated, she found an empty seat, but of course the chair and desk were too small for her. Still, she tried to listen to the lecture. The other witchlings seemed a little intimidated, whether by the age difference, the strength of Lilette's song, or her brief stint as an empress, Lilette wasn't sure. Perhaps all three.

When she returned to the house, Jolin was bent over her pestle and mortar, grinding something that smelled like a weed that grew around the chicken huts on Lilette's island. Doranna was busily scratching away at some parchment.

"Discover anything?" Lilette asked Jolin.

Jolin rubbed her neck. "Lots of things. Doranna's been recording our findings all day."

Lilette moved to the table and picked up a wooden cup, then filled it with water from a pitcher and took a drink. "They have me . . ." Her voice trailed to nothing as the world seemed to wrench to the side and pulse like an animal in its death throes. The cup slipped from her fingers, landing with a clatter on the floor.

"Lilette?" Doranna's voice sounded far away.

Lilette braced herself against the table, eyes closed as something oily and dark seemed to pool in her gut.

Suddenly, Doranna stood beside her. "Jolin, something's wrong with her."

Opening her eyes let in too much stimulation, so Lilette kept them closed as Jolin and Doranna guided her to a chair.

"What is it?" Jolin asked.

Lilette cradled her head in her hands. "It's like I'm dying, only I'm not." But that wasn't quite right. "No, it's more like a part of me is dying, or being tortured."

Jolin inhaled sharply. "You can feel it, can't you?"

"Feel what?"

"There are very few witches who are so tightly bound to the elements that they can sense their discord." Doranna sounded sad.

"It's your witch sense," Jolin explained. "You're feeling the manipulation of elements. It feels wrong, because it is."

"I've felt this before." Lilette wet her lips. "When Sash and the others were singing their curse. But it wasn't this bad."

"More witches are singing now. It's stronger," Jolin said.

Lilette finally dared open her eyes. "That's what this is, isn't it? Grove City is singing a curse." Her thoughts ran from her sister to her island to all the people she had met, even for a moment, while in Rinnish. She pushed back from the table and started toward the door.

"Where are you going?" Jolin asked.

"I can't just sit here." She shoved her feet into her boots.

"You can't stop them!" Doranna moved to follow her. "No one can."

Lilette didn't look back. "No. I want to be alone."

Doranna grabbed a cloak hanging on the wall. "At least take this. If you're out after nightfall, you'll be in the rain."

Lilette slung it over her shoulder. Ignoring the paths, she tromped right through Haven's mud. By now, the sky had darkened, the once-brilliant blue covered by a film of shadows. Eventually she found herself at the base of the cliffs, her heart racing. She prowled around, desperate for a way up. At last, she found it. Next to one of the waterfalls, stairs zigzagged toward the top of the cliffs. Hiking up her confounded dress, she started climbing.

By the time she reached the top, she was breathless and her legs ached. A sea breeze swept her hair behind her. The sky had darkened to the deepest turquoise, leaving an orange smudge where the sun had turned to embers. Another woman stood at the cliff's edge.

She recognized the woman's stance, her long gray hair. Lilette moved to stand beside her, watching the waves below batter the cliffs as if trying to find a way in. "Bethel."

"I wondered if you'd come."

"What is the curse?" It wasn't one to sink the island. It couldn't be.

Bethel closed her eyes and murmured in time with the twisted rhythm, "Rains to cease, winds to still, soil to harden, seeds to kill." She'd spoken in Kalari instead of the Creators' language, her words eerily echoing the discord.

Though they weren't sinking the island of Harshen, Lilette thought of the gardens and orchards curling up and couldn't catch her breath. With some of the men dead, her village would be hard pressed to survive off the sea. And Sash would suffer from this curse along with everyone else.

Bethel's expression was hard. "This goes against everything we were placed here to do. It's evil."

"It was my idea," Lilette said softly. "How could I suggest it so blithely?"

"The Heads were already planning to do it." Bethel drew in a deep breath. "What the emperor did was an act of war."

Clouds were rolling in from the west. A cool breeze picked up, chilling the sweat on Lilette's skin. She wondered where Han was, what he was doing. If he missed her as much as she missed him.

And then she looked further east, toward Harshen, and she wondered if Sash was still alive. If she was hurt or injured or scared. "How much longer will this . . . singing go on?" Lilette asked.

"If the emperor doesn't force his captives to counter-sing, not much longer. If he does—" Bethel shrugged "—it could go on for days."

Lilette wrapped her arms around herself. "Won't they just cancel each other out?"

"Let's hope that's all it does." Bethel was silent a moment. "What I can't figure out is what part you have to play in all this."

"What do you mean?"

Bethel studied the distant lights of Grove City. "All of us are just pieces on the board, Lilette."

Lilette swallowed hard. "Maybe we should get back. It's late."

"Don't tell me you don't see it. You were withheld from the game, and then you appear right as the final moves are being made."

"I don't think—"

Bethel's hand snaked out, grabbing Lilette's forearm. "What did she tell you to do? What are you here for?"

Lilette went still. "She?"

"Your mother."

Lilette's breath hitched in her throat.

Bethel's gaze narrowed. "I was right. She has sought you out."

Lilette took a sudden breath—somehow she'd forgotten to breath. "She said I was to save those I could." Lilette worried her bottom lip between her teeth. "I already did what she asked."

Bethel's gaze met hers. "Did you?" Her gaze revealed her disbelief.

Lilette held out her hands in a helpless gesture. "The witches are the strongest power on earth. How could they fall?"

Bethel scoffed. "Everything falls." She turned and started walking away. "Come on. I have something that will allow us both to get a little sleep."

Lilette cast a longing glance toward the sound of the song. It felt wrong to let this go on, but surely the pressure would force Chen to release Sash and the others. It was better than a war. Better that the witches send a message that any rulers who tried to use witches as weapons would suffer famine until they were disposed of by their own people.

As Lilette made her way back, the heavens opened and rain sheeted down. She draped the cloak over her shoulders and pulled up the hood. Bethel didn't have a hood, nor did she seem to mind the rain. They tromped down the slippery steps and into the soggy forest, stopping at a tree not far from Jolin's place. The inside smelled of minerals—like a cave—instead of tree resin. Rocks littered the floor.

Bethel opened a cupboard of dusty green bottles and rummaged around. "Now, if I could just remember where that sleeping tonic is."

"Ah." She pulled down a bottle and held up a finger. "One swallow. Two, and you won't be able to wake up in the morning. Three, and you won't be able to wake at all." She pressed it into Lilette's hands, but wouldn't let go until she nodded her agreement.

Lilette started for the dark beyond the door, but paused at the threshold and turned back. "Does this . . . feeling—does it have a name?"

Bethel's eyes met Lilette's. "Oh, yes. It's called the hassacre." She tipped back her own bottle and then wiped her lips with the back of her hand.

"How do you bear it?" Lilette's voice came out as little more than a whisper.

Bethel frowned. "You don't."

CHAPTER 26

Lilette was never happier than the time she spent on Haven.
She slept well and was filled with a quiet contentment. ~Jolin

The hassacre continued every night for the next week.
Despite the fact that it left Lilette sluggish and numb the
next day, she took a swallow of the sleeping potion every night.
Not only did it ease the wrongness twisting inside her because
of the hassacre, but also the ache in her heart for her sister and
her loneliness for Han.

The room was practically sweating when Lilette stepped
inside, even with the windows swung open to let in a stray
breeze. She set down the lunch tray and unloaded the contents on
the table. "Today, we have a surprise—fish. In this case, breaded
fish, with a side of yummick." Yummick was red as a beet and
tasted like squash. "And fruit."

Doranna took a plate, but Jolin barely looked up from where
she stood over a small, bubbling cauldron. Sweat ran down her
temples and dampened her hair. She'd long ago abandoned her
dresses for a tunic and trousers that looked suspiciously like the
ones from Harshen.

Lilette took her first bite, wishing she could have somehow
brought her eunuch with her. He would have shown the wastrels
how to make a brown sauce to sauté fish with some vegetables,
served over rice. Creators' mercy, Lilette missed rice.

She wiped a trickle of sweat from her forehead. "Jolin, lunch."

Her friend pulled a small rock out of the cauldron and dropped it into a crate full of rocks. "This time. I can feel it."

Rocks in potions? "Uh, what are you doing?"

Jolin smoothed a few stray strands of her hair. "I'm soaking raw steel in a compound to see if it affects the strength of the steel."

"She's going to send them to the blacksmith's to see if she can make an unbreakable sword," Doranna added.

Jolin shot a glare at the wastrel. "If I can manage to line up the particles of steel, it will strengthen the end product."

"And boiling rocks in a potion will help?" Lilette asked incredulously.

Now it was her turn to receive a glare. "That's what I'm trying to determine." Jolin dropped more rocks into the cauldron with a plunk. "Now clamp it. I'm working."

After making a face, Lilette took another bite of her lunch. Doranna smothered a laugh, and Lilette gaped at her. It was the first time she'd ever heard Doranna laugh—or seen her smile, for that matter. "Doranna, can I ask you something?"

"What?"

Lilette tapped the bread. "Why did you decide to become a wastrel?"

Doranna's smile became as brittle as glass. "You know, for someone on the fast track to becoming one of the discipline heads, you're blatantly ignorant."

Shame tore through Lilette. "I . . . just . . . there are wastrels everywhere. I don't understand why they would choose a life of servitude."

Doranna's mask of indifference slipped, darkening to something like hate. "You're lucky to be accepted as one of them, witchling." She stormed from the room, slamming the door shut after her.

Jolin stared after her. "You shouldn't have said that."

"What did I say wrong?"

"Wastrels aren't like eunuchs, Lilette. They didn't choose this."

Lilette gasped. "Surely they weren't forced?"

"No." Jolin dropped her tongs with a clatter and came over to sit at the table. She took a bite of her fish and started chewing. "Of all witch born, only a fourth are admitted as witchlings. Two-thirds of those never reach their apprenticeship."

"What happens to them all?" Lilette asked.

Jolin drained her cup of water and refilled it. "Depending on their skill, witchlings can become apothecaries, minor healers, herbalists. Apprentices—like me—can become master physickers, teachers, or researchers. Only those who graduate to full keepers sing the songs that rule the world."

Jolin's gaze went distant and she shook her head sadly. "Women like Doranna, who were never admitted at all, become wastrels because it gives them a chance to be a part of something. She and my mother have been fast friends since they were children. And my mother pays Doranna better than anyone else would."

For a chance to be a part of this, Lilette would have made the same bargain. "And those who choose not to join the wastrels?"

Jolin's expression tightened. "Become simply women, having babies and being wives." Her nostrils flared. "It is not an easy path."

Anger growled in Lilette's chest. All her life, she'd watched men measure out a woman's rights, taking what they wanted and giving far less. She would never willingly choose to be beholden to anyone. "Why would the keepers be so cruel? Everyone deserves a chance to prove herself."

Jolin scraped the last of her fish in her mouth and pushed herself back from the table. "That's exactly what Doranna and the others prove every single day."

***

Doranna didn't come back until the next day. Lilette stepped gingerly into the tree with the lunch tray and set it down. She, Jolin, and Doranna ate in smothering silence until Lilette couldn't stand it anymore. "Doranna, I'm sorry. This" —she gestured to everything around her— "is all still very foreign to me."

Doranna didn't respond.

Lilette sighed. "If what you say is true, if someone really has put me on a fast track to becoming a discipline head, I promise to try to change things."

Doranna softened a fraction and gave a curt nod. The rest of the meal was punctuated only by the scrap and clink of plates.

Ignoring her food, Jolin stared unfocused out the window. The bubbling cauldron was cold, the plants undisturbed. Yesterday, the blacksmith had sent word that their steel wasn't any stronger than regular steel. Jolin wasn't really talking to anyone yet.

Lilette finished her food. She was tired of Jolin's foul mood. What they needed was an expert on rocks and an expert on potions to work together. Lilette strode from the room without a word to Jolin or Doranna. After asking three different women where Bethel was, Lilette found her beside one of the cliffs' many waterfalls. Eyes closed, the woman sat perfectly still, nearly soaked through from the waterfall's spray.

Lilette crouched down in front of her, the spray cool against her damp face. "Bethel. It's Lilette."

"I know," the woman murmured without opening her eyes.

"Jolin is making a potion," Lilette went on. "But it seems no matter what she tries, it's not changing anything."

"That's because she's doing it wrong."

"Well, now I know were Jolin's bluntness comes from," Lilette muttered. She wiped the moisture beading on her brow before it could run into her eyes. "Can you help her?"

"Yes," the older woman said, "If she asks for my help."

Lilette pushed down her rising frustration. "Jolin is far too prideful to ask for help—especially from you."

Bethel's jaw tightened.

"And you're too prideful to offer." Lilette sighed and glanced up at the towering wall above them. It was made from solid black rock. A staircase had been carved into the side. "There's nothing at the top, so why build a staircase there?"

She started when she looked down and found Bethel staring at her.

"Because we're going to need them." Bethel paused. "Just like we're going to need Jolin's potion."

Lilette blinked. "What?"

Bethel hauled herself up with a groan and limped down the path, going faster as her limp faded.

Lilette had to hurry to keep up. "Where are you going?"

"You're right. It's fast becoming too late for pride. When everything ends, we'll need Jolin's discoveries."

Lilette threw her hands in the air. "Nothing's ending." But Bethel paid her no mind. Hurrying after her, Lilette huffed to keep up—she still hadn't recovered all her strength from nearly dying, and anything over a walk made her breathless.

Bethel entered Jolin's tree without knocking and went straight to the cold cauldron. Jolin's head popped up from the table, crease marks imprinted in her cheek from the book she'd been lying on. Her eyes were hazy with sleep. "Mother? What are you doing here?" Jolin's gaze suddenly sharpened and she glared at Lilette.

Bethel sniffed the potion, before dipping in a finger and sucking on it.

"I wouldn't do—" Jolin started.

Bethel spat it out, and Jolin's protest died on her lips. Bethel seemed to compose herself before turning to her daughter. "Potions are your area of expertise."

Jolin's jaw dropped.

Oblivious, Bethel knelt next to the rocks littering the floor. She closed her eyes and her body went still, as if she was listening. "But I know the earth. It's not like the other elements—full of life and vigor. Earth is more like a sleeping dragon. Slow to rouse and cumbersome when it wakes, but after it gets moving, it's explosive."

Jolin put her head in her hands. "I know that."

"No you don't!" Bethel turned, her face creased with anger. "The earth is alive, just like your plants or the waters. But it's so much bigger!"

"I'm simply trying to realign—"

"You're not listening!" Bethel rose to her feet and started toward the door. "You never listen."

Lilette stepped between Bethel and the exit, her hand up. "And where does she get her pride?"

Bethel shifted her weight from one foot to the other and took a deep breath. "Earth is simply too big to accomplish something so small."

Behind Bethel, Jolin mimicked her mother. Ignoring her, Lilette went on, "Then what do we need to do differently?"

Bethel rubbed her forehead with her fingertips. "You have to find a stone that's more awake. One that will listen to a potion and react more individually."

"What stone?"

Bethel paused for a few seconds. "I don't know."

Jolin threw her hands in the air and stormed into the greenhouse. Bethel closed her eyes until the last of her daughter's footsteps faded away. "And you should use a singer as well as a potion."

Lilette reached forward and put her hand awkwardly on Bethel's shoulder. "She's never felt like she was enough."

Bethel sighed. "She was always enough for me, just never for herself." Her gaze fell on Lilette's pendant. "What's this?" She was already reaching for it.

Lilette forced herself not to squirm. "The sun pendant. I wouldn't wear it, but Han—"

Bethel waved her to silence as she pulled it over Lilette's head and held it in her hand. "It's amber. Blood of the trees, frozen by the sun and wind. Hardened by thousands of years until it is something not quite stone but no longer plant. Something other."

Eyes closed in concentration, Bethel used her finger to trace a pattern through the stone. She sang, her voice commanding and clear as rainwater. The amber cracked, a crescent-shaped piece breaking off to leave an imperfect circle.

Lilette gasped. "That's mine!" Somehow, the pendant had come to stand for everything Harshen had given her—both the good and the bad.

Bethel pried off the setting and tossed it aside. She held the pieces in her hand, eyes closed. "It has been forced to be the sun, bright and hot and pumping blood, when it should have been the moon, layers of shadow and rivers swollen with life."

Jolin wandered back into the room, her footsteps hushed. Bethel turned, as if she'd heard her anyway. "This—this you could wake up."

Jolin stared at the two pieces. "What could I possibly accomplish with two pieces of amber?"

Bethel's gaze turned inward. "You cannot make a sword from coal. You cannot build a house on sand." She stretched out her hand and dropped the two pieces into Jolin's palm. "This is meant to be one piece, and it will fight to stay together. Wake up that need, give it life."

Jolin's mother hesitated a moment, as if she would say more, then shook her head and left.

Lilette bent down and picked up the discarded backing. It was solid gold—it ought to be worth something. Perhaps she could have it melted down into coins. She wandered back into their shared room and pulled down her sack of jewels, carefully adding the broken gold.

"She broke your pendant?" The voice came from behind her.

Anger pricking at her throat, Lilette nodded.

"Why would she do that?" Jolin held the amber in the palm of her hand.

Lilette reached out and brushed her thumbs along the precise edge. She curled her hands away. "She said your work was important, that many things in the future would depend on you, and that one of you should stop being prideful."

Jolin bristled. "Prideful? I'm not the prideful one." But there was no heat in her words.

Lilette shot her a look. "I've seen rocks more willing to bend than you."

Jolin wandered among her plants, her fingers skimming the edge of their leaves. "Wake up a need that's already there." Her hand stretched out, snapping a leaf from its branch.

Lilette followed her into the glass room and watched her pull a root free from the soil and lay it next to the leaf. "Wake it up. Strengthen its desire to be together." The brightness had returned to her eyes, the focus sharp enough to pierce shark skin.

A smile crept up Lilette's cheeks, but she was already late for class. She hustled to Political Studies, but her smile faded as her hand crept to the hollow of her throat. She felt empty without the familiar weight of her pendant around her neck. Empty and somehow free.

CHAPTER 27

I thought being strong meant never giving up. But it is really knowing when to fight and when to let go, and having the courage to follow through. ~Jolin

Lilette woke to a pair of hands shaking the dreams out of her. "It's ready. I know it's ready."

She cracked her eyes open and squinted at the lamp light not far from her face.

Jolin's expression was jubilant. "I've done it. I know I have. You have to sing, to wake it up."

Lilette dug the pads of her fingers into her eyes. "What have you done?"

"Created the potion to wake it up! Now get moving!"

Jolin hauled her out of the bed that had been shoved into the other corner of Jolin's room. When Lilette sat up, the hassacre slammed into her full force. She gasped in a breath as she stood, her underdress tangled around her thighs. Stumbling along after Jolin, she shook the dress to rights as best she could.

The glass garden was stuffy and hot again, but it smelled pleasant, somehow reminding Lilette of home. Doranna was there, looking exhausted and on edge. Sitting alone on a dirt-covered table was what remained of Lilette's broken pendant. The amber was dry, but a steaming puddle had formed around it.

Lilette stared blankly at it, fighting the grogginess of the sleeping potion. "What am I supposed to do?"

Jolin planted both hands on Lilette's back and pushed her forward. "I wondered the same thing after my mother left, but I just knew. How long to boil it and exactly what plants in exactly what quantity. I don't know how, but I did. And so will you."

Lilette picked up the pieces. They were hot in her hands and smelled of sweet resin. She shot a helpless glance at Doranna—surely she understood that this was madness. But the woman only stared back.

"It's like we were guided," Doranna said. "Like our minds didn't know what our bodies were doing. They just did it." Jolin shook her head in amazement, as if she still couldn't believe what had happened.

She and Doranna watched Lilette, waiting. Lilette shifted her weight uncomfortably, and then she closed her eyes as she'd seen Bethel do. She tried listening to the stone. Nothing happened.

But then something did. An image came to her mind, of resin seeping from the trunk of an ancient tree, hardening under the sun and wind until it became stone. All of the four sisters were present in this little weight on Lilette's palm. It had been one piece for thousands of years, until one sliver had been cut away. The pieces needed to be rejoined.

The comparison brought her sister to mind, and Lilette's eyes pricked with tears as she sang.

> Lost and lonely, you've gone astray,
> A part of you has been cut away.
> Until you find the other side,
> Peace and belonging will never abide.
> A song and vibration awaken your soul,
> Heal what's been broken and let it be whole.

Lilette knew she didn't need to sing the song three times, just as she knew the two pieces of amber would now find each other. "It's done."

Jolin didn't question her. She simply took the pieces of stone from her and set them on the table. She tapped the crescent with a fork. It slid across the table of its own accord and fit neatly against the other piece.

Jolin gasped with delight. She shook her fist triumphantly to the ceiling. "I did it! After all these years and all the doubters, I've finally done it!" She spun in a circle, the amber clenched to her chest. "They will have to make me Head of Earth now!"

"Well, you had some help," Doranna muttered.

Jolin laughed and kissed her full on the mouth. Doranna's eyes went wide in shock. Jolin whirled and zeroed in on Lilette. She tried to sidestep her friend, but Jolin's exuberance was greater, and Lilette too was kissed. "My friends, this is just the beginning," Jolin said. "Soon, kings will commission witches to sing them stone castles and ramparts. Soldiers will wish for our swords and bows. History shall never forget us and what we have done! We shall be written in the annuals of the keepers as the greatest, most advanced witches to have ever sung the songs."

Lilette's heart shrank away from such words. It was just too much power. Not wanting to ruin Jolin's happiness, she curled her arms around herself and said, "I think I'll go back to bed."

Jolin was already piling more leaves and roots onto the table. "Fine. Yes. Doranna, find me more amber."

Doranna rose slowly. "It's the middle of the night. There is no amber on this island."

Jolin paused before snatching a knife and slicing a root. "Ask my mother. She could find a diamond on the seashore."

As she left, Doranna grumbled something about going to bed and how Jolin could dig her own amber mine.

Lilette climbed under the cold blankets and lay awake as the hassacre throbbed around her. Sash and the others were countersinging. It was the only explanation for why the singing had gone on for as long as it had. Was Chen torturing the witches? Had he already taken them as his concubines?

Lilette watched the shadows slink away from the morning light as the bustle continued beyond her door. When she came out for breakfast, everything tasted like ash. Instead of going to class, she turned toward the cliffs. She was done waiting for Merlay and the keepers to save her sister. She was going to do something about it herself. And that meant she had to find Bethel.

***

Lilette followed the edge of the cliffs, her fingers skimming over the sculptures that seemed to be coming out of the rocks. Five stories high, they were mostly of women, but also some guardians. Their faces were so lifelike. She passed a group of four, their arms clasped and their mouths open in song. They were obviously part of a circle.

Next was a woman holding a perfect circle in her cupped hands. But no, the circle had a curved line through it. It looked like Lilette's pendant. Her gaze traveled up, resting on the woman's face. Lilette gasped and stepped back.

It was Jolin, her face suffused with joy. On one side of her was Doranna, on the other side was Lilette. Doranna looked determined and tired. Lilette found it harder to read the expression on her own face—sadness and trepidation, perhaps. It was a reflection of last night. But this sculpture was much older than that. Lichen grew along the folds of their clothes, and the sun and rain had bleached the raised parts, while the reliefs were darker.

Breathing hard, Lilette's gaze traveled to the next grouping. A single woman with three faces. The closest one was looking back, her face buried in her weeping hands. The middle face gazed serenely over the island. The one on the right glared at a wounded figure cowering before her. In her hand, she held a knife that dripped into a pool of blood at her feet.

"You should stand back."

Lilette had been so absorbed in studying the sculpture that the voice made her jump. A little farther on, Bethel stood flush with the cliffs, as if she was listening to secrets the stones whispered. Her black cloak made her nearly indistinguishable from the rocks.

Lilette scrambled over the scree toward her. "You knew about last night." Her breath turned white in the cool morning air. "How could you have known?"

Bethel didn't open her eyes. "The stone told me. Now go behind the largest tree. I can't always predict where the scree will fall."

Lilette knew what was coming. She was about to watch Bethel create the sculptures, see firsthand the source of the crashing sounds that regularly shattered the island's routine.

Lilette found the tree Bethel meant and stumbled behind it. Tucked safely behind the buttress roots, she peered out and had the sense she was witnessing something magnificent—something no one in the history of the world had ever seen before.

Bethel spent a few more silent minutes pressed against the rock. "There." She backed up behind a tree. Her eyes closed as if in concentration, she sang,

> I reveal what lies hidden beneath,
> Waiting too for the song of release.
> Rocks and stone,
> I've come to hone.
> Keepers of old,
> Show us our mold.

A thousand cracks filled the air like the sound of a hurricane, only louder and deeper. A fracture rent the rock, and a whole side of the cliff collapsed. Rocks tumbled down, dust billowing outward.

Lilette buried her face in the smooth bark of the tree, her fingers white as she pressed her fists into her ears to block out the deafening noise as the ground rumbled beneath her. When the world finally stilled, she peeked around the roots. The air was choked with dust that blocked her view. Coughing, she pulled her collar over her mouth and tried to take shallow breaths.

Bethel climbed over the rubble, her eyes glued to the cliff's face. Stepping cautiously up beside her, Lilette sang softly for the damp wind. The air cleared, revealing the cliffs. Her eyes went as round as the jumble of stones at the cliffs' base. The side had collapsed, exposing the lower half of a woman. Her feet dangled as if she floated in the air. But it was her clothing that made Lilette's heart stutter in her chest. The image wore slippers and a tunic with loose trousers, the patterns shown by subtle depressions in the stone.

Bethel reached out and pulled Lilette next to her. "Stay close."

Lilette sang again. More of the cliffs collapsed, revealing part of a face and releasing another cloud of dust. She impatiently sang the dust away.

Bethel's voice joined hers. Though their songs were different, the melodies enhanced one another. More of the cliff collapsed, revealing a woman's face. Lilette sat down hard, rocks bruising her backside.

It was her. The woman floating in the air was her. Her arms were thrown back, tears etching grooves down her cheeks. Her eyes looked up at the sky as if to ask how it could have come to this. How the world could ask so much. Lilette knew this was her future, and her soul ached with dread. She forgot all about Bethel until the older woman sat beside her.

"The stone told you this—that this is my future?" Lilette asked.

Bethel gestured to the sculpture of the three-faced woman. "It's recorded in every history book ever written. At a civilization's peak, the great and mighty destroy themselves."

Lilette swallowed a sob. "No."

Bethel's eyes were sad. "The moment I touched the amber, I realized it was meant to save you. You must take a piece. Another you must give to a guardian—one who has proven himself true to the end. That way, he will be able to find you when no one else can."

"I don't know how you did this." Lilette motioned to the cliffs. "Maybe you sang for the lichen, or have some way of aging the rock face like that."

Bethel picked up a rock, weighing it in her hands. "Some things you have to learn for yourself. I thought you had."

Lilette wanted to argue, but some deeply buried kernel of dread kept her silent.

"Why did you come here today, Lilette?"

She swallowed. "Because I'm done waiting for the keepers to free my sister. I'm going to do something about it, and I wanted your help."

Bethel met her gaze. "You already have all the help you need."

Lilette didn't know how to respond.

"We all have our own burden to bear. Mine is to create this."
Bethel held out her hands to indicate the island.

"Haven—a school?"

Bethel laughed softly, a bitter sound, and tossed the rock
away. "I'm not making a school. I'm making a last bastion of
defense."

Lilette looked back at the towering cliffs. "You're carving
history, so future generations will know what happened?"

Bethel studied the sculptures on the walls. "Stone lasts longer
than vellum. I hope that someday, they will see the message I
carved for them. We were once the strongest entity in the world.
But someday we will be the weakest."

The wars and destruction her mother had shown her. But Lilette
had freed the other witches from Harshen. She'd prevented that
disaster. Hadn't she?

Bethel's voice dropped. "I won't be able to say goodbye to
my daughter—she won't go if I do—and I fear I shall never see
her again. Will you tell her for me? Tell her I know she'll do her
part."

Lilette opened her mouth, then closed it again.

Bethel's hand rested on her back. "Take Doranna and Harberd
with you. You'll need the protection."

"Where is it you think we're going?"

Bethel sighed. "The stone didn't tell me that."

Lilette searched the one sculpture whose meaning was not
immediately apparent—the woman with three faces. "Is that
supposed to be a metaphor for the keepers?"

Bethel's hand fell away from Lilette's back "Yes. The one
facing out is our present, standing serene and calm in our power.
The one looking back is our past, grieving for what we shall lose
even as our future destroys itself."

"Bethel . . ." Lilette whispered.

"When the time comes, you must act," the older woman said
calmly. "We all must. Save those you can."

Lilette winced. Bethel had used almost the exact same words
her mother had.

Chapter 28

I needed Lilette, but I never stopped to consider that she might need me too. ~Jolin

"Lilette?"

A guardian stood a short distance away. Apart from the sailors who delivered supplies, men didn't come onto the island.

Lilette scrambled to her feet, her stiff legs straining in protest. "Yes?"

The man approached them. He was a little older than Lilette, with a heart-stoppingly beautiful face and an adorable cowlick that made a patch of his hair stand at attention. "My name is Pescal. If you will please come with me." His arm swept forward, indicating that she should go ahead of him.

Bethel looked up from her place on the hard rocks. She looked so small and lonely. "You'll remember to tell Jolin?"

Lilette studied the older woman. How must it have been to know dark things were coming, to prepare for them alone, while your peers called you a fool? "I believe you. And I'll tell her."

Bethel closed her eyes, tipped her face up to the sky, and smiled.

Taking a deep breath to steel herself, Lilette moved ahead of the guardian. It wasn't long before they were among the witches again and the path widened enough for Pescal to walk beside her. Remembering her training to become empress, she threw her shoulders back. "I'm waiting for an explanation."

Pescal's green eyes studied her. "The Heads have called you back to Grove City. You are to bring your personal effects."

Was it beginning already? "What for?"

Pescal hesitated. "I don't know."

Lilette closed her eyes. Hadn't some part of her known this was coming? She took in her surroundings. The shorter trees, the witchlings in dresses of green rushing to and from classes, their books clutched to their chests.

She had not been happy here. She'd been lonely and frightened and full of guilt for leaving her sister behind. And she'd drowned out those feelings with the tincture Bethel had given her. All her life, Lilette had dreamed of coming here. In less than two weeks, she was relieved to be leaving.

She stepped through the open door of her tree to find Jolin dumping a whole sack of amber pieces into a potion. Doranna was scrambling to pack books and notes into straw-filled crates.

Jolin glanced up. "There's a scroll for you on the table." She indicated it with a jerk of her head.

In a daze, Lilette went to the table and picked it up. On the thick, textured vellum was an embossed seal of a crescent moon in dark green wax. She broke the seal and unrolled the scroll. She'd been promoted from a witchling to an apprentice. "Did you know what this was?" she asked Jolin.

Her friend didn't look up. "Since witchlings aren't allowed to leave Haven unless they're being kicked out, I imagine you've been advanced to an apprentice."

Lilette glanced at Pescal, who stood just outside their door with his hands clasped behind him, and back to Jolin. "You're coming with me?"

A grin broke out over Jolin's face. "I sent a letter to the Heads informing them of my discovery. They've requested an immediate audience. I suspect they'll want to show off my discovery at the chesli harvest." That explained Jolin's frantic making of more potion. "They'll have to make me Head of Plants after this. My skill obviously exceeds Garen's."

When Lilette didn't comment, Jolin made a shooing motion. "Pack your things. We'll be ready for you to sing for this shortly."

Lilette stared at the scroll, not really seeing it.

Jolin straightened and her gaze narrowed. "My mother went crazy again, didn't she?"

Lilette hesitated before meeting Jolin's gaze.

"Did she start in on the end of the world or how we're going to save everyone?"

"Both."

"Well then," Jolin said, "let's get off this island before we're stuck spending the rest of our very short lives with her."

Lilette wet her lips. "Jolin, I believe her."

Jolin froze, a book in one hand, a handful of straw in the other. "Sometimes I miss social cues, so I'll just ask outright— are you being facetious?"

Instead of answering, Lilette moved toward the small room she'd shared with Jolin.

"Of course she was being facetious. Silly of me to think otherwise," Jolin grumbled to herself.

Lilette's gaze took in the books crammed on the shelves, the bed they'd brought in for her, even the lump in the middle of the floor that she'd stumbled over numerous times.

She pulled her bag of jewels out from behind the book, took her extra dress down from its peg, and she was packed.

She turned back into the main room in time to see Jolin hissing as she picked up a piece of hot amber. She blew on her fingers. "Oh! Creators' mercy!"

Lilette couldn't help but smile.

Jolin glanced around. "Doranna, tell Cori to care for my plants. I'll need you with me for this."

Doranna pursed her lips. "What if your mother needs me?"

"She'll be fine. She always is, despite your fussing."

Lilette hesitated. "Maybe she should stay." If they all left, Bethel would be alone.

Jolin rolled her eyes. "Doranna was part of this. She deserves some of the credit." She gingerly touched the amber. "It's ready. Sing for it while I finish packing."

"Must you really take all these books?" Lilette asked.

Jolin shot her a disbelieving look. "When I move into the Head of Earth's tree, I'll need my books. Everything will change after this."

Lilette's breath caught in her throat. "I hope not. I like things the way they are." Of course, the exceptions included being separated from her sister and Han.

"Well," Jolin huffed. "I do not."

By midday, they stood on the deck of the ship as it took them away from Haven. Lilette caught sight of a single figure standing atop the cliffs, one hand raised in goodbye.

"Jolin." She nudged her friend, who tore her gaze away from checking the books in the crates to look up.

"Who's that?"

"Your mother."

Jolin shielded her eyes with her hands. "Can't be. Mother never says goodbye."

A deep foreboding washed over Lilette, with the distinct impression she'd never see these cliffs again.

Before midafternoon, she stood in front of the Heads' pavilion, watching Jolin and Doranna march ahead of her. "Do you know a man named Han?" Lilette asked Pescal.

He hesitated. "The Harshen prince?"

"Yes. Can you find a way to bring him word that I am here?"

"I'll see it done."

She moved to follow the others, but Pescal stepped up beside her and cleared his throat. "Lilette?"

She turned to him. He smiled, and his teeth were straight and white and perfect. "At the celebration tonight, there will be dancing. Might I dance with you?"

She smiled uncertainly. "I don't know . . ."

"Just one." His smile grew even bigger, and Lilette noticed dimples on his cheeks. When she didn't immediately say no, he bowed to her. "Don't worry, I'll find you."

He turned to go before she could find the words to tell him no. He was certainly handsome, especially from behind, but she really wasn't interested. For one thing, he was far too pretty. And for another, he wasn't Han. She stepped inside the pavilion. Jolin was already demonstrating the amber, and Garen was glaring at her.

"Oh, that's amazing," Merlay said.

Tawny watched them, a suspicious look on her face. "Will it work over long distances? Does the effect wear out over time?"

Jolin rubbed her hands together in barely restrained glee. "All of that will have to be tested, but the technique itself can be easily replicated." Though only by Jolin, for Lilette knew she always left out a key ingredient to all the recipes for her potions.

The group chattered on excitedly, but Lilette tuned them out. She was tired of feeling dull from the tinctures Bethel had given her. Tired of using them to deaden her emotions.

Lilette felt a hand on her arm. Jolin shook her head and gave her a queer look. "I said Lilette was the person who finally pushed us all onto the right path. She deserves a small share of the credit."

Lilette shot Jolin an exasperated look.

"What? One moment of inspiration doesn't make up for a lifetime of study."

Lilette rolled her eyes.

Jolin straightened. "Fine. A slightly larger share of the credit. Will that do?"

Lilette didn't care either way, but it was fun to watch her friend squirm. "I believe it will."

"Very well."

Merlay watched the exchange with an amused crook of an eyebrow. "With all the trouble with Harshen, Grove City has been tense. Jolin's discovery is just the thing to boost morale. The chesli will begin to bloom tonight, and the inner courts will open to everyone for dancing and singing. Before the feast, we'll announce Jolin's discovery." Merlay turned to the four wastrels waiting off to the side. "See that they're properly dressed."

Lilette moved closer to Merlay. "I would like to speak to you about Sash, in private."

Merlay sighed and came down. They moved off to one side. "We're doing everything we can," she told Lilette.

"I want to help."

Merlay studied her. "That's part of the reason we called you here. I have a proposal for you, but Garen has been holding out—refusing to agree. That won't be a problem anymore."

Lilette glanced at Jolin's beaming face. "You're going to make her Head of Plants?"

"We don't have much of a choice. Even if she's not a full keeper." Merlay rested her hand on Lilette's arm. "Give me a few more hours to have everything settled and I'll tell you my plan. We'll go from there."

Lilette nodded, relieved to be doing something besides sitting back and watching everyone else bumble about.

Doranna stepped toward them. "I'll take care of Lilette."

Merlay handed her a money purse. "Very well."

"Come with me." Doranna turned away.

While Jolin and Harberd went with one of the other wastrels, Lilette followed Doranna from the inner courts into the city proper. Lilette paused in front of a tree with large windows featuring beautiful dresses, but the cuts and styles seemed wrong and foreign. She had a strong sense she was of two worlds and yet belonged to neither. "Not this."

Doranna hadn't even paused to consider the shop. "Of course not."

They wove through throngs of people, their excited chatter about the night's events making their voices louder and fuller than normal. Doranna stopped in front of a smaller tree.

At the familiar scent of incense, Lilette passed her and stepped inside. It was like coming home. Potted plants from the jungle, curved swords, jade combs . . . and linen sacks, the tops curled back to reveal a familiar grain. "Rice!" Lilette filled her hands with it.

A man came from the back of the shop. Seeing her, he called for his wife in Harshen. A woman emerged from behind a curtain. She wore the same style of cotton tunic and trousers that Lilette had worn most of her life.

Lilette's mouth formed the familiar words of the Harshen language. "I can't tell you how much I've missed rice."

The woman's face lit up. "You speak like one of us!"

Lilette smiled. "I am one of you."

The woman studied her through slitted eyes, then her expression went wide. "Empress!" She dropped to her knees and pressed her forehead to the floor three times. A beat behind her, her husband did the same. Lilette watched them so freely offer her such an honor, knowing she didn't deserve it.

They sat back on their heels, eyes downcast, and Lilette gestured for them to rise. "Please, I would like a tunic and trousers to wear to the celebration tonight."

The man rose to his feet. "I'm not sure I have the quality you require, Empress. Our silk is plain."

Lilette sighed. "But it is silk."

The man motioned for her to step behind the curtain. Amid the bolts of dyed silk, already-made tunics and trousers were draped across forms. There were three women's sets—one in yellow, one green, and one a deep turquoise the color of the sky at dusk. Lilette's fingers slipped across the silk. She had no more calluses on her palms to catch the fabric. "This one."

She stepped into a changing room and dropped the tunic over her head. The silk whispered over her skin before settling around her curves. The woman helped her wrap a pleated belt around her waist. Lilette pulled out the ruby brooch from her jewels and let it hang from its delicate chain. She hoped the sight of it would please Han.

She came out of the room and knelt on a mat that had been placed out for her. The man came with a clay pot of tea. He poured hot water over the cups to warm them while the woman worked on Lilette's hair.

The man placed the tea before her. Lilette lifted the fragrant cup to her nose and inhaled long and deep. She nodded in thanks and sipped her tea while the woman fixed her hair.

By then, the man had returned with a bamboo bowl of rice and vegetables with brown sauce and ginger. Lilette ate eagerly, her whole body sighing in relief at the familiar food.

The woman held up a mirror and waited while Lilette examined her hair. It was much simpler than what her eunuch had managed, but she liked it better. She pulled the comb Salfe had given her from her pouch and slid it in next to her scalp.

The woman prepared a pot of kohl and vermillion red. With a soft brush, she painted Lilette's lips and darkened her nearly translucent eyebrows and lashes. When she was finished, Lilette found herself looking at a version of herself somewhere between a fisherman's daughter and the empress she had been.

Doranna smiled approvingly. "You're more at home like this."

Lilette nodded. "I didn't realize it before now, but Harshen is my home, despite all its faults."

The other woman nodded sagely. "We feel the same way."

"I too know what that is like," Doranna said. She paid the couple while Lilette stepped into the twilight and inhaled deeply the delicate honey scent on the air.

Dropping coins into her pouch, Doranna stepped up beside her. "It won't be long before Merlay begins the feast."

They joined the throng of people flowing uphill like a backward stream into the inner courts.

"Do you know what Merlay has in store for me?" Lilette asked.

Doranna wouldn't meet her gaze. "I have an idea, but it's best not to speculate. Just enjoy one night of being a witch and let tomorrow take care of itself."

As soon as Lilette passed the barbed bushes, she started searching for Han. As evening descended, the small, white, bell-shaped buds of the climbing vines eased open, their stamens glowing golden. "What are they?" Lilette asked.

"Chesli," Doranna replied. "It only blooms once a year on a moonless night. The pollen extends the life of a potion indefinitely."

Amid the gaiety and laughter, strains of ethereal music were carried on a gentle breeze. The wastrels bent their backs to the harvest. Their glowing, pollen-speckled robes made them look like ghosts in the dim light.

Lilette paused to watch them, an unnamed discontent squatting on her tongue. Then the crowd pressed in on her and she glanced around, realizing she'd lost Doranna. Lilette searched as she was jostled to and fro, pressed in on from all sides. She was trapped. She couldn't breathe, couldn't think. Ever since she'd been trapped in a barrel for an entire night, she could not abide tight spaces.

She spotted Doranna through the crowd. Lilette called to her, tried to make her way closer, but the crowd kept pushing her back. Just when she'd truly started to panic, Pescal appeared at her side, that adorable patch of hair sticking up. "You look like you could use some help."

She pointed to Doranna. "My friend is over there."

His brow furrowed before he shook his head. "We won't make it through that. Come on."

Relieved, Lilette allowed him to take her elbow. "Doranna will worry." She had to shout to be heard over the din.

He glanced back at her. "She'll be all right. Come on." He pushed his way expertly through. In no time, they'd reached the pavilion, which was laden with tables of food. The Heads stood at the top of the steps, looking down on the crowd.

Jolin stood off to the side, a smug look on her face. Garen's eyes were red rimmed and swollen as if she'd been crying.

Merlay spread her arms. "The first day of the chesli harvest is for food and dancing."

As one, all four Heads bowed and the music changed from haunting to a lively dancing song. Lilette couldn't see Han anywhere.

Pescal grabbed her hand and hauled her up the stairs. They were among the first to reach the tables laden with a feast of fruits, vegetables, and pastries. After piling food onto two large, stiff leaves that Lilette had no doubt had been sung for this very purpose, Pescal managed to wrangle her past the guardians keeping watch on the Head's private gardens. They wove past important-looking people and found a spot to sit among the white flowers.

Lilette took her first bite of fruit, the juice and sour sweetness exploding on her tongue. They ate fruits she had never tasted before—and never the same one twice. Pescal regaled her with stories of famous guardians, his manner jovial. Every once in a while, he absently tried to smooth down his cowlick, but it stubbornly stuck right back up again.

Between the food and the laughter, Lilette forgot her worry over losing sight of Doranna. Feeling safe with Pescal, she kept an eye out for Han, hoping he'd know where to look for her.

When Pescal finished eating, he tossed his leaf plate out of sight. "You can eat them, but I'm stuffed."

Lilette was too busy watching the path from the pavilion to reply.

"Are you looking for someone, Lilette?" Pescal asked.

Lilette focused on him. "I'm sorry. I thought Han would have found me by now. Would you help me look for him?"

Pescal's grin faded. "Lilette, would I be correct in assuming you have feelings for the man?"

She didn't deny it.

He looked away. "Then I am sorry to say, he did not wish to see you."

The fruit Lilette had been holding slipped from her fingers and landed with a wet plop in her lap. "What?"

Pescal gently removed the fruit, which had left a dark splotch on her robes. He wetted a handkerchief and pressed it into her hands. "I am sorry. He said there is too much between you."

Her hands curled into a fist around the fabric, rivulets of moisture running between her fingers as the hurt washed over her, settling deep into her bones—so deep she wasn't sure she could ever shake it.

Pescal grinned wryly. "And here I was hoping to have a good time with such a beautiful woman."

She stared absently at the dark stain on her robes before daubing at it with the handkerchief.

Pescal sighed and handed her his cup. "Here, try this."

When she didn't take it, he held it to her lips. "It will help."

She held and sipped the drink, which tasted of sweet melons with a tangle of citrus and pear. She finished off the entire cup. He was right—she did feel better. Sort of floaty and warm.

He reached for her hand and helped her up. "You promised me a dance, remember?" He twirled her around and they danced.

Lilette didn't know the steps, but she picked them up quickly, laughing when she stumbled and fell into him.

He caught her against his chest. Before she knew what was happening, he bent down and kissed her. "You taste like melons!" Laughing, he pulled back and twirled her around before she could process what had just happened.

Dizzy, she backed away from him. "Stop, I can't breathe."

Pescal gave her a mock bow. "Then I shall bring you something to revive you and we shall dance again."

She watched as he trotted away, his hand on the sword at his waist to keep it from bouncing.

A breeze picked up and she leaned into it, grateful for the coolness against her damp forehead and the smell of crushed flowers and sap. Closing her eyes, she lay back and closed her eyes, the flowers soft as a bed beneath her. She turned her head to see if Pescal was coming back from the pavilion yet. There was no sign of him.

Everything was swaying gently in the breeze, so Han's stillness caught her attention almost immediately. He stood with his back against a nearby tree, his gaze intense. The smile melted from Lilette's face and something lurched within her. Had he seen the kiss? Part of her hoped he had, wanted him to see her with someone else. She pushed herself to her feet.

Han strode toward her, power in his gait. When he stood before her, he searched her gaze and the gentleness she'd seen before was gone, replaced with a wall she knew she'd never scale. The breeze washed over them, bringing Lilette the steel and leather smell of him.

"Chen has been using your sister and the others to fight back against Kalari," he said.

Lilette instinctively wrapped her arms around herself. "I know."

Han looked off in the direction Pescal had gone. "I don't think this can go on much longer. The hope for peace grows more fragile with every passing day."

She caught sight of Pescal weaving through the gardens toward her and let out a tiny breath of relief. "What do you think will happen?" she whispered.

Han watched Pescal, something dark crossing his face. "I don't know." He paused. "I'm surprised Doranna let you out here by yourself."

"I lost her."

Han cut her a glance. "Wastrels aren't allowed in the gardens unless their services are called for. I thought you knew that."

Lilette wondered if Doranna had been searching for her all this time.

Pescal arrived with light pastries and two cups filled with golden liquid. "I would have brought more if I'd known someone else was going to join us." Despite his friendly words, their undercurrent clearly said Han was not welcome.

Lilette wasn't sure how she felt about that, but Han had already made his choice, so she remained silent.

Han studied Pescal, his eyes glinting, and then he turned to Lilette. "You'll be staying at Sash's tree tonight?"

Panic stabbed through her. She didn't know where she was supposed to stay.

He must have noticed her hesitation. "You know how to find it?"

She mentally retraced the path. "Yes."

Han gave Pescal a hard look. "I'll be waiting to see you arrive safely." He turned and strode away without looking back.

Pescal didn't press the issue, just handed her the cup and guided her to a nearby tree. She drank the liquid eagerly. It tasted the way flowers smelled. Some layer of it was familiar, but she couldn't place it. Delicious.

Pescal handed her half of a pastry. The flakes dissolved in her mouth, and she licked the sugar off her fingers.

Her body seemed to be waking up, every sensation magnified. The gentle caress of the wind felt enticing. Pescal stroked her arm, sending tendrils of fire through her blood. He leaned forward and pressed his lips to hers, igniting a spark between them. "My tree isn't far from here."

"Mmm," she murmured, her eyes closed. Some part of her blared a warning, but it was overcome with the heat and the sensations.

He helped her to her feet, his fingers trailing down her side to rest on her lower hip. Unable to help herself, she reached up and twirled his cowlick around her finger.

He leaned down and breathed in her ear. "Come on, we'll go out the back way. Less people to fight through."

Desire ripped through her, nearly making her gasp. "Yes." She would go wherever he led her.

"What are you doing?" Lilette whirled around to see Doranna rushing toward them, her face red and her gaze furious. "You know you're not supposed to be out of my sight."

Pescal brushed his lips along Lilette's ear, and fire pulsed in her lower belly. She just wanted Doranna gone. Now. "I'm all right with Pescal." He chuckled and nuzzled her ear.

Doranna shot him a murderous glare. "She's an apprentice, and you know it. Your Lead will hear about this, I promise you."

He kept moving. "I'm just looking after her, making sure she finds somewhere to sleep tonight."

Doranna planted herself directly in their path. "No you aren't, and no you won't."

"Get out of my way, wastrel." Pescal put an unnecessary amount of venom into the last word.

Lilette pulled back, shocked at the hatred in his voice. "Don't talk to her like that."

Pescal's entire demeanor changed as he turned toward her—the meanness sucked back in like an oyster snapping shut. "Sorry, sweetling. I just want to do what's best for you." He stiffened as he turned back to Doranna. "You are excused."

Lilette ran her tongue over the roof of her mouth, her lips aching to be kissed. She pushed against him. "Let me go."

"It'll be all right—better than all right," he purred as his hold on her tightened. He stroked the back of her hand with his thumb, and the fight drained out of her.

"Let her go," Doranna said tightly.

A muscle in Pescal's face twitched. "Get out of my way."

Doranna's fist flashed out, connecting with Pescal's temple. He staggered back, knocking Lilette down. He scrambled to his feet and lunged at Doranna, but she skipped out of his reach.

"Guardians!" Doranna called. She rolled on the ground, coming up before Lilette, who was struggling to get on her feet.

Within seconds, high-level guardians had converged, hands on their ornate swords. "What's going on here?" one of them asked.

Doranna pointed a shaking finger at Pescal. "This man is trying to take advantage of an apprentice."

Pescal tenderly touched his temple, which was already swelling. "She hit me! That wastrel hit me!" There was no denying the hatred now.

They all turned to Lilette, whose emotions were so strong they made her shake. She wrapped her arms around herself to stop herself from stepping towards Pescal. "I–I think I'm going to be sick." Her eyes locked with Doranna's. "I *need* him," she whispered. "Why do I need him?"

"Creators' mercy," Doranna gasped. She gave Pescal a look that could flay the spines off a sea urchin.

One of the guardians strode to Pescal and gripped the collar of his shirt. "You think you can get away with drugging a witch, boy?"

He said nothing.

Lilette was quaking with the urge to be touched. Licking her lips, she stepped toward the guardian. "Drugging me?"

The guardian took a step back, dragging Pescal with him. "Can you get her home? I'd send some of my guardians with you, but . . ."

Doranna gave a curt nod. "I'll take care of her."

"Drugged me how?" Lilette asked. "What did he do to me?"

Doranna took a firm grip on Lilette's elbow and herded her toward the pavilion. "You were warned never to accept food or drink you hadn't seen prepared." Her words were soft, but they stung anyway. "You live among witches, child. Potions are easy to find—even the dangerous ones."

Tears pricked Lilette's eyes. "It was Pescal—I trusted him."

"Come on. I have something that will help," Doranna said. They left the gardens, passing a pair of guardians restricting those who could go in. Lilette found herself drifting toward the closest one.

Doranna held firm to her arm. "Keep your gaze down—it will help."

Lilette stared at the ground. "I thought you couldn't come into the gardens."

"Only if we're called for."

"But I didn't call for you."

Doranna didn't respond.

Inside the pavilion, only a scattering of food remained. Beyond, the crowd had thinned from a solid mass to clusters of witches who were far outnumbered by the wastrels still hard at work gathering pollen.

"Where'd everybody go?"

"Home, mostly. It's after midnight, and the festivities continue tomorrow. The gates will be closed soon, and the rest will have to leave as well."

Even with her eyes downcast, Lilette knew where the men were. Not going to them was physically painful. She tried to concentrate on the discarded leaf plates crushing under her feet and giving off the smell of sap, which mixed with the honey smell of the chesli flowers. "Doranna, I—" She pulled free and bolted toward an older man, not caring about the woman on his arm.

Doranna grabbed her arm and dug her heels in. "Han is waiting for us at Sash's tree. He's the one who sent me inside the gardens."

Lilette fixed her gaze on the path and started marching down it, not caring whom she passed. Han stood up from the table when she shoved the door open. She shot into his arms.

He stumbled back, surprised. "What—"

"Hold her," Doranna said.

Lilette buried her face in his chest and the pain ebbed away, but the desire flared up stronger than ever. She tried to stop her hands from tracing the bulk of his muscles. Tried and failed.

He trapped her hands against his chest. "Lilette?" He pushed her back to look at her face. "What's wrong with her?"

Doranna was busy searching through the shelves and didn't bother to answer.

His gaze locked with Lilette's, and his eyes widened. "Her pupils are solid black!"

Lilette didn't care. She tipped forward, brushing Han's earlobe with the tip of her nose. Creators' mercy, he smelled so good. "I want to taste you," she whispered before licking his neck.

He froze. "What did he give her?" His voice was deadly and cold.

Doranna set down a half dozen clinking bottles. "A love potion."

"So she's in love with him now!" Han roared.

"She's in love with the nearest man," Doranna corrected as she poured ingredients into the bowl.

"I'm going to kill him." Han pulled away from Lilette just as her lips found his collarbones. She cried out and moved to follow him, her hands outstretched.

"You leave and she'll be out searching for someone else! I barely got her here." Doranna added dried leaves and ground something in a pestle. "You can kill him later."

"Han." Lilette's voice was trembling. The smell of crushed herbs hung between them.

He slowly shook his head. "I'm not sure if I'm strong enough."

"Please," Lilette whispered.

"You want me to find another guardian to keep her occupied until I can make this potion?"

Han took one reluctant step toward her and another. And then he was holding her. She melted against him, his body next to hers sending a shock through her. She tipped forward and pressed her mouth to his neck, gently kissing him.

He moaned. "Doranna, hurry."

Knowing his resolve was weakening, that she was close—so close—to having him touch her back, Lilette worked her way up his neck to his jaw. He looked at her, defeat in his gaze.

She leaned forward and took his lower lip between her teeth, sucking gently. He moaned softly. Fire licked up Lilette's middle before settling into a warm ember in her lower belly.

"Try not to react," Doranna said.

Lilette chuckled on the inside. He'd already let go of her hands, and she was making good use of them, pulling up his tunic to run her hands across his broad chest. "Han," she whispered in a breathy voice. "Don't you want to touch me too?"

With a groan, he pulled her into his arms and kissed her— kissed her like she'd always dreamed he would, with no taste of goodbye, no regrets. Just need and want and the promise that he'd never leave.

Then Doranna shoved him. "Hey! She's had the love potion, not you."

Gasping for breath, Han pressed her forehead against his neck. "If you don't give her something, we're both going to be in trouble."

"Lilette, drink this."

She was too busy with her hands to listen.

"Lilette, drink it," Han begged.

She smiled against his skin. "Only if you promise me something."

"What?" His voice was low and gravelly.

"Promise to come upstairs with me."

He swallowed, his Adam's apple bobbing up and down.

"It's all right," Doranna said. "Promise her."

"I promise."

Without looking at the other woman, Lilette held out her hand. Doranna placed the mortar in her palm. Lilette wrinkled her nose at the sharp smell of crushed herbs mixed with some kind of liquor and tipped back the mortar, nearly gagging as the sludge crawled into her mouth. Her throat burned and her eyes watered. She scrubbed her tongue along the ridges at the top of her mouth to try to clear out the taste.

She started to put down the mortar, but Han tipped it up. Just the pressure of his fingers on hers was enough to convince her to finish the rest.

Once it was gone, Doranna took it from her and collapsed on a chair.

"What does it do?" Han closed his eyes as she took his earlobe in her mouth.

Doranna rubbed her face. "Something to make her sleep and something else to counteract any potion."

Lilette felt dizzy. She pulled back to look at Han, but her vision had gone fuzzy. A sudden lethargy weighed down her limbs. "You promised," she reminded him.

Doranna waved him off. "Go on. She won't do anything but sleep anyway."

"Come on." Cupping her elbow, he guided her toward the stairs. Her body was heavy and light all at once. Han gave a grunt of frustration before scooping her into his arms.

She nestled her head against his chest as they wound up the stairs. "Han?"

"Hmm?" he grunted as he maneuvered her feet first into a room.

"I think you're in love with me." His arms tightened around her and she sighed against him. "You shouldn't be. It's very dangerous to love me."

He eased her onto a mattress of rushes and pressed a kiss to her forehead. "I know," he whispered against her skin.

But Lilette was already dreaming, and his words burned to ashes that blew away before she could capture them.

CHAPTER 29

I would have done things differently had I known it was the last time I would see my mother and my home. ~Jolin

Lilette woke choking on her own scream. She shot up in bed, her heart pounding hard enough to bruise her ribs. Her head felt like it was full of boiling water. She twisted in bed just in time to vomit all over the floor.

Doranna was by her side in an instant. "What's wrong?"

Lilette pressed the back of her wrist to her mouth and swallowed to keep from vomiting again. "Hassacre."

Doranna reared back and squinted out the window. "This close, if the witches were singing, we would hear them."

Lilette's head pounded in rhythm with the horrible twisting around her. She pressed her fists over her ears and moaned. "Where's Han?" Creators' mercy, had she really thrown herself at him like that?

"Downstairs." Doranna rested a hand on Lilette's back. "Has it ever been this bad?"

"No." Lilette struggled to smooth out the waver in her voice. She would not cry. "This isn't the shifting of the elements to turn the seasons against themselves. This is using the elements as weapons."

"But you've felt that before."

Lilette nodded. "So why is this time different?"

Doranna's eyes widened. "The potion I gave you last night, it would have cleansed the sleeping tincture from your body."

"Creators help me, I cannot bear it!" Lilette pushed herself to her feet and started forward. She had no idea where she was going, only that the world was screaming its death cry and she had to stop it.

She stumbled down the stairs. Near the door, Han was sitting up, his gleaming chest laced with scars, some white with age, others a livid pink. Creators' mercy, she'd *felt* them last night.

"What's wrong?" He blinked up at her.

Lilette couldn't look at him. But what had happened between them didn't matter, not right now.

Doranna quickly filled him in while Lilette started toward the door. Han pulled his tunic over his head and grabbed his weapons and knives, struggling to juggle them while buckling them on. "Are they sinking Harshen?" he asked. His gaze locked with Lilette's, and her resolve hardened within her.

"If they are, I'll make them pay." She wrenched open the door and trotted down the steps. The chesli flowers were still open, moths and other night insects dancing from one to the next. But the people were gone. "Where is everyone?"

"They clear them out of the inner city after the witchling hour."

Using her witch sense, Lilette led them uphill, toward the source of the discord. "It's nighttime—why isn't it raining?"

"It never rains during the chesli harvest," Doranna said.

The closer they got, the worse the hassacre became. Lilette pitched forward and vomited bile into the foliage at the side of the path.

Han stood beside her. She held out a hand, trying to keep him away from the sight of her spitting vomit.

"Can't you help her?" he pleaded with Doranna. "Surely there's some kind of tincture."

Lilette shook her head. After what Pescal had done to her, she would never take a tincture again. She spit into the bushes and dropped her voice to a whisper. "Why? Why have you turned away from me—after everything we've been through?" She shouldn't care about this now, but she had to know.

"Turned away . . ." His gaze darkened. "Is that what he told you?"

She realized that Han hadn't even seemed to recognize Pescal last night. Pescal had lied about everything.

"I'm going to find him. And I'm going to kill him," Han growled.

Doranna picked a handful of mint leaves and handed them to Lilette. "Suck on these."

Shoving them into her mouth, she let go of some of her shame about how she'd acted last night. It wasn't her fault. And she hadn't lost Han. She took hold of his arm. "Come on. People are dying. Creators help me, I can feel their screams."

She staggered forward, picking up speed until she was running. Finally, they stepped into the ring of power. But it was empty. Lilette gripped the hair at her temples. "I don't understand."

Doranna took a step toward her. "Child, you have a lot of potions in your body. Perhaps—"

"No!" Lilette gasped for breath. "I know what I feel."

"Lilette," Han began. "There's no one here."

She turned a full circle in the moonlight. "Yes, they are. I can feel it." She closed her eyes and spread her witch sense. The wind tugged at her hair, bringing with it the smell of something burning. And as surely as she knew this chanting was destruction made audible, she knew it was directed at Harshen. And it was the strongest at the tree beside them.

Squaring herself, Lilette marched toward a large tree. The smooth expanse of bark seemed to mock her.

"Lilette," Doranna whispered, "we should go back."

Closing her eyes again, Lilette pressed the flat of her hands against the tree. Her witch senses combed it, searching for something different. "It's hollow."

"Of course it's hollow," Doranna said. "All the trees are."

Lilette opened her eyes. "This part of the tree isn't alive."

Han stepped up beside her. "What are you saying?"

Her searching fingers found a lip. "I'm saying this is a door."

Bracing herself, she pushed. It swung soundlessly forward, revealing a sliver of blackness. After glancing back at the others, Lilette slipped inside. They came in behind her, and Han pushed the door closed. Lilette couldn't see much, but far below there was a purple glow. Bracing one arm against the side of the tree, she felt the floor with her foot. It disappeared abruptly before her. Gingerly, she stepped down. "They're stairs. Come on," she whispered.

They moved toward the light, which shifted from purple to green and sent waves of fear through her that made her heart pound. Finally, she stepped into a huge cavern with the base of the tree serving as the roof. In the center was an opaque sphere in a shifting miasma of pastels. A strong sense of wrongness emanated from it.

A deep instinct warned Lilette to turn and run from this place. Here, there was no dawn—no warmth and light to chase away the shadows. Nothing but emptiness and death, like a soul forced to remain in its rotting corpse for all eternity.

She stretched out her hand to touch the sphere, but Doranna pulled her back. "Don't."

Lilette glanced around at shelves of books and tables with potions. She paced to a table, picked up a vial, and sniffed the contents. She quickly jerked back at the rotten egg smell.

Doranna stared at the sphere, sweat beading her brow. "There is something so wrong about this."

A sudden wave of discord slammed into Lilette and she pitched back, coming up hard against one of the tables and knocking something over. She gritted her teeth.

Han gripped her shoulders. "We need to get out of here."

Lilette glared at the sphere. "What is it?" She turned to right whatever she'd tipped over, but froze, her hands hovering above an open book. "No."

She leaned forward, scanning the pages. Her eyes widened before she snapped the book shut and stuffed it down her robes. She took a handful of vials and shoved them into her pockets. "We need to go, now."

She was already running for the stairs. Han jogged behind her. "Why, what—"

She didn't slow down. "It's a barrier! If the witches inside stop singing, it will come down and they'll see us."

"But barriers are cylinders. That's a sphere," Doranna protested.

Lilette didn't bother answering. When they were halfway up the stairs, the light shattered, leaving them in complete darkness. They could hear indistinct voices.

Her mouth pressed in a thin line, Lilette concentrated on moving quietly. They reached the door and Doranna pulled it open, letting in a stream of moonlight that Lilette hoped didn't alert those below to their presence.

They darted into the night. "Split up and hide," Han hissed.

He took Lilette's hand, but she resisted. "I have to see."

He pulled her into the brush, ducking behind a plant with huge, deeply scalloped leaves. Lilette peeked over the top as eight women streamed out and began to go their separate ways. She strained to make out their faces, but they were swathed in shadow.

One woman reached out and grasped the arm of another. "Merlay, wait."

Lilette stifled her gasp. Merlay turned.

"What will we tell everyone?"

Merlay ran a hand down her face. "The only one thing we can tell them—that they're dead."

Lilette couldn't hear anything over the rush in her ears. She knew who they were speaking of. Knew it in her core.

Her sister was dead. They were all dead.

She thought of the sister she'd never know. Of the witches who'd stayed behind so the rest of them might escape. Her throat made a strangled sound. Han pressed his hand over her mouth and held her tight against him.

Merlay glanced around, as if looking for the source of the sound, but the others were already leaving. After a moment, she turned to follow them.

"It's my fault," Lilette whispered through her tears. "I numbed myself to the pain when I should have been fighting."

Han held her against his chest to muffle her sobs.

CHAPTER 30

*Regrets are like a parasite living inside you. You have to find a
way to stop feeding them or they eat you alive. ~Jolin*

L ilette sat beside the window in Sash's house, watching
the chesli flowers curl shut and the moths flutter away,
watching the night die in the morning light. She felt as if a part
of her had died with it. Her hand rested on the book she'd found.
She hadn't looked at it again—she couldn't bear to.

Han sat in silence across from her. Someone else might have
said he was sorry and tried to console her with words or gestures.
Han just stayed close, sharing Lilette's grief with her.

When morning finally came, she tucked the book back into
her tunic and stood.

"Where are you going?" Han asked.

She strode toward the door. "To find answers."

Doranna had finally gone to sleep upstairs, and Lilette had
no desire to wake her. She stepped into the weak morning light.
Han came up behind her and checked his sword before strapping
his baldric over his chest.

Together they walked up the path. People gave them strange
looks as they passed. Lilette hadn't bothered to change her
clothes or wash her face. Her eyes were probably smeared with
kohl, and her hair had fallen from its bun to lay in messy waves
around her shoulders. With his armor and his impassive face,
Han looked the part of the warrior.

The pavilion was empty, so they strode to Merlay's tree. Lilette didn't knock, she just thrust open the door. A wastrel with a smudge of flour on her nose hurried into the front room but stuttered to a halt when she saw Lilette and Han.

"I will see her. Now," Lilette demanded, her voice shaking.

Just as the wastrel began telling them to leave, Jolin stepped into view. Lilette wasn't surprised to see her. She blinked sleep from her eyes. "Lilette, Han, what are you—"

Lilette held out the book she'd found—the one Jolin had written. "How many of us have you betrayed?"

Jolin's face went deathly pale. "Bani, go away."

The wastrel disappeared back the way she'd come. Jolin dropped her gaze and started up the winding stairs, Lilette and Han silently following. At the second floor, she knocked on the door. "Lilette is with me. She knows."

Several seconds later, Merlay walked out wearing a dressing gown. Lilette took a vicious pleasure in her matted hair and bloodshot eyes. She held up the book. "You've found a way to hide your songs from the others. And you attacked Harshen last night."

Merlay didn't deny it as Lilette had expected. The Head of Light just sighed, her shoulders sagging as if the load she carried was too heavy to bear. "Bani," she called down the stairs, "please bring us some tea."

She asked Lilette and Han to follow her and strode to another room, a library. She crossed the room to step onto a balcony surrounded by flowers. A branch bridge connected the balcony to the listening tree. Merlay stared out over the city as the morning light glinted off the tops of the trees and shone on the distant sea. "I'm sorry," she said to Lilette. "It was a very long night last night. I'm very tired."

"Don't lie to me," Lilette said. "You attacked Harshen—I felt it."

Merlay sighed. "I did."

It took everything Lilette had to control her rage. "You killed my sister?"

Merlay turned to face them, tears streaking down her face. "The emperor did. He killed all of them."

Lilette staggered back, and Han said, "No. Chen is many things, but he isn't a murderer."

Merlay looked at him. "Our spies confirmed it. They were all killed yesterday evening, just after the chesli harvest began."

Suddenly, Lilette found it very hard to remain standing. She slumped into a chair. She'd been feasting in the pavilion, trying to climb into the nearest man's lap, while her sister had her head cut from her body? How had Lilette not felt it? How had she not known that a part of her had died?

Han hadn't moved from his place by the door. "What did you do?"

Merlay looked away, as if she couldn't bear the sight of Lilette in pain. "We shook the city to its knees."

"And Chen?" Lilette choked out.

Merlay glanced at her. "Our spies have searched what remains of the palace. I think it's safe to say you are a widow now."

"Chen wouldn't do this," Han repeated, but this time without conviction.

Lilette buried her face in her hands. "I watched him kill his wife."

She felt Han's gaze on her. "He saved her the humiliation of a public execution," he said. "Gave her the chance to be buried by her father instead of sold for curses."

Lilette shook her head. They were brothers. Even if Chen was guilty, Han would naturally stand up for him, believe the best of him. She refused to dwell on the fact that Han's brother had killed her sister.

Jolin finally spoke up from behind them. Lilette had almost forgotten she was there. "You see why I had to help them?"

Lilette refused to look at Jolin. "You've never used that barrier before?" Lilette asked.

"It's called the veil. They couldn't," Jolin said. "They didn't even know about my research into barriers until a few months ago."

Lilette directed her words at Merlay. "Why keep their deaths a secret? Why not tell everyone—why not tell me?"

"Because I didn't want to ruin the celebration. Because we wanted to respond without the burden of public debate. Because I couldn't bear to spoil your first chesli harvest."

Lilette sagged. When she'd seen the book in Jolin's handwriting, when she'd realized what the witches were doing, she'd assumed they were secretly cursing Harshen. She'd been wrong. "That veil—it's offensive. Evil even."

"I designed it that way," Jolin spoke up, "to repel anyone who happened to stumble upon it."

"Surely you knew I could sense it," Lilette said to Merlay.

"I was informed of your . . . condition . . . by the guardians. I didn't think you'd have the awareness to realize what was going on."

"That's another thing," Han growled. "What that man did to her—"

Merlay cut him a look. "Believe me, he will be severely punished."

Lilette stared at the harbor, ships coming and going as if the world wasn't falling apart. "Why not make the counterattack public?"

"That's . . . complicated." Merlay said.

Lilette glared at her. "I think I can handle it."

"Because if the world begins to view witches as weapons, they'll start using us as such. From greedy rulers down to jaded farmers, they'll know they can capture one of us and torture her until we do their bidding. How can we stop it? We risk becoming slaves to the very people we rule."

"That's why you did it," Lilette said. "Because Chen was using his captives to sing a counter-curse. You couldn't let the world know that. Couldn't let them know that with their own group of witches, they don't need you—that you couldn't stop them."

If she hadn't been drugging herself, she would have realized all of this from the beginning. Perhaps she couldn't have changed anything, but perhaps she could have. Now she would never know.

Lilette closed her eyes as she imagined her sister's terrible death. "What did Chen do to them?"

Merlay's head dropped. "Our spies have indicated that Sash and the others turned on Chen. Most of them died in the aftermath, and some killed themselves when they realized they couldn't escape. There were only two left—we don't know who. He had them beheaded."

Han was staring out the window in the direction of Harshen, his face troubled. But he didn't argue.

Merlay moved to sit behind her desk. "Jolin, Han, if you will wait outside, I need to speak with Lilette alone."

After they had gone, Merlay studied Lilette over her steepled fingers. "We now find ourselves dealing with a conquered nation, a ruined city, and a downtrodden people."

Lilette could well imagine the devastation. She'd seen Rinnish destroyed before.

"I don't have the time or the inclination to mince words," Merlay went on. "Harshen is in need of a new ruler. I'd like that ruler to be you."

Lilette gaped at her. "Women don't rule in Harshen. They don't have any power at all."

"Well, perhaps it's time you changed that. If the Harshens want rain, if they want their seeds to sprout, they will do what I tell them to."

Lilette's insides seemed to sink into a puddle around her feet. "You want Harshen at your mercy."

"They are already at our mercy," Merlay huffed. "You would be a good candidate. You're already their empress, and they consider you one of them. But you are also one of us."

Lilette fisted her hands at her sides. "All I've ever wanted was for my sister to be safe. Beyond that, I wanted to be a keeper—the best of them." And she just couldn't give up on that dream.

Merlay inclined her head. "We can send you a tutor. Nassa has been begging for the job. And you'll have the opportunity to really change things for the better. How can you refuse?"

Lilette rubbed her temples to try to stop the headache forming behind her eyes. "If anyone should rule Harshen, it should be Han. He's the best man I know."

Merlay's gaze shifted to the window, which overlooked the Heads' garden, the circle, and beyond that, the city itself. "He doesn't have the ties to the keepers that you do. But . . . it would strengthen your claim as empress to have one of the emperor's sons as your consort."

Lilette's heart fluttered in her chest. "I'm not sure Han would agree."

Merlay chuckled. "He risked his life, betrayed his country and his brother for you—a man doesn't do that unless he's hopelessly in love.

"He never betrayed his country." She tried to think past the shock of Merlay's proposal. "If I agree, Harshen would be free of the keepers?"

"If they stay in line, yes."

"What do you mean, stay in line? Harshen will never be a puppet nation. They are too scattered and too stubborn."

Merlay lifted her brows. "As long as they pose no threat to Kalari and pay Vorlay for the loss of their armada, they'll be free."

From what Merlay was telling her, in the end Lilette would have everything she'd ever wanted. "I'll do it."

Merlay pushed up from her chair and headed toward the door. "Good. Now, if you'll excuse me, I have a lot to do before we announce this at the chesli harvest. Why don't you take one of the guest rooms downstairs? It'll be easier if you're close, and you look like you've had less sleep than I have."

Lilette followed her into the hall. Jolin and Han were nowhere to be seen. "No. I'll stay at my sister's home. Besides, I won't be able to sleep."

Merlay went into her room, which was filled with tasteful furnishings and muted colors. She opened a side drawer beside her bed and took out a bottle with familiar-looking sprigs of herbs inside.

Lilette met the other woman's gaze. "A sleeping tincture?"

Merlay nodded and Lilette took the bottle wordlessly. Her head was pounding, and it took every remaining bit of her strength to keep her emotions at bay. She descended the stairs just as the wastrel went up with a tray of tea and scones. Her face fell when she saw Lilette.

"I'm sorry it took so long. Would you like breakfast with your tea?"

Lilette's mouth watered, but she now believed Bethel and would never eat anything she hadn't seen prepared. "No. Thank you."

Jolin was waiting for her in the receiving room, her expression pensive. "Lilette, I'm sorry."

Lilette couldn't respond at first. "I'll see you tonight." She left the tree, shutting the door behind her. Once outside, she glanced around to make sure no one was watching and tossed the tincture into the foliage.

CHAPTER 31

Did she ever forgive me? ~Jolin

Lilette smoothed her silk robe. It was gorgeous, with images of the sinuous, five-clawed dragon in black and gold. Doranna set a headdress inlaid with gems and turquoise on her head, strands of clinking pearls dangling past her ears.

She already wore the ruby brooch and the dragon ring. Wearing a copy of Laosh's ring made her cringe, but Merlay had insisted.

It had taken nearly every Harshen craftsman Merlay could scrounge up to create this ensemble. And they all had orders for more. Dozens of robes, a smaller headdress, slippers, even little things like pots of kohl and scrolls for Lilette's mandates.

"You must look the part," Merlay had said when she inspected Lilette earlier. "They have to feel you're above them if they're ever to follow you."

Lilette hadn't liked that, but she hadn't bothered arguing.

Doranna touched her arm, startling Lilette. "You're ready." Doranna opened the door to Merlay's library, and they stepped inside.

Outside, night had fallen. The chesli flowers on the balcony were open, and moths and other night insects flocked from one to the next. A trail of glowing pollen drifted from their wings and lent an otherworldly glow to the inner city.

Lilette slipped forward, keeping out of sight behind the chesli flowers. On the balcony on the opposite side of the woven-branch bridge was the listening tree. All four Heads were there—Jolin with them.

At the sight, Lilette's stomach twisted in knots. "I don't feel ready." She wished Han was beside her, but no one had seen him all day. Merlay had dispatched dozens of guardians to search for him, but so far they hadn't found him.

Lilette knew how capable Han was. How strong. But she still worried. Something wasn't right—she knew it deep in her bones.

Her gaze shifted to take in her surroundings. From this vantage point, she could see everything from the Heads' pavilion down to the city surrounded by an ethereal glow that ended at the liquid darkness of the ocean.

Despite the breathtaking view, Lilette's eyes kept being drawn to the wastrels, cloths in their hands to gather the pollen. It didn't seem fair that they had to work from the inner city to the outer until the flowers closed off at dawn, then snatch a few hours of sleep before being up to prepare the feasts.

There had to be a better way. A more fair way. An idea began to take shape in her mind. "Doranna, can you gather as many wastrels as possible under this balcony?"

The wastrel raised a single brow. "Why?"

"Just trust me."

Doranna took a deep breath and headed to the door. She swung it open, and Lilette heard footsteps. A moment later, Han was ushered in by three native-born Harshens, all of them carrying silk robes and other finery to match Lilette's.

Han's gaze flew to her face, to the robes and headdress. He froze, his face expressionless. Doranna gave Lilette a nod and stepped out of sight.

Lilette's heart raced. Han still didn't know. What if he refused to marry her? She took a steadying breath and looked at the Harshens. "Leave them and go."

One of them bowed nearly in half. "Empress, the announcements will start any moment."

She forced a patient expression on her face. "I know. Thank you."

At least he didn't miss the dismissal in her tone. They departed without a word, leaving her alone with Han.

She crossed her arms over her chest. "Where were you?"

"I went looking for Pescal."

"Looking for him?"

"He escaped the guardians. No one told you?"

"No."

Han's mouth tightened. "I've been searching for him all day, but it's like he disappeared. No one has seen him and no one knows where he might have gone, which probably means someone is sheltering him." Han paused. "Something's not right here, Lilette."

She shivered. "I know."

At the other balcony, Merlay had begun her introductions. Lilette was running out of time. "They've made me empress."

"You never stopped being the empress," Han replied.

She couldn't look at him. She took a step deeper into the room. "Han . . . I'm leaving. As soon as the ships are prepared."

He moved to stand before her. "I thought you wanted to be here more than anything."

She picked one of the gleaming flowers and twirled it between her fingers. "It doesn't matter what I want. It never has."

His brows arched. "It matters to me."

She finally turned to face him. "Are you in love with me?" *Because I'm in love with you.* She didn't say it. She wanted his answer first.

His breath caught in his throat. "Lilette . . ."

Just to make sure he knew exactly what choosing her meant, she stepped forward and pressed her lips against his. He returned her kiss, breathing her in as if she intoxicated him. She liked that, liked the barely contained restraint she could taste on him. What would he ever do if that restraint were gone? She shuddered deliciously at the thought.

She broke away from him and savored the smell of him in her nostrils, the taste of him on her tongue. "I need you, Han. I always have."

He pressed his forehead against hers, as if finally surrendering. "Where you go, I go." She heard the promise in his words.

A smile spread across her face. "Where you go, I go." It felt like a bargain had been struck between them. He wrapped his arms around her and pulled her close, their bodies and hearts entwining as he kissed her, lighting a smoldering coal deep inside her chest.

In the background, she was vaguely aware of Jolin launching into her speech about her pendant, Merlay announcing the first apprentice ever promoted to a full keeper in order to become Head of Plants. The crowd cheered wildly.

It was almost Lilette's turn. Breathless, she broke away from Han. "There's more." She let out a slow breath. "I . . . well, they want me to take you as my consort."

Shock crossed his face. Lilette forced herself not to look away, to wait as the disbelief melted away into something else.

"We have one other announcement to make," Merlay cried out over the sounds of the crowd.

Creators' mercy, I took too long. "I have to go. It's my turn." She backed away from him onto the center of the balcony.

"A new leader has been chosen for Harshen," Merlay continued. "This leader has strong connections to us as well as to this errant land. May I present Empress Lilette." She threw out her arm in Lilette's direction.

Thousands of eyes fell on Lilette, their scrutiny burning through her. She threw her shoulders back and kept her expression blank. Now it was her turn to amaze them. She opened her mouth and called for a wind to come through the trees. She gathered pollen from the flowers, curling it into a cocoon, much as the witches did when they sent messages with the wind. A glowing gust twisted through the trees, dancing among the crowd until all conversation ceased. She directed it toward the few dozen wastrels Doranna had gathered at the base of the tree.

When Lilette judged it close enough, she abruptly stopped singing. The wastrels held their jars to the sky as pollen drifted down, dusting their skin like glowing freckles. It fell across Lilette as well, sticking to the tiny hairs of her arms and making her gleam.

Below her, the wastrels' faces glowed with happiness and pollen. The sight brought a lightness to Lilette's heart. Other wastrels came to dust the pollen into their overflowing jars. "Now," Lilette said with a smile, "perhaps you can enjoy the celebration with the others."

The wastrels cheered, and many in the crowd joined in. But Lilette noticed a woman staring at her with something close to contempt in her eyes. And she was not the only one. Then the multitude parted to reveal the Harshen man and woman who had dressed Lilette the evening she met Pescal. The man and woman were kowtowing in respect. There was another disturbance in the crowd as more native-born Harshens bowed to Lilette. The keepers murmured among themselves.

"She has already been accepted by those Harshens among us!" Merlay shouted. The other Heads clapped. That seemed to be all the direction the crowd needed to break into applause. Merlay caught Lilette's gaze before looking pointedly behind her. Lilette turned to find Han wearing the tunic that had been laid out for him.

"Han?" she said, her voice trembling. He caught her face in his hands and kissed her.

Merlay cried out, "And it appears she will have a Harshen prince as her consort to strengthen her claim!"

The people roared in approval. Lilette gripped Han's wrists and pulled back. "Is all this for them?" She tipped her head toward the crowd. "For Harshen? Or is it for us?" she finished in a whisper.

Han rested his forehead against hers. "All three."

She searched his gaze. "You're sure?"

"Since that day in the cherry tree."

He kissed her again. Lilette couldn't hear the crowd anymore. Couldn't feel the night air. There was only Han, his gentle kisses as soft as the moth wings that brushed against her pollen-dusted skin.

CHAPTER 32

Sometimes things are broken so badly they can never be put to rights again. ~Jolin

"That bit with the pollen and wind was brilliant. If any question your appointment by the Sun Dragon, they won't any longer."

Han and Lilette broke apart. Merlay was standing on the bridge, one hip resting on the railing. Lilette blushed as she lifted a hand to hide her tender lips.

Merlay laughed at her expression. "And the kiss at the end." She shook her head. "Breathtaking showmanship and a knack for politics." She stepped into the library and began looking through a sideboard. "I'm lucky you're going off to Harshen. Between that public display of your song and your prowess with the crowd, you'd have my job within a month of graduating to a keeper."

Feeling uncomfortable, Lilette took a step back from Han. "So you're displeased with how I handled things?"

Merlay spun around, a bottle in her hands. "On the contrary, I'm just glad not to have the competition." Her smile softened her words a bit, but the tension in Lilette's chest didn't ease.

Merlay gave a slight nod to Han. "We appreciate your willingness to serve your country."

"It's easy when you offered me what I wanted all along."

Merlay poured the liquid into two cups. "Yes, well, ruling in your brother's place won't be easy after the mess he's made."

Han stiffened, and Lilette wanted to slap Merlay.

Strains of music came from below as Merlay handed them cups of dark wine. Motioning for them to follow her, she started down the stairs.

Waiting for them at the bottom were Doranna and Harberd. Merlay gestured to them. "I have a wastrel and a guardian assigned to you from now on. These two volunteered."

Lilette blinked. "Why?"

"To see to your needs and your protection, of course."

Lilette studied Doranna's face. "Are you sure? You'd be leaving Bethel."

"This is what Bethel wants."

Merlay smiled. "Everything's arranged then. Tomorrow, we begin preparing you to rule Harshen. Now I have a very handsome man I have to bring down a few notches."

Lilette watched Merlay depart, and she felt the future she'd planned for herself in Grove City crumble to ash. But when she glanced at Han, the loss didn't sting as much.

She motioned to Harberd and Doranna. "You may both have the evening off."

Doranna stepped forward to take both of their wine glasses and dump the liquid outside.

Harberd watched Lilette, his brow drawn. "I'm sorry, empress, but outside your tree, my orders are to keep you within sight."

She sighed. "Does Merlay think me in danger even here?"

"I don't take my orders from Merlay," Harberd responded.

Lilette grunted, and gratitude warmed her. Bethel she trusted.

Han crossed his arms behind his back. "Don't worry—I'm sure Harberd is excellent at his job. You won't even know he's there." He shot the guardian a significant look.

The man gave a curt nod and melted out the doorway.

"I don't—" Lilette began.

"Merlay's right on this," Han interjected. "He'll do a good job at being unobtrusive. Besides, another pair of eyes would lessen the pressure on me."

Just as Lilette felt herself giving in, Jolin appeared in the doorway, her breath short. "Did you see? I held them completely captivated."

Lilette lifted a single eyebrow. From what she'd heard, Jolin had been completely condescending. "You could have been a little more respectful."

Jolin waved her comment away. "I'm sure they didn't even notice."

"There's a reason you don't have many friends, Jolin." Not the least of which was her propensity for betrayal.

"Oh, please. The mindless masses are only here for the food and the drink." Jolin must have finally noticed their disapproving looks. "Nothing like you two, of course." She glanced between Lilette and Han. "Is it true? Are you really going to become an empress and marry?"

Lilette felt Han moving close, as if drawn to her. "It's true," he said, his voice oddly husky. He cleared his throat and said louder, "The amber you used in your demonstration?" His fingertips came to rest at the hollow of Lilette's throat.

Guilt shot through her for letting something precious to Han be used this way.

"Ah." Jolin pulled it from her pocket.

Han studied the two pieces, sadness in his gaze. "I'd like it back. It has been in my family for a very long time"

Jolin hesitated. "Six hundred years, if you believe the historians, which I personally never do. Historians are like hired portraitists. They always skew the depiction to please the subject." She set the pieces in Han's open palm.

Lilette cocked an eyebrow. "And you would do differently?"

Jolin grunted. "I would write it exactly as it happened. No glossing it over or shifting of facts."

Lilette made a noncommittal noise in her throat.

Han was still staring at the broken pieces in his hands. "Lilette, would you excuse me. I've something I need to attend to."

She studied him, trying to read all the thoughts and emotions that went on beneath his hard exterior. "Will I see you later?"

He gave a small nod. "I'll find you." He stepped closer and pressed a kiss to her forehead. "I promised I always would, remember?" He strode from the room without looking back.

In the silence, Jolin suddenly clapped her hands. "I'm going with you."

Lilette started. "You're what?"

"Going with you. You're going to need me."

"But you're the Head of Plants, and your research—"

"Can be done there just as easily as here. Well, almost. I'll have to practically empty the library, but Merlay wouldn't dare refuse me that. Not with everything she has planned for this new technique."

Lilette dropped her gaze. "Jolin, I don't think I can ever trust you again."

Jolin paled. "I was part of that circle—I felt the destruction. I still believe helping Merlay was the right thing to do, but if I can help Harshen rebuild—help them become something better—I will. Besides, you need me."

Lilette took a deep breath to steel herself. "I don't want you there."

A sound of pain slipped from Jolin's throat. She turned away. "I don't expect you to understand. You make friends as easily as breathing, but I don't. I'm cocky and have no tolerance for stupidity. And I'm lonely."

Lilette knew how hard it was for Jolin to admit this, but it wasn't enough. Not after what she'd done.

"Merlay is the only friend besides you that I've ever had," Jolin went on. "She's been there for me when no one else has. When she asked for my help, I gave it." Jolin turned to face her, and Lilette was shocked by the sight of tears on her cheeks. "I will do the same for you, whether you ask me to or not."

Lilette was silent for a long time, debating, but then her shoulders sagged. "I'll try." It was the most she could promise. "Do you think I can do this? Rule an entire country? I grew up in a fishing village."

"But that's not your heritage." Jolin scrubbed her cheeks. "You were born to rule the world. A small country will be no problem." A grin broke across her face. "Plus, as empress, you'll have unlimited access to Harshen's amber deposits."

Lilette chuckled.

"See? I can be funny on purpose."

When Lilette didn't respond, Jolin nudged her with her elbow. "Stop worrying! You've just become an empress—again. This is cause for celebration."

Lilette shook her head. "I don't really feel like celebrating." And she wasn't ready to spend time with Jolin again. She begged off and went back to Merlay's balcony. Grove City was filled with golden light, warmth, and music. The night beyond was filled with liquid darkness.

So why did Lilette feel the opposite was true, that everything around her was false—like gold leafing over rotted wood?

CHAPTER 33

I wanted everything, and the want blinded me to what I stood to lose. ~Jolin

This was the third time Lilette had seen Rinnish destroyed. Her heart ached at the sight. Parts of the city had been burned black, and most buildings had collapsed completely. Much of the ramparts around the palace had crumbled, only part of the north ramparts remained. Miraculously, the palace itself appeared to still be standing.

The city was hushed, as if hunched under the angry clouds and waiting for a blow. Lilette shook her head. Merlay had said the clouds and lightning would ensure the people cowed before her. But Lilette didn't want them cowing. She wanted them to look at her and see hope.

And she didn't completely trust Merlay. Lilette would do this her own way. Standing at the bow, she sang, forcing the clouds back until the air glittered with sunshine. Finished, she looked down at the beautiful horses they had brought for her. Tears pricked her eyes when she remembered her elephant— how proud she had stood and how hard she had fallen.

She stepped forward, Han on one side, Doranna on the other. Both of them had hands on their weapons.

Jolin edged up behind her. "You don't all really expect me to ride one of those, do you?"

Lilette smiled. "I do, in fact."

Jolin groaned. Beside her, Galon gave a mischievous grin as he helped her mount. Lilette noticed his hands lingered on her outer thigh, and Jolin gave him a secretive grin.

Han rode beside Lilette, for this was more than just an empress riding through the streets—it was also her and Han's wedding procession. They wound up the city's streets, from the mostly gutted slums by the docks to the affluent houses with inner courtyards.

Over fifty witches and a small army of guardians surrounded them—and that didn't count the two hundred gray-clad wastrels, all of whom had eagerly followed Lilette after that bit with the pollen.

Lilette couldn't help but see this for what it was—an invasion. But she'd come prepared for that too. More than once, Harshens suddenly attacked—a few of them wearing the uniform of an imperial guard or an elite. The guardians beat them back almost effortlessly.

Finally, they passed the ruined palace gates. Inside, the courtyard was filled with the rubble from the three fallen walls, though the dead seemed to have been cleared away. The harem was practically gone, crushed beneath the falling north ramparts.

Lilette wasn't sure how, but the palace still stood, looking vulnerable with only the east ramparts to safeguard it. Even the stone dragons remained.

Lilette leaned toward Han. "Where are the eunuchs—the concubines? Surely some of them survived."

Han's gaze was fixed on the harem. "The guardians already swept the palace grounds. They were abandoned."

"Where would they go?" Lilette asked.

Han made a sound low in his throat. "My guess is they're either hiding in the city or dead. I'll put out feelers with some of my friends and see if I can't hear anything."

She hesitated. "And Chen?"

Han let out a deep breath. "They haven't found a body."

"What if he's still alive?"

Han studied her for a long time. "I've considered it."

"And?"

One side of his mouth crooked up. "It won't change anything, little dragon."

A sad smile curved the corners of her mouth. She reached out and took Han's hand, giving it a squeeze. "Thank you."

She dismounted and turned to face the two hundred wastrels and the few Harshen-born women she had managed to round up. "You may see to it now."

The women started toward the palace or the outer edges of the palatial compound. Lilette had promised them a life in Harshen if they stayed with her. She'd been surprised how many of them had eagerly agreed.

"Where are they going?" Merlay asked in disbelief.

Lilette hid her smile. The wastrels answered to her now. "To prepare the wedding feast." And also to clean up the palace, but that didn't sound as grand. She flashed a smile at Han. "Let's announce my presence to the city."

He took her arm to help her over the rubble-strewn courtyard to the stairs that crisscrossed the east walls. At the top, she gazed out over the city. She didn't see a single Harshen, but she knew they were watching.

A crier announced her as the empress and brought out the empress's crown with six bobins. He spoke the words that would bind her to Han.

A new emperor was supposed to hand out sweet things to bless the people—oranges or sweet rolls, perhaps. Lilette didn't have that—she had something better. She wasn't sure how the Harshens would react to her song. She just hoped they didn't storm the palace, because the guardians and the witches would put them down.

Lilette had planned to ask the witches to gather in a circle and sing. But the familiar stirring was in her breast. She didn't need them.

She sang out for the wind. From all around the compound, wastrels threw seeds into the air. The wind caught them and carried them out over the city. Taking a deep breath, Lilette sang again, but this time it was a song of growing.

All over the city, thousands of seeds took root between cobblestones and courtyards. In the muddy slums by the docks, stalks of rice shot to the sky. In the courtyards and open green, mango and pear trees took root, their boughs filling the air with fragrance before bowing heavily with fruit. Vegetables grew in the marketplace. Wheat sprouted up between the cobblestones.

By the time Lilette had finished her song, the city had grown a fat harvest. Lilette sang.

Eat and be filled,
For tonight I wed your prince.

The people didn't cheer. They didn't call out. But a few ventured into the sunlight. They gathered the armfuls of food before disappearing again.

Satisfied she'd done all she could, Lilette started back down the stairs. Her eyes scanned the guardians, passing over a familiar face and a telltale cowlick before her gaze whipped back. But he was gone.

"What's wrong?" Han asked.

Lilette breathed out. It had to have been someone that just looked like Pescal. He couldn't be here. Shaking it off, she smiled at Han. "Nothing. It was nothing."

Inside the palace, she'd had the wastrels arrange a feast, nothing as extravagant as her wedding feast with Chen, but it was the best she could do.

They sat down to fruits and vegetables in a room that had been picked clean of even the low tables. Lilette grieved for all the lost silk screens and intricate statues. The only ones still remaining were the great stone dragons before the palace—and those only because they were too heavy to lift.

They sat on the wooden floor, eating off leaf plates and drinking out of tin cups in a room that smelled of smoke and death. And yet Lilette was happy. Against all odds, she had finally married the man she loved.

As evening fell, Han helped her to her feet and they bid everyone goodnight. He led her up the stairs to the fourth story. "This entire floor is yours now."

It had once been opulent—evidence of that was everywhere. Now, it had been looted to the bare walls. The wastrels had rolled out a couple reed mats. That was it.

Lilette walked to the windows, looking out over the city as sadness and guilt assaulted her, for she'd been part of this destruction—unwilling or not.

Han rested a calloused hand on her shoulder. "Not everything was ruined. Come with me." He turned and led the way to a silk screen.

She stood before it, but he only stared at her as if she wasn't real, as if at any moment a puff of wind would take her away. Self-conscious, she wrapped her arms around herself. "Well, are you going to open it or not?"

He grinned—something she'd never seen before. It pulled at his scar tissue, tugging his eye down and twisting his face. He was not beautiful, and she was glad. She didn't trust beautiful things.

He pushed open the screen, and Lilette was suddenly overcome with the scent of growing things. She breathed in a gasp. It was a potted garden, and despite the drought in the city, this had obviously been well-tended. A few plants had been tipped over, but there was nothing here of value to the looters, so they'd left it mostly untouched.

She took a few steps inside and stopped to smell a gardenia, its sweet fragrance making her eyes slip closed in pleasure. She turned slowly toward Han. He held out his hand and opened his fist. Something fell out, swinging from a chain. As she took a step closer, her mouth came open in surprise. It was the crescent of amber from the pendant Bethel had split. Now it was attached to a silver backing instead of gold, and instead of the sun . . . "It's the moon!"

He clasped it around Lilette's neck, the long chain allowing the pendant to dangle between her breasts. "It's the token of the emperor," he explained. "That's why I told you to keep it. As long as you had this, you had a claim to the empire."

Han lifted up his piece—the larger one—from underneath his shirt. "I told you I would follow you anywhere. Now I can."

She took a step toward him and pressed his lips to hers. The kiss quickly went from soft to something more, something deeper, and Lilette had no intentions of stopping.

CHAPTER 34

*Han and Lilette rarely showed affection in public. Yet they
communicated more in a glance, in a simple touch, than
anyone ever shared in more amorous ways. ~Jolin*

A hand rested on Lilette's shoulder, shaking her softly. But
Han felt so good lying next to her. Solid, strong. For the
first time in a long time, she was safe. Then she realized both of
his arms were wrapped around her body. With a cry of warning,
her eyes shot open. By the time she was halfway up, Han had
bolted to his feet, a look of death leaping from his eyes.

But Lang only glanced up impassively at Han before his gaze
was back on her. "You must come with me."

"My mother?" Han said breathlessly.

"She's fine. I've hidden her in the city."

"I want to see her," he demanded.

Lang stood. "Then you better hurry."

Han didn't put away his sword. "And why should I trust you?"

"I saved your mother's life," Lang replied. "Isn't that
enough?"

In answer, Han passed Lilette a pair of his dark trousers and
a tunic. "What's going on?" she demanded as she donned the
clothing.

Lang studied her. "I know how your sister really died. And it
wasn't Chen."

The world seemed to tilt. Han's hand shot out to steady her.
"What?"

"I have proof. If you'll come with me."

"Why can't you just tell us now?" Han pulled his helmet over Lilette's pale hair and strapped on the faceguard.

"Because you won't believe until you see for yourself." Without waiting for a response, Lang trotted to the rail that surrounded the garden. A thin rope dangled from a grappling hook.

"You climbed four stories?" she asked in surprise.

Lang grunted. "You need to speak to these guardians about security."

Lilette looked far below them and felt dizzy. "I'm the empress. We can just go through the front door."

"You have no idea the danger you're in," Lang scoffed as he swung his leg over the side. "Can you climb?"

Lilette peeked over the edge. "Um . . ."

Lang turned to Han. "Tie one end to her and we'll lower her down." They tied the rope around her middle and slowly lowered her to the gardens behind the palace. She hid herself behind a dying bush—obviously this garden hadn't been as well-tended as the one above.

The two men came after her in no time, and the three of them took off at a run through the destroyed garden. At the ramparts, they simply scrambled beneath a triangular space left by two sections of wall. A short run down the rise, and they were in the city. Everything was eerily silent and deserted.

Lang led them through mangled streets until Lilette was hopelessly lost, but judging by the grim look on Han's face, he knew where they were.

Finally, they arrived at a modest home that was more or less standing. Hand on the door, Lang paused. "You must promise to remain silent when you see what's inside. I can't risk attracting attention."

Lilette nodded, and Lang opened the door to the modest home. Ko rose from the low cushions, which were surprisingly elegant. She rushed to Han and embraced him. He held her, a look of profound relief on his face.

But Lilette's gaze was locked on Salfe—the boy from her village who'd been banished for trying to help her escape her betrothal to Bian. Unconsciously, her hand went to the comb Salfe had given her, her fingers tracing the ridges on the jade.

He strode toward her before his gaze shifted to Han and the joy bled out of him.

"You're alive!" Lilette managed to say. "I don't understand."

Ko grasped Lilette's hand. "I want you to know how glad I am for you—both of you."

"Ko," Lang said almost apologetically, resting his hand on her arm.

She took a step back. "You're right, there isn't time. This way." She pulled back a worn but clean curtain hanging across the doorway. Lang stepped through first. Following him, Lilette gasped at the stench of rotting meat that assailed her. She lifted her arm to her nose and took shallow breaths through her sleeve. It was a small room. She leaned to the side to look around Lang.

What she saw sent her whirling around and reaching for Han's sword. Before she could pull it free, he shoved her aside and strode into the room, his sword snaking free of its scabbard, but then he froze. Lilette scrabbled for his knife and lunged forward, but Lang caught her and deftly twisted it from her grip.

From the pile of rushes, Chen laughed. Trapped in Lang's arms, Lilette cursed him, using every vile word she'd ever heard.

"You swore to keep silent," Lang hissed.

Lilette gritted her teeth as Chen's laugh shifted into a cough that rattled around in his lungs.

Han's sword slowly fell to the side. "How?"

Lilette thrashed against Lang, but he rode her assault out. "He's nearly dead anyway! Stop!"

She went limp, the murder leaking out of her. "Why? Why would you help him?"

Lang released her but stayed between her and Chen. "I found him when I went searching for survivors. We dragged him here under cover of dark days ago."

"His legs are crushed," Ko said.

Lilette realized the stench was coming from Chen. The thought made her gag.

Lang's gaze rested on her. "And I helped him because I wanted to know what happened the night the witches destroyed us."

"You need to hear what he has to say, Lilette," Ko added softly. Lang handed the knife back to Han, hilt first.

Lilette wiped her arm across her mouth. "Fine. Speak. Then I'm going back to the palace and returning with a contingent of guardians to arrest all of you."

Chen's dark gaze was fixed on her. "In my tenth year, my father received a very important guest. She bade us orchestrate the deaths of one Lellan, and her daughter, Lilette."

Speaking seemed to wear him out. He reached for a cup beside him. Ko rushed forward to help him drink. After only one swallow, Chen lay back, clearly exhausted. "Success would guarantee us prosperity the likes of which few empires ever see. Failure meant a disaster of our own—one that would destroy all our people."

Lilette knew what he was implying. Anger surged through her, so strong it nearly swept her away. She braced herself until it ebbed. "I don't believe you."

"Despite what you may think of my father," Chen went on weakly, "he didn't relish the idea of murdering a little girl. He came up with another plan—simply faking the witches' deaths and adding them to his harem. The woman would be his. The girl would go to me when I came of age."

"And having a witch as a wife was no motivation," she said angrily.

"To add the power of witches to our line seemed like a good idea at the time." Chen's gaze went to Han. "My younger brother overheard my father being ordered to kill you. He warned your parents, and you all fled into the night."

Lilette couldn't stop shaking her head. "It's a lie."

Chen went on as if she hadn't spoken. "No ship can catch one sung by a witch. Not unless they are aided by another, stronger witch."

Lilette closed her eyes, trying to shut down the memories assaulting her. It didn't work. Her mother had stood between her and the battle going on before them—her face ashen, eyes haunted. "We've been betrayed," she had whispered.

Lilette had thought she'd meant someone from the ship had let the elite onboard. But Chen was right. No ship could catch them, not without the aid of another, stronger witch. Her mother must have realized that moments before she'd died.

Lilette slowly raised her eyes to Chen's.

"You believe me." He nodded and relaxed into the rushes. "You must understand," he pleaded, as if her opinion of him really mattered. "We had no choice. The safety of thousands makes even the most heinous price palatable."

He wet his lips and took another drink. "There was no saving your father and the other guardians, Lilette. And for that I am sorry. But we would have taken you and your mother and hidden you away. But then the ship caught fire and we found your mother . . ."

Lilette shut her eyes tight, trying to close out the image seared in her memory, even though she'd never seen it. The image of her mother, floating face down in the water, her flesh badly burned, her face purple and bloated.

"The price was paid. And Harshen was blessed," Chen finished softly.

"Who would do such a thing?" Lilette asked.

"Who has the most to lose if you live?" Chen said. "Who is strong enough to best your mother?"

Lilette bent over, her hands on her knees as the world spun. "Merlay?" she breathed. She scrubbed away the tears on her face. "How did you find me?"

Chen's gaze shifted to beyond the door. She whirled to find her old friend standing behind her. "Salfe? How could you?"

He stared at the floor. "You deserved better than to be the fourth wife of a fisherman. You deserved to be with a prince." He finally raised his eyes to hers and Lilette saw the pain there. He'd told her he loved her once, had risked and lost his future for her. "Please. Please forgive me. I didn't mean to start all of this."

Lilette closed her eyes as two heavy tears plunged down her cheeks. "You didn't start it. I did. Fa warned me what would happen if I sang, and I did it anyway."

She turned to Chen. "That's how they found me—that's why they came looking. Because I sang."

Chen's gaze was faraway. "I always wondered why they finally came for you, after all those years of nothing."

Lilette clenched and unclenched her hands, feeling sweat building on her palms. "My sister . . . if you didn't kill them . . ." She couldn't finish.

This time Chen's voice was filled with pity. "The witches did. They sang an earthquake that brought the ramparts down on them and the harem. It also brought down nearly every building in all of Rinnish."

"No!" Lilette finally said, her voice coming out hoarse. The night she'd felt the world dying. She wavered on her feet.

Han reached out, holding her steady. She looked into his fathomless gaze. "Han." The word was so full of pain and need. She hadn't cried for her sister, for everything she'd lost and gained over the last few weeks.

He drew Lilette into his arms, holding her tight as the sobs slowly started. And once they began, she couldn't stop.

They took her back to the main room, and Ko fixed her something hot and soothing. When Han seemed convinced she wouldn't fall apart again, he straightened his shoulders and returned to his brother's sick room.

Unfortunately, the rooms were divided with silk screens, so Lilette could hear every word.

"So how are you enjoying my wife, Brother?" Chen asked.

Han was slow to answer. "She's not your wife anymore, Chen. I'm sorry. I truly am. But I thought you were dead. And I won't give her up."

"I thought I loved her too," Chen replied so softly Lilette could barely hear him. "But then, I don't think she ever let me see the real her. All I ever saw was a silent, compliant woman with a mischievous streak. But that's not really who she is."

"No," Han agreed.

"Well, Father would be pleased that after all this trouble, at least one of us can bring a little power into our line."

"Don't," Han warned.

They were silent. "I'm dying, Han."

"I know."

"I'm sorry Father lost his temper. I'm sorry he scarred your face. He was afraid and he was angry."

Han didn't reply.

"Brother, swear to save Harshen," Chen said clearly, "no matter what it takes. Our people deserve our protection. And if you can, find a way to make the witches pay."

"I swear," Han said, his voice breaking.

Chen seemed to have lost all his strength. "Don't come back here. You can't risk it . . . and to be honest, I don't want to see you or Lilette ever again."

Han came from behind the curtain a moment later. His gaze found hers, and his face changed. He knew she'd heard, had accepted it and moved on. He glanced at the silk screen windows. "We need to head back."

Lang rose from his place on the cushions beside Ko. She embraced Lilette and Han once more.

Lilette looked at Salfe, at a loss for what to say or do. "If things had been different, if I had been ready . . ." She gave a helpless shrug.

One side of his mouth crooked up, a shadow of his former cocky manner. "Really, Li. You're married now. You shouldn't be pining after me."

She nearly choked on her laughter. At least Salfe hadn't changed. She shook her head as she left.

Han and Lang were waiting for her outside. Han searched her face. "He's the one who gave you the comb you always carry?"

She nodded. "Out of everyone on the island, he is the only one who tried to help me."

Han moved to her side and guided her into the street, Lang beside him. "Then we both owe him a debt."

Lilette let out a silent sigh of relief.

"Lilette and I are too wrapped up in this to escape," Han said to Lang. "But you're not. I want you to get my mother out of Harshen. As far away from the islands and the witches as you can."

Lilette rested a hand on his arm. "He can't. We need him."

Han took a deep breath and stared up into the night sky. "Lilette . . ."

"The world needs to know what Merlay has done." Lilette told them her plan.

When she finished, Han dropped his head in defeat. "Merlay is the most powerful person alive. We'll have to be careful."

Lilette met Lang's gaze. "You're the only one I can trust with this." She gave a wry smile, seeing as how she'd threatened to have him arrested a short time ago.

After a moment, Lang nodded curtly. "They destroyed our city—killed nearly everyone I know. I will do what I can, but after that I'm leaving."

For a time, there was only the sound of their light steps. Han cleared his throat. "Thank you, for saving both of them."

Lang looked into the night. "I wish I could say my motivation for helping your brother was kindness, but I only wanted him to live long enough to understand why the witches had destroyed us. I never could have imagined the real reasons."

Han hung back to walk beside Lilette. "I'm not sorry. Not about us."

Lilette stepped a little closer to him, and their shoulders brushed. The comfort in that simple touch strengthened her resolve. "Nor am I."

CHAPTER 35

I had no idea what they planned or what they had seen. It pains me that Lilette didn't trust me enough to share the truth, but I can't fault her logic. ~Jolin

Lilette woke in the predawn light. She was still tired, but sleep was already leagues away. She rolled over and found Han asleep beside her. She'd hardly seen him in the last three days. He'd been too busy gathering up every remaining elite or imperial soldier he could find. The ones who'd been willing to swear allegiance to Lilette had been drafted into her service. She didn't completely trust them—after all, they'd helped hold her captive, had fought against her. But Han trusted them to do what was best for Harshen. Right now, they all had the same enemy. That would have to be good enough.

Han looked younger, almost boyish, his long lashes brushing against the skin under his eyes. He was a huge man. She liked that about him. Liked that he was strong and solid—like the earth. Here was someone she could sink roots into, someone who would stand strong and steady as the winds beat against her.

As if sensing her gaze, he rolled over and gathered her into his arms. She traced the line of his scar—strangely enough, the feel of it beneath her fingers was comforting. He was strong and good no matter the consequences—he wore the proof of it on his face. "Stop worrying," he said, still not opening his eyes. "We've done everything we can."

Lilette sighed. In three days of searching, Han and Lang had only rounded up two people who'd survived that night at the palace. If eunuchs weren't so easy to spot, they probably wouldn't have found any witnesses. It had been harder still to convince the eunuchs to share what they'd seen. They had only agreed after Lilette promised to expel the witches responsible from Harshen. She didn't fail to notice they didn't really consider her one of the keepers. And for once, she was glad.

Lang had tucked the two witnesses away and promised to bring them to her when it was time. Arranging everything had been difficult. But the hardest part for Lilette was sitting at the same table as Merlay and not strangling her with her bare hands.

Lilette propped her head up on one hand. "We could just poison Merlay and be done with it." It wasn't the first time she'd suggested it.

Han sighed. "No. This is about more than just us. This is about the rot inside the witches that allowed this kind of thing to fester. It's about never letting something like this happen again." He growled and pushed her onto her back. "And now that I'm irrevocably awake, we may as well make good use of our time." He kissed her neck, and it wasn't long before Lilette had forgotten all about their schemes.

***

Hidden behind a curtain, Lilette watched the crowd filling the courtyard. While Han and Lang had been rounding up witnesses and elite, Lilette and the guardians had spent the last three days gathering up all the island leaders so they could swear fealty to her. They, along with the people of Rinnish, filled the courtyard by the hundreds.

Judging by their sullen silence and the palatable threat of violence in the air, Lilette was certain they weren't here of their own free will. Between the palace and the unhappy crowd, the guardians had gathered five men deep, each of them armed to the teeth. On the floors below Lilette were the other witches, all of them prepared to subdue the crowds if necessary. If those two groups weren't enough of a deterrent, Han had ordered all the elite and imperial soldiers to weave through the crowd, whispering for the people to hold their peace, promising a reward for their patience.

She felt Han step up beside her. "He's late," he said.

Her insides were full of knots. There were so many ways this could fail. "Lang will be here." She wouldn't consider an alternative.

"Lilette!"

Steeling her expression and forcing her fists to relax, she turned to face Merlay as she stepped into her apartments and came to stand beside her. Lilette knew she should say something, but she didn't trust her voice.

Merlay raised her eyebrows. "People are starting to grow restless. I don't need to remind you that the Harshens do not trust us. The island nobles are starting to act like we're going to murder them all." She laughed at her own joke.

Lilette tried in vain to join in.

Merlay's laughter trailed to silence. "Well, shall we go on with it?"

Lilette opened her mouth, to say what she wasn't sure, but Han leaned in and whispered in her ear, "He's here."

She turned to find Lang and Salfe slipping inside, two eunuchs between them. Each of them carried a bucket of soapy water. Lang gave her a slight nod—she didn't doubt that all four men had hidden more than one knife in the buckets.

"Who's this?" Merlay asked, a hint of mistrust in her tone.

"Servants," Lilette answered smoothly. "After all, the wastrels can't stay with us forever, and my apartments are a mess." The four men immediately began scrubbing the soot from the walls.

Apparently satisfied, Merlay snaked her arm through Lilette's and leaned in. "You seem nervous—much more so than when you addressed the crowd at the chesli harvest. Are you all right?"

The air felt thick and hot, not filling her lungs like it should. The edges of her vision were tight and distant. But her reactions had nothing to do with the crowd she was about to address, and everything to do with Merlay's arm linked in hers.

"Just a little nervous, that's all." With a small smile, Lilette slipped free of Merlay and moved into view on the porch.

Silence swept through the crowd, but not one Harshen kowtowed to her. It was a blatant show of disrespect, one Lilette ignored altogether. "I was born a witch," she said as loudly as she could. "I thought it was my heritage. But I learned honor from Harshen. I learned strength from Harshen. And when I returned to Grove City, I realized I *was* Harshen."

She paused as the criers carried her words to the back of the crowd. Han stepped up beside her. "I have taken a son of the emperor as my husband, so that his line may continue, and because I know there is no stronger man on earth who I would have by my side."

She took a deep breath to steady herself. "Harshen—my people—I am your empress." They did not cheer, but they hadn't booed her either. They were listening. "With the help of the witches, I have fed you, cleaned your city and begun repairs."

When the criers had gone silent, she made a slicing gesture. "There is only one thing left for me to do as your empress, and that is expel the witches from our presence."

The crowd stirred with disbelief. Lilette could practically feel the agitation of the witches on the porch below hers. A handful of guardians broke away from the perimeter to disappear inside the palace. Within moments, they would be pounding on the door.

Merlay stepped up behind her. "Lilette! What are you doing?"

"Silence!" Lilette shouted. Merlay jumped in surprise, and Lilette turned from her. After today, she never wanted to see that face again. "This woman's name is Merlay," Lilette continued. "Long ago, she committed a murder. Her attack on Harshen was, in part, a plot to cover that up."

Merlay moved as if to physically stop Lilette, but Han blocked her. Merlay turned and said to the crowd, "We have made a mistake in choosing Lilette as your empress. We will find ano—"

"You did not chose her!" Han roared. "The Sun Dragon did!"

Merlay took a step back. That was Lang's cue. The eunuchs moved onto the porch, as far away from Merlay as they could get. One of their feminine voices rang out. He told how he had been in the palace, sleeping in the kitchens, when the world began shaking. He described how the ramparts had crumbled, killing all the concubines in the harem, and crushing the witches in the garden.

"Lies!" Merlay cried. "All lies! I—"

Han stepped forward. "You will be silent—one way or another."

Merlay looked Han's massive frame up and down and made to move toward the door.

"No." He blocked her again.

Merlay's jaw tightened, but she remained quiet.

Another eunuch came forward. His story was the same, only he had been fetching the court physician for his concubine, who was about to give birth. He'd just crossed the bottom set of steps when everything had come crumbling around him.

Both of the eunuchs' stories ended in the same way, with them running from men dressed in black who had slaughtered anyone they came across—eunuch, lord, or witch alike—including one witch who'd begged for her life.

A black hate stained Lilette from the inside out. Had the woman been her sister? She couldn't bear to ask. "So the captive witches were not fighting Chen?"

Both eunuchs shook their heads.

The door behind them flew open and Brine marched in, a dozen guardians at her back. Shock and distrust and outright hostility shone on their faces.

Lilette backed farther onto the balcony. Han stood before her, Lang and Salfe on both sides. Even the eunuchs stood their ground, soapy knives in their hands. They didn't make her feel any safer.

If Brine attacked her, the crowd would see it, and a battle would erupt. She had been willing to bet Brine wouldn't risk it.

Merlay was talking fast, trying to explain. Lilette ignored her, focusing on Brine. "Jolin created a barrier, called the veil, which could only be sensed by a level seven. Merlay used it to hide her attack, bringing down the ramparts and crushing my sister and the other captives—forever silencing them." Lilette's voice trembled, but she forced herself to go on. "And in the process, she destroyed the city. In the ensuing chaos, she sent your spies to kill everyone in the palace—it's the only way to explain how everyone died even though the palace is still standing."

Merlay stepped back. "I would never do such a thing!"

Lilette shook with rage and grief. "And she did it all to hide the fact that she'd killed my parents in an attempt to murder me—along with dozens of other level sevens—to protect her place as a Head."

"Creators' mercy!" Jolin cried. She and Galon, along with at least a dozen more witches, had come inside at some point.

Brine turned to her. "Jolin, is this true? Did you create a veil to hide songs?"

"Merlay came to me, asking if it could be done, telling me the witches could do much more good if we could use our powers to destroy evil."

Brine frowned. "Did you hear this song—the one that destroyed Harshen?"

Jolin's face went white. "I helped sing it."

For a time, the only sound was the cries of the crowd. Finally Brine stepped forward. "Merlay?"

"The emperor killed her family." Merlay scoffed. "I had nothing to do with it."

"More lies." Han held out a sealed scroll. On it, Chen had written his testimony and signed it. Brine scanned it, her face growing tighter with each line she read.

"Brine—" Merlay began.

"Silence! The truth is easy enough to uncover." Brine turned to the crowd. "Were the witches in the palace compound singing the night of the tremors?"

A thousand different voices denied it. The evidence was mounting. The witches packed into the room were staring at Merlay, their disbelief slowly changing to disgust.

"Merlay," Jolin said softly, "what have you done?"

Merlay turned to the other witches. "You know me. I couldn't—wouldn't—do something like this."

Jolin's face was pale. "Creators' mercy, how much blood have you stained my hands with?" Beside her, Galon moved closer.

Merlay shook her head, but the crowd outside was screaming now, demanding justice. "I swear to you, I didn't do this. After all my years of service, how could you not believe me?"

But it was clear the witches didn't. And neither did the crowd.

Merlay turned to Brine, who was watching her, arms folded, a horrified look on her face. "Brine, I swear, I—"

"Silence!" Brine hissed. She motioned to two guardians who had finally reached her side. "Take her into custody—and make sure the crowd sees it or we'll have a riot on our hands."

"Brine," Merlay said, her voice low. The guardians bound her hands.

Brine's eyes glittered with rage. "Be quiet! We'll be lucky to get out of this alive, thanks to you." She stepped up next to Lilette and looked over the crowds until they went silent. "The keepers of Grove City had no idea one of our own could orchestrate something like this."

"Get out of our city!" someone shouted.

Brine searched the crowd with her gaze, but whoever had spoken was not to be found. She closed her eyes, her shoulders heavy with the burden of regret. "We will leave our guardians to protect you from any retaliation from Vorlay or elsewhere. Some of our witches and all of our wastrels will remain to help rebuild. The rest of us will go."

Lilette ducked as something exploded around her, something horrible. A rotten egg had hit Merlay square in the chest. Brine had chunks in her hair.

Han stood up to the rail. "If you had hit the empress, I would have found you, and I would have killed you."

His words sliced through the crowd. He had been a prince of Harshen, respected and known for nearly two decades. "Your empress has spoken. She has protected you. We will rebuild— better and stronger than before."

He looked at them, meeting one gaze after another. "Now go home." The crowd milled for a bit, but their anger seemed to be dissipating.

Merlay glared at them, clotted eggs dripping from her breast. Even the guardians didn't seem to want to touch her. "You don't know what you've done," she said bitterly. "You haven't saved your people, you've condemned them!"

The guardians started taking her away. Jolin marched right up to Merlay and slapped her. Galon pulled Jolin back before she could hit her again. "You used me!" Jolin shouted. "You pretended to be my friend, but you were just using me."

Merlay glared at Jolin. "I did what I had to, for the good of the witches."

Lilette clenched her fists at her sides. "You did what was good for yourself."

Brine maneuvered herself between the three of them and gestured to the guardians. "Get her cleaned up and on the fastest ship we brought. Our guardians will guard our exit . . ."

"No," Lilette interrupted. "You send armed guardians through my city and the people will fight. I will send imperial soldiers—the ones who survived. My people will not attack them."

Brine hesitated before slowly nodding. Galon shot Lilette an unreadable expression before pulling Merlay away.

Lilette spared a glance at Merlay's retreating form. "What will happen to her?"

"Do you realize what you've done?" Brine asked.

"I haven't done anything but reveal the truth."

Brine chuckled bitterly. "You opened the door for the world to see that we are vulnerable and corrupted."

"Merlay opened that door."

Brine was silent a moment. "Maybe so, but you pointed it out to everyone." She studied Lilette from head to toe. "Since you no longer need our guidance to govern your nation, I'll take Grove City's leadership, but leave the rest of the witches with you." More guardians had arrived, and Lilette recognized them as the ones who usually accompanied Brine. The Head of Water ticked off a list of witches to accompany her, and a guardian went to fetch them. Brine turned back to Jolin. "You're coming too."

"I'm staying," she said.

Brine's expression hardened. "I will need you to testify."

Jolin turned to Lilette, her eyes haunted. "I wish I'd never created the veil."

Lilette wasn't sure how she felt about Jolin, who had helped the witches kill Sash and hundreds of Lilette's people. But she hadn't done it knowingly. "Don't let Merlay get away with it," Lilette told Jolin.

Jolin nodded, then pivoted and walked toward a waiting Brine.

When they were out of sight, Han came to stand beside Lilette. "Do you think they'll try anything?" she asked.

He shook his head. "If they do, the elite will step aside and let the city have at them."

Lilette let out a breath. "It worked."

"Let's hope so."

Within an hour, the leaders of the witches were hustling through the city. The people threw things at them, rotten food, mostly. But they couldn't do much damage unless they wanted to hit the imperial soldiers, which they seemed unwilling to do. With the witches singing, the ship snaked out of the harbor.

Long after the first ship had disappeared, a smaller ship slipped out of the harbor. Lilette noticed the way Han's gaze followed it. "Your mother?"

He watched them depart. "Lang thought it was safer to go. I agreed."

CHAPTER 36

Lilette was like a star—full of light and distant beauty. Han was like the shadows around the stars—he let her shine. ~Jolin

Lilette spent the rest of the day organizing the guardians into teams to clean up the city. The wastrels were dispatched as healers—their knowledge of herbs were far superior to any Harshen physickers. The rest of the witches went to work rebuilding the groves and fields. By nightfall, the city already looked better. Most of the main streets had been cleared, and green things grew everywhere.

Lilette watched the sun set—without mountains to hide behind, the sky plunged from pale blue to velvety navy within minutes.

Han came up from behind her and snaked his arms around her waist. "What are you doing?"

"We did it. They're really gone." His voice was gravelly and he sounded tired but happy. He nuzzled her neck and a warmth built in her chest. With so many guardians and witches left behind, the city would be rebuilt in a matter of months.

Lilette licked her lips as Han's nuzzling went from loving to something deeper. She leaned back, giving him better access to her neck. She lazily watched a ship slip into sight, backlit by the twilight. It headed toward the harbor, its white sails almost looking peach. "What if they try something else?"

Han started untying the sash around her robe. "They won't. Not with as many of their people as they left here."

Lilette straightened as she watched the ship come closer. "Han?" It was moving fast—too fast to be just any ship. She pointed to where it now rested in the open waters. "What is that ship doing?"

His brow furrowed as he squinted at it. "Fishing?"

Her gaze swept over the conformation, the lay of the sails, and her breath caught. "It's Brine's ship."

Han stepped up beside her just as a wavering column of blue and purple shot up from the deck. He leaned over the rail and shouted, "Sound the alarm!"

The guardians in the compound whipped around, unsure what to do. But the elite knew. One struck the gong that had been repaired earlier.

As the percussion broke out over the city, Han snatched Lilette's arm and half dragged her toward the stairs. "You have to create a circle. Deliver a counter song!"

Her mind kept stumbling on the fact that the witches were launching an attack. It didn't seem real.

They reached the second level of the palace, where the remaining witches were staying. It was a wide room divided by dozens of silk screens. Most of the witches were still out in the city, but a few had returned for the evening. The thought of them dying jarred a protective instinct inside Lilette. "Witches! To me!" she called.

A few screens slid open, and a handful of witches rushed out of their rooms, Nassa and Doranna among them. "What's going on?" Doranna asked.

"Brine is singing against us!"

"That's not possible!" Nassa said.

Lilette didn't have time to argue. "Help me or we're all dead!" she cried. She rushed into the courtyard, the handful of witches behind her, just as the world bucked beneath her. She found herself face down on the brick-paved courtyard, her nose gushing blood into her mouth.

She could see Han's lips move as he screamed at her, but she couldn't hear him over the din. He started pulling her away. She looked back. Looming over them, the palace pitched violently.

What if it fell on top of them?

She dragged herself forward as the ground heaved again. The skin on her elbows tore, but she couldn't feel anything past the bone-numbing fear of being crushed.

Movement in front of her caught her gaze. The last remaining rampart shook itself to pieces and leaned toward them. With a deafening roar, it shattered against the brick courtyard. Han snatched her into his arms, shielding her with his body as broken bricks pounded them.

The shaking subsided a bit. Her ears ringing, Lilette dared to lift her head. She couldn't see anything through the choking dust. Groaning, Han pushed himself up beside her. Pieces of brick and dust cascaded off his back. Blood coated his scarred ear.

"What are they doing?" Lilette gasped.

Sometime between when he'd been kissing her neck and now, Han had thrown on his death armor. "They're going to destroy all the witnesses."

His words refused to penetrate the thick layer of disbelief that held Lilette captive.

"Keepers!" his voice rang out in the unnatural stillness. "To me! If you want to save your lives, to me!"

Lilette pushed herself up. This was happening. And if she didn't do anything to stop it, everyone was going to die. Wiping blood and dust off her face, she pivoted, searching for Doranna and Nassa. They had to start a circle. Now.

Lilette stumbled over broken bricks, coughing as dust filled her lungs. Her foot caught on something too soft to be rubble. She bent over, her hands grazing clothing. She found an arm and pulled on it. It was Doranna. "Are you alive?"

Doranna moaned. Lilette shook her. "There's time to be hurt later. Get up."

The wastrel blinked open her green eyes—the color a shock in a world of yellow dust.

"We have to sing," Lilette said.

Doranna grimaced and pushed herself up. "Why would they attack us?"

Afraid of being alone—of losing her—Lilette dragged Doranna along as she searched for Nassa. "Because we know too much." *Brine must be in on it. All the Heads must be.* Lilette suddenly thought of Bethel—of the history she carved into her cliffs—and wondered if the older woman would engrave this moment as well.

They stumbled upon Nassa, wandering and confused. Only a few minutes must have passed since the tremors had ceased, but Lilette felt the songs building in the elements, building until everything would burst.

"Drop!" she commanded. They hit the ground just as it started moving again. They clung to each other, their cries of fear drowned out by the deafening roar of the earth in pain.

Lilette felt it subsiding. She popped her head up, silently begging to see Han again. *There!* He was coming through the dust, one arm bracing a witch, another witch thrown over his shoulder.

He gently set down the barely conscious woman. "Is it enough?"

Nassa leaned over her, pressing her hands against a wound in the woman's head that gushed blood. "We need eight to even begin to fight."

Belatedly, Lilette realized she could clear the dust. She sang and the breeze picked up, clearing the air. She could see down to the city, or what remained of it. It was gone now—nothing but a pile of rubble. Her eyes swept over the harbor. Some of the piers had collapsed, dragging the ships down unnaturally into the water.

But the worst part was that what had once been a crescent-shaped harbor was now open to the ocean—the outer rim had completely sunk underwater.

Han looked at her, realizing what was happening a beat before she did. "They're sinking the island."

His words finally broke through the fog that had descended on Lilette. "Five will have to do. Get her up," he said, motioning to the dazed woman.

Nassa shook her head. "She's hurt too badly."

"There isn't time to be hurt." Lilette grabbed the injured witch's arms and hauled her to her feet. She swayed, one hand on her head, but managed to stay standing. Her eyes were wrong, one pupil much larger than the other.

Power hummed through Lilette. "Find more of us, Han." She commanded the others, "Sing me up."

Shuffling, already broken, they did. Her voice joined theirs, and she wobbled into the air. She could feel Merlay's song building, feel it aching to be released. Lilette didn't attempt to stop the building tremor. There wasn't time for that.

Instead, she called the wind, making it cocoon around her words. She shot them to the city, instructing the people to flee for the ships. She directed another song toward the harbor, telling them to cut the ships free before the island dragged them down with it.

The Harshens obeyed. Some of the ships jerked back up to float free as their mooring were cut. Others sailed away. Lilette told them to wait. To take the people.

And then another tremor hit. Lilette's fragile circle broke apart as the women inside it were thrust to their knees.

Lilette fell from the sky. She sang for all she was worth to slow her descent. She hit the ground so hard everything went black.

When she came around, Han was bent over her, shaking her so hard her head was flopping. She shoved him away. The panic in his eyes faded. She glanced around. He'd found five more witches.

Lilette staggered to her feet. Something was wrong with her lower leg. She turned her focus inward. It was broken, but it held her weight. Though the pain was biting, it was bearable. Not waiting for her command, the witches simply linked arms and started singing again.

She tried to go on the offensive, tried to call in a lightning storm, but the next tremor was so bad that half of what remained of the island fell away. And Lilette knew thousands of Harshens had died in that one moment.

She couldn't stop this. But she could slow it down—give some of her people time to get to the ships. Her mouth set in a grim line, Lilette steeled herself, making Merlay battle hard for every inch of the island that fell, every wave that swallowed a bit of Lilette's empire.

A few people made it to the ocean. Some dove straight in and swam for the ships waiting in open water. Others grabbed broken bits of wood and settled children on top before paddling out to sea.

Merlay would hunt them mercilessly, but Lilette had to believe some of them would make it. Her circle was weakening. The witch with the different-sized pupils had collapsed long ago. If she wasn't dead, she would be soon.

The ocean beat against the upper city now. The harbor, the slums, the market—all of it was gone. The only buildings left were a few of the fine, walled-in homes and the palatial compound.

Directly below her, Han was watching his homeland slowly sink under the waves. His hair was caked with blood.

Lilette reached out with her witch sense and felt the power building around her. So much power. And then the tremor hit with such force it broke her circle apart. Lilette fell from the sky.

Han was waiting, his arms open. He collapsed when she hit him. Her hand smacked into the ground, and the blast of power rising up hit her with such force as to make her gasp. The island tipped sideways and started to sink so fast she could feel the ocean spray on her face. "It's over," she said.

Caked in dust, Han pushed himself halfway up and let out a cry. Lilette could see it too. The water was so full of debris it was black as it hurtled toward them. Pinching her eyes shut, she turned away.

CHAPTER 37

Watching Harshen sink, knowing Lilette was there, I saw myself clearly for the first time—my selfishness and my conceit. I ripped away that part of myself. I was done being used. Done being naive and malleable. I swore I would make them pay.
~Jolin

The crashing wave didn't touch her, didn't swallow her whole. Lilette let out a gasp and opened her eyes to see churning black waters surrounding them on all sides. They were sinking into the deep, the barrier a solid line of demarcation between them and water choked with the remainder of the dead city.

The remaining witches had managed to grab one another and sing. Han eased his death grip on Lilette. Together, they watched the sky grow farther and farther away. After what seemed like forever, the island stopped sinking. She could see nothing except a shaft of blue sky above them.

The barrier flickered, and water started to seep in. It was weak because the witches were weak, but it was holding. Feeling crumpled and damp, Lilette struggled to her feet, careful not to put weight on her aching leg.

The witches were humming to keep the barrier up, their faces pale and resigned. "Now what?" Lilette asked.

Han looked up at the distant sky and then back at the choked, black water. Lilette caught sight of a dead water buffalo hitting the barrier before bouncing back into the debris. She looked away before she saw something worse.

"How long can you hold it?" Han asked.

Nassa struggled to sit up, careful not to let go of the witch next to her. "Until we give out." She craned her neck back to get a good look at the sky. "But eventually we'll have to let go, and then the sea will come rushing at us."

Han stared up, as if gauging the distance. "I think we could reach the surface before our air runs out."

"I can't swim," Doranna said, her eyes wide. She seemed to be barely keeping it together.

Han gestured to the fragments littering the ground around them. "We'll tie you to a board. It will carry you up. Matter of fact, we'll tie you all to a board."

Lilette motioned to the wreckage still slamming into the barrier. "I don't think anyone could survive a swim in that."

He rubbed his chin. "So we wait—hold the circle until the debris settles. Then we swim for it."

"Harberd?" Lilette said.

Doranna gave a slight shake of her head. "He was in the city."

So he was probably dead. Lilette's body was threatening to collapse. She sank to the ground, her hand wrapping around her leg just above her ankle, the pain hitting her hard now that she wasn't fighting anymore. "Merlay will see the barrier. She'll be waiting for us."

Han knelt before Lilette and pulled up her trousers to inspect her swollen leg. "She won't dare come close, not with all the wreckage."

Lilette lay back, resting her palms on her eyes. Her mother had shown her the island sinking. Lilette had thought she'd stopped it when she'd rescued the captive witches from Chen. She had been wrong. And now all those people were dead.

Han went about finding bits of broken wood inside their circle and tying them to the witches with ripped bits of their clothes.

Lilette stared at the blue sky as the debris slowly settled, enough that she caught sight of the palace. Miraculously it still stood.

The stone dragons stood guard at the entrance, their lips pulled back in an eternal snarl. Beyond them, the leaves of trees waving gently in the water. Lilette couldn't wrap her mind around the fact that she was lying on the yellow-brick courtyard—which was now and forever underwater.

Han knelt before her. Using her sash, he tied a board to the front of her robes. "Lilette, look at me."

She kept staring at the palace, wondering how many were dead now because of her.

He lay both his palms on her shoulders and shook her. "Lilette!" She finally turned to face him.

His face was tight. "The others—they're not going to be able to hold on much longer. Better to let go now, while they have the strength to swim, than to wait until everyone is too exhausted. And the water is clearing."

She pushed her head back into the rubble beneath her, the physical pain a relief from the emotional one. "Han, I don't think—"

"Don't you give up!" he growled. "I've seen battles where men give up. And they die. You have to fight to survive. You have to live!"

She slowly shook her head. "Why? I already failed my purpose."

He cupped her face in his hands. "Did you? Your mother said you were to save those you could. Maybe that's just the witches here. Maybe the others who managed to escape. Lilette, if your purpose was over, you wouldn't have survived this."

She looked at the devastated city. That they were still alive was a miracle. "You're right," she breathed. She forced herself to stand, her bad leg bent to take less weight. "Han's right. We need to swim for it now, before we're too exhausted to reach the surface."

The other witches exchanged wary glances, but no one argued. Staying wasn't an option.

Lilette stared at the sky, as Han had done. She was raised by a fisherman—she knew the sea. "You're going to be tempted to breathe. Fight the urge. When the water comes in, everything will be blurry, and the debris will probably be stirred up. Follow the bubbles. And don't stop kicking."

The witches nodded.

"When we reach the top," Han said, "swim for each other. We'll be safer if we stay together."

"What about . . ." Nassa cleared her throat. "What about Merlay and the others?"

Han took a deep breath. "If they're up there, hide. It's all you can do."

They all nodded grimly. Lilette tried to prepare herself, but how did one prepare to die? She looked at the surface, speckled with flotsam and so far away. And she accepted that she might not make it. If so, she had at least saved some of her people. She could die knowing that.

Han took her hand. "Sometimes you just have to move."

The other witches stopped singing. Cracks appeared in the barrier's surface, and it was as if the pastel purples and blues caught fire and smoldered to ash.

Lilette took a deep breath and held it as water roared toward them. She instinctively turned away from it, burying her face in Han's chest. He held her tight as the water slammed into them. But even the strength of his arms couldn't hold her as the water hit, ripping them apart. When it stopped dragging her, she was blinded by debris again.

She spun in the water, pain piercing her ears. When she finally came to a stop, she was surrounded by debris, so thick she couldn't see up or down. It was too dark to even see bubbles. Her lungs burning and raw, she turned in a circle, searching for the surface.

And then something registered in her brain. There was tension at her neck. The chain attached to the pendant was pulled taut to the left and down. It had been activated. Han was trying to find her. That meant up was that direction. The thought shocked the fear out of Lilette, and she clawed and kicked at the water. She suddenly broke free of a pocket of wreckage. Morning light shattered across the surface in golden waves.

But she'd been down too long. Of its own volition, her body took a breath. She coughed more water into her lungs, the brine abrasive and foreign inside her. Her eyes fixed on the surface. Just as everything began to grow dim, something touched her head. A hand latched onto her hair and yanked.

Her body was pulled through the water and she surfaced. Han squeezed her chest violently, forcing water from her lungs and sending a blaze of pain through her. It made room for her to draw a little air, which she devoured greedily. She coughed more water from her lungs and gasped in the barest trickle of air. Han wrapped his arm around her upper shoulders just as a wave slammed into them, forcing them underwater again. But the hands holding her never let go. His legs kicked, and she forced hers to do the same. She came up again, choking out half the ocean. Water streamed down her face, brine filling her mouth.

Han swam with powerful strokes as the coughs locked up her whole body, making it a struggle to keep her head above water. He hauled a chunk of wood through the water toward her. "Grab onto this." She hugged it to her chest, too consumed with coughing to do anything else. "We have to get away from all this flotsam!"

She realized with a shock how loud everything was compared to the stillness of the water. She could hear cries in the distance—people and animals. "We have to help them," she said between coughing fits, her voice sounding rough and raw.

Han made a helpless gesture. "How?"

He was right. There was nothing they could do. "Where are the others?" Lilette asked.

"There."

She turned in time to see four of them holding onto ropes that pulled them onto a Harshen ship Lilette hadn't noticed before. Nassa and Doranna were among them. Her relief was immediately overshadowed by sorrow. There had been eleven of them on the ocean floor. "Are you sure that ship is ours?"

A broken piece of wood came rushing at them, and Han had to let go of her to shove it away. "We don't have much of a choice. It's too dangerous to stay here."

He lugged her toward the ship. As they came closer, Harshens shouted at them and threw ropes over the side. Lilette took hold of a rope and held tight as they pulled her onboard. She collapsed onto the deck and lay panting in a puddle of water.

One of the Harshens stared at her in horror. "Empress!" His face contorted with fear. "Jump!" he cried, waving his arms.

Lilette gaped at him in confusion. Then the hatch opened and Pescal stepped into view. He took one look at her and shouted, "It's Lilette!"

More guardians rushed from below, one of them killing the sailor who'd warned her. She pushed herself up to jump overboard, but Pescal grabbed the ankle of her broken leg. She screamed and went down.

Han brandished his knives and lunged at Pescal, but he was swarmed by at least five guardians and knocked down. While another guardian bound Lilette's mouth, Pescal pinned her arms behind her. She cried out, sure he was tearing her arms from their sockets.

Pescal was breathing hard—she could feel his chest rising behind her. "I've got her."

She cocked her foot to kick him, but he wrenched her arms up higher and an involuntary cry slipped from her throat. Han gave a shout of outrage, but the guardians had him pinned to the deck. Lilette struggled against Pescal, tears of pain and fear coursing down her face.

Merlay came from below decks and surveyed her in disbelief. "You just won't die, will you?"

CHAPTER 38

*Learning that Lilette was alive and about to be executed
burned all the fear out of me. ~Jolin*

Merlay drew back her hand and slapped Lilette. "You
think you saved any of them? You're just forcing me to
kill them, one at a time. Soon as we're clear, I'll have to send
a storm that will sink every ship for a hundred miles, and even
more will die!"

Lilette could taste blood from where her teeth had cut her
cheek. "I'm not the one soaked in blood." Her words came out
muffled around her gag.

Shaking, Merlay wiped her face. "I risked so much to spare
your life for your sister. I sent you to Harshen—made you an
empress. All you had to do was stay out of my way."

Rage boiled inside Lilette. "You murdered my entire family!
Sent Pescal to drug me, and who knows what else."

When Merlay looked away, Lilette realized it wasn't just
Pescal. "You sent Laosh after me too?" She shook her head in
disbelief. "Sash trusted you! I trusted you!"

Merlay took a step back, and her eyes clouded over for the
smallest moment. And then her face hardened. "I did what I had
to do. What I've always had to do."

Lilette ground her teeth around the gag. "You've been playing
God."

Merlay made a slicing gesture. "We are Gods! The Creators endowed us with the power—us and no other! Nations can either obey us or they can feel our wrath!"

The guardians hauled Han to his feet. "Like Harshen felt your wrath," he growled.

Merlay's glittering eyes met his. "Yes. Like Harshen."

"Having power doesn't make us better," Lilette said through her gag.

Merlay raised a brow. "Of course it does!"

Lilette's gaze shifted to Brine as she came up from below decks. "What's all the commo—" Her gaze lighted on Lilette. "Oh."

Lilette tossed back her head. "And you? You knew what was going on, didn't you?"

Brine only grimaced. Beside her, Nassa growled through her gag, "Brine, if you're going to murder me, I deserve to know why."

The stolen zhou turned, probably toward the next batch of survivors. Brine took a shaky breath. "This isn't about Merlay or your family. This is about the fact that Sash and the others were singing a counter-curse that rendered us completely powerless."

Brine pressed the heel of her hand into her forehead. "What do you think will happen if the world realizes how vulnerable the witches are? We risk becoming slaves to the very people we rule."

Nassa shook her head desperately. "I won't tell anyone. I swear I won't! Take me with the rest of you."

Brine looked toward the back of the ship, and Lilette realized the stern deck was coated with blood. "I'm sorry, Nassa. But the others have proven their loyalty. You haven't."

Brine tipped her head toward the stern. "Cut their throats and throw them overboard like the others. We have more of them to dispatch."

Pescal dragged Lilette to the back of the ship. "Merlay sent you to drug me into oblivion," Lilette muffled around her gag, "so I wouldn't realize what she was doing."

Pescal leaned in, his breath whispering against her neck. "You would have enjoyed it immensely, I promise you."

She threw her head back, but he dodged her. "Easy now, there's no point in adding any more pain. You look like you've suffered enough."

Lilette gasped in horror as tacky blood squelched beneath her bare feet. How many other survivors had they "rescued" only to murder?

The other four witches were screaming and begging as a guardian pulled out a knife and stalked toward them. Lilette pinched her eyes shut and turned away as one of their cries was abruptly cut off.

Merlay and Brine headed below decks, most of the guardians following. The ones who remained were either guarding the prisoners or had hidden themselves on deck, their weapons trained on the captive sailors maneuvering the ship toward the next batch of survivors.

Han was struggling, fighting. He wasn't any closer to free, but he was distracting the guards from killing them.

And then Jolin climbed from below decks, Galon beside her. The two of them rushed toward Lilette.

"What are they doing?" Merlay's shout could be heard from below. "Get her back here!"

Her friend had betrayed her. Lilette rose up, her anger cresting. She threw herself back and kicked, but Jolin dodged her and slammed into one of the guardians holding Han, just enough to knock him loose.

Galon tossed Han a sword and stabbed the other guardian holding him. Han caught the sword, whirling about so fast Lilette couldn't follow his movements. The two of them cut through the guardians holding them. Pescal scrambled away from Lilette just as Han grabbed an extra sword.

Galon and Han turned to face the guardians constraining the crew. A dozen against two. Pescal exchanged an amused glance with another guardian and they started forward. But then one of the sailors tackled him. As if it was the cue they were waiting for, the rest of the sailors jumped into the fight. One of them even managed to batten the hatch and trap the rest of the guardians below.

Jolin produced a thin knife and cut Lilette's and Han's gags, then rushed for the hull, her small knife frantically working at the ropes holding a small dingy to the side. "Help me," she cried.

Lilette wanted to kill her instead, but there wasn't time. The three of them scrabbled and pulled until the ropes slithered and the boat crashed into the waves.

The guardians busted free. They streamed from below, quickly overpowering the sailors.

"Han! Let's go!" Lilette shouted. Galon cried out. A guardian had broken through, slicing his arm. Galon stumbled back. The guardian cocked his arm for the killing strike.

One of Han's swords snaked out, deflecting the stroke. The movement cost Han. His right flank was open. Pescal sank his sword into Han's side.

"Han!" Lilette started toward him, but Jolin grabbed her and hauled her toward the railing.

"Go!" Han growled as he countered with a blow to Pescal's thigh.

When Lilette hesitated, Jolin tightened her hold. "They won't break away until we're safe."

Han's blades twisted about him like a whirlwind. Nassa had already jumped into the water and was pulling herself into the drifting boat.

Doranna wasn't far behind. "Come on!"

Gritting her teeth, Lilette leapt off the side, her legs and arms windmilling as she fell. She crashed into the water hard, slamming into more flotsam. Pain, old and new, flared inside her. She pulled herself out of the water, pushing flotsam out of her way as she swam to the boat. She pulled herself in and turned back.

His swords crossed, Galon forced a guardian back. Then Galon jumped.

With the scrape of steel, Han twisted Pescal's swords to the side and head butted him. Pescal stumbled back and Han's sword whipped forward, stabbing him in the throat.

Mouth open in shock, Pescal gripped the sword, blood welling between his fingers. Han threw himself back. Pescal grabbed something at his waist. Even as he tipped forward, he threw a knife.

Lilette didn't see where the knife landed. Han hit the water hard. The boat had drifted from the ship, so she snatched an oar. "Help me." They brought it closer. "Han!"

Merlay appeared at the railing. "Stop them!" Other guardians jumped in after them.

Galon climbed into the boat and went to the stern, his swords at the ready. Holding the oar like a club, Lilette scanned the water for Han. He would come up. He would.

And then he did. She barely recognized his face, it was so dark. With both swords clamped in his teeth and red surrounding him, he swam for the boat and pulled himself inside. Lilette saw blood streaming from his body and panicked. He barely spared her a glance.

Doranna snatched the oar from Lilette. She and Jolin started frantically rowing. More guardians were coming through the water. Han and Galon hacked at them as soon as they came within range. The rest of them stomped on their hands as they gripped the boat.

Lilette's gaze swung to the ship as it turned toward them. Nassa kicked one of the guardians in the face. "You have to bring that ship down—now."

Lilette hesitated.

"You have the power to do it," Nassa cried. "I've seen it!"

The panic in Lilette's chest turned to something else—something dark like the shadows around the stars. As her chant built, the elements turned toward her, eager and hungry for her command—almost as if they knew they'd been used for evil and were eager to right the wrong.

Her voice lashed out like a whip, calling down lightning from the clear sky. It slammed into the ship. Once, twice, three times. Flames licked across the bloody deck.

Their boat picked up speed, fast enough that they'd left the guardians in the water behind. And Lilette knew what she had to do. She sang a current, one strong enough to pull them to her island.

The fire grew higher, spreading faster than the guardians could fight it. The screams started. It was the screams that brought the memory crashing down on her. This wasn't the first time she'd escaped from a burning ship. Not the first time those she loved had died. Her eyes wide with horror, she swung around to face Han.

"You're safe," he said, relief in his voice. And then he collapsed.

CHAPTER 39

*Han fell from his father's grace and wore the brand of that
encounter on his face the rest of his days. ~Jolin*

The boat was packed with survivors. Through the dark
night, no one spoke. No one made eye contact. Besides
Lilette and the others, none of the Harshens seemed to know
each other. They were a smattering of living who survived their
dead.

Lilette was crammed in one end of the boat, Han's head on
her lap. He hadn't opened his eyes since he'd collapsed. Hadn't
even flinched when she'd wrapped his wounds with strips from
her robe. And that knife wound in his chest—she couldn't think
about that. She was safe here in this empty place. If she allowed
herself to think, the emotions would kill her.

"There!" Nassa cried. "I see it."

Everyone in the boat whipped around. Lilette didn't need to.
She knew the shape of her island by heart. They drew closer,
passing battered ships and boats. Hundreds of haggard Harshens
lined the beach, their forms dark against the moon-bright sand.

Some of the men in their boat took the oars and steered
them neatly between the other vessels. Their boat pushed right
up against the beach and began tipping to the side. The people
inside spilled out onto the sand.

Galon knelt before her and gently lifted Han, passing him
carefully to another man. The two of them carried him to a bright

spot of fire, Lilette following numbly. The people made room for the men to set Han down beside the warmth. She took up her place beside him, watching his breath rise and fall for what felt like days.

Jolin suddenly appeared, plants filling her arms. She set them down and came back with two rocks, which she used to crush some of the plants. Others she laid whole on Han's wounds.

Lilette watched her. "Why?" she finally asked.

Jolin froze and then started working again. "I didn't know. Not all of it."

Galon looked between them. "I'm going to see if anyone needs help. Call if you need me." He squeezed Jolin's shoulder and left.

Lilette felt no anger, no pain. She was in a place as vast and empty as the night sky. "I don't believe you."

Jolin's shoulders slumped, but she didn't stop working. "I helped them develop the veil. I gave them all my research. Dozens of new concepts—including one with variations of sulfur, saltpeter, and charcoal." She looked over the ocean. "They tricked me, but only because I let them. I'm smart enough to put the pieces together—smart enough to know the pieces didn't fit into the picture they were showing me. But by then I had already done so much for them."

"And now they don't need you anymore." Lilette's words tasted bitter. "They have all your potions and research."

Jolin gently opened Han's mouth and set the mashed leaves inside. "No. I wanted credit for my discoveries, so I always supplied some of the potions—I'm the only one who knows all the ingredients. It's why they took me with them when they left."

Lilette stared off into the darkness. "Did you know they were going to sink the island?"

"No," Jolin said simply.

Lilette rested her hand on Han's cheek. It was cold, but she had no blanket. She took off her robe and laid it over him, leaving her in nothing but her smallclothes.

Jolin watched her. "When they turned our ship and I realized what they were going to do, they locked Galon and me in my cabin. We dumped every single one of my books out the porthole."

Lilette's head came up in surprise. There was nothing Jolin treasured more than her books.

Suddenly, Han took a deep breath and opened his eyes. His hazy gaze searched the darkness before finding her.

A small sound of joy cracked her throat. "Han!"

His eyes were bright and wide. "Lilette."

Her hands fluttered over him, wanting to touch him, but not daring to. She finally took his face between her palms. "Does it hurt?"

He spit out the wad of herbs Jolin had put in his cheek. "Lilette—it's not over yet."

Tears pricked the back of her eyes. "Of course it's not over. We have our whole lives before us."

He slowly shook his head. "You cannot defeat Kalari. You must retreat."

She smoothed back his hair. "I'll let you work that out. You're the great military mind."

"I won't be here."

Something in Lilette tightened, so tight she was sure it would break her. She met Jolin's gaze. "Fix him."

"I can't."

Lilette snatched her arm, squeezing so hard Jolin winced. "You fixed me. You created potions and songs no one else could. You can fix him!"

Someone touched Lilette's arm, and she whipped around, ready to pummel whoever had dared lay a hand on her, but it was Han. "She's right," he said, his face so chalky she barely recognized him. "I'm falling."

Lilette took his hand and pressed it to her cheek. "Don't. Please don't."

He wasn't looking at her anymore. His face was distant, his gaze fixed on the stars above him. "I have fallen every day since the day I met you. Following a falling star."

"Please." She had hovered in the space between life and death before. If her mother had brought her back, she could bring back

Han. Lilette closed her eyes. She'd never begged for anything, but she was begging now. *Please, Mama, don't take him from me.*

"You always were my downfall," he said softly. "I went willingly to it, and would do so again."

A scream built in her chest, but she forced it down. "No. Fight it, Han. You're the strongest man I know. The best man I know."

He turned to her, a stillness stealing over his face. "Remember what I told you, little dragon? Fight the battles you can win. Retreat from the ones you cannot."

The tension in his hand went soft, and his eyes grew unfocused. Something shattered in Lilette, wounding her so deep no one would ever heal it. "Han?" Her voice came out shaky and pleading.

She reached out and touched his face, his stubble scraping against the pads of her fingers. He felt alive. His flesh was warm and giving beneath her, but the emptiness in his eyes said something had gone. Whatever was left wasn't Han. He had moved beyond her reach. All the fight went out of Lilette, and she collapsed on top of his body. Somewhere, someone was screaming, screaming, screaming.

It wasn't until Lilette tasted blood on the back of her tongue that she realized it was her.

CHAPTER 40

Han was right. He did fall.
I believe he saw the pattern—that those who loved Lilette, truly
loved her, always saved her life at the cost of their own. In the
end, he accepted his fate long before his death. ~Jolin

Lilette rubbed her soil-caked thumb over her whole pendant.
She leaned heavily on her cane as Galon settled the last
shovel full of earth. Next to it, Fa's grave had settled, becoming
indistinguishable from the rest of the jungle floor.

Beside her, Jolin cried softy. Lilette couldn't bring herself
to. Crying meant she had accepted Han's death, and she would
never do so.

Days would pass and Han's grave would look just like Fa's.
It was like they were never here. Never living and breathing and
loving.

"Lilette?"

She turned to see Pan standing at the edge of the village, a
bowl of fruit in her hands. She dropped it, mangoes and coconuts
rolling around her feet. She rushed forward, a light coming on in
her face. "It is you." Then her gaze faltered over the new grave
and she halted. "What happened?"

Lilette took a deep breath and let it out in a rush, but the words
wouldn't come. "I can't . . ." She lifted her hands helplessly at
her sides.

"Her husband died," Jolin said for her.

Pan took the last step and enveloped Lilette in her arms. "I'm sorry. I'm sorry for what I did and for what you've been through. I'm sorry."

Some of the pain Lilette had shoved behind a barrier of her own making leaked out, making her eyes tear. She shook her head. She couldn't let this barrier fall, not if she was to keep going. She stepped away from Pan.

Beside her, Jolin shifted from one foot to the other. "Lilette, what are we going to do?"

"If Merlay survived, she won't stop," Galon added.

A shudder wracked Lilette so deep it rattled her bones. They wouldn't even allow her time to grieve. "Tell them not to sing. No matter what, they can't sing."

Jolin took a step toward the beach, Galon shadowing her. He hadn't left her side since they arrived. "I'll tell Nassa to explain it to the others."

All the wastrels and any witches to be found had gathered together around a shared fireplace the night before. The remaining guardians had taken up residence around them.

"I'll be back," Jolin promised. "I'll only be gone a moment."

It was as if she was afraid to leave Lilette's side. As if the absence of one more person could possibly make a difference.

Jolin and Galon rushed toward the beach, where most of the refugees were, and headed to the fire where they'd spent the night with Han's cooling body.

Pan searched her eyes and Lilette noticed her old friend's deep and lasting pain—the same look Fa had carried with him every day of his life. Now they carried it too.

"We're no longer the girls we were," Lilette said.

Pan shook her head. "No, we're not." She hesitated. "Lilette, did the witches really sink Rinnish?"

She opened her mouth to answer, but she turned at the sound of footsteps. Jolin was leading a marching elite toward her. His uniform was ragged, and he didn't have a weapon, but his pride was unmistakable. He dropped into his kowtows. "Empress, I'm the highest ranking elite to survive. I must know your orders."

Pan gasped and covered her mouth with her hand. "Empress?"

Lilette nodded slowly, an answer to both of them. "We need weapons. Men who can fight." She steeled herself. "Find them. Make them."

His hand twitched. "Empress, there aren't enough men. We have no ore to make weapons."

Lilette closed her eyes. Han should be here, issuing these orders. Instead, he was dead. She looked up again. "Then make staffs and bows out of the trees. Find a wastrel named Doranna. She will help you train the women."

The elite watched her, fear touching his features. "Empress, we cannot fight them. There are less than four hundred souls on this island."

His words hit her like a punch to the gut. The witches had two thousand guardians—and they wouldn't even need to use them. A dozen songs, perhaps less, and this island would slip beneath the waves like the last had. The only reason it hadn't happened already was because Lilette had sunk Merlay's ship.

The elite bowed to her. "Empress, we must retreat."

"And go where?" she snapped. She remembered what Han had said. *Fight the battles you can win, retreat from the ones you cannot.* But they had nowhere else to go. "Their listeners and level sevens will find us." She was suddenly angry, so angry it bled into the cavity left over by Han's death. She held onto that anger, because anger didn't hurt as much as pain.

She was a woman, and she would surrender like one, which is to say not at all.

"Are you certain they'll come after us," Pan asked quietly.

"Oh, yes," Lilette breathed.

Jolin nodded. "Even if Merlay and Brine were dead, which I doubt, Tawny won't risk exposure." She passed a hand over her eyes. "You burned the ship they'd stolen, not their other ship. They're probably already looking for us."

The elite's jaw tensed. "How many days do we have?"

"Two. Three at the most," Jolin replied.

"There has to be something," Pan said in her quiet way, her gaze going between Jolin and Lilette. "You're witches."

Jolin cast her eyes heavenward, as if asking for help. "We have a handful of witches and a few dozen wastrels. What you're asking would take hundreds."

Lilette remembered her mother visiting her, pressing her lips to her forehead. And days afterward, her song had grown in strength, until it had moved beyond a level seven—perhaps even approaching the power the Creators themselves possessed.

Lilette gasped and held onto Jolin for support as one pattern after another clicked into place. Her mother had shown her Harshen sinking. Shown her wars and terrors that would bring the world to its knees. Lilette had thought she was meant to prevent all of that by saving her sister and the others from Chen. But now she understood. Those events were inevitable. She was only meant to preserve a portion of the keepers. To pave the way for another to take up the fight.

She realized Jolin was calling her name. They locked gazes, and the spark of all that had passed leapt between them and bound them together.

Lilette turned away from her and surveyed the others. "The veil."

Jolin's eyes went wide. "What?" Her mind seemed to catch up to what Lilette was implying, and she shook her head. "We can't hide the entire island. And certainly not indefinitely."

"No," Lilette said. "We're not going to hide the island. We're going to hide all of them."

"But—but that's impossible! And who even knows how long it will last."

Lilette squeezed Jolin's arms. "You'll find a way—you're meant to. It's why you're with me, just as your mother said."

"My mother?"

Lilette cupped her face. "She's a part of this. We all are."

Jolin rubbed her lips together, her gaze distant and intense—the look she got whenever she was concentrating. "I'll need help."

Lilette gestured to the shore. "You have four hundred people. What do you need to create the veil?"

Jolin nodded, a determined expression stealing over her face. She faced Pan and rattled off a list of plants.

"Yes. I can find them," Pan replied.

"Go. Quickly," Jolin said, then started marching off with the elite and Galon.

Lilette's hand shot out, catching Jolin's arm. "Wait." Her hand went to her pendant. She always became lost after a tragedy. Bethel must have seen that, must have known it would be important that someone, somewhere, be able to find her. So she and Jolin had created the pendant. Lilette stroked the pendant once more, hating to part with something that had touched Han's throat—even for a moment. Yet he had gone where it would never find him, and she didn't need it anymore.

But perhaps someday, someone else would. Lilette pulled the pendant over her head and handed it to Jolin. "I want you to take this."

Jolin gasped. "Lilette, I can't—"

Lilette pressed it into her hands. "It was your mother's gift to you as much as to me." Lilette could see that wasn't going to be enough. "I can't bear its weight, not anymore," she lied. "But I won't see just anyone with it. Please."

Jolin closed her mouth and slipped it over her head. With more tears filling her eyes, she turned and walked away.

Lilette faced the graves. "I can see what it is I'm meant to do," she told Han and Fa. "And I know how to stop them." Bending down, she rested her hand on Han's grave. "Where you go, I go." With that, she turned to limp after the others.

All day, Jolin and the surviving wastrels were in a flurry, gathering plants to make the potions required to form the veil. Lilette worked beside them—staying busy was the only way she remained sane.

Wounds were treated. Food was gathered. More people died. That night, Lilette found herself staring at the star-swept sky. But she didn't look at the stars. She looked at the darkness between them. And she thought of Han.

Jolin sat beside her, knees drawn to her chest.

"Do you ever feel like it's wrong?" Lilette asked.

Jolin turned to her, the firelight making a line across the side of her face. "What?"

Lilette didn't look away from the sky. "Using the elements like this. They're so strong, so powerful, and we bend them to our will, for good or evil. Just like we bent Jia Li to our will."

"The elephant?" Jolin said. When Lilette didn't answer, she sighed. "They aren't alive."

Lilette felt the connection with her witch sense throbbing inside her. "Aren't they? Then why can I feel them writhing in pain during the hassacre?"

Pushing past her exhaustion, Lilette forced herself up to follow the witches gathering in the circle. Everything had happened for a reason. She was just a piece of the puzzle, and now she knew where she fit.

Jolin followed her to the center, wringing her hands together. "Are you sure this is wise? If we sing, it will draw them to us."

Lilette nodded. "Are you sure we have enough of the powder?"

In answer, Jolin held out a large covered bowl.

Lilette peeked inside. "So this is the stuff you use to create the veil?"

"Yes. It takes song and this potion to make it work. Over the next few hours, the men will spread it across the beaches on the perimeter of the islands. Then you'll spread it around when you're airborne to seal it into a dome." She took a deep breath. "But for now, you have to bring in the islands. What . . . what if you're not strong enough?"

Doubt slivered inside Lilette. What if she was wrong? What if, after everything, they failed? "There's nothing else we can do, Jolin." Her voice faltered. "Sometimes you just have to move."

Jolin stepped back and joined the circle. Lilette was surrounded by witches and wastrels. She wasn't sure the circle would be strong enough to launch her into the air, but she pushed her doubts aside and followed her own advice.

She nodded to them and they gripped hands. Their voices rising together, they sang. Lilette knew the listeners would hear this. But it had to be done. Their voices moved through her, their thoughts in her head. The wastrels were elated and terrified.

They'd never been allowed to practice their magic—small as it might be.

More than one keeper was disgusted with the off-key singing. To them, it was tramping on something sacred. Lilette didn't care. It didn't work as well, but it was working. And that was all that mattered.

The first stirrings of wind thickened beneath her feet, but it wasn't strong enough to take her up. *Concentrate,* Lilette commanded them silently. *We need each other.*

Follow my lead, Nassa said. She held herself rigid, her mouth open wide, the song coming from deep inside her. The wastrels copied her. And the notes might not have gotten any better, but their power certainly did.

The wind lifted Lilette's robes, tugged at her hair. She felt light—light as a cherry blossom spinning on the wind. And then she was airborne, twisting and twirling up. Closer to the stars far above. She wanted to keep going, until she could finally touch the shadows between the stars. But she forced herself to concentrate, to find that hum beneath her breastbone where her power resided. As their songs filled her with more power, she stretched her witch senses out, grasping onto each island.

When she opened her mouth, she sang, and it seemed even the moon in the sky stopped spinning so it might listen.

> Harshen, raise thy stakes.
> Winds, a path to make.
> Earth, compact thy soil.
> Plants, thy roots uncoil.
> Waters, thy waves divide.
> Islands line up, side by side.

Even with the power humming through her, filling her with light until it looked like day, it took her singing until her voice was hoarse before the other islands of Harshen began to appear. All of them flashed into sight, all of them close enough to reach by a good swimmer. It would have to be enough.

The circle slowly sang her down and then it broke apart.

"You did it," Jolin said in awe as she handed Lilette a cup of tea.

She rubbed her scratchy throat. Not wanting to risk speaking, she nodded. Boats were immediately dispatched with the powder, which was to be spread along all their shores. They had until morning to see it done. If they failed, all they'd accomplished was making themselves easier targets for the witches.

CHAPTER 41

Sometimes I hate her for choosing Han over me. It's selfish. It's weak. But knowing that doesn't stop the anger from flaring up so strongly I choke on it. ~Jolin

"Ships!" someone shouted. "On the horizon!"

No sooner had the cry gone out than clouds rolled across the sky. Lilette glanced up, at the lightning flashing beneath them.

"They're here!" Jolin echoed the words ringing through Lilette's head.

"Run for cover!" Guardians and elite cried out, ushering people off the shore and deeper into the jungle.

"Is the powder in place?" Lilette asked. Not all of the men had checked in yet.

Jolin shoved a pot of it into her hands. "We're about to find out!"

Witches and wastrels ran toward them, grasping hands, fear and hope mingling on their faces.

Once again they sang, and once again Lilette twirled into the sky. At the apex, she tugged the lid off the last of the powder. The witches sang again, and Lilette spun so fast she was certain she was going to be sick. But it worked. The powder swirled around her, shimmering a poisonous purple as it plumed out over the sky. The other witches shifted their song, adding their strength to Lilette's.

The power built inside her, slowly filling her up. The other ship was just offshore now—close enough Lilette could make out the witches from the guardians. The clouds billowed in, thicker and heavier.

The other witches sang their barrier into place. Lilette could see a witch in the center, rising toward the sky. When the two of them were level, Lilette recognized her. It was Merlay. Even from this distance, Lilette could see her shake her head, pity in her gaze. "I have the most powerful witches in all of Grove City with me," Merlay called out. "What chance do you stand against us?"

Lilette ignored the fear scrambling for purchase inside her. "I am meant to stop you."

Merlay tipped back her head and laughed. "Time to teach you about real power." She opened her mouth and a chant beat out.

Lilette ached to stop her, but the song she must sing required so much—she couldn't risk lessening her reservoirs to fight Merlay. Lilette could do nothing as the clouds turned black, as lightning slammed down again, and again, and again.

The few people who'd been foolish enough to ignore the warnings to seek shelter cried out in fear and ran for cover. Lilette catalogued each scream, determined to make Merlay pay.

The wind picked up. Safe inside the barrier, Lilette wasn't touched. But the wind scrubbed across the islands. Huts collapsed and blew out, scattering across the sea. Thunder boomed so loudly the world shook with it.

A wave as high as a mountain rose up in the sea. It rolled forward, crashing against the shore. Only the circle was safe. The wave tore through Lilette's village, taking everything with it. Her only comfort was that she'd moved the villagers deep into the mountain in the center of the island. Hidden in an open air pit, they were vulnerable to the lightning, but safe from the wind and the earth tremors that were sure to come.

The tempest stilled. Head tipped to the side, Merlay watched Lilette. "Are you not even going to try to stop me? Not that you can, but I expected at least some resistance."

Lilette used her witch sense—the song was close. So close. "Merlay, sometimes a fall is required to change our path. The witches will fall. I can't stop that—I was never meant to. But I can delay our utter destruction until someone comes along who can rebuild us into something better."

Merlay's brows rose. "We are too strong to fall."

A sad smile graced Lilette's lips. "Everything falls." Han had taught her that.

"After I'm through here, I will remove your songs from the very elements. It will be as if you never existed."

Lilette was ready for this to be over. The darkness was waiting for her. So close. So tantalizingly close. Merlay's gaze narrowed. "No more games. This ends now." She sang again. The ground trembled.

In the circle below Lilette, the keepers were shook to the ground, but they held on and continued singing. She could see them down there and knew if she didn't finish it, they would all die. She closed her eyes. And waited . . . waited. Now.

She opened her mouth. The storm stopped. The tremors stopped. Even Merlay stopped. There was no sound besides Lilette's voice. Around the edge of the islands, the powder began to glow with purples and blues.

Lilette sang the veil up, up, up. But instead of growing in a column that shot into the sky as the barrier did, this curved into a dome. It was going to completely cut her off. She saw the realization come over Jolin as she gaped up at her. In order to hide the veil, Jolin had created it to be completely enclosed. And when Lilette moved the island, there would be nothing beneath her.

"No," Jolin mouthed.

For such a brilliant woman, Jolin was sometimes rather obtuse. Lilette had realized her fate before she'd ever suggested the plan. "The witches need a martyr," her mother had said.

Lilette lifted her hand in farewell. Jolin cried out, and the veil warbled. Lilette couldn't make out the words over the sounds of her own voice, but the lament was obvious.

She thought of her parents, her sister, of Han. All of them had died for her. No more. Never again. That was the pattern she had to break. That was the sacrifice she must make.

Not trusting herself to respond, she sealed the veil, making it self-sustaining. Then she sang storms and foreboding around it like a dark shadow—like Han. It would take a witch as powerful as herself to find it, let alone remove it.

Lilette's voice holding steady, she sang a song to move the islands. In a flash of blinding light, they disappeared below her. She hadn't taken them far—even she wasn't strong enough for that. But they were far enough the keepers would never find them.

Water rushed in to fill the void left by the islands, dragging Merlay's ship down with it. With an explosion, the water met in the middle and shot upward before rolling out in an enormous tidal wave.

Merlay and her ship were gone. Lilette wished she could say the same for the damage the woman had left behind. But that was not her battle. That battle was for another.

Lilette was alone, with nothing below her but leagues of water, shimmering like the surface of a mirror. She could continue singing, keep herself afloat until her voice grew thin and thready. But she refused to linger.

The darkness between the stars was waiting for her.

EPILOGUE

Lilette fell, shooting through the sky like a falling star. There was a brief, exquisite moment of pain. A flash blinded all her senses. She floated in a space of nothingness.

She became aware of the music first. Soft and haunting, it washed over her. Then everything rushed toward her, filling her with light and power and song and leaving the emptiness behind.

When the last of it throbbed beneath her skin, she opened her eyes to find Han standing before her. She gasped in the silence and reached out, touching smooth skin where his scar had been. She withdrew her hand, for he was beautiful, and she was afraid.

Then he smiled at her, and her sadness shattered in a thousand pieces. She leaned toward him and he gathered her in his arms. "Lilette."

She closed her eyes, reveling in the sound of her name on his lips. Then a sob caught in her throat. "I wanted so badly to save them."

He tipped her head back and kissed her gently. "You did." His hand dropped down to take hers. Their fingers laced together. "Your sister, father, mother, even Fa—they're all waiting for you."

She turned toward the music with him by her side. And she knew that death was not the end. Only another realm—beautiful and perfect. Someday those she left behind would find her here.

***

Lellan had been right about the islands of Harshen. They remembered Lilette in their songs. With each passing decade, she became more powerful, more lovely. The actions of those around her were attributed to Lilette—from Jolin's making of the song pendant, to her creation of the veil.

Among the keepers of Grove City, Lilette was spoken of with a hiss, for she was seen as the reason for the dissonance brewing around them. Then her name was blotted from the records, her song unwoven from the world. She was purposely forgotten. Merlay and the others were not. Records were changed to make it look as if they survived, as if the horrors they inflicted never happened. To this day, the witches refuse to take blame for those atrocities.

Over the long centuries, wars were fought. Keepers were taken captive and used for their powers. Thousands died. The keepers of Grove City broke into factions. The ramparts of Grove City crumbled. The thorns and trees burned.

Over time, the witches fell from the most powerful and revered entity on earth to the most hated and feared. Witches were no longer safe, for the world only wished to use them or kill them. Some of Jolin's notes must have survived—probably protected by Bethel—for after Grove City was overrun and destroyed, Haven was moved to a newly formed country called Nefalie.

Creators are patient, but so much time had passed that Lilette began to doubt anyone could ever reunite the witches and return them to their former splendor. Unable to watch everything she'd hoped and worked for disintegrate, she turned away, focusing all her attention on the man who had taught her how to surrender.

But then someone called for her help. Lilette turned back and saw the world on the brink of collapse. Nature was a ruin of droughts, darkness, and floods. All the witches were captured. All but one—a young, untrained girl who had been hidden away by her mother.

A girl who had crossed oceans and fought armies.

Her name was Brusenna.

A Note from Jolin

I cannot guess how long the barrier will hold, so I have taken to ensuring that the people who remain with me are as strong as I can make them. All witches, wastrels or not, are learning the songs. If necessary, we can unite and wield a meager strength. Doranna is training a faction to fight—something that would have never been tolerated in Grove City.

Part of the weakness of our system of government was the total power the Heads held. I have spread that power out—giving equal power to the wastrels, who have formed into orders that serve their element in a different way.

But I knew these two groups would cancel each other out. There had to be a higher power—one who was as accountable to them, as they would be to her. A higher power that could be deposed with the unanimous vote of both these groups. So I invented the office of a listener. Instead of singing and controlling the world, she would listen to what the world and her people needed and act accordingly.

Both groups unanimously voted me into the position. I tried to maneuver myself out of it—I have no head for crowds, and I had already made so many mistakes. But they wouldn't be dissuaded.

I threw away all my notes and books before I leapt into the sea after Lilette. I could rewrite them, I suppose. Begin the experiments again. But I will not. I will never again be part of creating something that can be twisted in such a way.

I cannot fathom what the Heads have done to Lilette's name. Some part of me doubts they have made her a villain of unnamable horrors—it would mean admitting that someone was strong enough to shake their perfect world.

No. I suspect they will simply wipe her name from the records. Remove her song from the songs woven throughout the world—at least the ones they can reach.

As for Lilette—I hope that wherever she is, she can forgive me. I wrote her biography for her so people would know the truth, free of adornment or hatred. So that her sacrifice would not be forgotten.

THE END

# # #

Acknowledgements

Thanks go out to:

My awesome readers: JoLynne Lyon, Julie Slezak, C Michelle Jefferies, Melonie Rainwater, Lani Woodland, Cathy Nielson, Tiffany Farnsworth, and Rachel Newswander.

My fellow artists: Laura Save, Devon Dorrity, Kathy Beutler, Linda Prince, Mark Penny, and Robert Defendi for using your artistic talents to enhance mine.

My amazing family: I love you!

WINTER QUEEN
Fairy Queens Book 1

---

1. CLAN MISTRESS

I lyenna's horse danced nervously beneath her, the animal's hooves clicking against the snow-covered stones that coated the land like dragon eggs. Reaching down, she patted her mare's golden neck. "Easy, Myst. What's the matter, girl?"

"There." Her father pointed at the base of a forested hillock not fifty paces beyond the road. Ilyenna saw the shadowed form of a large animal.

Bratton soundlessly pulled an arrow from his quiver and nocked it. "Bear?" He directed the question at their father.

The word stirred currents of tension in Ilyenna's body. The cold stung her cheeks and formed a vapor no matter how shallowly she breathed. As she glanced up and down the road, her hand gripped the knife belted around her bulky wool coat.

"I think it's a horse," Bratton finally said.

Ilyenna eased her mare forward for a better look. It was a horse—a bay. "Then where is his rider—" The words died in her throat when she spotted a motionless gray lump at the horse's feet. Without thought, she rammed her heels into her mare's ribs.

"Stop!" her father cried at the same time Bratton called, "Ilyenna!"

But the healer in her couldn't be denied. In three of the horse's strides, she was in the forest. She pressed herself flush against Myst's muscular neck. Still, larch trees managed to slap her, leaving the sharp scent of their needles in her hair and clothes. Clumps of snow shook loose from their sagging boughs, falling across her horse's mane and into her face. Yet Ilyenna barely registered the icy shock.

The other horse shied away. Myst tossed her head and balked, but Ilyenna didn't have time to hesitate. She jumped from the saddle, and her heavy boots sank into drifts up to her thighs. Grateful for her riding leggings, she struggled toward the man, whose face was blue with cold.

Her heavy riding skirt spread around her as she knelt beside him. Strangely, even in this frigid weather, he wore no coat. Beneath him, the white snow was stained crimson. An arrow shaft stuck out of his left side, and his mouth was coated with bloody foam.

A quick assessment revealed the arrow head had passed completely through his chest, but the shaft was still lodged inside him. Ilyenna couldn't imagine riding in that kind of pain. Each of the horse's strides would've reopened the wound and spilled more blood.

Fear rose in Ilyenna's gut, and she wondered what had driven this man to ride himself so close to death. The lump rose higher when she recognized the knots in the stranger's clan belt. "An Argon," she announced as her brother and her father reined in behind her. Instantly, her mind went to the Argon clan, and her brother's best friend, Rone.

At the mere thought of the boy from her childhood, a hundred memories came unbidden. Memories she wished to banish forever. But over the last six years, that had proven impossible. She bit the inside of her cheek, forcing herself to concentrate as she pulled her sheepskin-lined mittens from her hands and probed the man for additional wounds.

"You can't just run off," her brother growled as he dropped beside her. "What if his attacker was still here?"

Ilyenna kept her expression neutral. Even though she was seventeen, her brother would never see her as anything but a child—one incapable of caring for herself, let alone their clan. Thankfully, the calm sureness that always accompanied her healing steeled her voice. "He's not breathing well. Get him on your knees."

Despite his obvious annoyance, Bratton quickly obeyed.

"Why would an Argon appear in Shyle lands with an arrow in his side?" she murmured as she worked to stop the bleeding.

Bratton's grip tightened around his axe hilt as his gaze probed the forest. "Only Raiders would attack the clans."

Ilyenna suppressed a shudder at the mention of the Raiders, men who survived by pillaging and enslaving those they conquered.

"Raiders don't come this far inland," her father said. He handed his coat to Ilyenna, who draped it over the man. Her father pointed to the arrow that rose and fell with each of the Argon's labored breaths. "Besides, I saw a Raider's arrow as a boy. This isn't one."

"Then whose arrow is it?" Bratton asked.

Ilyenna eyed her brother carefully. There was something odd about his expression, as if he suspected more than he was saying.

Her father frowned. "It looks clan made."

Neither Ilyenna nor Bratton had a response for that. It was an impossible thought. The Clans didn't fight among themselves; they banded together to fight against outsiders. Pressing her ear to the injured man's chest, she listened to a sound like the gurgling of a gentle stream. She sat back on her heels. "His lungs have filled with blood. He's drowning."

Even as she said it, the urge to fight against death pulled at her, though she knew all too well how useless fighting it was. All things served the Balance. Life and death were no different. Though Ilyenna's calling was to battle for life, without death, there would be no birth.

Her father bent down and gently shook the man's shoulder. He moaned softly before settling back to his labored breathing. The death rattle. Her father looked at her questioningly. "Should we take him to the clan house?"

She shook her head. "You know he won't make it."

With grim determination, her father leaned over the man and shook harder.

Had something happened to the Argons? To Rone? Ilyenna had to know. She applied pressure where the wounded man's thumb met his palm. His lids fluttered, revealing the whites of his eyes. She pinched harder. His eyes opened wide.

"Who did this to you?" Ilyenna's father asked.

The Argon's gaze focused on his face. It was clear he didn't understand.

Ilyenna brought her face so close she could smell the blood on his breath. She gently brushed his hair from his forehead. "You're in Shyle lands."

The man snatched her hand, his icy grip surprisingly strong. "I didn't fail?"

Ilyenna wasn't sure what he meant, but she shook her head anyway. "No. You didn't fail."

He guided her hand to his pocket. She reached inside and pulled out a piece of rolled vellum. Her hands shaking, she slid off the leather band and unrolled it. The dying man echoed the words she read, "The Tyrans attacked us during the night . . . Clan Chief Seneth sent me to call for aid." The man seemed to be fighting to keep his eyes from rolling back. "So much dying . . ." The words strangled from his lungs with his last breath.

Death had claimed another. Somewhere, a child filled its lungs for its first squall. Ilyenna handed the vellum to her father, then closed the fallen man's eyes and rested his hand on his axe hilt. "So passes a warrior," she said.

"So passes an Argon," her brother and father replied in unison.

After gently laying the man's head back on the snow, Bratton leaned toward her father and read the note with him. A plea for aid that was written in Seneth's own hand. It affirmed the truthfulness of the dead man's words.

The Tyrans had attacked the Argon clan.

Bratton shook his head. "It doesn't make sense."

Ilyenna couldn't understand either. Undon, the Tyran clan chief, might be renowned among the clans as a dangerous man with a short temper, but this was far beyond killing a man in a drunken brawl. This treachery made him and his Tyrans even worse than Raiders.

She studied her father and brother, like twin images in a mirror. The only real difference was their age. Both men had the clan's typical blond hair and blue eyes. They even had the same braying laugh.

Ilyenna had inherited all of her mother's foreignness, right down to her dark brown eyes and black hair. Tears pricked the back of her throat. Her mother—the other half of her mirror— was dead, and it was her fault.

Her father gently retrieved his coat, then hauled himself into his saddle. Bratton wasn't far behind.

"Hurry, Ilyenna. We're near the border. It's not safe."

She heard the warning in her father's words. If the Argons had been attacked, the Shyle could be next. Even now, the killers could be close. But her eyes stayed fastened to the dead man. One death, one moment, and the peace of decades had been shattered. "We should take his body."

"We'll come back if we can," her father said sternly.

She squeezed her eyes shut. Her father was right. But the man had died trying to find help. He deserved better than for the wolves to pick him apart. "I'm sorry," she mouthed, hoping his ghost would hear and understand, that he wouldn't come for revenge against her family for this insult.

"Ilyenna!" Bratton snarled.

She turned and shoved her foot into the stirrup, then pulled herself into the saddle. Myst pranced impatiently. Ilyenna leaned low over the mare's neck to shield herself from the wind that whipped away warmth and breath.

Continue Reading in:

WINTER QUEEN

Fairy Queens Book 1

About the Author

Amber Argyle grew up with three brothers on a cattle ranch in the Rocky Mountains. She spent hours riding horses, roaming the mountains and playing in her family's creepy barn. This environment fueled her imagination while she was writing her debut novel.

She has worked as a short-order cook, janitor, and in a mental institution, all of which gave her great insight into the human condition and has made for some unique characters.

She received her bachelor's degree in English and Physical Education from Utah State University.

She currently resides in Utah with her husband and three young children.